THE
MARKETPLACE

B rian remained at attention. Shame flooded through him. Clamps, leather, straps, boots, chains, yes!

But pink ribbons and bows?

All over his body. His naked, shaven body. No. Oh, god, no.

Rachel stepped in front of him and pulled gently on the ribbons cascading down his chest. Pleasure shot through his nipples, and she smiled at the tension in his face. Wrapping the ribbons around her fingers, she led him, stumbling, across the room, where there was a large table used for folding laundry. She edged up against it and released him, leaving him standing at attention in front of her.

Carefully, she lifted the edge of her black dress, revealing that she wore stockings, not pantyhose, and that she had no panties on whatsoever. She slipped herself neatly onto the table and reached out to get another grasp on those damned ribbons. With a sudden harsh tug, she pulled him onto her, and then pressed his head down.

"You heard him," she said, her voice raspy with pleasure. "Get to work, pretty boy."

Also by **SARA ADAMSON**

The Catalyst

THE
MARKETPLACE

SARA ADAMSON

RHINOCEROS

ISBN 0-7394-0822-4

Cover Photograph © 1993 by Robert Chouraqui

Manufactured in the United States of America
Published by Masquerade Books, Inc.
801 Second Avenue
New York, N.Y. 10017

For Adam & Gillian
and
Ann & John

who bring reality & fantasy to my life.

Introduction

Merchandise does not come easily to the Marketplace. It never has. In years past, just *finding* the Marketplace required a mix of personal dedication, passion, and the investment of a great deal of time. The creators always intended it to be that way. If it were easy to find, we would be overwhelmed by applicants.

As it is, far too many intermediate applicants appear on the edges of the Marketplace, their eyes wide with pleading and frustration. They hear of us, they instantly believe in us, and they then spend months, sometimes years, trying to find their way to us. They haunt the clubs and the organizations, their need so real and desperate that they exude sensual tension when they glide through the crowds. Some of them are so ripe that they intimidate the poseurs, the weekend sadists and the furtive dilettantes who are so endemic to that world. And they never stop asking where we may be found.

So few of them are truly ready. They may have flirted with the trappings of a subculture and found it to be an extraordinary aphrodisiac. But a steady diet of aphrodisia is far too overwhelming. To survive and to thrive in this world, applicants must need it more than they need pleasure, more than they need the companionship of peers, more than they need even the barest personal satisfaction. And the very best of them understand that the mark of the very best slaves is infinite patience.

Those of you who have toyed with or even lived a term of service may wonder at just how hard it could be to attain the level of excellence required by the Marketplace. After all, you muse, these are people who will be called slaves. Owned chattel, their lives formed and polished for the pleasure and use and amusement of those whose need is to control and improve. Many of you believe that the right attitude combined with some physical charm would be more than adequate to the task.

It is not. Even the most gifted of naturals, those individuals whose wrists are naked without restraints and whose souls are bleak without guidance, need to be trained.

That is why we exist, actually. We are a gateway to the Marketplace, one of the few ways to be a part of it yet still be outside of it. We are also easier to believe in, easier to access, easier to afford.

If you work hard enough and your devotion is genuine, one day you may ask someone where the Marketplace can be found. They will consider you, perhaps ask one small service of you or a deeply personal question, and they will judge whether you are ready. If you show some slight potential, they may take you home and give you what you desire. Or, if the need is very strong in you, they may grant your wish and take you on a long drive, a soft blindfold locking out the light. At the end of that drive, your entire body in a state of sexual hunger and your mind obsessed with the fruition of all your deepest fantasies, you may come to our household.

I shall be awaiting you.

You will learn to hate me.

And you will remember your stay in our house for the rest of your life.

Chapter One

"May I serve you tea, ma'am?" The girl's body was bent slightly forward in a subtle, exquisite, inquisitive posture. Her small white hands held the china teapot firmly, waiting for an answer. That was excellent, too. An untrained girl might have started pouring as soon as she asked the question.

"Yes, of course," the mistress of the house replied. Her eyes followed the movements of the girl as the liquid poured into the cup. The tea made a distinct sound while it ran into the cup, another perfection. When the cup was three-quarters full, the pot was replaced, and the ritual continued.

"Would you like sugar, ma'am?" Then lemon, then cream. Each refusal was met with a slight bowing of the girl's pretty head. When the options were finished, she backed away from the table, her steps small and carefully placed, barely disturbing the slender golden chain that wound between her white, high-heeled shoes.

She was pretty, small and delicately shaped. She was well suited to the serving ensemble she wore, the tight, corseted bodice and the lightly ruffled apron. Her curly light brown hair cascaded down her back, the pert lace cap pinning it back. Her deep green eyes were always lowered in humility, long lashes charmingly fluttering. The wisps of hair, which seemed to carelessly escape from the cap to frame her heart-shaped face, were in fact cunningly arranged to suggest disarray.

Cute, Alexandra Selador thought, as she drank some tea. Far too cute for her own good.

"That will be all, Claudia," Mistress Madeleine said, her voice strong and tightly controlled. Alexandra nodded and her major-domo came forward to leash the girl and remove her from the room. The two women waited until the servants had gone to relax back into their chairs. They laughed together at the conceit.

"It's good to see you, Alex."

"And you, Madeleine. It's been far too long. You should come out and visit us more often. And Claudia is simply enchanting. It's rare you see such grace in that form of service these days. At least here in the States."

That comment was answered with a simple but elegant shrug. "You should come and visit us," Madeleine insisted. She smiled, her face transforming in a way few of her slaves had ever witnessed. "Did you know that we finished the pool and the deck? It's beautiful, especially at night. We light torches—it's very romantic."

"Hm, I bet it is," Alexandra murmured. "And you bring in some extra property? To serve at poolside?"

"We invite people to bring their own, but of course we try to have someone for everyone. You should have come to the last party we threw! We had some friends in from the Netherlands. They had just bought a pair of twins, big blond beauties. We had them dressed in nothing but slender, black chains, wound all around their bodies."

Alexandra tried to imagine that, and the image of them standing next to the tall, dark mistress. She nodded. "That must have been nice. Boys?"

"Boy and girl. Barely spoke English, actually, but very well trained."

Alexandra whistled slightly. "Very nice indeed. Twin brother/sister combinations are very, very hot right now, especially if there's a strong resemblance." She waited politely for Madeleine to begin the business discussion. Over such an elegantly served tea, it didn't feel right to just ask what the woman wanted. Was she interested in a set of twins herself? Alexandra did a quick mental inventory. There was one pair she knew about that might be ready for training, but they were in San Francisco, a continent away, and there was no telling what kind of contracts they wanted.

"Well, there was a strong res emblance here, honey." Madeleine flashed that brilliant smile again. "Both of them had long hair, shaggy almost. They looked primitive, very ... raw. I told David to have their noses pierced. That would have completed the image. But even without that, they were a great success. Wherever they walked, people admired them. David even got a few offers."

She sighed, and finally put her cup down. "Shall we get on to business?"

"At your service, ma'am." Alexandra reached for her note pad. "What can we do for you this time?"

"I want you to take Claudia."

Alexandra's eyebrow shot up in surprise.

"Claudia?"

Madeleine nodded, her smile gone. "I want her trained."

Alexandra considered for a moment. "I have to be honest with you. I don't think we're the ones you want, Madeleine. We're entry-level, undergraduate. Claudia, if I might say so, is already past the level of many of our graduates." She smiled ruefully. "But I can put you in contact with one of the master trainers, if you'd like. I think Anderson is accepting new applicants next month."

"No, I want you to do it," came the confident reply. "Anderson is wonderful, her slaves are always perfection, but that's the problem."

Alexandra waited for the explanation. It was not every day when a client protested that they didn't want perfection. Her eyes scanned the table. There wasn't a drop of moisture on a serving utensil nor on the tablecloth. In fact, the teapot, creamer, sugar bowl and everything else seemed to be pleasingly arrayed, something she hadn't noticed before.

Madeleine stood up, looking toward the door as though she could see her property through the walls. "Claudia was meant for perfection," she began, walking away from the table. "From the first time I saw her, I could tell. It wasn't just her attitude, you can see she's a slave to her soul, but the way she devoted herself to being attentive to the slightest details. Adequate was never acceptable to her. Every once in a while, I would find her practicing—how to move, how to curtsy, how to speak. She would watch herself in the mirror and do something over and over again until it satisfied her."

She turned to look at Alexandra. "It was intoxicating for a while. Of all my slaves, she had the most desperate drive to be perfect for me. It was worth the challenge to find fault with her. A fray on an inch of lace, a scuff on her shoe, a grain of sugar on the table, it didn't matter. I punished her heavily for every imperfection.

"And the punishments! What else could I do to such a creature but have her bent tightly over a bench and caned until she cried? And she *would* cry, just like the little girl she is. Every time, early on, but with grace. I taught her to stand for the cane and kiss it prettily when I was done—they were wonderful sessions.

"With stripes across her bottom, she was even more perfect." Madeleine paused. "Do you understand?"

"I understand that you made a perfect slave," Alexandra said cautiously.

"Yes, and no. I took a perfect slave and made her more perfect. And now ..."

"Now she bores you."

Madeleine nodded, a blush faintly discernible on her cheeks.

It was a rare but classic dilemma. Alexandra began to jot down some notes. She had heard of this happening, but had never seen the results. What did happen, owners would ask each other, if a slave actually achieved the perfection they were supposed to be searching for? Would the master be happy? Or would the slave have surpassed the master in one of those unquantifiable ways that makes people unworthy of each other?

"So what do you envision for her?" Alexandra asked when she finished writing. "Do you want her changed into something more challenging?"

"If possible."

Ah, Alexandra thought, making another note. "So you've already tried."

"Well, of course. As soon as I realized what was wrong, I tried to see if there were some other areas I could explore with her. But she ... resisted me." Madeleine frowned slightly at the memory. "Not directly, of course, that might have been interesting in itself. But somehow, anything outside of her role would just make her sad, or confused. I love her dearly, but she's so limited!"

"Yes, of course," Alexandra murmured sympathetically. "You'll want her back then?"

Madeleine turned back to look at Alexandra, her face composed. "If she cannot be taken beyond the role she is in now, I will want her sold."

"Does she know that?"

"No. I want her to change because she wants to please me, not because she is afraid of the possible results. Besides," Madeleine waved one hand toward the hallway, "a new owner may be what she needs. After all, I can't pretend that I had nothing to do with the state she is in. Although she came to me as a novice little maid, I was the one to enhance her training to the level she has achieved. I was the one who decided to seek perfection in this role. Perhaps with someone new, she can break out of it. Be more complete, more useful."

Alexandra underlined 'useful'. "We'll want her for one week of evaluation. After that, we'll send you a report and you can decide whether to accept our recommendations. If you decide to go through the whole program, we suggest four to five more weeks, depending on how intense you want the experience to be."

Madeleine nodded, coming back to sit down. She reached into her bag to draw out her calendar, and began marking down dates.

"And you know the rules here," Alexandra continued. "You will not be able to call or visit her."

"That's perfectly acceptable. Here is her file." The folder was filled with sheets of heavy, cream-colored paper and photographs. "I can't tell you how much she means to me, Alex. If you can do it, I'll be in your debt."

"You certainly will," Alexandra said with a smile. "You'll get the invoice for the evaluation tomorrow, and an estimate for the training will come with the report. As you know, it's a business doing pleasure with you." The two women laughed and finished their tea.

Grendel read through the file before him, scanning relevant parts and occasionally glancing at the two photos on the desk. One showed a young dark-haired man in black leather, looking in what he must have imagined to be a defiant way at the camera. It came off more petulant than angry and proud. The second was a nude shot, the same man standing in a stiff position, his arms at his side. The file wasn't very long.

"Well, you were right about one thing," he said lightly, closing the file. "This is a classic example of raw goods."

The man on the other side of the desk shrugged. "I told him he wasn't ready." Paul Sheridan was wearing his own black leather. But in sharp contrast to the picture on the desk, Paul looked as though he lived in his leathers. They were old, well crafted, well formed to his hard body. His only concession to the summer heat was that his shirt had short sleeves. "But when he decides he wants something, he just keeps asking and asking."

"How submissive."

Paul shrugged again. "Oh, he can be submissive when the situation is right. But he's really just a greedy bottom most of the time. A real 'stand and model' type. In fact, that's where I first saw him. It was at one of those events, you know, Mr. Leather something-or-other."

"And this was the best they had to offer?" Grendel waved over the file. "Now I know why those things never interested me."

"Yeah, well it was pretty awful. He wasn't the best maybe, but he was hot looking. Also, he had that nice bratty attitude. Made me want to pull him off that stage and spank him till he cried."

The master of the house nodded, familiar with Paul's tastes. "So what do you want us to do with him?"

"Make something out of him if you can. Break through that bullshit smugness he has, get rid of that 'I want, I want' nonsense. If you can bring out his real submission, I know he can fetch a nice price somewhere." Paul examined his fingernails for a moment. "All I'm interested in is the finder's fee."

"I bet. You know, we don't usually work with talent this shallow." Grendel leaned back, his smile genuine but his voice hardening with business. "I don't think you've got market quality here, frankly. Hot leather boys with selfish needs don't rate very high in value."

"He's not all like that, Gren. There is something real in him. I've seen it, I've brought it out. Besides, I'm not asking for three months of real training here, just the basic six weeks. Just enough to fetch a nice starting price. Have I brought you any dogs before?"

Grendel grinned. "Only that puppy."

"Right!" Paul pointed at Grendel, emphasizing his words. "And he went into a two-year contract right out of training, didn't he? And traded at a twenty-five percent increase out of San Diego last year."

"So he did." Grendel flipped open the file again. He looked back at Paul from time to time. The man had a point. Paul had yet to bring someone who didn't have some real potential in him. But taking an entry-level trainee like this was always an iffy proposition. If he didn't fetch a high enough price at his first sale, Paul only lost an agent's fee. Grendel and the house stood to lose the cost of training, and the loss of face if the training didn't help.

"You say he's bisexual," Grendel said, still thinking.

"Well, he says he is. But his preference is men."

"Does he know that preferences aren't allowed here?"

"Of course."

Grendel tapped the folder a few times and then looked up and reached for the intercom button. "Chris? Bring him in, please."

The door opened immediately, and the man from the photos walked in, followed by the major-domo. He strode to Paul's side and knelt next to his chair, keeping his eyes lowered. He was dressed in artfully worn jeans covered with stylishly cut black leather chaps. His chest was bare except for a harness made of silver chain. A matching chain was around his neck, with a silver lock, and small silver rings adorned his nipples. His hair was shorn boot-camp short, and he had a black mustache.

No imagination, Grendel thought. "I didn't tell you that you could kneel," he said, his voice soft and reasonable.

The man looked up, then toward Paul. Paul groaned and rolled his eyes in frustration. "I warned you not to embarrass me, you scumbag. Get up!"

With a jingle of harness, the man did so, and then stood, his arms behind his back and his head lowered.

"I didn't tell you that you could avert your eyes, either," Grendel said, smiling. "Paul, why don't you introduce me?"

"Sure. Grendel Elliot, meet my latest boy, Brian Cohen. Brian, this is Mr. Elliot, the master of this place. If you're lucky, he'll accept you for training. But thanks to your spectacularly stupid entrance, he probably thinks you're nothing more than a cheap, thrill-seeking little leather clone, and he'll kick both of us out in the next ten minutes. After which you'll be walking the sixty miles back to Manhattan." Paul compressed his lips into a smile. He'd do it, too.

"Uh. Pleased to meet you, sir." Brian exposed a mouthful of large white teeth as he extended his hand across the desk. His attitude had gone from stylized subservience to game-show host in one second. It took him two more to realize that Grendel had no intention of shaking his hand. Awkwardly, he pulled back. Unsure of how to stand, he put his hands behind his back again.

Grendel studied the man before him. He was not particularly stunning, but handsome in a dark, ethnic way. His skin didn't show evidence of a lot of time out in the sun or at a tanning salon, and his waist showed a lack of time spent in a gym. Grendel's face didn't show the slightest spark of interest as he rose and walked around the desk to study Brian a little closer. He looked as though he was dutifully examining an incomprehensible piece of art at the behest of a loved one.

Brian was clearly not used to such dispassionate observation. Within thirty seconds he began to tense. In another thirty, he began to fidget.

"No discipline," Grendel snapped from behind him. Brian almost jumped, but managed to remain still.

"He's just shy," Paul offered.

"Are you? Shy?"

"Well, it depends, sir, I've competed in contests, and I don't think I could win if I was really shy. I, um, get nervous sometimes, but I try to get over it as best I can...."

"That is not an answer to the question I asked, Mr. Cohen. That is a series of personal observations referring to yourself far too many times in one sentence. Try answering yes or no." Grendel remained behind Brian, speaking to the back of the man's neck.

"Uh, no, sir!"

Grendel raised an eyebrow at Paul, who merely grinned and shrugged again.

"This is not very promising, Paul."

"Well, I'm sorry to waste your time, Gren. Listen, I'll make it up to you, real soon. I'll find you a muscle stud like you wouldn't believe, a god. Some guy that would eat this twinkie for breakfast." Paul started to rise, but Grendel waved him back down. Before he could begin to speak, Brian piped up.

"Please, sir, please reconsider me! I'll do better! I'll learn. I can be better, much better. I'm just nervous today, I promise you, I'll be the best slave you ever trained!"

"I wasn't speaking to you, Mr. Cohen. And if whining and making impossible promises is any indication of how you plan to be the best anything I've ever trained, you are badly, badly mistaken." Grendel put his hand out and grasped the back of Brian's neck. The man's first reaction was to stiffen up, but then he relaxed and leaned backward into the hand.

"Hm. First thing you did right."

Paul smiled.

Grendel let go and walked back around to his seat. "All right, Mr. Cohen, I'll give you one more chance. Tell me what you're good for."

Brian looked startled at the question. Although Grendel asked it of all new applicants, many of them didn't know how to answer. They invariably felt intimidated by the question, some of them afraid of boasting, others simply mystified at the implication that they should know their own capabilities.

Brian started to say something, but stopped himself on the first syllable. Some instinct in him told him that "whatever master wants" wasn't going to fly here. Not with this man.

"Well, I can take a good beating, sir." Grendel nodded and gestured for him to continue. "And ... and I can obey orders. I can take care of a man's leather, polish boots. Um. I can service a man...."

"Don't be evasive!"

"I can suck cock, sir. And work over a man's body, I can make love to every part of him, sir." That came out in a rush. Paul nodded, obviously agreeing.

"Can you? Show me."

Brian looked startled again, but recovered quickly and looked at Paul. When Paul made no invitation or protest, he glanced at Grendel, and then began to walk around the edge of the desk.

"Not on me, Mr. Cohen. On Chris."

Brian turned to the major-domo, who had remained standing inside the door until this time. They had not exchanged a single word in the time that Chris had been watching him, but Brian had had plenty of time to study him.

Chris was a very small, compact man. He was dressed in a suit with a crisp, high-collared white shirt and a long, dark jacket, which seemed to emphasize his heavy shoulders and hide his waist and hips. His hair was dark, thick, and curly, his eyes shadowed by tinted glasses with heavy steel frames. It was Chris who had answered the door and brought them to this office. After announcing Paul in a mellow tenor voice, Chris had stayed with Brian in the antechamber, silent and watchful.

Blow him? That would be easy. Little guys tended to have undersized dicks too. It would look good for Brian to dive in with enthusiasm. As the major-domo moved forward, unfastening the fly of his pants, Brian slid to his knees and moistened his lips.

He put his hands behind his back as he had been taught, and waited for Chris to pull out his cock. The first indication that things were not as they should be was when Chris's hand had to actually slide into his fly to grasp it. Maybe he's not that tiny, Brian considered, giving his lips another swipe. No big deal, I can handle it.

But he couldn't handle what came out of those pants. For although the size was indeed respectable, it lacked one important element for any devoted cocksucker. His eyes widened as he gazed at it, and without a single cognizant thought, his head snapped back and his hands loosened from behind his back. Instantly, he gasped and then compressed his lips in trepidation. He screwed his eyes shut for what he knew was coming.

"You stinking, good-for-nothing fuck-up!" Paul exploded. "You're going to be lucky if anyone ever takes you home as anything but a cheap trick, you lousy son of a—"

"Paul, Paul, please." Grendel held up one hand as he jotted down one more note. "No need to raise your voice. Chris, you may put that away."

Still mute, the major-domo did as told, tucking it back into his pants. Brian remained where he was, a deep blush growing at the back of his neck and a trickle of sweat sliding down his back. I screwed up big time, he thought, grinding his teeth. I don't believe my big, fucking mouth. Oh, that was rich, Brian buddy, just shout it out like this was the first time you ever tried any of this. What's the big deal if the guy ...?

He glanced up at Chris, who seemed entirely unaffected by the exchange. Brian shuddered involuntarily and then ducked his head down again. *Whatever* this guy was didn't matter any more. Brian wouldn't have to worry about ever seeing Chris or Mr. Elliot ever again. Paul would kill him when they got out of here.

It took me four months to get him to admit that he knew about this place, and I blow it in the first ten minutes, Brian thought in a flurry of self-condemnation. He lowered his chin until it almost touched his chest and didn't look up as Chris walked away from him.

But Paul was smiling. Grendel hadn't stopped taking notes, and that was an excellent sign.

"This is what I'm offering you, Paul," Grendel finally said. "We'll evaluate him as usual. If he passes, and we think he can get better, we'll take him on as a total novice. Your commission will be cut by fifty percent for our trouble. If he fails and proves to be a loss, you owe us his estimated value on your next find."

Paul laughed. "Cut the commission only ten percent and I'll guarantee your choice on the next one. If he fails, I'll cut my fee fifty percent on whatever I bring you."

"I hate to quibble. Twenty-five percent, plus our choice on the next one with a ten percent decrease in your fee. No change on the failure, take it or leave it."

Brian trembled.

"OK. But only because I know that he's quality and that you're the only people in the world who can bring it out. And get a mark up worth my time." The two men shook hands over the desk.

Brian was almost in shock as Chris reappeared, bearing a key. The chain around his neck was taken off and returned to Paul. He was so flustered that Paul's voice had to filter through his confusion gradually, like light coming through a dense fog.

"... and do as they say, boy. Did you hear me?"

"Yes, sir!"

"You'll see, Gren. He's got the potential."

Grendel stood up and closed the file. "We'll let you know in one week, Paul. Chris, take Mr. Cohen to the dorm, please."

Brian turned back as he got up. "Thank you, sir, you won't be sorry...," and immediately knew that he had made yet another grave error. Paul's grimace told him so.

"And gag him," Grendel said softly. The major-domo nodded and pushed Brian out the door. As they were exiting, Grendel turned back to Paul with a devilish glint in his eyes. "Our choice for your next find? How about a pair of twins...?"

"May I serve you tea, ma'am?" The server's body was bent awkwardly forward. His large hands held the teapot gingerly, aware of how much more fragile it seemed when those blunt, calloused fingers were wrapped around the delicate handle. He started pouring at once.

Alexandra cut off her reply as he poured and

studied him some more, unabashedly amazed at the sight.

He had to be over six feet tall in his stocking feet, so the grotesquely large high-heeled shoes he was wearing made him seem like a giant. The corset-style maid's costume he wore emphasized the broad expanse of his back. A beautiful wig gave him styled locks of bleached-blond hair, which contrasted with the barely discernible shading on his cheeks and chin.

"Would you like some sugar, mistress?" His voice was scaled up to approximate something feminine. Alexandra declined, and he offered the sugar tray toward the woman who brought him, who waved it away. With a slight rattle, he replaced it on the table and reached for the lemon. His offering was stiff, and his hand trembled, and when he replaced the lemon, the china rattled some more. He whimpered.

Alexandra narrowed her eyes as he lifted the creamer. They followed his shaking hand as he poured a little cream into the other woman's cup and droplets spilled down the side.

"Oh dear, oh dear! I'm so sorry, mistress!" That comic-opera voice grated.

"Just serve the sweets, Roberta," came the icy reply.

The creamer quickly found its way to the table, where it left a growing stain. The man in the maid's uniform hurried in ridiculous little steps to the sideboard, where he picked up the waiting tray and turned around. But as he stepped toward the table, the stiletto heel of his right shoe caught on the edge of the carpet.

Alexandra closed her eyes.

The man stumbled, lost his balance, and the tray shook in his hands. His face a mask of horror, he tried to regain his feet and succeeded, but the tray had tilted too far already. A plate of cookies slid neatly off.

Alexandra heard the dull thumping of the tray hitting the floor and sighed. What a stereotype. But when she opened her eyes to see the damage, the only thing on the floor was the tray. The plate of cookies was in the man's hand. His knees were still bent. He had caught the plate before it fell, sacrificing the tray. Nice move. But totally irrelevant in the context of the scene.

He had also started to cry.

"Oh, dear! I'm so sorry, mistress! I am so bad! Please don't punish me, I didn't let them fall! Please?" He sniffed.

"That will be enough, Roberta. Chris, please?" She beckoned, and Chris came forward, picked up the tray and replaced it on the sideboard, and then took the plate from the man's hand. Placing it on the table, he gave a slight bow to the two women and then took the sniffling man by the elbow and led him from the room. Alexandra watched them leave with a sigh.

"What was that?" she asked, ignoring the tea.

"That was a perfectly good slave, absolutely ruined—ruined!—by some amateur bimbos who called themselves 'mistresses'!" Ali glared at the closed door. "Do you believe it? The first time I saw him, I thought it was a joke, some kind of one-time role-switching, maybe a punishment. The woman who 'owned' him," she raised her fingers to make imaginary quotation marks, "was, well ..." She sighed and said a well-known name and Alexandra nodded. "You know, Ms. Famous All Around the World, I've been on *Donahue,* and I charge $400 an hour to do this stuff so I'm much better than anyone at it?"

Alexandra laughed and nodded. Yes, she knew the type, and knew the particular woman involved as well.

Ali continued. "But then I realized that this woman was *proud* of the way he was trained! She actually wanted to take him on some sleazy talk show and show him off as her great success! I tell you, I almost smacked her I was so angry!"

Ali Cruz was an expert in a specialized field. She had not been born a woman, but achieved that status after years and years of effort. Her skills in teaching others in similar positions made her a much sought-after mentor, but her focus was on those who not only desired a change in gender but in lifestyle as well. Any transgender property of Marketplace value could be traced to Ali or one of her former students. They were all uniquely qualified to deal with the combined needs and pressures that their clients had. Ali had been to the house many times before.

"He ... Robert? ... He doesn't really want to change, does he?" Alexandra asked, opening his file. It was very brief.

"No! Oh, God, no. Could you imagine? He'd be an Amazon!" Ali rolled her eyes. "He'd be a silly-looking Amazon. But can you believe it? That ... woman he was with wanted him to go for electrolysis. And he has got to have beautiful body hair—when it grows back. You'll see. And Alexandra ... his cock.

It's beautiful. Huge. Mama, men would kill for such a cock. And he's ashamed of it. That's how I met him. He was actually attending meetings asking about where he could get it cut off! To please his mistress, he said."

Alexandra shrugged. "Not unheard of."

"You're telling me? I hear it all the time. But he's not really like that, Alexandra. He's all man, inside and out. He's just a little confused, about the slave part. I know, believe me. He's a natural slave. Trust me on this, babe, have I ever lied to you? Of course not! It's just that he needs to be ... deprogrammed."

"Ah. You mean, he's stuck."

Ali nodded. "Too many women told him that he should behave like that and look like that if he was going to be submissive to women. And Mistress Prime Time, She Who Must Know Everything, told him so. What else could he do? He wanted to be a slave, and that's how he was told slaves should act." She shook her head.

"Well, somewhere in there, he made the decision to put those clothes on," Alexandra commented. "You can't blame it all on the tops."

"Of course not! But still, it's a sin. I want you to do whatever you do, find out what he's good for, and get him out of those stupid clothes. He wants to be owned, Alex. He needs it. But like this? You couldn't move him for play money."

"Do you know," Alexandra asked in between making marks on her note pad, "he's the second maid I've seen today? But we'll take him."

"You're an angel. A miracle worker! Have a good time with him." Ali brought her checkbook out, bracelets jangling. "If he gets through the evaluation, keep him as long as you need to. He wants to be sold to a woman, but I told him about house rules. I told him everything." She stressed the last word, glancing up to give it extra meaning. The check slid neatly in between the edges of the file folder on the table, and the two women shook hands warmly.

"It's always good to see you, Ali. I'll call you in a week and let you know how Robert does in the evaluation. Now, how about if we step outside and have some iced tea? Served without the embellishments?" They laughed and left the room together.

Robert had followed the little man, sniffling and sobbing, away from the scene of his disgrace. At some distance from the room they turned a corner, and his escort stopped and let him go. Robert immediately gave a long whimpering moan and slid against the wall.

I embarrassed her, he thought as he mourned. And myself. I'm such a bad slave, I can't do anything right! I'll never get sold, I'll never find a mistress, I'll never get it! Tears continued to flow, and the sounds he made as he sobbed were alternately harsh and deep and high-pitched and whining.

Finally, he realized that Chris wasn't reacting. Cautiously, he opened his eyes.

Chris was holding out a clean white handkerchief. Robert reached out and took it, his hand shaking, and hurriedly dried his eyes. Shadow and mascara stained the linen.

"Th-thank you," he sniffed, dabbing at the wet spots on his face. "I'm sorry ... I didn't mean to be a trouble ... oh! Look at what I did!" He stared at the soiled square in shame and then crumpled it in his hand and dropped to his knees. "I'm sorry, I'm sorry, it's all my fault!" The bend of his body ill suited his tall frame; the position was comical to the point of ludicrousness.

The major-domo calmly extended a hand. "At this time, this behavior is inappropriate, Mr. Grafton," he said. "Please get up and accompany me. If you are accepted for training here, we will discuss your behavior and faults. Now, you are a guest."

His voice was soft and edged with a city accent. Robert looked up in confusion and then allowed himself to be raised. "Um. I'm sorry. I didn't realize ..." He sniffed one last time and offered the handkerchief back. "I'm really making a big mess, aren't I?" His voice remained in the stylized "maid" aspect.

"I couldn't say, Mr. Grafton. Now please come with me. You will be informed how the meeting went when the ladies are through." He gently took the handkerchief back and folded it before putting it into his pocket.

"Yes, yes, of course. I'm sorry. You're very kind. Much better than I deserve. Are ... are you a master here?"

Chris, who had started to turn away, twisted back to look up into Robert's eyes. He smiled, his eyes dark behind the glasses.

"Not today."

"How did I end up with two French maids, that's all I want to know," Alexandra complained.

"Just lucky, m'dear." Grendel put Robert's file

back on the table. They were in the garden, the late-afternoon sun warming and pleasant. Just past the ornamental hedges and along a stretch of lawn, the brown rails of the paddock could be seen. They were far from the public roads, and the sounds of birds and an occasional snort or cry from the stable made a soothing background for their consultations. From inside the house, they could also hear the cook preparing a meal for their three applicants.

"At least you have Claudia to work with. That's certainly a consolation for you. It's not often we see such perfection."

"Ah, not true."

Grendel looked up for a moment and then winked. "You're right, you're right. But still, she's the star of this group. My second interview never even showed up. I told Chris to contact the next on the list. Have you noticed how quality continues to plummet? We never had so many no-shows before."

Alexandra nodded absently.

"And this Brian!" Grendel sighed dramatically. "Barely acceptable. If Claudia bores you so much, maybe you'd like to trade?"

"Ah, no. That kind leaves me cold. Let me see him when you put the fear of god into him."

They both looked up when Chris politely cleared his throat. He was standing between the open glass doors. "Excuse me, ma'am, sir. Ms. Sharon Brosa is here."

Grendel raised one eyebrow. "What time is it?"

"A quarter of five, sir."

"Great start," Alexandra commented wryly.

"I'll see her in my office. Tell her I'll be there in ten minutes." He turned back to Alexandra before

Chris left. "See what I mean? No more quality. An hour and a half late, and she didn't even call. Didn't even ask Chris to deliver her sincere apologies and beg our forgiveness."

"And she's all yours," Alexandra said with a malicious grin.

Sharon followed the guy who answered the door, smoothing her skirt over her hips. He was real short. Bad enough it cost so much for the car service and they got lost anyway, bad enough her skirt was wrinkled and her hair was starting to uncurl from the heat. But the least she expected was that the door would be opened by some tall, muscled, naked slave or something like that.

Nope, only some quiet guy who looked at her like she was from New Jersey or something. And he wasn't a butler or anything, because he wasn't dressed up like one. And she knew he wasn't the master here because she had descriptions of the two people who ran the place.

He didn't even offer to take her bag.

He had taken her to a small room where she waited with nothing but a large, fresh flower arrangement and a hard bench for company. She sat down and tapped her feet impatiently.

All this way and they keep me waiting. You'd think they'd send people out looking for me by now. I hope they realize it wasn't my fault. Maybe they're trying to psych me out? Maybe this is some kind of power thing already?

The guy from the door came back, his sudden appearance startling her.

"Jeeze!" she said. "Give some warning, will you?"

"My apologies," the guy said smoothly. "Mr. Elliot will see you in his office in the north wing. You may leave your piece of luggage here. Please follow me."

More surprises. She had expected rich furnishings and a castle, like in the story books. Instead, the house was clearly modern and decorated in a light, contemporary style. Large windows allowed the afternoon sunlight to penetrate the corridors. When they passed a dining room with open doors, she saw someone laying the table. Disappointingly, she was also fully and plainly dressed.

"Don't you have slaves to do the work around here?" she asked as they reached the stairway.

"Sometimes." Chris turned down a wide hallway, opened a door and indicated that she enter the room. She walked into an office showing a lot of use. File cabinets lined one wall. A table was piled with papers and folders and stacks of correspondence. There was a computer in one corner, and at least two phones that she could see. A large oak desk dominated the room, with a sturdy leather chair behind it. Two more chairs were angled in front of the desk, and she walked over to one. Sunlight poured in the large windows behind the desk. There was a view of a driveway and a grove of trees beyond.

"Mr. Elliot will be here in ten minutes, Ms. Brosa. Please do not seat yourself or disturb anything in the room."

She stopped herself as she was sitting down. "I can't sit?"

"No."

"For ten minutes?" But Chris was already leaving, closing the door behind him. She walked over to the door and reached for the handle, her indignation growing. But she stopped herself.

It's a trick, she realized. If I chew the little guy out, I won't be acting submissive. She grinned. Ten minutes? He'll come in five. He'll be expecting to surprise me, like I'd be sitting down and he'd come in all of a sudden. Not *this* babe, buster.

She put her purse down on the floor next to one of the chairs. I'll just wait here like it's the most natural thing in the world. Five minutes isn't that long. She checked her watch.

As the seconds ticked past, she glanced around the room. It was obviously a working office. It wasn't dirty, but it could probably use some organizing. Where were the house slaves, anyway? This wasn't anything like in the books. In the books, everyone was drop-dead gorgeous, and the slaves walked around naked, or wearing bikinis and stuff like that. They lived in pristine palaces or in Victorian mansions with luxurious playroom dungeons in the basements, and masters and mistresses lolled around being waited on. They didn't hang out in boring offices surrounded by paperwork.

She checked her watch impatiently, and then wandered over to the table and looked at the items spread over it. Maybe there were slave files here. Maybe some pictures? No such luck. Bills. Lists. A diagram of something, she wasn't sure what. A Rolodex was open to some guy's name and number somewhere in Maine.

Boring.

The bookcase was also dull. No mysterious books on the training of slaves. In fact, there weren't even any of the classic books that she had read. Instead, it was all computer books. And some sailing books, a big dictionary, a bunch of business books. She looked at her watch again. It was already five minutes, thank god, but the guy wasn't there.

Huh. Double psych-out, she thought. Like he figured I'd figure him to be here in five, but he really meant ten. Damn, this stuff could get confusing. She picked up a small glass dog, looked at it and put it back. Was he really going to make her wait a whole ten minutes?

Over to the desk to see if there was anything interesting there. Ah-hah! Right on top, a file folder with her name neatly typed on the label. She glanced at the door, and then at her watch. Two minutes to go, just enough time to take a peek. She picked it up and opened it to find only one sheet of paper inside. It had her name at the top, and absolutely nothing written on it anywhere else.

Damn! She carefully put it back. Where was the letter she sent? Where were the pictures? How long was this guy going to make her wait?

Pacing filled out the rest of the ten minutes before she considered the effect all that walking would have on her hair. She touched it up neatly and had the brush back in her purse before she realized that ten minutes were up. Now *he* was late! And her legs were starting to hurt. It was almost a two-hour ride in the car, and she was tired and stiff.

Minutes dragged by.

Is he going to make me wait an hour? That horrified thought came to her about the tenth time she checked her watch. Standing up? She walked to the door and reached for the door handle. Enough was enough. But as soon as her hand touched it, it turned by itself. Sharon shrieked and leapt back from it.

"Jesus! You scared me!" she cried. Expecting to see the little guy again, she found that she had to look up. The man standing in the doorway was taller and broader, his shoulders at the height of her nose. He was casually dressed, in jeans and a button-down shirt. His hair was black and longish, his beard a close-cropped mass of black salted with silver.

Oh shit. He fit the description she had been given. She composed her features at once and knelt gracefully, the skirt swirling around her legs in an elegant way. She had practiced this move hundreds of times, and knew that it was beautiful. She bowed her head slowly. Don't speak until spoken to, she reminded herself.

Grendel looked down and then walked past her. "I'm glad to see that you aren't injured, Ms. Brosa." He sat down behind the desk, the leather chair creaking.

Sharon raised her head a little. He had just walked by, without noticing what she did! She turned her head, but the angle was wrong, she couldn't see him. Now what? What should she do?

"Why don't you take a seat?" The suggestion was slowly and firmly made, in a way that suggested that she was a child. Biting her lip, she rose with the same grace she used in kneeling and then took one of the chairs facing the desk.

Grendel opened a drawer and brought out the real file on her and laid it out on the desk. When no apology seemed forthcoming, he began to lay out the pages, putting the photographs to one side. Now that she was here, he realized that they didn't do her justice.

Oh, they were well done, a class act. The photographer had known what he was working with and had done very little to distract from her natural beauty. But in the flesh, she was absolutely stunning. From the gentle waves of her deep auburn hair to the curves of her toned body and her lovely legs, she was quite a prize. Her eyes, under thick lashes, were hazel.

"When you failed to appear, Alexandra and I thought that there might have been an accident," Grendel prompted.

Sharon smiled in thanks. "Oh, I'm OK. The driver was totally lost, though. I'm really sorry you had to wait."

She doesn't get it, Grendel realized. He sighed and referred to the papers before him. "I see you've never had any formal training," he began. And stopped when she frowned. "Yes?"

"Yes, I did," she said, leaning over the desk. "With Jerry! And Frank. I know I put that in there. Do you need another copy?"

"No. Your experiences with your lovers don't count, Ms. Brosa. When we refer to formal training, we are talking about a more intense and structured form of living. What you did with those two men was more of a negotiated fantasy relationship between partners who were on an equal footing." Grendel tapped the sheets of paper. "These kinds of experiences are fun, but they aren't what the Marketplace is about. And if you had approached us in the proper way, I wouldn't have to explain that to you."

"Well, I couldn't get anyone to train me the way you need," Sharon protested, trying to keep the whine out of her voice. "I asked everyone I knew, and they never even heard of you! You wouldn't believe what I had to do to just get your names!" She sat back, trying to regain her composure. Be humble, she said to herself. Be like a slave. "All my life, I've wanted this, master. All my life. But I keep running into guys who, like, do it on the weekends, you know? I want to live it. Like in the books." She nodded toward the papers. "Like I said in the letter."

"So you stole information about this house from the office of a friend of ours," Grendel noted.

Sharon visibly trembled. Did he really know that? Or was he bluffing? This wasn't going the way she planned. What was going to happen now? Was all this for nothing?

He leaned back in the chair and watched her. She would fetch a high price if she were gagged, he thought. But the minute someone got her home, her flaws would become as apparent as her physical appeal. He remained impassive as she bowed her head (very prettily) and said, softly, "Yes, master."

"I am not your master, Ms. Brosa. And frankly, your behavior isn't impressing me. I train people to act like that. It's nothing new to me. If you wanted to impress me, you might have tried it with genuine contrition for your inexcusable tardiness, and swift admission of your felonious behavior." He suppressed the incredible desire to grin at his own pomposity, but it had the desired effect.

Sharon withered a little and then became angry.

"What do you want me to do, Mr. Elliot?" she shot back. "You want me to say I'm sorry? It wasn't my fault, but OK, I'm sorry. You want me to say that I took the stuff about you and this place from what's-her-name's house? OK, I did. But that was the only way I was gonna get in. All the people who know about you keep you a secret. Like you're the president, or something."

"There's a reason for that. When someone comes to us untrained and unprepared, it wastes time. For us and them." Grendel pointed at the papers and photos. "This is a good attempt at faking our file format. And I have to admit that you would make a nice decoration in someone's hallway. But you have no idea what you might be getting into."

"I know exactly what I want to get into, Mr. Elliot." She picked up her pocketbook and pulled out a folded sheet of paper. She smoothed it out and placed it on his desk. "OK, so I need some real training, maybe. But I can be the best thing that ever happened to you. Everyone who ever knew me says I was the best pleasure slave they ever saw. Take a look at that and tell me I don't know what I'm doing!"

Grendel picked the paper up and read it through. It was a contract, written in proper Marketplace jargon. He read it through once and then scanned it again. Then he placed it carefully on the stack of papers in front of him.

"Who wrote this?"

Sharon looked down. "I can't tell you that."

"Well, at least you didn't try to claim that you did. This interview is over. Chris will call you a cab."

"What?" Sharon's voice scaled up in genuine surprise and anger. "You can't—I mean, why?"

He closed the folder with the contract inside of it. "Because how could I ever expect you to be trainable if you are incapable of telling a simple truth to the people you might be training under? Ms. Brosa, this isn't a game. But never mind. I'm sure you'll be happy with someone outside the Marketplace. You might even find a situation like the one outlined in this contract. But for now, investigating who exactly wrote this document has to take priority."

Sharon panicked. "No, wait! Wait. I didn't know it was so important to you. It's just, I promised I wouldn't tell anyone about him, OK? But I won't let it screw up my chances to get in here. Could you promise that you won't tell him I told you?"

Grendel hit the intercom. "Chris, please call a cab and come and get Ms. Brosa."

"It was Joe, Joe Manelli, OK? From Forest Hills! I got his number!"

Wimp, Grendel thought, suppressing a smile.

"Aren't you going to tell him to cancel the cab?" Sharon demanded.

"I never said that I would, Ms. Brosa." He leaned back, still impassive.

"But you *have* to! I mean, please, please, master, I mean, Mr. Elliot, this is the most important thing I ever did in my entire life! I told you about Joe, didn't I? And read those papers, they're true, every word! I'd give up everything for a chance, OK?"

"That's what the contract says," Grendel reminded her. "Do you understand what it means?"

"Yeah! I get sold to a place and a guy like it says

in the bottom, and I'm a pleasure slave. For at least two years, but preferably five."

"That's what it says about your life. But do you understand about the fee?"

Sharon nodded. "You get it all."

Grendel nodded. "And you understand that this isn't the usual way we do things."

"Yeah. It's like that book about the resort hotel, isn't it? Usually the slaves get the money after the contract is over."

A long sigh. "You really got all your information about us from those fictionalized fantasy books, didn't you? My god, I don't know if they do ten times more harm than good." He shook his head and pulled the contract out to read it again.

She just gazed at him, a confused look on her face. "I just wanna get trained and sold," she finally said. "And I know I can be worth a lot. Come on, Mr. Elliot, look at me! Guys fight over me."

"We will have to alter your gender preference in the contract," Grendel noted. "Slaves out of this house may not negotiate the sexual preference or gender of their future owners; it's a house rule. If it's that important to you, come back in six months with some real training and I'll refer you to a trainer who will accept that limitation with the rest of them."

She shook her head. "As long as they're single, I don't care. I've had my share of women, too. I can do it."

Grendel considered. She was hot. Very attractive, with an edge of feral rut around her, and that always went over well. She was young enough so that the lack of real records wouldn't hurt her that much. And the way the contract was written wasn't so difficult that they'd have trouble placing her. It was just her attitude! Was she submissive at all, underneath her playacting? He wanted Alex's opinion on this one.

"We'll accept you for one week of observation and testing," he declared. "After which, if you look promising, another four to six weeks of training. But under this agreement, if we feel you need more training, we may keep you as long as we like. And you understand that you will receive absolutely no part of whatever we arrange as a selling price for you."

She nodded, her eyes sharp with anticipation.

He leaned over and hit the intercom again. "Chris, please put Sharon with the others."

"What about the cab?" she asked, helpfully.

"Chris will take care of it," Grendel said, as the door opened. "You will find that Chris takes care of a lot of things here."

As they left, Grendel picked up the phone and punched in a long number. As he waited to be connected, he read the contract that Sharon had given him, shaking his head. It was very neat. It was very good.

"Hello, is this records? This is Grendel Elliot, from New York. I just accepted an applicant with a contract drawn up for her by Joseph Manelli, from Forest Hills." He spelled the last name. "No, the contract is fine; in fact, it's constructed to give the maximum benefit to the house. But the merchandise is incredibly shoddy. I'm talking barely, barely acceptable, and even then, I'm taking a gamble on it. I think this is the third time I've heard that he's working with unsuitable clients, isn't it? Yes, I thought so. Well, I just wanted to let you know. Thank you."

The beauty queen princess and the Christopher Street clone, he thought as he put the phone down. Alex *always* gets the interesting ones.

Chapter Two

Claudia woke to a frightening, unfamiliar sound. For a second, the image of a snarling lion invaded her already confusing dream. Then, she was awake, in darkness, the vicious snarling noise unabated. She gasped and clutched at the firm pillow, her naked skin cool against the soft but light bed coverings. It took her a minute to realize that the noise she heard was snoring.

What am I doing here? she wondered for the thousandth time. She had sobbed last night, her neat, gentle tears a contrast to the comic blubbering of the man who was undoubtedly filling the dorm with such a racket. Tears and sobs were the only sounds they had been permitted to make yesterday. The awful sight of the other man being forced to wear what looked like a very uncomfortable gag for hours was a concise object lesson for the other three. They had avoided each others' eyes for most of the time they had been together. Or at least, they tried to.

Claudia had fallen to her knees and begged her mistress not to leave her. It had been an awful scene. Mistress Madeleine had to actually raise her voice to stop Claudia's first cascade of tears and restore her to obedience. Afterward, when Chris brought Claudia to this bare, functional dormitory room, she had resolved not to embarrass her mistress any more, to be even more perfect than she had ever been. Then, surely, Mistress Madeleine would be pleased and take her home swiftly.

But it was so hard to concentrate on being correct and brave when that large man was making such an awful noise! Shivering under the covers, Claudia pulled them tighter around her and tried to snuggle down. But the mattress was hard, the pillow thin. She was too long used to the softness of her own bed back home, with its pristine white cotton sheets and the thick comforter and the oh-so-big soft pillows....

Just as she was beginning to doze off again, the lights came on.

"Good morning, applicants."

Claudia blinked and squinted, knowing that it screwed her face up horribly and hating it. But the lights were a cold, white fluorescent, allowing no relief. The other three stirred in their own beds, making various sounds of waking.

"You have exactly one minute to meet me in the hallway. Tardiness is not permitted."

It was Chris, the major-domo. Through her now wide-open eyes, Claudia could see that today he was dressed in dark jeans and heavy boots, and a short-sleeve shirt and a tie. He looked like a common laborer dressed for a job interview. His hair was still wet. As soon as he finished speaking, he turned and left the room, the door ajar.

Claudia and Robert immediately jumped out of their beds, shivering. They looked across the room at each other, and then looked away in simultaneous embarrassment.

Brian groaned and stretched and scratched between his legs. It took him a moment to notice what was going on, but he was no fool. He got up and followed Robert, trying to remember exactly what the little guy had said. The three of them were out in the hall, rubbing their eyes, well before the minute was up.

"Tomorrow, you will have thirty seconds," Chris said as a welcome. He wasn't alone. A woman in a conservative housekeeper's uniform stood next to him, with a laundry tray at her feet. "By the end of the week, I will expect that you will be awake before I arrive. This," he said, indicating the maid, "is Ms. Rachel. She is our housekeeper, and second to me. As with any house servant, she is to be obeyed immediately and with all respect."

Claudia tried to keep her eyes focused on the major-domo, but they flickered back to the dorm. Where was the other woman, that beautiful woman she couldn't help sighing over last night? The one who tossed and turned so much. The door was still open, but there was no sign of her.

"Eyes front!" Chris snapped suddenly. Claudia turned her eyes back to him in anguish. But she maintained silence. She had not been given permission to speak. For the first time, she noticed that a short, doubled strap hung from one of his belt loops.

"Each of you will take one bundle from Rachel and proceed to the showers at the end of the hall. This morning, I would like to see you trot. Wait for me inside the room, with your bundles in your arms. Go!"

The three of them collided as they all tried to turn toward the maid. But Robert stepped back to allow Claudia to take the first bundle. I don't know how to trot, his mind screamed. Oh, please, you lovely, sad little thing, show me what I'm supposed to do!

Claudia took the neat bundle (something wrapped in a towel), and turned up the hall. Immediately, she began a high stepping fast walk, almost a run, her legs jerking up like a Tennessee walking horse, her head high.

I can't do this shit, Brian thought. But he took his bundle with a nod and tried to follow. The stupidity of the gait got to him though, and half down the hallway he changed to a loping jog. Robert followed, trying desperately to create the proper movements. His pounding feet seemed to make an exceptional amount of noise, and he whimpered all the way.

Chris watched them go, and then dismissed Rachel. She took the tray, with the last bundle still in it. Chris casually unhooked the strap from his belt and walked into the dorm.

Sharon was still asleep. She was curled up on one side, her arm clutching the thin covers around her head and her knees drawn up.

Down the hall and in the bathroom, Brian heard the sharp whacking sounds and identified them even before Sharon started screaming. He turned to the other two, standing naked beside him, and grinned. "Someone's in trouble," he said.

"Oh, my goodness, that poor girl!" Robert said. He was trying to cover his genitals by holding his bundle very low. "We should have gotten her up!"

"Shhh!" Claudia lifted a finger to her lips.

Brian sneered at her. "Oh, please. Listen to Miss Goody-Two-Shoes. Or better yet, listen to Miss Thing, down the hall." They all did.

Sharon screamed again, and cursed, even as her butt hit the floor next to the bed. "Jesus fucking Christ!" she managed to get out, before the strap caught her on one thigh. Chris immediately reached down and took a handful of her hair, jerking her head back. She screamed again, the cold and the pain and the fear overwhelming her.

"Be silent," Chris hissed. He bared his teeth for a moment. "This kind of behavior is unacceptable."

"What the fuck …"

He slapped her. Heavily and slowly, across the mouth, her head firmly held by his hand in her hair. "And your language is also unacceptable. Get up and *present*."

She started to get up, fully awake, trembling and confused. It's starting, she told herself. It's just the first day. They want to scare me. I can handle this.

"Today, Sharon, today!"

She stood, taller than him, trying to get into a humble posture. From the corner of her eye, she could see a broad scarlet mark on her thigh. She looked down at it and her hand naturally floated over to touch it gingerly.

In an instant, she was turned around and pushed

firmly down, until she rested with her elbows on the surface of the bed. "Ow!" she complained.

"I told you to *present*, Sharon. Ten for lateness. Five for discourtesy. Five more for ineptitude. Try to control your hysterics."

She did. The first blows of the strap were light, but as Chris counted them out loud for her, she realized that they were getting heavier. They all caught her on her rounded, soft buttocks, expertly aimed, and each new one was an explosion of heat, the impact driving her forward. This was nothing like the wonderful, loving spankings she had gotten from some of her previous lovers. And although she was always able to go along with a scene that rose in intensity and take a pretty good butt-warming, it had never been like this! This was sudden and hard and relentless. She tried to muffle herself at first, but it only took three strikes to get her to cry out. Before the first ten were finished, she started to beg.

"The poor girl," Robert repeated. He was shivering, shifting his bare feet against the cool tile floor.

"Lucky bitch," Brian muttered. "I'm sleeping in tomorrow, if that's the wake-up call. I mean, she's getting all the attention while we're standing here getting chilled. And you don't even have your fur, Babette." He aimed that at Robert, who blushed and lowered his head again.

"Shhh!" Claudia insisted.

"Oh, suck my dick!" Brian turned his attention toward the sounds coming from down the hall again. Claudia shrank back in horror.

"Please! Oh god, please stop! I'm sorry! I'm sorry!"

Sharon was on the floor again. She had tried to stay bent over, but the pain was just too much! No one had ever hit her like that, ever! She had tried to turn, tried to get away, but instead, she just slid down, bending her body to try and cover her vulnerable areas.

"You have six remaining, Sharon. Get up." He pulled her up, the strength in his arm surprising. She fell against him, giving him her best utterly defeated slave girl look, but his eyes were still cold behind his glasses. "Out into the hall. The others are waiting."

She sniffed and nodded, wiping tears from her eyes. The glow from her beating was beginning to rise, and she craned her head to catch sight of the redness on her cheeks. She failed to notice that Chris had never put the strap back. He aimed and swung as soon as her bare feet touched the hall carpet.

"Trot, girl! That way! Move!"

She yelped and started to run. "Not that way, you idiot! Knees up! Head back! Shoulders straight!" All the way down the hall, Chris followed her with the strap. She tried to do as he commanded, throwing her shoulders back, pumping her arms and bringing her legs up smartly. Hadn't one of the books mentioned something like this? But every time she thought she had it right, that damn strap hit her across her ass, and she faltered. Her cries became steady and wailing, until the last strike caught her neatly across the backs of her thighs and she collapsed in front of the bathroom.

Brian, Claudia, and Robert all shrank back at the sight of her falling almost through the door. Chris stepped in behind her, clipping the strap onto his belt. He took a fistful of her hair and propelled her into the room, her knees banging against the floor.

"That," Chris said, keeping his eyes on the assembled party, "was inexcusable. The next time *one* of you is late getting out of your room, *all* of you will share in the punishment. Because you have not been informed of the rules, let this serve as a lesson. There are no exquisite punishments here, only uncomfortable, painful, and inconvenient ones. Do you all understand?"

Claudia nodded.

Brian snapped back, "Yes sir!"

Robert whimpered, "Yes, yes, I understand."

They looked down at Sharon, who was still on the floor, her eyes narrow with shock and anger. She nodded, but by the time she did, Chris was already speaking again.

"My name is Chris," he said. "Not sir, not master, not mister. I am the major-domo of this household and you are part of my responsibility." He reached over to a counter and picked up a Lucite clipboard. "I have been given instructions for each of you, and I will be obeyed. In the future, if you do not understand an order, you will remain still and admit your ignorance. Part of the reason why you are here is to learn proper behavior. If you attempt to do something you have no skill in and your attempt is unsuccessful, you will be punished twice. Brian," he looked up, "I noticed your pathetic attempt at trotting. You and Sharon will both join me this afternoon at 4:15 for a lesson in that skill."

No punishment? Brian thought. How disappointing.

"For this week, you are applicants to this house. You will be tested in various ways, and observations about you will be recorded. At the end of the week, we will inform you or your owners of our evaluation. If it is determined that you have some value, you will stay here for a period of four to six weeks, and we will improve you." He stressed the word "improve."

"Standard rules of behavior will be posted in your sleeping area. You are expected to learn them and follow them in addition to any special orders given to you individually. This morning, you will be interviewed by Master Grendel or Mistress Alexandra. This afternoon, you will be assigned your goals for the week." He looked at them, sweeping his gaze across the four. They were all shivering now.

"Every morning, you will rise at five. You will assemble in the hallway and then proceed here. You will have thirty minutes to shower and clean yourselves—inside and out." He pointed at the bundles. "Your personal articles are here. When you are finished today, you may place them on these shelves. While you are in this room, you may speak to each other only in low tones. You are required to help each other maintain cleanliness, and you are each responsible for how the others appear. Is that understood?"

More nods. Sharon looked up, her hair falling over her face. Carefully, she got her feet under her and rose. Her ass and upper thighs were cherry red. She crossed her arms over her body and hugged herself. Then she raised one hand.

Chris ignored her. "When you are finished here,

return to your room. If there is any clothing on your bed, dress yourself. I will be back to retrieve you at that time."

Sharon spoke up as he turned to leave. "Please … I don't have a towel.…"

Chris paused, his back to them. He turned back around and took a pen out of his back pocket. While the four would-be slaves watched and trembled, he wrote something down on his clipboard, and then put the pen away. He said, "Put your hands behind your back."

She did, and very nicely, too. Her back arched slightly, and her beautiful breasts rose gently. Her nipples were hard.

"You will stay in that position until the others have finished bathing. Then, and only then, you may ask them if they care to share their supplies with you." He smiled suddenly, teeth flashing. "I would advise you to beg. Nicely. Because all four of you will be punished later on for *your* bad manners. You three," he said as he turned to the door again, "are not in any way obligated to help her. Or," he shrugged, "to deny such help. A bell will ring in exactly one half hour. You may begin preparing yourselves now." He left.

"Welcome to boot camp," Brian said. He unfolded the towel to look at what was inside. Robert shrank back to do the same, and Claudia looked around nervously. The square room had two shower heads in an open area with three drains, two plain, gleaming toilets and two white sinks. There were no modifications for modesty. No place to hide.

"Well, don't just stand there, princess, we only have thirty minutes." Brian picked up a specially designed tube and glanced over at the two shower heads on one side of the room. Silver coils ran alongside them. He hooted and walked over to one. The nozzle fit perfectly. "Talk about hygienic," he said cheerfully. "We all have our own butt irrigators."

"Oh my," Robert said weakly. "And we have to do this ... in front of each other?" His voice scaled up.

"Not only that, big guy, but we have to help each other!" Brian chuckled and turned the water on, adjusting the temperature as it ran. "Anyone wanna help me out? Toss me the soap." Robert squatted down to pick up the soap that Brian had left on his towel and tossed it to him. Brian winked in thanks and rubbed a little soap on the tip of the nozzle.

Claudia pulled her own soap and shampoo out of her bundle and went to the other shower. But even as she turned the water on, she kept looking back at Sharon, who was still standing with her hands behind her back. She was already fidgeting, and the look on her face was murderous.

Oh, this was just horrible! To have to bathe and ... and ... her bundle had *two* nozzles in it; and even though she tried to turn her body away from the room, Brian's coarse laughter followed her. What if I don't do it today, she wondered. What if they check?! Oh, that would be much worse! Fingers trembling, she tried to thread one of the nozzles onto the cable. She dropped it twice.

"Oops! Don't bend over to pick up the soap around here, sister!" Brian turned around to show that he had stuck his cigar-shaped nozzle up his rear. He shook his butt like a dancer. "Sorry about the indelicacy, ladies, but it's almost time to open the gates of heaven!"

"Will you shut the fuck up!" Sharon shrieked. Over the sound of the running water, her voice reverberated around the sterile room. She twisted, but tried to keep her hands behind her back. "This is not one big joke to some of us!"

"Yeah," Robert chimed in. He was holding his own soap, almost protectively. "Please ... we don't need to be in any more trouble!"

Brian jerked the plug out of his ass and walked with exaggerated dignity over to one of the toilets. Sitting down, he stuck his tongue out and laughed. He leaned forward with a sigh and began to play with his nipple rings.

This is a nightmare, Claudia thought, as tears began to form again. She turned to the wall and gasped as she felt a touch on her shoulder. It was Robert. He screwed the nozzle onto the silver cable for her and then retreated to the other shower head. There was no avoiding it. Claudia adjusted the flow and temperature of the water and cleansed herself. Front and back.

Mistress will be proud of me, she thought, tears streaming down her face. I will be very, very good.

Robert hurriedly showered. His kit did not contain a razor, and he wondered what to do about the stubble that was already appearing. One of his usual morning rituals was to shave all of his body hair off, and he felt strange not doing it. But he was used to cleaning his nether regions for Mistress, just in case she deigned to make use of him. He just wasn't used to having another man ... or a young, pretty woman, for that matter ... watch him.

To his horror, as tepid water flowed into him, his nasty-thing started to misbehave. He turned to the wall, but there wasn't really enough room. He blushed and tried to cover himself. Frantically, he turned the water off. Then, he glanced quickly at the remaining toilet and dashed for it, his hands covering his growing embarrassment. Sharon, from her vantage point in the middle of the room, made a snorting, derisive sound.

"You'll never make it if you're that shy," she said, shifting from foot to foot.

"Hey, sweet tits, you better be nice to him," Brian said, punctuating his words with a flush. He went back to the shower to wash and rinse off. From under the water, he continued, "Because I sure as hell ain't giving you my stuff to help make you all nice and spanking clean. You'd better charm the socks off these two shrinking violets, so they'll be nice to you." He stepped out, shook the excess water off and began toweling himself down. Deliberately, he let his towel drag along the floor.

"Bastard!" Sharon spat.

Claudia ignored both of them as she went about her humiliating duties. She washed her cleaning implements in the sink with very hot water, and then brushed her teeth. When she was finally finished, she dried herself off and looked forlornly around for grooming tools. The only one in her bundle was the toothbrush. There was no hair dryer, no brush, not even a comb. And there was no cream rinse, and no conditioner, and no styling gel. No soft creams to rub into her skin and make it velvety and sweet-smelling. She ran her fingers through her hair, trying to get it to fall attractively, and then stowed her toothbrush, the two nozzles, and her soap and shampoo on the lowest shelf.

"I still don't hear you begging anyone for their stuff, Miss Thing," Brian taunted as he picked up his supplies and put them away.

"Just shut the fuck up!"

He shrugged, "Suit yourself."

Sharon closed her eyes and tried to count to a hundred. She was exhausted, stiff, and despite the steam in the room, still chilly. And her arms were beginning to hurt. And her feet. But she would go to hell before she asked any of these assholes for anything. She looked around. Were they finished? Chris had said that she only had to wait until they were finished. But Robert was still washing, back under the shower like Brian had done, to rinse off. She ground her teeth.

The bell went off, and Claudia and Robert scrambled for the door without looking back. Brian sauntered, blowing a kiss to Sharon on his way out. With a heavy sigh, she shook her arms out and dashed for the shower. She purred under the steaming water. There, she thought, reaching for the soap that Robert left behind. I didn't need to ask any *slave* for permission to do anything.

She took her time, running the bar of soap over her body and luxuriating in the feeling of heat that ran through her limbs. Then, as her hands slipped across her beaten asscheeks, she realized that they might be waiting for her. The image of Chris with that damn strap flashed into her mind, and she rinsed off. All of the towels were damp, but Claudia's had been folded neatly, so she used it to dry off as well as she could.

When she got to the dorm, she had to smile. Not only wasn't Chris there yet, but the other three looked unhappy and uncomfortable. And no wonder.

Cute little Claudia was wearing a simple gray cotton dress, with no frills and no real decorative elements. Flat shoes were on her feet. Brian was wearing a gray T-shirt and plain cotton pants. His feet were bare. Robert had pants but no shirt. His arms were crossed over his chest.

"Great fashion sense," Sharon said as she walked over to her bed. She didn't expect to find anything there. After all, she was going to be a pleasure slave. And she was beautiful. When you have beautiful things around, you show them off. No problem with that. But laid out on the bed was another gray dress. She sighed and picked it up.

Well, she thought, while pulling it over her head, at least I'll look better in it then Miss French Maid over there does. She barely has any tits. But instead of clinging to her body and falling to mid-thigh, like she expected it would, the shapeless frock settled over her body like a tent. It fell below her knees. It was unmistakably hideous.

Brian smirked and started to say something, but Chris suddenly appeared in the doorway.

"Knees up against the edge of the bed, backs to me!"

They moved into position, and he passed among them, touching as he went. He stopped in front of each of them, telling them to move or drop or raise clothing as he desired. He poked and ran his fingers along their bodies, made them bend and twist to offer themselves to his observation. When he finished with Sharon, he walked back through them and turned to face them.

"Disgraceful," he snapped, pulling his pen out. "Your backs and the backs of your calves are still damp. Your hair is tangled, matted, and unevenly dried. One of you failed to conduct a thorough cleansing. Another didn't brush his teeth. None of you is in any shape to meet your trainers, let alone eat breakfast with them. I think you'll break your fast alone this morning."

Claudia and Robert both lowered their heads. Brian stiffened.

Sharon's stomach growled at the word "breakfast."

"When you are ordered to help one another, follow that order. If you had done so instead of wasting time in meaningless modesty and pointless chatter, you could have dried each other's backs and examined each other. This may be the only time when you are permitted to aid each other; I suggest that you use it. Now. Who loaned their cleaning supplies to Sharon?"

The question was fired off as strongly as the criticisms. Brian's mouth twitched into a slight smirk.

"I asked a question!" Chris tucked the clipboard under one arm and reached for the strap.

"No one!" Brian said immediately.

Chris's eyebrow edged up over the rim of his glasses. "No one? Is that so?"

"Well, uh, oh dear, I didn't tell her that she *couldn't* use mine," Robert said, his voice slipping further into his falsetto.

Chris nodded. "I see. Sharon, report back to the bathroom at once. I will come and get you after breakfast. The rest of you will follow me. In silence, please. You have made enough noise this morning."

"Wait … wait." At the sound of Sharon's voice, the three applicants sighed. Brian rolled his eyes back. How much trouble was this bitch going to get them in?

"What do you mean, after breakfast? Don't I get to eat?"

"Eat?" For one second, Claudia saw a gleam of pleasure in the majordomo's eyes. "Oh, yes, my dear. You'll eat."

The three followed Chris to the stairway, where he stopped to signal Ms. Rachel to his side. She was carrying a box of supplies in her arms. Chris said, "I've sent you a little helper, Rachel. Have her clean that room from corner to corner. Feel free to use whatever means necessary to get her to behave."

The woman nodded seriously, but all three slaves could see that she was pleased.

"Oh, and Rachel?" Chris hooked a finger into the box, rummaged around, and pulled out a round ball of decorative soap. "Don't forget her breakfast." Pleasure turned to cruel delight. Rachel smiled sweetly and dipped her head courteously before going down the hall.

Chapter Three

It was hard to believe that after all they had gone through, the day was still very young. They blinked in the sunlight as they followed Chris out the back door of the house, through a roofed courtyard, and into a formal garden. When he pointed, they obediently preceded him to an open area of flagstones and turned to face the owners of the house, who were seated. A coffeepot and two cups were on a table between them, and each of them held a clipboard.

Alexandra raised her head inquisitively toward Chris. Her blonde hair shimmered in the morning light. "Where is Sharon?" she asked.

"She has been delayed, ma'am."

"Discipline problems already?" Alexandra smiled.

"Didn't you hear her serenade this morning?" Grendel asked. He poured himself more coffee. "Go and get her, boy."

"Yes, sir."

"All right now." Alexandra glanced at her notes. "Since my two are here, I'll begin. This is the official start of your evaluation period at this house. From now on, everything you say, do, and are will be noted. Before we cover some basic rules and explain what's going to happen, does everyone understand why they are here?"

Robert and Brian nodded. "Yes, mistress," Robert added, his voice pitched high.

"I'm not your mistress," Alexandra replied. "'Ma'am' is good enough for the queen and it's good enough for me. What about you, Claudia?"

"I ... I think I understand, ma'am," Claudia said. "Mistress wants me to receive further training."

"Good enough," Grendel murmured. He turned when he heard the sound of Chris's boots on the stone walkway. Chris appeared, pushing Sharon ahead of him by a firm grip on her upper arm. Her shapeless gray dress was so wet in so many places that she left a trail of drops. There were still bubbles evident around her throat and in several places on the dress. She looked even more exhausted than before, and very, very angry. Chris pushed her to stand with the others, and she gasped, choked, and expelled a small bubble from her mouth.

Brian barely managed to suppress a giggle. Alexandra caught his eyes.

"I hope you receive equal commiseration when you find yourself being disciplined, Brian," she said.

"I'm sorry, ma'am," Brian managed.

"Getting back to what I was saying. I'm sure Chris went over some of this with you, but there are some fine points you need to hear from us. During the next week, you are required to maintain absolute respect and obedience. We have all your records, we know what you can and can't do, as well as what you can take. You are not allowed to ask questions unless given direct permission to do so. You are not allowed privacy, the freedom of discussion, choices in anything, or pleasure, unless it is directly given to you. You may not touch yourselves or each other without permission. Is this all understood?"

"Yes, ma'am," they all chorused.

Grendel continued. "Furthermore, you are under strict discipline. Anyone in this household has the right to correct your behavior in any appropriate manner." He glanced at Sharon. "You have no rights. At the end of the week, if things work out, we might permit you to try and earn some. But don't count on it."

"You'll have chores to do, practical ones." Alexandra handed a sheet of paper to Chris, who studied it. "You will also be tested in a number of ways, then trained and tested again. This isn't a fantasyland, kids, this is a vocational school. Think of it that way and you'll do much better."

"When you're given an opportunity to do things that are forbidden, take it," Grendel advised. "In a moment, we'll let you ask us some questions. Think very carefully about what you want to ask."

Alexandra touched the back of his hand gently. "Let's get the questions over with now. Chris can fill them in on the rest of the rules during the day."

"What a good idea." Grendel turned to the applicants and picked up his coffee. "I'm ready."

"Look, master, I think there's—" Sharon began.

"Address me correctly, Sharon. Especially when asking questions." He sipped, and Sharon wiped her lips with the back of her hand.

"Right," she sighed. "Sir. Look, *sir*, I think there's been a mistake here. Can we talk about this in private?" She jerked a thumb toward the house.

"That's an easy one. No. Next question?"

Alexandra laughed.

"Hey, wait a minute!" Sharon's voice scaled up slightly. "I mean it! I mean—this is *not* what I signed up for, OK?"

Chris began to come forward, but Grendel held up one hand. He gestured to Sharon to continue.

"Like, I understand why you do a lot of this stuff. But I am not in this to become Suzy Homemaker-slave, OK? I am a *pleasure* slave, and I'm not used to this stuff. I thought we had a deal. And you never said anything about getting up at five in the morning and cleaning bathrooms, or, or ..." She wiped her mouth again. "Or anything!" She brushed back her thick hair with one hand, trying to find some pose that made the sack she was wearing seem even vaguely flattering. Grendel noted that despite the difficulty of the task, she did manage to retain some measure of beauty.

If we can train her, he thought, just a little, she can move out of here like an Armani suit at Barney's during the warehouse sale. He turned to Alexandra. Did she want to field this one? No way. She was taking a little pleasure in the fact that he had accepted the woman for training—now he was stuck with her.

"First of all, Sharon, those were not questions, they were comments. But seeing as you don't have the wherewithal to form them into questions, I'll discuss the matter with you anyway." He stood up. Might as well make this good.

"Whatever you were before you came, whatever roles you played, who you lived with, what you did—doesn't matter here. You are here to be improved, not entertained. What you want to be when you leave here, or what your owners want you to be, is also irrelevant. Right now, you are nothing. Do you understand that?" He stepped closer to Sharon, and she gulped. And nodded.

"Then I want to hear you say it, girl."

"Yes. Yes, sir."

"Yes sir, what?"

She trembled. He stepped closer, lowered his voice. It made him more menacing. She stared into his dark eyes and whined, "Yes! What you said! Wadda you want me to say!"

"That you're *nothing*," Grendel gently prompted.

"I'm nothing!"

He shouted into her face, sending her stumbling back. "You're nothing, what?!"

"Sir! I'm nothing, sir!" She whimpered and looked down and then had a sudden inspiration. She dropped to her knees and lowered her head to his feet.

The other three gazed at her, bent into a sexy, trembling package. Claudia nodded approvingly. Robert felt a stirring between his legs and bit his own lip.

Grendel went back to his chair and sat down.

"Now, as I was saying," he began. Sharon stirred and started to raise her head. "No, stay where you are, Sharon, that's the first correct thing you've done since you got here, and I want to enjoy the moment. As I was going to say, you are especially nothing this week. At the end of the week, *if* you stay, your education pattern will change."

"Except for one thing," Alexandra noted. "You will still be required to obey everyone else in the house, and you will still be subject to whatever discipline is necessary to help you remember what your place and purpose is."

Brian raised his hand, sneaking a glance back at Sharon. God, but that bitch was a laugh and a half. When Alexandra nodded at him, he asked, "Sir, ma'am, will we always get punished for someone else's, um, mistakes?"

"Maybe," the two of them answered at once. The dominants looked at each other and laughed.

Alexandra said, "During this week, absolutely. You can worry about next week when it comes."

"Think of it as an incentive to encourage good behavior in your fellow applicants," added Grendel.

"And … if I may? What about safe words?"

Sharon's head snapped up at the question, and Grendel sighed. He snapped his fingers. "Crawl over here, Missy Pleasure Slave. Get your head down there." He pointed to a spot near his left foot. She did as he said, her body slinking across the patio like a cat. When she put her head gently down, he raised one booted foot and planted it between her shoulder blades, pushing her down further.

"Now stay put for once! I'll let you know when

you can get up." He looked back at Brian, but Alexandra had decided to take the question.

"This is not like your old life, Brian," she began. "There are no safe words here. Grendel and I—and Chris—know what we're doing. And if you are driven to the limit of your capacity, we will know it. If you experience some physical problem that requires attention, you will say so, immediately, and it will be attended to.

"But you have no way of changing what is going on because it's uncomfortable, or boring, or difficult, or because it hurts and you don't like it. You aren't here to like it. You may like the life, you may love it and never leave it, but we will not be your owners, this will not be your house. You are here as a student, and you will leave—hopefully—as property."

Brian nodded and lowered his head. "Yes, ma'am. Thank you."

"Are there any other questions right now?" Grendel shifted his foot to a more comfortable spot on Sharon's back and leaned on it a little. Her moan sounded muffled; no doubt her cheek was pressed against the stone. He relented a little and eased up.

The other two, the "goodies," as Alex had phrased it, were silent for a moment. Then, timidly, Robert raised one hand, still trying to cover his chest. Alex nodded at him.

"Ma'am? Um ..." He shifted nervously and almost whispered his question. "May I have a shirt, please?"

"No," Alexandra answered. "I want to see your chest. Be thankful you still have your pants."

"Oh!" Robert gasped, horrified. It was so difficult

to be naked, even half-naked! He blushed, and low-ered his head.

"Any other questions? Claudia?" Alexandra turned her sharp blue eyes toward the little slave, who shook her head. "Well, then that's it for now. Did you want to say anything else, Gren?"

"No, I think they have enough to consider for a little while." He turned to the three and said, "Go back into the house and wait in the main hallway. Chris will join you momentarily and explain the rest of the house rules to you, and we will have some private interviews later on today, after you get acquainted with the house and the staff." He waved, and kept his foot firmly on Sharon's back. The three looked slightly confused, but then walked toward the house.

Alexandra was taking notes.

"Your two are quiet," Grendel said.

"They have some manners."

He nodded and drained the last of his coffee. "I seem to have the losers."

"Think of them as challenges. Besides," Alexandra smiled and winked, "this one can at least make a good ottoman."

Grendel looked down and sighed. "No, she can't. Too bony." He lifted his foot and nudged her. "Follow the others. Quickly."

She got up, her hand reaching up to caress her jaw, and then turned and fled. She looked quite graceful as she jogged past a silent Chris, who never moved from his stationed spot by the pathway. Grendel beckoned to him, and he approached, to stand about a foot away. Chris put his hands behind his back expectantly.

"Don't sulk, Chris, it makes you look cross," Alexandra said, pausing in her writing.

"Yes, ma'am. Forgive me."

"What's the matter, boy, upset over their bad behavior this morning? Think it reflects badly on you? Or are you just jealous of the attention pretty Sharon was getting?" Grendel's voice was light, but his eyes seemed to get harder. Alexandra looked up to watch the exchange.

Chris's face remained impassive. He didn't answer, but cast his eyes down respectfully. Grendel pushed his foot out across the stone, making a light scraping sound. Chris remained still.

"You'd like it if I let you get down there, wouldn't you, boy? Wouldn't you like to feel your back under my boot?"

"Would it please you, sir?"

Alexandra smiled. "Give it up and let him get back to work, Gren."

Grendel glanced at her and sighed. "Right. Get on with it, Chris. You have a lot of work ahead of you this week."

"Yes, sir. Thank you, ma'am." Chris turned to leave and unhooked the strap from his belt.

"Now look what you've done, Grendel" Alexandra said, pointing. "Now he's going to take it out on them."

Grendel shrugged and then got up to stretch. "That was the point."

"Here comes the bad girl," Brian announced softly to the other two. "Aw, did the little girl have her mouf washed out wif soap?" He snickered.

They were waiting in a high-ceilinged hallway,

near the main stairs. When Sharon approached, they all looked up. She glared back at them.

"Why ... um, why don't you leave her alone?" Robert asked. "Shouldn't we be trying to get along?"

"Why should I be nice to her?" Brian hissed, glancing back down the hallway. "We're already going to suffer for her dumb-ass bad manners, right? And you, sister, you just don't fucking get it, do you?"

"Get off my case, asshole," Sharon snapped back.

Brian lifted his hands in mock surrender and turned away. The reason for his capitulation was clear. Chris entered the hallway several seconds later, the strap in his hand.

"Let's begin the tour of the house, shall we?" he said. His voice seemed a little scratchy. "Your interviews start in one hour, and you will *not* be late."

Brian got his beating in the main dining hall, the sharp reverberations of the strap echoing around the room like gunshots. He was bent over at the waist, his hands braced on a mahogany sideboard, his clothing neatly folded between them.

The three watched, their backs stiff and their hands held tightly behind them. Chris quickly, almost savagely, brought deep red marks up on Brian's ass, and Brian growled and grunted with each shot. He twisted slightly from time to time, but maintained his position, lowering his head and groaning when Chris caught him with an especially strong whack. It seemed to take a very long time until Chris appeared satisfied.

The major-domo stood back and looked at his

handiwork and then turned back to the three standing applicants. "You will not eat in here," he said calmly, as though he had not halted the tour to beat a man viciously. "Unless you are in training or permitted to eat in the company of the owners, you will take your meals in the servants' dining room, after they have finished. This room is mostly used for entertaining." He turned back to Brian, who had held his position. "You may thank me and put your clothing on, Brian."

Brian knelt and then looked up. Chris nodded, and Brian bent swiftly forward and kissed each of Chris's boots. "Thank you, sir. I mean, thank you, Chris."

Chris started walking while Brian was still pulling his pants on. Tough little guy, Brian thought, pulling his T-shirt on as he caught up to them in the next hallway. Heat spread all along his ass. His cock was at half-mast, nicely awakened by that strap. Gives one hell of a nice beating. I wonder if he's pissed about what happened yesterday? When Brian flashed on the scene in Grendel's office, he wondered if any of the other slaves knew. Did they get the same test? He tried to pay attention to what Chris was saying about the rooms they passed through.

Claudia was ordered to take her dress off in the library. Positioned so her small, dimpled buttocks extended behind her, she lowered her head and held herself very stiff. A tear was already slipping down her cheek as Chris let the strap slide along her curved bottom.

"For Sharon's lack of manners," Chris said. He had said the same thing before starting on Brian.

The first stunning slap of leather sent Claudia stumbling forward. She cried out, a very harsh, unladylike sound, as she fell forward and hit the table she was supposed to be bracing against.

It hurt! Oh, god, it hurt too much! It wasn't like Mistress' cane, which whistled and cut in sharp, electric seconds and then went away. It was *hard*, it was so hard, and flat, and stinging and, and, it wasn't *dignified*! Claudia burst into tears.

"Please, Chris, please, I can't take it, please!" Claudia slipped to her knees alongside the table. "Please ..."

Chris looked a little surprised. He placed the strap on the table and bent down to look at her. Then, he straightened up and motioned to Robert. "Pick her up. Lay her over there, on her belly." He pointed to a long, brown leather sofa flanked by several imposing windows. Robert helped Claudia up and took her over to one end of the sofa, looking back at Chris for confirmation. When Chris nodded, Robert whispered to Claudia, and positioned her over the arm of the sofa, her head almost resting on the seat. The rich scent of the old leather filled her nostrils.

"When we received your records," Chris said, addressing the four, "we also received a description of how and why you have been disciplined. For many of our applicants, *fetishes*, theirs and their owners', played a large role in how they were treated. For Claudia, her preferred form of discipline was the cane." He picked up the strap again.

"Here, the cane is a tool, like this strap. But it is impractical from my point of view, as it has a tendency to produce lasting marks, something I am not authorized to do this week. You will get very used to this strap, regardless of whether you can withstand it, or if it makes you cry." He walked past them to Claudia's side, and ran careful fingers over her ass. There was a pink trail where he had struck her before.

"Claudia, this is nothing. You will compose yourself with discipline for the remainder of your punishment or be gagged."

"Yes, Chris," she started to say. But the first blow of the strap caught her in mid-acknowledgment, and she gasped. It was another line of punching pain, like the first. But this time, she was fully braced, and didn't have to rely on her arms to hold her in position. She turned her face to the cushions of the sofa and made a series of muffled cries as the rest of the flashes of pain coursed through her bottom.

How humiliating! How awful! Her tears flowed copiously down her face, wetting the leather below her. She tried not to squirm, and then made little fists in her agony. Then, as suddenly as the beating began, it was over, and Chris was pulling her up to stand in front of him. She didn't wait for his direction, but dropped to her knees and kissed his boots. And how inappropriate his boots were, she thought, even as she pressed her lips to them. Mistress had such lovely footwear, shiny black patent leather sometimes, or lace-up Victorian boots with stiletto heels. Chris wore common workman's boots.

Her tears landed on them and glistened. This was not the elegant domination she was used to at all!

"That will be enough, Claudia. Now, we will proceed to the north wing of the house, Master

Grendel's wing." He walked away from her while she was still on her knees, and she scrambled to catch up with them.

The tension was making Robert shake as they proceeded through the archway that led to the north wing. The sound of Chris's voice describing the rooms that they passed through became a steady drone. None of it registered. He gazed at the paneled walls and looked wherever Chris directed their attention, and tried to remember what his mistress had told him before she left.

"These people can make a real slave out of you," Ali had insisted, petting his head. "If they can't, no one can. Listen good and do everything they tell you, and you'll be on your way to a real mistress in no time!"

And as he padded obediently behind the group taking this tour, he knew that deep in his heart being owned was a dream of immense magnitude. But maybe he just wasn't cut out for it. He was such a failure at everything! He certainly couldn't take a beating like Brian did, so manly and strong.

They had reached the end of the wing, where Chris merely showed them a closed door. "This is Master Grendel's workshop, where you will not have any need to go. Beyond is the garage. Robert, please remove your trousers, brace yourself on this door, and present." The strap appeared in Chris's hand once more, and the other three got out of the way.

Robert unfastened the drawstring of the loose gray pants and lowered them, blushing all the while. He hurried over to the door, hoping no one could really see his nasty thing, and leaned over, placing his broad hands against the oak finish.

Aiming the first blow, Chris said, "For Sharon's lack of manners," and then struck. It was a wide, even swing that brought the length of the strap neatly across Robert's extended cheeks.

As he felt the sharp pain and the thudding impact, Robert gasped. The second blow brought out a whimper, but his arms stayed where they were put. He twisted his ass slightly, and the third blow landed more on one side than the other. Immediately, Robert began to react the way he had been taught to. He started to cry.

"Oh, oh dear!" He managed to whine between shots. His voice was high pitched again, strained by his posture. "Oh, p-please! Oh, I'm sorry, I'm sorry! Uph!" He bit his tongue as the strap hit him lower down.

Abruptly, the strapping stopped. "Be silent, Robert." Chris ran the edge of the strap across the larger man's back. "Your ass is not the only place on the body I may pay attention to."

Robert bit his lip and tried to be quiet through the rest of the beating, but whimpers, whines, and squeaks came through his lips with every blow. Oh, he tried, tried so hard, but it was so frightening! And with everyone watching, it was ten times as bad.

Finally, it was over. And when Robert straightened up for a moment, the state of his nasty thing was yet another embarrassment. He crouched down to kneel at Chris's feet and tried to hide the awakening of his cock, but he knew that they all saw it. When Chris turned away to lead them to the east wing, Robert deliberately stayed behind a moment more so that no one could look at him pulling the pants back on.

"This is Mistress Alexandra's wing," Chris said, when they had passed through the main house again. "It was added on in 1977, but the architecture and construction are consistent with the Dutch Colonial design of the main house. Her studio is, as Master Grendel's workshop, off limits to you. Here," he opened a set of wide double doors, "is the solarium and exercise room. Some of you may be assigned to tasks here. It is also one of the three places where you may spend your free time, if you have any."

They looked around, curious and impressed. One entire wall of the long, narrow room was made up of broad windows. Light poured in and bathed an assortment of gleaming equipment. A bar was on one end of the room, and a curving staircase going down was on the other. Chris pointed.

"The stairs lead to the pools. We have a small swimming pool and a jacuzzi, both of which are off limits to you." Sighs and one barely audible "aww" answered that announcement. Chris smiled briefly and then showed them the various equipment. When they followed him out of the room, they all glanced at each other. Surely Sharon should have been punished there?

But the tour continued, through the media room (off limits), and then to Alexandra's study, and then a brief nod toward her master suite. The third floors of both wings held guest bedrooms and storerooms. The third floor of the main house had servants' bedrooms, the dorm the applicants slept in, and the shower room. They hadn't seen anything that looked or sounded like a dungeon or playroom.

When the tour ended, Chris glanced at his clipboard and said, "Brian, to Master Grendel's study. Claudia, to Mistress Alexandra, in her studio. Robert, to the kitchen, to be directed in duties by the cook, and Sharon ..." He looked up at her for a moment. The slaves felt a moment of tension start to build.

"Sharon, to the main library. There, you will find a binder containing the standard rules of decorum for *property*. You will begin to study it." Chris snapped his fingers. "Go!"

They obediently ran off in different directions.

Chapter Four

"But can't you do anything else?" Alexandra asked. She glanced down at the folder on the table and shook her head. Obviously, no matter how many times she asked that question, the answer was always going to be that pathetically perplexed face and a shivering shake of that pretty little head. The interview was already an hour and a half long. Claudia was simply a slave with very, very limited uses.

But she was a cute thing. Standing in the slanting morning sunlight, her body free of that shapeless gray dress, she looked like a little doll, pink, smooth, and sweet enough to want to sweep up and take home. But then what?

"You know all the rituals of various teas. You can squirm delightfully when you are teased and you can take a formal caning with some panache. You

80

can do light housework, such as dusting, but your mistress never insisted that you do the real work." Alexandra reviewed the salient points again, expressing her amusement with every line. "After all, washing dishes might ruin your nails. Vacuuming was just too strenuous and inelegant for a delicate little thing like you."

Claudia squirmed, just a little bit, and lowered her head, blushing.

She does that very well, Alexandra thought. The mistress of the house took a step closer to the girl. "In other words, Claudia, you have been spoiled rotten, haven't you? You did practically no labor and performed no meaningful task other than to carry a tray every once in a while and manage to do it with some grace. Your other skills, if we can call them that, are blushing, simpering, being obsequious to the point of saccharinity, and looking cute in an erotically designed maid's costume. Is that an accurate evaluation?"

Claudia lifted her head a little. "If—if ma'am says so," she said softly.

"Well, you can be voice trained," Alexandra mused. Voice training was valuable in a property. It meant that the slave would never answer a question or voice a comment that would indicate a personal desire. Some owners liked that, it could add to the value of an otherwise uninteresting or limited offering. Alexandra realized that she was already assuming that they would have to sell Claudia. That wasn't fair, not to Claudia, not to Madeleine, and certainly not to the house.

"Tell me, Claudia, did it ever occur to you to ask for more duties or responsibilities?"

Claudia shook her head. "No, ma'am. I did what my mistress told me to do."

Alexandra smiled at that. "Oh really? That's not exactly true, is it?" She stepped in closer and ran one light, gentle finger along Claudia's shoulder. It produced a shudder, a nice, rippling response. "You did have trouble obeying her whenever she tried to take you out of these limited areas, didn't you? For example, when she wanted to see you play with yourself?"

"Oh!" Claudia lowered her head again, so fast her hair flew around her head. "Mistress ... Mistress told you?"

"Yes, of course she told me," Alexandra replied. "Pick up your chin, I don't like talking to the top of your head." Claudia did so, her cheeks red with humiliation.

Alexandra walked back to the table and pulled a sheet of paper from the folder and scanned it. "You couldn't perform when she commanded you to; instead you burst into tears. On a later occasion, when she honored you by taking you to bed, you did the same thing when she gave you a dildo and told you to use it on yourself." Alexandra looked up for a moment. "Did you end up staying with her that night, or did she send you away?"

"I stayed, ma'am," Claudia whispered.

"Spoiled rotten," Alexandra muttered again. "In fact, any time your mistress decided that you should be more interesting sexually, you rebelled, didn't you? You used your tears and your whimpering and your charm to manipulate your Mistress into letting you dig yourself into this rut of a role, where you expected to stay for as long as you continued to like it."

"No!" Claudia gasped as the word escaped her lips. "I mean, please, ma'am, it wasn't like that. I loved … I love my mistress! But some things are so very hard for me!" Tears had started welling up in her eyes.

"That's not going to work here," Alexandra commented, indicating the tears. "Grendel loves it when slaves cry, and it doesn't affect me in the slightest. Not from you or from Robert."

"I'm sorry, ma'am."

"Don't be sorry. Just stop it. Your first charge is to stop crying every time something unpleasant happens. Learn to express your emotions with your posture, your attitude, and your mouth. For the rest of the week, whenever you cry, you will be given additional work to do." Alexandra beckoned and Claudia came to her, frantically blinking away tears.

Alexandra ran her finger along Claudia's body again, this time over her throat and along her arm. Her skin was soft, and a little pale. "You'll also start spending some time in my solarium. I'll tell Chris to put some sunblock on your shelf tomorrow. You'll find a workout regimen prepared for you every day at … four o'clock. Don't make it necessary for me to watch you."

Claudia said, "Yes, ma'am."

The finger continued its journey. Alexandra traced a line from Claudia's hip to one small breast, circling the erect nipple and then gently pinching it. That elicited a slight moan from the girl, and Alexandra smiled gently. Slowly running her finger down Claudia's belly, she was not surprised to find that the shivering little maid was hot and very wet between her thighs.

Claudia gasped slightly and arched her back a little bit. She was blushing again, how sweet. Alexandra flicked her finger across Claudia's swollen clitoris and then eased two fingers between the folds of her damp lips. When she brought them out, they glistened.

"Clean me off," Alexandra said, holding them up. Claudia licked at them with tiny catlike strokes, tasting herself and her excitement, and continued to lick until Alexandra took her hand away. Claudia's body shifted slightly, her hips moving just a little closer. But her hands remained at her sides, where they had been during the entire interview. Still, every inch of her begged to be drawn into an embrace.

Alexandra stepped away suddenly, leaving Claudia to sway slightly on the balls of her feet. "Get dressed. That will be all for now," Alexandra said. "After lunch, Chris will assign you some duties. You may go directly to the kitchen and see if Cook needs any help." She watched the girl pull the dress over her head and slip her feet back into the shoes. Claudia gave a polite nod before exiting the room, but her face was still flushed with erotic expectations.

Altogether, it was not an unpromising interview. Despite the fraidy-cat exterior, there was some strength and discipline in the girl. It took practice and dedication to create art from a form of service, and it took some strong resolve to take regular canings. And she did have a kind of enticing sensuality, that little pout in her lips and her delicious reaction to being humiliated. It was just a little difficult imagining what to make of her after one interview. I need to see her working, really working, Alexandra thought, and then see what kind of a sexual plaything she could be. That's something to look forward to....

But she's the best of the four, Alexandra reminded herself. And as promising as she might be, she was still far from Market material.

Sharon was starving by lunchtime. Not that she was ever a big eater (keeping slim and fit had been a very large part of her life until now), but being denied breakfast made it her priority thought while she had been waiting in the library. All alone for hours! She had found the binder after about twenty minutes of looking around, flipped through it, and scanned the pages of lists. There were literally hundreds of little details in there, some of them only applying to certain types of slaves and some of them only applying to certain situations. Some of them were just so silly that she giggled out loud. Reading through them wasn't even a turn-on, although some of them sounded hot. She got bored and started examining the room, spinning a large globe around, looking in the drawers of the two desks (nothing interesting), and then actually looking at the other books. The topics of most of them didn't meet with her standards of "interesting." And once again, as in Grendel's office, there weren't any books about bondage or SM or slaves and masters.

Her stomach growled through the rest of the morning. By the time Chris came to summon her at 12:45, she was ready to pull her hair out with boredom and hunger.

The four applicants met in the servants' dining room at precisely 1:00, after washing up. Robert and Claudia brought in a meal of sandwiches and mounds of raw vegetables and fresh fruit. They had ice water to drink. They didn't speak to each other when they sat down, each concentrating on the food. There were brief glances exchanged, and tension was high, but no one spoke.

"After lunch, you will have one hour of free time," Chris announced from the doorway. They all turned to him. "Free, of course, is a relative term. You may spend it resting in your dorm in silence, reading in the library, or you may take a walk with me around the grounds. After that, Robert will see Mistress Alexandra in the solarium, Brian will report to Ms. Rachel for his duties, Claudia will report to me for hers, and Sharon will return to her studies." He paused and looked them over. "At 4:15 this afternoon, Sharon and Brian will report to me in the paddock for a lesson in trotting. Your evening schedules will be given to you at dinnertime. You may speak to each other this week while you eat, but keep in mind that you only have a half hour for meals. Any questions?"

Sharon nodded, swallowing a bite of sandwich. "When do I get interviewed?"

"At Mr. Elliot's pleasure, Sharon. Kindly address some of your studies to section three of the manual, on patience and the control of curiosity." He looked back at the others. "Any more questions? No? Then I will see you in one half an hour." He left, closing the door behind him.

"Oohh, I hate him," Sharon said after he left. She drank deeply from her water glass. "I don't believe it. I need a fucking cup of coffee. How do we get coffee around here?"

"You don't," Robert answered. "I spent the morning with the cook. She's a real nice lady." He picked up a large pear and put it on his plate. "She told me that we get no coffee, no soda, no sugary things, nothing that's unhealthy or fancy."

"I am going to die without coffee," Brian moaned. "That was the hardest thing today, facing that interview without a cup of coffee in me." He sighed and looked at the table. "And all this rabbit food is gonna kill me. I'm dying for a cheeseburger deluxe already."

"What about diet soda?" Sharon asked. Robert shook his head. "You mean, this is it? *Water?*" Her voice scaled up sharply.

"W-well, in the morning, we get fruit juice," he stammered out. He lowered his head and then fidgeted nervously. "A-and they can give us, um, little portions of forbidden foods as rewards, and we can have herbal tea at night, and, um, stuff like Gatorade when we're in the gym." He said all of that in a rush and then took a long drink from his glass. God, it was difficult dealing with all of this! And to have a fellow slave looking at him in such a—*dominant*—way, demanding answers from him, oh it was just not to be borne! And with his interview coming up so soon!

Sharon stared at him for a moment as he tried to concentrate on his plate. "You know, you really are a big sissy, aren't you?"

"Sharon!" Claudia cried out in horror. "Be nice!"

"No, it's true," Robert sniffed. "I *am* a big sissy. I'm sorry." He pushed his plate away and buried his face in his arms. The bulk of his shoulders shook as he sobbed loud, falsetto tears.

"This is gonna be a long week," Brian said out loud. He took a carrot stick and munched, trying to figure out what had happened during his own interview. It was easy to tune out the tirade that Sharon was starting.

Grendel had asked him a lot of questions about things he had done before. Where he worked, what sports he played, which bars he went to. Brian answered all the questions truthfully, quickly, and with nicely snappy "sirs" punctuating his speech. But as the interview went on, he realized that he was being asked to talk more and more about what he liked to do and what he wanted out of life, and he began to wonder if he was being led into a trap. Brian tried to slip in some comments about how much he wanted to be owned and have decisions made for him, but Grendel casually brushed these answers off and always returned to what Brian enjoyed, what Brian did, what Brian ate.

It was very strange.

And then the interview changed. Grendel ordered him to strip and show himself, and savagely criticized his body and mannerisms. Called him a soft, lazy dilettante with no real direction in life and no idea how to commit to anything. Brian had panicked and tried every trick he knew to mollify an angry master, but Grendel laughed at him and called him on every one. Shit, Brian thought, remembering. That guy really knows his stuff. Even Paul wasn't as tough as Grendel. By one point, Brian was begging to do anything to prove his sincerity, suck cock, lick boots, kiss ass, drink piss, anything.

And Grendel had merely sighed and told him to get dressed and get out. It was lunchtime.

Did I pass or fail? Brian mused. And what do I have to do to get on around here? I have to figure it out soon, or I'll never have a chance like this again.

At least, he thought, watching Sharon browbeat poor Robert, I have a much better chance than she does. Hey, maybe we should keep her in control, so she can be my bad example! Compared to her, I'm wonderslave. He snickered.

"And what are you laughing at, faggot?" she turned on him with a snarl.

"Oooohhh!" Brian threw his hands up in mock horror. "The bitch called me a bad word! I'm shattered! I'm dismayed!" He turned serious and lowered his voice. "And I am thoroughly sick of your attitude, Miss Thing. You just don't get it, do you? We're here to be trained to be slaves, OK, honey? If you don't like it, just tell them and get your ass back to Scarsdale or Teaneck, or wherever the hell you came from." He glanced up at the clock and took a handful of grapes and began popping them in his mouth.

"Stop it! Just stop it!" Claudia cried out. Her hands were clenched in anxiety. She had barely eaten anything. The sandwiches tasted like sawdust in her mouth. She had nibbled at a piece of an apple, but set it aside soon after Sharon got into her litany of outrage and complaints. All of this anger and spite made her lose her appetite.

By the time Chris came back, there was an aura of gratitude from at least three of the people at the table. The cook's helper cleared the table and Chris asked them where they had decided to spend their free time.

Robert sniffed and said, "The library, please."

Claudia thought. "I'd like to rest for a while," she admitted softly.

"Me too," Sharon said. Claudia looked horrified at the prospect, and raised her hand. Brian looked at the three of them and then at Chris.

"I think I'll take that walk," he said lightly. Chris nodded and was about to dismiss them when he noticed Claudia's timorously raised hand.

"Yes, Claudia?"

"Can I change my mind? I would like to go to the library, too."

Chris nodded. "Fine then. Everyone to your place. Sharon, you may not leave the room or make any noise while you rest. Robert and Claudia, follow the standards of behavior you've been given and do your reading away from each other. Brian, you may go to the storage room on the third floor next to the dorm and get a pair of boots. Meet me out by the stable in five minutes. When the hour is over, you will proceed to your next task or appointment, and you *will* be punctual."

Robert carefully folded his trousers as he was instructed and placed them on the floor next to a chair. When he drew himself back up, he was even more conscious of the beginning of stubble all over his body. He kept his eyes down, the better to avoid looking at Mistress Alexandra, who stood to receive him in a long white skirt and a sensuously light, rose-colored silk blouse. She was holding what looked like a short brown riding crop.

His nasty-thing was already hard, despite his efforts not to look.

Alexandra raised his chin with one finger. He was much taller than she. Naked in the daylight, shorn of all its hair, his body was formidable. His shoulders and upper arms were broad and muscular, his back strong and his chest deep. He was in good shape, his stomach flat. And Ali had not lied. His cock was quite a thing of beauty.

It was thick, and, even flaccid, it looked like a meaty sex machine. Now, tumescent and stirring, it hinted at a respectable length when it reached its full potential. Without a tangle of curly dark hair to distract from its size, it looked fat and heavy.

Alex tapped it with her crop, very lightly.

Robert moaned and whimpered. His cock grew more, and a deep blush began to rise in his neck and face.

"You have a very nice body, Robert," Alexandra said. "Turn for me and show me what you look like."

Robert closed his eyes and began to pivot awkwardly, automatically rising on his toes.

"No, not like that! Turn slowly and carefully. I want to see you do it proudly, gracefully. Try again."

He did, but his feet seemed to get in his way and he almost tripped over himself. He caught himself neatly and regained his balance, but didn't miss the look of disappointment that crossed Alexandra's face. Tears formed in his eyes, and he saw that disappointment turned rapidly into what he thought was disgust. He immediately started bawling, dropped to the floor, and tried to kiss her feet.

What did I do to deserve this? Alex thought as she walked away. She put the crop down and started talking. "First of all, you are going to stop this behavior, Robert...."

Didn't she give this lecture already? She hoped that Grendel was having a better time with his "losers." So far, it looked like she was going to spend all her time with a couple of crybabies who weren't of any use in bed. She paused in her instructions to him and studied his bent form.

"Kneel up, Robert. And get your cock in your hand," she announced suddenly.

Robert drew himself up and grabbed hold of his cock, grateful for the opportunity to hide it from view. His face was red from his blubbering and from keeping it so low to the floor.

"Show me how you jerk off," Alexandra commanded. "Take hold of it and work it for me." She leaned one elbow against a drawing table and waved a finger at him. "Go ahead, get it really big and hard. Show me how huge it gets. You can spit in your hand if you want to."

Robert gasped in horror. Show it off? He grasped it tightly, feeling the jolt of pleasure shoot through him, and closed his eyes. Carefully, he tugged at his cock, drawing it down and away from his body in a motion he liked. It was hot in his hand. Never, never had he been permitted to touch himself like this in the presence of a mistress.

"That's it, work it. A lot of mistresses like a well-hung slave around, and you might be sold to a house where you need to be able to get it up on a moment's notice." She watched his efforts with interest. Oh yes, he had a real machine between his legs. No wonder Ali was horrified at the thought of lopping it off.

Robert squeezed his nasty-thing hard again and began to move his fist faster and faster along the shaft. The idea that a mistress would like it, would want him because he had it, was intoxicating. An involuntary groan escaped his lips, and he opened his eyes to make sure Mistress Alexandra wasn't displeased.

On the contrary, she looked very attentive. Trying to please, he worked faster and harder, and began to feel the stirrings of an orgasm. He looked up, pleading with his eyes. Alexandra seemed unaware of his condition, or perhaps uncaring. He kept the tempo up but loosened his hand a little. His breaths were coming in gasps now, his chest rising and falling in a double-time rhythm. He tried to catch her eyes again, failed, and began to whimper.

"Did you want to tell me something, Robert?"

"Yes, ma'am! Please, I'm about to, ah ... please, I'm almost there, ma'am!"

"Do you mean you want to come, Robert?"

He squirmed and his hips bucked forward, but his hand didn't stop. "Yes, ma'am, please ma'am!"

"No, I don't think so. Just keep yourself on the edge. It's very presumptuous for you to just announce that you're about to come, Robert." She smiled, lesson delivered, and Robert's gasp of pleasure and frustration was very rewarding. There was something to this potential slave after all. "In fact, I think you should stop right now."

Robert gave a high, sharp cry, almost a yelp, but took his hand away. His cock stood away from his body, engorged and curving upward.

"Now let's see how long you can keep it that way without touching it," Alexandra said, sitting down. "Keep your eyes open, and put your hands behind your back."

He struggled to put himself in that position, his chest expanding outward, his groin area shamelessly exposed. His breath came in short gasps.

"We're going to work you hard if you stay," Alexandra said softly, stroking the length of the crop. "That body of yours needs schooling. Your attitude and behavior needs shaping. But I'm inclined to believe that you have some real potential. The first step in realizing it is to understand that the training you have had before coming here is not relevant. To hammer this home, you will not be permitted to wear the garments you brought with you, the teddies and the costumes and bows."

To her dismay, his cock began to lower. Was it so deeply ingrained, this fetish? Well, she might as well find out this week, before he was accepted.

"You will wear male-identified work clothes. You will do real, meaningful work."

The cock drooped and lowered further. What a shame.

"You will remember to address me as 'ma'am,' and never as 'mistress,' and you will serve an equal time with Grendel and with Chris as your studies increase."

Robert whimpered as his erection faded away. Alexandra sighed.

"Very disappointing. By the end of the week, I want you able to hold onto that for longer than," she checked her watch, "two minutes." She jotted down a note. "You may dress and go now, Robert."

He practically crawled out of the room. He felt like he was in hell.

After spending an hour in silent study in the library,

far across the room from Robert, Claudia was almost grateful to find herself in Chris's company again. The silence, after that wretched luncheon, was unbearable. She found that she couldn't concentrate on anything, and ended up aimlessly turning the pages of a randomly selected book, never really reading what was printed there. To be assigned a household task was so wonderfully familiar! She followed the major-domo back through the formal dining room and kitchen, and he showed her where the cleaning supplies were.

"Your records show that you have limited housekeeping skills," Chris noted, taking her to a sunny alcove off the west side of the kitchen. "However, polishing silver seems to be one of your strong points."

Claudia nodded eagerly. "Mistress has some fine silver," she said proudly.

"I didn't ask for that information, Claudia." Chris's eyes bored into her and she shrank back. "It's not like you to volunteer such useless information. Control your anxiety in silence, please." He continued as though he hadn't just scolded her and humiliated her to the core of her being.

"Without making judgments on the quality of the silver you're going to be given, you will proceed to clean and polish it. The time you have is just over three hours. If you don't finish it all today, you'll be disciplined and then you will continue the task tomorrow, and the next day until you are finished. Place the cleaned pieces on towels on that shelf. Ah, here's the first box."

Claudia looked up to see Brian enter the alcove with a large box cradled in his arms. As he lowered it carefully to the floor, it made a loud clanking sound.

"Ms. Rachel says there are two more like this, Chris. Should I get them now?" Brian asked. His shirt was gone, and the nipple rings glinted in the afternoon sun.

"Yes. Better to let Claudia know what she's in for, so she can pace herself properly. Deliver them here; you can fit them under the table." Chris pointed and Brian nodded. Then Chris turned back to Claudia, who was eyeing the box with a growing sense of trepidation.

"Are your instructions clear, Claudia?"

"Um. Yes, I mean yes, Chris."

"Then go to it, girl."

Claudia waited to open the box until Chris had actually left. Silver-polishing in the home of her mistress was a task utilizing pristine, beige polishing cloths, small amounts of creamy pink fluid, and loving, gentle wipes. The silver was never allowed to become truly tarnished.

The box was full of ancient-looking, heavy pieces of silver blackened with old tarnish, stained, and scratched. It looked like a box of burnt junk salvaged from some basement of family castoffs. And it was full to the top, with goblets, trays, serving pieces, and a tangle of eating utensils.

Claudia sat down heavily. She looked at the box and felt a touch of nausea. She could never finish all this work in one day. She couldn't finish it all in a year! And it was so, so dirty! Filthy! Despite Alexandra's warning, tears sprang to her eyes. How could she do such work?

And what had Brian said? There were two more boxes of this … this mess.

She was in hell.

As Brian went hunting for the second box of old silver pieces, his mind was on the walk he had shared with the major-domo.

He had originally decided to take the walk in order to get to know the mysterious little man better. It was also, he reflected, a good chance to get away from his fellow "slaves." He had gone to the storeroom and found his own clothing neatly on a shelf marked with his name. Pulling his boots on, after only half a day of wearing these soft, loose garments, had been a startlingly pleasurable experience. It had also given him his second thorough beating of the day.

Chris had been waiting for him at the paddock adjoining the stable. The strap on his belt was missing, but he held a short riding crop, a style Brian knew was called a "bat." As Brian stepped forward, a smile on his face, Chris's expression went from acknowledgment to disgust.

"What? What did I do?" Brian asked, pausing.

"What did I tell you to do, Brian?" Chris questioned.

"Meet you here in my boots," Brian said, puzzled.

"No. I told you to meet me here and to *bring* a pair of boots. You have to learn to listen when someone speaks to you, Brian." Chris turned as a young man with long blond hair led a chestnut mare out of the stable. The mare was saddled with an English-style cross-country saddle, stirrups run up.

"Jack, would you please bring me a dressage whip?" Chris asked, taking the reins.

"Yessir, Mr. Parker." His voice rolled and dipped, a slight accent emphasizing a tone of amusement.

Chris looped the horse's reins around the top rail of the paddock and pointed toward a sunny spot some twenty feet away. "Trousers down, shirt off, and bent so that your arms are braced on the top rail, Brian."

Such an amazing experience, being so naked in the sun. The boots seemed to emphasis his vulnerability. Brian had waited, his arms braced, for several interminable minutes, reveling in the sensations. The sun was hot against his back, the wind sensuous against his thighs and belly. His cock rose and trembled. By the time Chris came to him with the whip, a drop of moisture had formed at the tip, and sweat had appeared at the back of his neck. It all felt so good, so right!

Until the whipping started. The dressage whip stung, a sharp, annoying, cutting pain that made him yelp. Chris laid it on with steadily increasing force and rhythm, from the backs of Brian's thighs to his shoulders.

This was not like a beating with a strap or a belt or a heavy flogger. Those were manly instruments, meant to cause impact and bruising. In the right hands, whips and straps had coaxed monstrously pleasurable orgasms from Brian's body.

But this whip hurt in an entirely different way. Without causing the thudding repercussive effect that made his cock stand at attention, it hurt him lightning fast, with terrible accuracy.

Brian tried to control himself after the first surprising bite of the whip. But the swiftly flying single tress kept catching him in one sensitive spot after another, until all the discipline he could muster just faded away to nothing. Clenching his hands tightly around the smooth wood of the fence, he lowered his head and tried to keep as quiet as possible, but whimpers and gasps soon began to break through. Sharp, whistling breaths between clenched teeth gave way to actual cries as his body began to accumulate long reddish lines of stinging intensity.

And then, it stopped. Brian gasped and shook, but did not break his position.

"Good," Chris said. "Now, put your clothing back on and wait for me."

And that was it. When Chris returned, he was leading the mare. Chris mounted and rode, and signaled Brian to walk beside him, and Brian did. His trousers and shirt felt hot, confining, and irritating against the marks on his skin. The sun seemed glaringly hot all of a sudden, and if Brian had ever intended to start a conversation with Chris, the intent fled with his confidence. The mental gag he felt was as efficient as the physical one Chris had pushed into his mouth the day before. He kept his pace with the horse and took deep breaths and tried to figure out what the hell he had to do to make it here.

This was nothing like he had expected. Ruefully remembering Sharon's outburst of the morning, he found that he was in agreement with her. This was not what he had signed up for. He had figured that the house was going to be heaven.

The fiery condition of the back of his body was a testament to his error.

When they got back to the house, Chris examined him and told him to leave the shirt off for the rest of the afternoon. Ms. Rachel was brisk and efficient and very cold, and there was amusement in her eyes as she ordered him about. Although Brian felt a moment of sympathy for little Claudia, stuck rubbing smelly chemicals over the most disgusting pieces of silverware he had ever seen in his life, he spent most of the afternoon feeling enormously sorry for himself.

Sharon waited. And waited. And waited. Spending an hour dozing on that sorry excuse for a bed was hard enough. Being stuck in this totally boring library without even a radio to listen to was excruciating! How could people have so many books that were so boring? Back home, she had three shelves of books, famous ones and cheap, dirty ones, all about slaves and masters and kinky sex. She even had some books of photos, and one really hot version of The Story of O done up in drawings. These people, supposedly "real" masters, didn't have even one hot book in their entire stupid library.

She looked at the binder containing the stuff she was supposed to be studying, flipped through it again, and put it back. She had seen all that shit this morning! How many times did they expect her to read it? Or maybe they thought she was slow or something.

She tried to sleep again, but was too tense. First, I get awakened like I'm in the army or something. Then, some bitch of a *maid*, for crying out loud, gets her jollies stuffing soap in my mouth while I crawl around doing *her* job. Then they leave me all alone in this stupid, boring, so-called library, feed me dull, boring food for lunch with no coffee, and then wham, I'm back in this room. Maybe they're gonna train me to be a slave by boring me to death.

She did finally manage to doze, thinking of a beautiful castle full of gorgeous, California-blond, deeply tanned, and muscular young masters who wore soft, tight leather pants. And I would wear a jeweled thong, dipping low and arching high, with a sparkling collar around my neck, and maybe gold rings on my nipples, and everyone would just die when I walked by, but they couldn't touch because they know I belong to the king, who loves only me, and they're all jealous....

"Are you ill, Sharon?"

She came out of her reverie with a snap. Grendel was standing by the couch she had been dozing on, his hands in his pockets, a thoughtfully concerned look on his face.

"Huh? No, no, I'm all right, I'm awake." She sat up, trying not to yawn, forcing a small, slightly embarrassed, slightly shy smile. "I'm sorry, ma—sir. I guess I didn't get enough sleep last night."

He nodded. "And you're not used to studying this much?" he offered.

Her smile broadened, and she bowed her head in the way that all the men she'd ever played with found so charming and submissive. She knew what would come next. He'd smile back and stroke her hair. She arched her neck to give him a better angle.

"We can begin by your explaining to me how to show yourself for examination," Grendel said. She looked up and found that instead of moving closer to caress her, he had actually turned away. He took a seat in a large, comfortable armchair and crossed his legs.

She looked at him in utter confusion.

"How to present yourself for examination, Sharon," he repeated patiently. "For example, by a prospective buyer."

Oh! Shit, how was she supposed to know that? Wait, it was in that binder, wasn't it? Something about kneeling? She tried to remember, but the very concept was vague. But there was something about it in one of her books, wasn't there? Stalling for time, she stood and smoothed that shapeless jumper over her legs. An image came to her from the book she had at home, and she gracefully sank to her knees and placed her hands on her thighs with the palms turned up. She tilted her head down in humility.

"Whenever you're ready, Sharon."

Her head jerked up. "Um, this is it, sir."

"First of all, I didn't tell you to *do* it, Sharon, I told you to *explain* it. In words. And if that is how you think it should be done, you're incorrect. Let's try another one. Tell me how you would stand if told to be at attention. That one is a little easier." Sarcasm dripped from his words.

"I ... I'd stand up straight," Sharon said.

"And ...?"

"Uh. With my head up?"

"Are you asking me, or telling me?"

Sharon bit her lip. "With—with my head up and, and my hands straight at my sides."

"Sharon," Grendel said softly. He uncrossed his legs, leaned forward slightly, and beckoned to her, and she moved toward him on her knees.

"You didn't really study today, did you? In fact, you've probably wasted every minute that you've been here, haven't you?" He kept his voice very soft.

"I looked at it, sir," Sharon said, bowing her head again. "But I'm not real good at studying. I forget. I'm sorry." Her voice lilted upward in supplication. "Please don't punish me."

"All right," Grendel said easily. "I won't."

Sharon's head snapped back up. "What?"

"I'm granting your request. I *won't* punish you. In fact, after we conclude this interview, I won't even see you privately again until you've memorized the first two pages of this manual." He swept the binder up and tossed it on the floor between them. It fell with an unnerving clatter. "Don't forget that I know you, missy. You're a spoiled little princess who's gotten men to do precisely what she wanted them to do while deluding them into believing that they had some power over her. I said it yesterday, and I'm reminding you today—*That shit doesn't work with me!*"

She gasped as he raised his voice.

"You were given hours alone today and one simple task. And not only didn't you do it, but you lied to me, directly and indirectly. Let me tell you one thing, girl, and listen to me very carefully." He kicked the binder so it landed against her knee. "If you lie to me one more time, Chris will have your bags packed and your sorry ass in a cab so fast you'll think this place was an hallucination. Am I making myself clear to you?"

"Yes, yes sir!"

"You seem to think that the phrase 'pleasure slave' means you are exempt from responsibilities and duties. The truth is, my girl, the route you've chosen is harder than you think. Not only will you have to memorize every position and style in this manual, but you'll have to execute them, perfectly, with no regard to the nature of your owner, whether you love or hate them. You have to learn to endure discomfort and pain and still manage to look exquisite and inviting. You have to be ready to serve at every moment of your life, waking and sleeping. Do you really think you're ready for that?"

"Yes," Sharon whimpered. "I want it so bad!"

"You want? *You* want? Your wants don't matter, Sharon! That's part and parcel of the whole scene, and you don't get it. Do you think that you really want what I've described? Well then, study when you're told to. Act when you're told to. Stop bitching and sulking every time you think we're not watching." He leaned back again. "This stuff is only the beginning, missy. In addition to all the behavior and language that turns you on, you're also going to have to learn how to dance. And play games. Do you play tennis? Golf? Do you swim? Can you dive? Do you ride? Can you play poker? Backgammon? Bridge? Mah-jongg?"

Each question was met with a frantic nod or shake of her head. There were many more noes than yeses.

"And then there are your social skills, what little there is of them. You have to work on your atrocious accent, and learn to stop centering every conversation on yourself. You'll have to learn how to address people naturally, so that everyone who hears you knows that you belong to someone. On top of that, you'll have to learn how to converse, from the basics of communication to how to welcome, flatter, and otherwise receive guests. You're going to have to know about topics ranging from opera and theater to current events and politics."

Sharon's back began to stiffen. "But why?" she asked.

"Because pleasure, Sharon, doesn't begin and end between a person's legs." Grendel stood up. "If you have any hope of getting into a situation like you described in your contract, you need to be educated. And believe me, Eliza Doolittle was a Rhodes scholar compared to you."

He sighed as a veil of incomprehension settled over her face.

"When someone has the money and time to invest in a pleasure slave, they're assuming that their new property will be alluring, captivating, submissive, and utterly available. But they also want them to be *interesting*. A pleasure slave has to serve all the pleasures of their owner, and share them from time to time. Normally, we don't handle strictly pleasure slaves here, their training tends to be very time-consuming for the return on the investment. In your case, *if* you manage to stay here and *if* we manage to make something out of you, prospective buyers will know just what a novice you are, and that makes the return even less."

Grendel watched her reactions. She was listening intently, thank god. Maybe something would get through.

"Well, that's enough for now," he said as he rose. "You have about twenty minutes before you're due to meet Chris for your lesson in trotting. I suggest that you start memorizing. When you can recite the first two pages to me, I'll see you for another private interview."

After he was gone and well away, Sharon picked up the binder and threw it with all her might across the room. Her curses followed it for a full five minutes.

"That's a nice bit o' fluff, ennit?" The man's voice startled Claudia so much that she dropped the candlestick she was holding. It banged against the table, and the sound made her jump. The man laughed.

She turned toward the door to see a stranger standing there, a cup of coffee in one hand. He was tall, had long blond hair, and smelled faintly of horse. Cook's voice, coming from the kitchen, answered him.

"She's with the new ones, Jack. The name's Claudia. Now don't you disturb her, she's got work to do!"

Claudia flushed and turned back to the polishing and cleaning. She was going very slowly. Each piece needed a lot of rubbing, and the polish smelled like something evil and noxious. Streaks of tarnish marked her dress, and a pile of rags made filthy by their use was growing on one corner of the table. Yet the number of pieces finished could be counted on the fingers of one hand. Three boxes full, and she hadn't even begun to make an impact on the task.

"Aye, she's got 'er hands full all right," agreed the stranger. "Looks like she'll be busy through the judgment!"

Claudia silently agreed, and the tears that she thought had all been cried out returned.

"Eh now, at least you're inside where it's nice and cool, fluff! Not like your compatriots out by th' paddock, stamping about in th' hot sun!" He chuckled. "You should 'ave seem them, Cook. And that Chris, layin' into them like a thresher. Two of the new ones, that pretty boy and the lass with the model look. He had 'em dancin'! Not like this 'un, sittin' pretty in the cool shade." He finished the cup of coffee and wiped his mouth with the back of his hand.

"Well, be good, fluff. We'll be runnin' into each other now 'n' again." With another chuckle, he turned away from her, leaving her flushed from his attention and the stream of moisture that streaked down her face. When she was alone again, she put the silver and the rags down and leaned her head against her arms and cried. Again.

Just a little while after she had stopped crying and turned back to the task at hand, Chris came in. His tie was slightly askew, loosened as a reaction to the sun and heat. His boots were dusty. He looked grimly at her and at the row of five silver objects that she had managed to finish all afternoon.

"This...," he started to say. He sighed and ran one hand through his hair. "This is intolerable."

Claudia's mouth dropped open in terror. She tried to say something, but couldn't get the words out, and lowered her head in contrition.

"You were supposed to know what you were doing, Claudia. How do you explain this ... this ... inefficiency? Did you forget how to polish silver? Did you find something *else* to do this afternoon?"

"No, sir! I mean, no, Chris!" She swallowed hard, and sniffed. "I tried, I'm trying, but it's all so ... so ... dirty!" More tears. "Please, I'm sorry, I'll do better tomorrow!"

"I certainly hope so." Chris looked at his watch,

felt for the strap that wasn't at his belt, and grimaced at the inconvenience. Then, a slight smile
curved up one corner of his mouth. He strode over
to Claudia, grasped her upper arm, and dragged
her out of her seat. Ignoring her astonished cry, he
pulled her into the main kitchen, across the spotless
tiled floor. They passed an astonished Robert, who
was shucking fresh corn, the husks filling a basket
between his feet.

With one wrenching jerk of his arm, Chris propelled Claudia through the room and away from
him. She fell with a graceless thud and cried out as
she hit the floor next to a large cupboard. Robert
squeaked out a shocked, "Oh my!"

"Cook! Stir this!" With one last disgusted look at
Claudia, Chris left the room.

Claudia gasped in her pain and confusion before
looking up into the eyes of the motherly woman
who had thus far been given no real first name.
With a sigh, the woman plucked a wooden spoon
from a ceramic jar on the countertop, and reached
down to pull Claudia back up.

"I'm sorry," Claudia whimpered as she was
helped up.

"Not as sorry as you're going to be, little one.
Over you go!"

The cook neatly turned Claudia around and
pushed her against the countertop. Claudia reached
out to avoid falling, and felt the back of her shift
being pulled up. The next moment exploded for her
in a driving stab of pain as the stirring end of the
spoon smacked against her left cheek with an
unnatural, loud slap.

"Ow!" Claudia jerked forward, her hands leaving

the counter. Cook placed one heavy, warm hand at the back of the girl's neck and pushed her back down.

"You're not going anywhere until we're finished, my girl, now hold still!"

Claudia actually screeched as a rain of sharp blows fell on her ass, peppering the twin globes with spots of intense, biting pain. She whimpered, bit her lip, and ended up yelping as often as she could catch her breath.

Then, as suddenly as it started, it stopped. Claudia's tears were genuine tears of fear, shock, and pain now, and she coughed out loud, blubbering sobs as Cook flipped the back of her dress down again.

"Get along, child, you're done. Get back to work, before Chris catches you lollygagging around!" Cook tossed the spoon into the sink and turned back to preparing dinner.

It had taken less than a minute. Claudia felt like someone had held fire to her rear end, and the shame of it all made her head pound in agony. That was it? That was her punishment? Didn't she get to beg for forgiveness, receive it, and get a gentle reminder to be better in the future? Where was the ceremony in that? The ritual? Who knew—or cared—how she took it, how genuinely contrite she was, and what a good girl she could be?

She looked at Cook, who was taking some salad vegetables out of the refrigerator. It was like nothing had happened to disturb her afternoon. Robert was staring intently at the floor, deliberately not seeing anything. Claudia sniffed again and left the room.

Dressing like a maid, or like a poodle, bending

over for her righteous chastisements, adorned in ribbons and bows with cunning clips and clamps attached to make her vulnerable and ever-so-enticing, sent to her room like a naughty child and lectured with infinite patience, all this Claudia had endured in her years of service.

But now, after this afternoon, she was certain of one thing.

She had never been more humiliated in her entire life.

"Before dinner each night, you will have twenty minutes to rest and clean yourselves." Chris, dressed in a clean outfit, his tie correct and tight against his throat, addressed the four applicants in their room. "Tonight, Claudia, Brian, and Robert are to come to dinner nude."

They all glanced at Sharon, but she bit her lip, maintaining silence. Both she and Brian were a mass of aching muscles, their bodies striped from shoulders to calves from Chris's dressage whip. The trotting lesson had been an aerobic exercise in pain and humiliation. Chris smirked and nodded slightly.

"After dinner, there will be another hour of free time, which you may spend in the library, this room, or with one of the owners, if an invitation is extended. After the free time, you will assemble out on the eastern side of the garden, and you will receive any punishments you have accumulated for the day. After that, if you are not chosen for service ... which you will not be tonight ... you will return here. Lights out will be at 9:30." He glanced up. "Any questions?"

And that was the way it went. Dinner was taken

by themselves, three of them stripped to the skin and Sharon sitting in her shapeless gray frock. Sharon alone avoided the library (having spent most of the day there already). And when they went out to the garden, electric torches made the whiteness of their skin seem luminous against the darkening sky. With Grendel and Alexandra in attendance, they stripped down again, and Chris went to work on them with the strap. He had a long list on that clipboard of his. And, as he had told them, neither Grendel nor Alexandra asked for their company when it was all over. Sore, heartsick, and awash with self-pity, all four of them went to their room in silence.

But it didn't stay that way for long.

"So, how did *you* end up here, Miss Thing?" Brian asked as he stretched out on his bed. He was lying on his stomach, the backs of his thighs and his ass still a dark red and very tender from his final strapping of the day.

Sharon turned coldly away from him, refusing to answer.

"Oh, for crying out loud, we might as well get to know each other," Brian said disgustedly. "We're going to be roomies for a whole week, you know. It wouldn't *hurt* to be a little human." He winked at his terminology, and Robert responded with a moan.

"I would like to know you all better," Claudia said. She sniffed and shifted her body around, finally leaning on one elbow and keeping her pretty butt as much off the bed as possible. "I think we should get along."

"Oh, you would," Sharon sighed. "What did you

call her, Mr. Kissy-Face? Miss Goody-Two-Shoes? It's a good name for you. Like, between the two of you and the sissy in the corner, I'm surprised these people don't come down with diabetes. 'Yes sir, no sir, right away sir, let me kiss your ass sir!'" Her mimicry was crude and vicious.

"I hate to remind you, Sharon dear, but that is the way slaves—remember slaves?—are supposed to behave." Brian rubbedhis back. "I guess that wasn't included in your guide to the scene, huh? Back where you come from, masters are probably used to their property delivering a seven-point critical review after each torture scene." He began a mimicry of his own. "Oh, and by the way, master, sir, you hit the left side of my butt six times more than the right! Master, hit me harder! No, softer! A little lower now! Now fuck me! Harder! Faster! Oh, god, I love it when you dominate me!"

Claudia and Robert snickered, although Robert hid it by burying his face in the pillow.

"That's not the way it was at all, asshole, OK?" Sharon sat up, gingerly. "You don't know shit about where I came from!"

"So, like I said, enlighten me, sweetie," Brian answered easily. "We'll take turns. If we don't finish tonight, we've got the whole rest of the week. And if they keep us, we've got the rest of the summer."

Sharon played with her lip, a gentle movement that pursed her lips prettily. She looked around the room, and then pulled her pillow up to lean against. "OK," she said, easing her way back against it. "I'll tell you. Just so, like, you know where I'm coming from."

They all sat up to listen.

Chapter Five

Sharon's Story

I was always into being dominated. Back when I was a little girl, I used to tie myself up in my own closet, you know, looping belts and a clothesline over the clothes bar? By the time I was ten, I knew I was a pervert, but it was like the best secret in the world. I used to stay awake for hours every night, making up these fantasies, only they were like soap operas. I was always this rich girl who was kidnapped, or taken prisoner by pirates, or stuff like that, and I would have adventures, you know? But my adventures always got me stripped naked, or whipped, or gang raped, and stuff like that.

So anyway, in junior high, I was over at a friend's house and we snuck into her older brother's room to look at his magazines. We expected, you know, the usual T&A stuff, some *Playboy*s, some cheap rags. But he had a lot of these really sleazy newspapers with pictures of women tied to stakes, being whipped, having rings in their nipples, and stuff like that.

My friend was, like, totally grossed out. She wanted to just leave them all and forget about the whole thing, because we had another friend who had some normal magazines, and we could always go look at those, OK? So I kind of went along with her, made her believe I thought these things were the grossest things in the whole world, and when she went to the bathroom later on, I snuck in and stole a couple. I mean, who was her brother gonna tell, right? Anyway, I guess he never noticed, because she never mentioned it.

Meanwhile, I go home and I read these things until the ink starts coming off the pages. I mean everything! The letters, the stories, the ads, and all the personals. It was just amazing, you know? Like finding out that the totally cool guy you've been looking at for weeks is really turned on to you. I mean, there were all these people who were into the same stuff I was. I couldn't wait until I grew up, you know?

So I started collecting these things. I would go into a busy store, like one of those little cigar shop places where they sell lottery tickets? And I'd just grab anything weird and kinky and bring it up to the guy and pay for it. Mostly, they didn't notice. Once, I, like, blushed and told the guy they were for my brother, who had a broken leg, and he couldn't tell my mom to get him stuff like that. The guy laughed, like it was the funniest thing in the world, and whenever I went back, he'd ask about my brother. And I don't even *have* one. A brother, I mean.

In the meantime, I really filled out. I mean, every girl in school hated my guts. I was always real thin, but my tits came in kind of early, and guys would really just glom onto me all the time. And, like, I couldn't be bothered with most of them. They were all so *immature*! I knew what I wanted. I wanted an older guy, rich, who had a car and his own place, who was into all this kinky stuff. I didn't want some pimply faced, all-hands-and-mouth high school brat who was gonna live at home until he was thirty, you know? Like, they had no *imagination*. If you asked them to do something kinky, they'd probably think you were talking about moving to the back seat, OK?

So I waited, and I kept buying these books and magazines and things. I even rented a P.O. box so I could order by mail and not have my mom open them by accident. I mean, she would have died! And I had this whole drawer of my dresser that was full of my own toys. I had a bag of clothespins. I used to put them all over my body before I jerked off. I dropped candle wax on myself, and I got really good at figuring out ways to tie myself up so I could let myself loose, you know? Like, no good getting stuck and having to call dad to come get me out, right? I had this really neat leather gag, like it cost me all of my allowance and two weekends of baby sitting, but it was really worth it. I just got off on that fat thing stretching my mouth open while I came.

Oh yeah, I was a real jerk-off artist. I mean, that was my sex life until I met Jerry.

I was hanging out at the local community college. Like, it was either that or get a full-time job, you know? So I was there killing time, and I took this course in literature for idiots, or something like that. A whole class full of airheads, you know? But the teacher was way hot. He dressed up to come in, and he had the best clothes, like designer pants and Gucci belts, and silk shirts. And he was like, *incredibly* strict in class. He had this real short haircut, just when it was really cool to do that, and dark eyes, and this really square jaw. He had this way of looking at you that was totally scary.

I fell in love with him the first day. I mean, really in love. He was just like the masters I made up when I was a kid, you know? Older, smarter, he made money, and he was totally in control. So, I waited a few days to make sure I was right, and then I hung out near the teachers' parking area until he was going home, and I stopped him. I told him all this stupid stuff about how much I liked his class, and I was starting to, like, come on to him, and he totally put me down. He started telling me all this stuff about how it was real nice I liked the class and all, but he thought I was acting inappropriately. That's how he put it, too, *acting inappropriately*. That he was my teacher and I was a student and that was it, you know?

So the next day, I dropped the class. And three weeks later, I moved in with him.

He was *so* cool. Like, he knew right away what I was into. The first time I ever had sex, I was tied to his bed, I mean really tied down, ropes everywhere. I was crying and laughing and coming all over the place that night, it was just fucking incredible. He would get me real hot, and then stop and make me like, beg and beg, and then he'd do mean things like pinch my nipples, or pull my hair, and then he'd start making love all over again, like from the beginning. He was really strong, and he worked out and had a great body, and he was just the hottest thing I could imagine.

And he was really good with, like, talking to me the right way. He never said, "Oh, honey, would you mind going to Pedro's tonight for tacos?" He'd just take me there, you know? And then he'd order for me, without asking me what I wanted. And then, he'd make me eat it! At home, he'd have all these little rules, and I'd forget them—because they were stupid, sometimes—and he'd spank me until I couldn't sit down. I mean, this is for not hanging a towel up, or for not talking nice to him, or stuff like that. And he used to call me names all the time, like slut, cunt, and bitch. I really got off on that, because he did it so casually. It was just, "Hey, slut, get me a beer!" and off I'd go! But the best was when he called me all those names while we were having sex. He used to fuck me real slow, telling me how slutty I was, what a cheap, dirty whore I was, and all sorts of stuff like that, until I was just screaming.

But after a while, I realized that he was only into it *sometimes*. Like, he'd begin to talk regular to me during the week, or he'd have temper tantrums and not spank me or do anything but yell at me. I woke up one day and I thought about it, and it was suddenly clear to me. He really only did that stuff on the *weekends*. During the week, he wanted me to be like a regular girlfriend or a wife even, and not have to deal with ropes and chains and spankings and stuff.

He even started calling me sweetheart. I mean, he was a teacher in a tiny college, OK, and he was sounding like he wanted me to be his wife. No way, baby, I was in this for thrills, not for a lifetime of K-Mart shopping, OK?

And I got so bored, so fast. I began to find rules to break, and, like, I'd make it obvious? I say hello to him when he got home, or I'd leave the stupid bath mat on the floor, or something like that. But he'd just forget it, or not notice, unless it was when *he* wanted to play. Then, I tried to get him into some more stuff. I got some catalogs and showed him some toys we didn't have, like whips and leather blindfolds and dildos and buttplugs and stuff. I mean, we were still using my old clothespins for nipple clamps! But nothing seemed to interest him, you know? Then, in the back of one of my magazines, there was a listing of these kinky clubs in New York, so I went out one night to check out what they had.

And that's how I joined the, um, Equivocal Coalition. I mean, I don't know what the fuck that name is supposed to mean, but that's what they called it, OK? The first time I went, I thought it was the hottest thing since rollerbladess. I mean, it was like hundreds of people into this SM stuff, and they had meetings and parties and stuff. But it was at my third time there when I realized that it was really this club of total dweebs who were trying to get some kinky nooky, like *right now*. I mean, I'd walk in and there'd be this parade of men growing around me. And they'd all be 'masters,' you know? Because I told them I was this total slave bitch, and they all became instant masters. Like instant coffee. Just add bullshit.

They weren't really masters, not most of them. If I walked in there with boots and a riding crop, they'd all be slaves, you know. They were just regular guys who liked their sex a little kinky and needed to get laid real bad. I played with some of them, and it was just like Jerry. OK, now we're master and slave, and now we're like, Bob and Sharon, OK? I mean, nothing was ever real for longer than a couple of hours. But these guys did do one thing right. They showed me the sex clubs.

They were great! I went to one, and this night there were these guys just rolling around on the floor, dressed in rags and shit? And this woman was tied to this really weird bench, with, like, thousands of feet of rope? And all these pervert guys into feet were crawling around licking boots and stuff. Everyone was dressed in tight leather and sexy clothes, and some of them even carried whips and handcuffs and stuff. And I went to this other one, and they gave out play money and pretended they had a slave sale. I did that a couple of times, and let me tell you, if that money was real, I'd be a fucking millionaire, OK? It was a lot of fun, though. The sale part. Seeing all these guys fighting over me, borrowing this play money from all their friends and stuff. And the best part was seeing that other people did this, well, seriously. Like they were masters and slaves, and the slaves wore little collars, and masters wore black boots, and it was so much better than what I had with Jerry.

So, I'd find some way to get time to go out, and I'd do all this stuff. I bought new, sexy clothes and some cheap silver chain jewelry, and I would just go in and take over the place! Every time I went out,

I'd meet tons of guys who would do anything for me. I'd make them fight with each other just by, you know, not making up my mind. And then I'd get up and do the sale thing, and do some hot scene with the guy who had the most play money.

But then it would go back to the same old problem, you know? I'd get off the stage, and they'd just be regular guys who want a little kinky touchy-feely session and then go home and fuck. And a lot of them wanted to go to *my* home to fuck, too, because it turns out that they're married or some shit.

This kinda became a problem with Jerry. I was still living with him, but I wasn't telling him where I was going all these nights. I mean, I'd tell him I was going out with girlfriends, or shopping, or to the movies, or something. Like, he wasn't stupid, you know? So he caught on, but he thought I was cheating on him with someone regular. It was really cool for a while, because he would sometimes get into playing master when he was really pissed, or he'd threaten to chain me to the bed for the whole weekend and stuff like that. But he finally just lost it, and I had to tell him what was up.

So we went to the clubs together after that. See, he always knew about them, but he was afraid of his, you know, reputation. Like, what if his students showed up there, or another teacher, right? So I told him, hey, who gives a shit? I mean, they're there too. And you've got this total slave babe on your arm while they're probably crawling around licking some old woman's boots, OK? And he saw I was right, so we started going out together.

And that was really cool for a while, especially when he led me around on a collar and leash, and

made me call him master all night. He even sold me
once, brought me up on stage and all that. But that
was like the biggest mistake he ever made, because
that's how I met Frank.

Frank bought me that night, and it was like my
biggest fantasy coming alive. I mean, he looked the
part even better than Jerry did, and he acted it 100
percent. And Jerry was cute, you know, I liked him,
but Frank was a total fox. And he was rougher than
Jerry, you know, not so cultured. But he was really
educated, like he was this building designer or
something, and he had this loft in Manhattan, with a
dungeon and a slave's room and a jacuzzi.

So anyway, that night, he bought me and he totally dominated me, right there in the club. It was really hot, with Jerry watching and everything. But
when we got home, I really expected Jerry to be
angry and jealous and get up in my face about it.
And he didn't. He just acted like everything was
cool, same as usual, good night sweetheart, see you
in the morning!

So, I went to the, um, Equi-whatever Coalition,
and I asked around, and they told me that this guy,
Frank, was probably gonna be teaching this special
seminar on masters and slaves in about a week. So I
went there, and I saw him again, and like a week
later, I was living with him.

He was the best. I mean, I thought he was a real,
100 percent master when I moved in with him. He
had his own little playroom, and there was leather
everywhere. He even had a table with a wheel on it,
like a rack? And he had tons of equipment, I mean
an entire wall of whips and paddles and bondage
cuffs and things.

And he was ready for me. He had me dress the way he liked, walk the way he liked, and every day when he got back from work, I had to be kneeling naked in the hallway, waiting for his cock.

That cock became my entire life. I had to be ready for him to fuck me, or I had to be ready to blow him, all the time. And he'd spring it on me when I wasn't expecting it, like during dinner, or while he was watching TV, or once, when he was talking on the phone to his fucking *mother*. I mean there he was, saying things like, "Sure, Mom," and "Hey, Mom, that's great, and how's cousin Susie?", and there I was slurping away on his dick! And he liked to do things that Jerry didn't get into, like put a vibrator in me and take me out to dinner, or spend a whole day just tying me up in different places. And he liked to whip me, too, and that was something else Jerry really didn't do.

But the best part was that he loved to show me off. We went to the clubs every weekend, and we were the hottest sensation! He'd walk in with me on a leash, dressed in something really, um, skimpy, with gold chains around my ankles and my belly? And he'd be in all black, with, like, whips and riding crops on his belt. Sometimes, he'd handcuff me, or put these really pretty nipple clamps on me. They had little pearls hanging from them, they looked *so* hot. And he'd do a scene with me in the middle of the biggest room, and everyone would watch. Guys would just drool over me. At this one place, they'd just whip out their cocks and start pumping.

And once in a while, Frank would have a play party at the loft, and people would come over. Those were the best. He would tie me up really fancy, and make me a centerpiece, or he'd make me wear this really stupid costume, or maybe crawl around all night like a dog. And he'd let everyone touch me if they wanted to, and sometimes even whip me or spank me. He'd say things like, "My property is available for loan tonight," and people would be so fucking impressed. And I was real good at being a slave now, so all the guys would get really jealous.

It was at one of his parties that I first played with a woman. He and this other master who had a slave thought it would be real hot to watch some girl-girl action, and they put us together. She was shy, but I really got into it. I just did stuff that I liked, and she went crazy. Afterwards, the guys pulled us apart and fucked us silly, like for hours. Soon, all these mistresses were asking to play with me, too.

And for a while, it was like living a dream. But it *was* a dream, you know? You begin to wake up and realize that things really aren't that great. For me, it started when Frank began to talk about getting another slave or two. Like, he always wanted what he called a "stable." And I'm not exactly the most, you know, *monogamous* girl in the world, and it didn't bother me if he wanted to play with other women, but living with them was kind of out of the question. And when I raised the issue, he kinda just dropped it, and just like Jerry did, he started to only do this stuff part-time.

I call these guys "weekend masters." Like they're two separate people, and one is totally normal and dull and vanilla, and the other is a walking fantasy.

But you have to understand, I was always a real sex slave to them. I mean, a pleasure slave. I didn't do the dishes and stuff all the time. The way I figured it, my job was to keep them happy below the belt, you know? And they thought I was the best. My two masters always told me I was the best slave they ever had, and all their friends could just burst from being jealous. The problem was that they were never really enough master for me.

So anyway, Frank and I went to this private party one weekend, at this woman's house down by the shore. And the minute I walked through the door, I knew that there were, like, two kinds of people there. There were people like Frank and me, and there were these really different people. I can't explain how they were different, except that they seemed to be more intense. And at that party, I met this guy named Joe Manelli. I was, like, coming out of a bathroom, and I heard him talking on the phone, telling someone about this hot deal. So, I thought it had something to do with the stock market or something, but then I realized that he was talking about people. And that was the first time I heard about the Marketplace.

I, like, cornered him later, you know? When Frank wasn't looking. And I asked him, you know, what was he talking about? And he just totally went into denial, like I hadn't heard him right, he didn't say anything, and besides, it was none of my business. And from then on, anyone I thought was in on it, they treated me like I was some kind of idiot, and they all laughed. Even Frank, when he heard about what I was asking about, even he laughed at me. He bought me more books and told me to be happy with what I had.

So the next time we went to that woman's house,

I kind of found this file cabinet in this office and there was a folder in it marked "Market," and I just kind of borrowed it for a while. I took it to the bathroom, and I wrote down some names and addresses. And I put it back, real nice. I mean, if no one was going to tell me anything, if they were going to all pretend it didn't exist, how the fuck was I supposed to get in, you know?

So, in the folder was Manelli's name again, and some stuff about contracts. I called him first. When he wouldn't talk to me, I went to see him, because I had his address now. And he tried to brush me off, but I just stripped down and knelt on his carpet and looked up at him and called him master, and boom, he was all mine.

And he told me about the whole deal, how this thing is international, and old, and really secret, and how contracts work, and who makes money, and how slaves live, and *everything*. He even gave me some lessons on how to act, although he wasn't right at all. I mean, now I realize that he probably was some kind of Marketplace nerd, you know? Good for the shit work, but not part of the, you know, inner circle, or whatever.

But basically, I let him fuck me and he wrote me a contract, the way I wanted it, and then I wrote to this place. My contract is totally great, like it says that I'm a pleasure slave and I shouldn't be doing, like, the windows? He showed me how to make up a file like the slaves had to have, and he even got a photographer to take my pictures for me. About a month after I wrote, I got a postcard back, with the date and time I was supposed to get here. It said I should pack a weekend bag, and that was it.

So I packed up my favorite books and toys and stuff and told Frank I was lending them to a friend, and that she thought he was really hot. He didn't even ask who! I put them in long-term storage, and paid for two years' worth. And I really concentrated on being the best slave for Frank, so that when I was gone he'd have lots of good memories.

I called Frank from the railroad station and told him I was visiting my family out of state, and I'd be back in a month or two. I figured one way or another, it'll be easier for him if he thinks I'm coming back.

But I'm not. I can't. I need the real thing. And what's more, when I get what my contract says, it's going to be the real thing forever. Because I'm not an idiot, I know how guys work. And if they sell me like it says in my contract, I'll have myself a master who wants no one else but me for the rest of his life!

Chapter Six

This was the pattern for the rest of the week: Each day, they met privately with either Alexandra or Grendel, and either answered questions or underwent some form of testing. One morning, they might be assigned to some mundane household chore; the next might find them doing a series of poses intended to be erotic or defining. Questions seemed random, partly about their experiences and hopes, and then suddenly about current events and philosophy. They were grilled, constantly, on the most basic kinds of submissive behavior, and the blue binder in the library was frequently consulted and sections memorized by them all, although it had taken a while for Sharon to apply herself to it seriously.

Claudia found herself drowning in that ancient

silver, a task that was assigned only to her. And each night, she received more than her fair share of punishment for not finishing the job. Chris taunted her constantly, openly questioning her ability to do anything right. In time, her tears slowed, but they never seemed to really stop. She began to hunger for a kind touch or word, and would shiver at a gentle tone in anyone's voice.

Robert missed the comfort of his role and his costumes, and seemed to be in tears as often as Claudia. Whenever he was given a task, he always seemed to do it best when no one was looking. But whenever Cook turned to see what he was up to, or Alexandra wanted to watch just how he was going to sweep the porch, or (worse yet!) when Chris came by and just stared at him with those cold little eyes, he just fell to pieces. Suddenly, the knife would slip and weird chunks of vegetables would drop onto the pile of neat slices he had already cut. Or clouds of dust would rise where only clean floors had shone a moment earlier. A bag would shift in his arms, seemingly of its own accord, and curios would clatter as he set them back on a shelf. He was positive that he had his own personal gremlin. It was the only way to explain how all these things only happened when someone was there to watch.

And they were tightly controlled, like prisoners, Sharon commented one night. But not like slaves. And on this point, they all agreed. They clothing, their sleeping arrangements, the manner in which they were spoken to and even the punishments they received, all seemed devoid of the stuff their fantasies had conjured. And even as they were stripped of what little clothing they were issued from time to time, no special distinction was ever made between the clothed and unclothed.

There were no collars, no leather cuffs, no sexy, threatening whips, no delicately painful nipple clamps. No costumes were affected, ever, and even their periodic nudity went so unnoticed that it lost its power to make them "other." And although Grendel and Alexandra made it clear that they were interested in the ability of the applicants to be salaciously interesting and available, neither they nor Chris made the slightest carnal use of them. The most attention they got in that area was a cursory acknowledgment of their ability to get aroused by their treatment. But nothing ever came of it. The four walked a constant path of pain, arousal, and frustration. And each night, they retreated to their room, aching and exhausted. Despite their assurances to get to know each other better, after their first night, no one had enough energy to continue their personal narratives. They barely had the energy to get into a comfortable position to sleep.

It was baffling.

Grendel remained true to his word and only saw Sharon when she was with the other three. But she was no longer left in the library all day. She too found herself peeling potatoes, polishing furniture, and folding laundry as she rotated household tasks with her fellow applicants.

Two days had passed before she realized that Grendel had every intention of keeping his word to her. Her fit of anger that night got them all ten additional blows from Chris's strap. The following morning, when Chris came to wake them, he threw a piece of Sharon's luggage at the foot of her bed and left it there, making no comment.

That day, she went to the library after lunch and started really studying.

As the week drew to a close, the anticipatory tension became maddening. They received no encouragements and no hints that any of them had been accepted for a longer stay. In fact, the inclination of the master and mistress of the house to take any of them to bed or demand some sort of sexual service weighed heavier and heavier on them, especially on Sharon and Brian, who at last found something they had in common.

"I just don't get it," Brian moaned one night. It was just before lights out, and he, Sharon, and Robert were all seated on their beds. There was one more day left in their evaluation period.

Robert was more or less seated—he had gotten one hell of a strapping just moments before for bursting into tears at what Chris had called "an insignificant level of chastisement." Robert's entire body, now covered in a light layer of new hair, ached. He shifted from time to time, trying to find a spot that didn't hurt.

"I mean, Paul told him I was a great cocksucker," Brian said, leaning back against the wall. "Told him I was a great man-lover. But the only time he ever even suggested that I show him was ... that first day in his office!" He controlled what felt like a blush growing on his cheeks. Could that be the reason why he wasn't allowed to show off how well he could suck? Because of what had happened with Chris? No, it couldn't be, he thought. No one else is getting either sex. He wondered briefly if anyone else had been given the same test. "I mean, how the hell can they tell if we're worth anything if they don't have any ... experience with us?"

"My mistress almost never permitted me to ... be that way with her," Robert said.

"Yeah, well my masters never got enough of me," Sharon said spitefully. "I could have a dozen guys fighting over me on any Saturday night! I could make them insane; guys would get off just looking at me. I'd walk into this club on a busy night and instantly, all these guys would just run up and they'd wanna worship me. Understand? Like I was a slave and everything, but guys would line up to lick my boots and stuff. And the sex? I could tire any guy out. One night, my master brought two friends over and they all fucked me, you know? I told you all this, right? And girls, too, every once in a while." She sighed. "Not that *Grendel* would know, I mean he decided to look in on me today, and the only thing he wanted was for me to fucking recite this stuff I'm memorizing. Like memorizing things is high up there on the list of stuff masters want from their slaves, right?"

"Way up there next to knowing how much fabric softener to use," Brian added bitterly.

"You two shouldn't talk that way," Robert said softly. "How do you know you won't be sold to someone who just wants a pretty face to do the laundry? How do you know you won't be sold to someone who just wants labor out of you? Once you're a slave, you're a slave! You have no choice in what you end up doing."

"Listen, sissy," Sharon snapped, "I may have to

listen to them when they lecture me, but I don't have to hear it from you!"

"Sorry." Robert lowered his head and turned away from them.

"You know, you could lighten up," Brian said to her. "By tomorrow night, we could be out of here. Back to whatever you used to have to do to get through the night." He made jerk off motions with his right hand. "But come on, prima donna, didn't any of them do anything to, you know, test you or something? Even on the first day?"

Sharon shook her head firmly. "Fucking *nothing*. Like I was some ugly old hag or something. I swear, Grendel has to be gay, and Alexandra ... she's just jealous."

"Whoa!" Brian chuckled. "You'd better hope this room isn't bugged, Sharon baby, or you just got yourself a first-class ticket home."

"I don't care!" Sharon cried. But then her face screwed up and her eyes glistened with tightly restrained tears. "I want to be wanted! I want them to want to fuck the shit out of me! What the fuck is wrong with that? It's not right that they're not ... not ... interested!"

"You're just pissed because they're probably the first people you couldn't wrap around your little manicured fingers, darling. For your information, Grendel isn't gay and Alexandra is." Brian announced this with all the confidence his voice could carry.

"How do you know that?" Sharon and Robert echoed each other, Robert finally lifting his head.

"Because Paul told me so. He said that Grendel had a woman slave a few years ago, and that

Alexandra has girlfriends. Grendel is kinda bi, actually, because he and Paul used to go out to the gay sex clubs, but Paul thinks he's mostly straight. And I don't know where you get off on the jealousy thing, either, because Alexandra is one classy piece of work. You may be prettier in the mirror, but you're all shine, no substance. Alexandra is ..." He paused and considered. "Elegantly beautiful. And no fool. Definitely not the type to fall for a pretty face. So you struck out on two counts, babe." He grinned.

But he knew better. What Paul had really said was that he didn't know what they were and only had the barest information about what some of their preferences might be. But there was no chance that Sharon was going to bump into Paul and get that information out of him. And besides, if this was going to be their last night together, he might as well sink a few good lines into her for posterity's sake. She fumed and tried to compose a retort, but Robert's voice cut in.

"Do you mean that they're not, um, married?" Robert asked. "They seem to be a couple to me."

"They have different last names," Brian pointed out. "And different bedrooms. On opposite sides of the house. Does that sound like married to you?"

"What would you know about marriage, fairy?" Sharon sneered.

"Enough to know what *you're* up to, sweetie," Brian answered smoothly. He turned a knowing smile toward her.

Before she could retort, the door opened, and Chris came in with Claudia, who looked forlorn. She went over to her bed and sat gingerly on the edge.

"Tomorrow is the last day of your examination period," Chris began, glancing down at his ever-present clipboard. "Tomorrow evening, you will be informed as to your status. Those who will be leaving may choose to leave tomorrow night, or you may spend the night here in one of the standard guest rooms. If you are asked to leave, you must wait a year and a day before you can reapply to this house, unless previous arrangements with the owners have been made.

"Those of you who are permitted to stay will be given a contract delineating your wish to enter a strenuous training program here, lasting from four to six weeks. Signing the contract will make you an official part of the Marketplace, and the records of your examination period will be made available to the master database. The only way out from that point is failure to make it through the training course." He paused, took a long, lingering look at the four of them and suddenly grinned. "Of course, if you are accepted, you will not do this house the disservice of failing the course."

Claudia shuddered.

"I have always given prospective applicants to this house my opinion of their level of acceptability on the night before their final day of examination."

They tensed and looked up at him.

"You have been the *sorriest* most *unsuitable* applicants I have ever had the misfortune to supervise," the major-domo declared. His light voice had hardened. "You have displayed every fault I could possibly imagine in an applicant with the exception of a venereal disease."

Robert buried his head in his arms.

"From extreme narcissism to cultural illiteracy, from nearly pathological introversion to a stunning lack of basic motor skills, you have all managed to catalog a veritable banquet of unsuitability. In all my years of service here, I have never seen such an array of incompetence."

Each word was like a hammer blow. Robert shook at the end of each sentence. Claudia bit her lip, all out of tears at last. Brian clenched his fists and cursed at himself, the sound and repetition drowning out the panic that was rising.

Sharon just glared.

But Chris seemed totally unaffected by their reactions. He tucked the clipboard under his arm and continued. "My opinion, of course, is meaningless. Grendel and Alexandra are the ones who will make the decisions regarding your futures."

He grinned again.

"But keep in mind—if any of you do stay on, you will still be under my supervision. Sleep well."

They all looked at the door as it shut behind him, and then looked at each other.

"Yeah, right," Brian said, his voice slightly shaky.

"What about training him as a butler or major-domo?" Grendel asked, tossing Robert's file on the table. It was the third hour of their deliberations. "He'd look good in the uniform."

"Yes," Alex admitted with a sigh. "But somehow, it doesn't fit him. Not now, at least. If we're going to make something worthwhile out of him it has to be light-years away from his former role. We have to break him totally away from it, give him something new to focus on. And honestly, I hate to let the potential in that body go to waste. He'd be a beautiful showpiece."

"We've already got a showpiece," Grendel noted.

"You really want to keep her, huh?"

"Do you really want to take that vacation this winter?"

Alex nodded thoughtfully.

"The potential profit on her is worth the other three combined!"

"That's *if* we can do something with her. Big if."

"Well, yes." Grendel leaned back and thought for a moment. "She did manage to memorize those two pages in a little over a day. That does indicate some level of skill."

"When she's properly motivated. But how do we make sure she won't revert to her natural state as soon as she leaves our hands? Do we really want to have to handle a return procedure? Risk our reputation? For her? It's not worth it."

They looked at each other, both frustrated. Together, they reached for the other files.

"We can keep Claudia," Grendel said hopefully.

"I don't know what for." Alex sighed again. "She is almost as hopeless as Robert. That role is so much a part of her nature, she just can't let it go, not even when her record of perfect obedience is at stake. And Chris tells me that she is next to useless in any practical skill." She played with her pen, spinning it carefully through her fingers. Her sense of balance was perfect.

Chris looked up when his name was mentioned. He was seated comfortably on the floor, his back resting against Alexandra's chair. When he realized that Alexandra didn't want him to elaborate, he checked his watch and went back to his patient waiting.

"Maybe we can work with that," Grendel said. "Elaborate on her chosen role in some way."

"What, make her a better French maid?" Alex shook her head. "Not something I want to spend my time doing. We can't just keep any of these people unless we know what the hell to *do* with them. Claudia is an interesting challenge, I suppose, but I have no idea what to make of her. And let me tell you, speaking to Madeleine about this isn't going to be easy. Maybe we should keep her on as a favor? After all, Madeleine is responsible for a lot of referrals. Do you want to train her? Maybe she needs a man, something different from what she's used to."

Grendel looked down at the table for a moment and ran a finger along his jawline, bending and stroking down his beard. "I guess I can do that, if I'm sending Brian back to Paul. But damn it, I hate to do this to Paul. He's usually very good at spotting them. And then, of course, we lose the favor he'd owe us if we make something out of the kid." He thought about it for a moment and then met Alex's eyes across the table. "Unless you want *him*, of course."

"I don't think so. From what you've told me, there's nothing exceptional there. Every move he makes is so calculating. It's shallow. He knows the right sounds to make, but I don't think he knows why he's doing all these things, unless he thinks it's the best way to get sex. Give him a few more years, maybe he'll grow up and stop thinking the world revolves around him."

"Then I guess we know what to do," Grendel said, closing the folders and piling them up. "Unless you have anything to add, boy?"

Chris looked up again. "Keep Brian," he said simply.

"That's it?" Alex asked, a little smile curling around her lips.

Chris nodded.

Grendel frowned for a moment and then relaxed it into a grin. "Did you like his cocksucking so much?" Chris grinned back but didn't respond.

Grendel sighed, and pulled the folders apart again. "OK, let's reconsider. What about Robert, again? Do you think we can make a bodybuilder out of him? There's a run on bodybuilders these days."

Alex shrugged eloquently. "Or maybe we can just make up something as we go along."

The following afternoon, Chris made four phone calls. That evening, the applicants were gathered in the library after they ate.

"Is there anyone who wants to voluntarily leave the program?" Alexandra asked. The four stood still. "Then we'll cut through the dramatics right away. We've decided to keep you all."

Four bodies expelled breath at once. Claudia's knees almost buckled. Robert's did, and he went to his knees.

"Oh, thank you, ma'am, thank you!" he cried.

"Robert, control yourself!" Grendel snapped. "Get up and get back in line." The shamefaced man did so, but he couldn't hide the incredible look of relief and gratitude on his face.

"You may be congratulating yourselves now, but Grendel and I want you all to understand something. None of you were automatic selections. You are all, in some way, below our usual standards for applicants. In fact, that was a part of our decision to keep you all together. The amount of remedial training needed is extensive, but your deficiencies overlap. You will all benefit from each other's training."

"Tomorrow starts a whole new way of life for you," Grendel said. "Some of the rules you have managed to learn will change. But the basics remain the same. You will offer your absolute, trusting obedience, your most profound and genuine submission, and your greatest respect and gratitude for everything you are taught and everything you receive. Are you all absolutely sure you wish to stay?"

The four nodded, and murmured "Yes, sir."

"Then receive your training collars."

Chris handed Alexandra and Grendel lengths of heavy silver chain. One at a time, the applicants stepped forward and bent at the waist. Four muted snaps locked them on. As they stepped back, their fingers went up to fondle the smooth links, and they looked at each other to see how they looked. Grendel nodded when Alexandra locked Robert into his collar, and he turned to her with a smile.

"Now the fun begins."

Chapter Seven

Many aficionados of the scene imagine that being trained to be a slave is a journey through a magically erotic kingdom. They envision an endless stream of sensual stimulation ranging from the most common sexual encounters to prolonged sessions of agonizing torture. With all the participants suitably costumed, of course.

It is disillusioning for these people to realize that masters and mistresses do not often feel compelled to conduct their affairs in gleaming black leather or latex, complete with jackboots or stiletto heels. Their faces fall in disappointment when they are made to understand that a slave's life is mostly composed of patience and study.

Yes, study. If not with actual books, then following the example of greater, senior slaves. Or learning every nuance of their owner's character, so that they can more completely and seamlessly offer themselves at the right time and in the right manner.

True slaves, those who will be cherished and valued, will never allow their skills and talents to become stagnant. They will never be satisfied with their level of competence. And they will always be willing to follow their owner's lead, quickly, respectfully, and to the best of their ability.

To be thrilled at the touch of leather, aroused by the sound of harsh words, or satisfied by the security of rigid bondage is the mark of a lover.

To be thrilled at the opportunity to provide useful service, aroused by a pleased nod, and satisfied by the proverbial job well done is the mark of a slave.

It may sound severe. Almost anti-erotic. Until you see two people, owner and owned, existing in a complementary relationship where each suits the other like balances on a delicate scale, until you feel the energy of their rapport, you cannot understand how they fulfill each other, take and give in ways no negotiation could possibly express.

Then you will understand that singular intimacy that drives such people on their search for perfection. It is beyond orgasm. Beyond love. It can almost be called rapture.

To achieve that level may require many years of training. But in the end, there is nothing that compares to it. At our house, we know this, and we construct our training with that exact goal in mind. We demand that applicants leave behind their foolish dreams and expectations, and we strip away any falseness that may linger. Those who survive and go on must be implanted with the urge to go further. Our name and reputation depend on it.

But it's so hard to get good material these days.

Chapter Eight

When the four slaves tumbled out of bed and into the hall for the first morning of their formal training period, Ms. Rachel was standing next to Chris, as she had the first morning they arrived. New bundles were neatly folded in a large basket at her feet.

"Since this marks the start of a more personalized training period, you have been issued some new items," Chris said, pointing down. "If you have questions about how to use anything, ask me immediately. Assume that anything you've been given is meant to be used every time you bathe." As Chris pointed, they gathered their new supplies and walked quietly but quickly down to the shower room.

Razors and shaving gel were in everyone's bundle except for Robert's. He looked downcast when he realized that he had been left out. He ran a hand through the short but thick hair on his chest and sighed.

Claudia sighed as she smelled the sweetness of the new soap and shampoo they had been issued, and eagerly dipped under a shower head to begin bathing. So far, training was proving to be better than being examined.

Brian asked Chris, "Should I shave all over?"

"Yes. Chest, legs, underarms, groin, and ass. You're to be completely shorn below the neck. So are Claudia and Sharon. Oh yes, and your mustache will come off as well, Brian. Robert, Mistress Alexandra will decide if she wants you to shave your face by the end of the week." Brian blanched and reached up to touch his thick black mustache. For a moment, his mouth worked, but no sound came out. Chris waited for more questions, and when none were forthcoming said, "You will all continue to practice your usual exercises in cleanliness, and keep yourselves clean inside and out." He left them to bathe in what seemed like luxury.

By now, they had gotten used to helping each other. At least for the most part. As razors slid through hair and water swirled, Claudia and Brian spotted for each other. Robert almost offered to do the same for Sharon but changed his mind just before he opened his mouth.

She's never said a nice word to me, he thought, lathering up under the shower. Why should I do anything for her? The new soap felt wonderful against his skin, and smelled so nice. Why didn't they let him shave? He'd feel so much more, well, *natural,* with all this ugly hair off. He glanced enviously at Brian, who was staring at his face in the mirror and hefting the can of shaving gel, but finished his shower and internal cleansing in silence.

"Today, you start some new assignments. At the end of next week, Ms. Rachel, Mr. Shaw and all of our part-time help will be taking three weeks off, and you four will replace them, taking over all duties except for cooking and stablekeeping."

Chris addressed them as they stood naked in the morning sun, near Alexandra's side of the rear gardens.

"Some of the tasks you will be performing will be practical, others will be educational. Free time, as of today, has ceased to exist. Any time you are not working or being worked, you will be studying, exercising, or sleeping." He looked at Brian, who had raised one hand. "Yes?"

"Chris, what does 'being worked' mean?"

"That's the term we use to refer to any time spent with the mistress or master that is designed around your erotic or sexual use, Brian. And you knew that, and asked the question facetiously." Chris raised one eyebrow, and waited for Brian to deny it.

Brian's entire body tensed, and his mouth opened, but he held it back. In silence, he lowered his head.

His cock stirred against his freshly shaven groin. Chris ignored it.

Chris continued. "Your assignments are as follows: Brian, to Ms. Rachel and laundry duty. Robert, since Cook thinks highly of you, to the kitchen. But don't get too comfortable there; Mistress Alexandra has some other plans for you eventually. When

Cook doesn't need you, you will be used outside, so also see the gardener, Mr. Shaw.

"Claudia, you're under me directly, dealing with the maintenance of the main house and various staff duties, which I will explain to you in time."

Claudia pressed her lips together, biting back a moan.

"And Sharon ..." Chris looked directly at her and smiled gently. "To the stable, if you please. Jack is waiting for you."

Brian ended up downstairs, in the spotlessly clean laundry room. And how do we know it's spotless? he asked himself. Why, because we scrubbed every square inch of it just last Thursday—floors, walls, and ceiling, with Sadistica Supreme as our personal devil with a pitchfork. Ms. Rachel, so composed, so polite, and so utterly disagreeable. So accurate with a wet towel, so quick to take offense, and ever so eager to shove something unpleasant in your mouth.

He closed his eyes for a moment, and tried to compose himself. But this is it, he thought, tensing and relaxing. You made it, pal, you're in the program. From here on, it should be easy, and then in no time, you'll be off to what you want.

As long as what I get isn't anything like this, he mentally noted. He opened his eyes as he heard footsteps coming down the stairs. It was Rachel, Chris, and Claudia. Claudia was holding Chris's clipboard under one arm, and she had a leather bag, like a mail satchel, hanging from one shoulder. Otherwise naked, and shorn of hair, she made a funny sight. A site inspector who had forgotten to get dressed that day. Brian tried to control the twitch that struck his face. He failed, but managed to keep from laughing out loud. The thought that his face was as naked as the delta between her legs struck him as rather sobering.

"Stand at attention, please," Chris said. The major-domo held a hand out toward Claudia, who began taking things out of her bag and handing them to him. Rachel looked amused.

"Master Grendel has ordered that you be adorned, Brian." Chris brought his hand forward and showed Brian two objects that the younger man didn't recognize. Swiftly, they were attached to the silver rings through Brian's nipples. Brian looked down to see what now looked like upside down silver bows with little strands of satin ribbon hanging down from them. The ribbons extended down his hairless chest all the way to his belly. They were baby pink, and curled at the ends. The weight of the adornments was negligible, but from the way the ends of the ribbons bounced with every movement of his chest, he knew that he would never be able to forget that they were there. His head began to pound.

"The next one, Claudia—I shouldn't have to ask." Claudia hurriedly pressed another item into Chris's hand, and a pink bow of the same color and texture was tied around Brian's throat. Chris took a moment to adjust the knot of the bow so that it fell neatly into the hollow at the base of Brian's throat. The ends were split, and curled up.

"Very nice," Chris said. But the look in his steel-framed eyes was vicious amusement. "What do you think, Brian?"

"Please, Chris," Brian choked out. "I ... I don't ... I never ..."

"Yes?" Chris prompted.

"Please. I ... I hate this. Can I speak to Master Grendel? I can explain—"

Chris shook his head. "It's very impertinent for you to express such a judgment about your master's desire to adorn you. You hate it? That's just too bad." Without taking his eyes away from Brian's face, Chris held his hand out again. When Claudia didn't drop something into it instantly, he gently smacked her across the top of her head, the way teenagers take shots at each other in play. His hand returned to the open position by her while his eyes pinned Brian to his spot on the chilly tile floor.

The last thing to be added for adornment was another length of ribbon. Chris let it unravel from the ball that Claudia belatedly passed to him, and gathered up Brian's cock and balls in one hand.

Brian closed his eyes.

The ribbon went around them, and then crossed to separate the cock from the balls, and then one ball from the other. The ends of the ribbon crossed each other neatly around the whole package securely but not tightly and then tied at the top. Another bow. A neat, crisp one.

"There!" Chris announced cheerfully. "That finishes the look. You may continue your work, Brian." Without another word, Chris and Claudia left the room.

Brian remained at attention. His hands were locked at his sides, his entire body as erect as his cock wasn't. Shame flooded through him. Clamps, leather, straps, boots, chains, yes!

But pink ribbons and bows?

All over his body. His naked, shaven body. No. Oh, god, no.

Rachel stepped in front of him and pulled gently on the ribbons cascading down his chest. Pleasure shot through his nipples, and she smiled at the tension in his face. Wrapping the ribbons around her fingers, she led him, stumbling, across the room, where there was a large table used for folding laundry. She edged up against it and released him, leaving him standing at attention in front of her.

Carefully, she lifted the edge of her black dress, revealing that she wore stockings, not pantyhose, and that she had no panties on whatsoever. She slipped herself neatly onto the table and reached out to get another grasp on those damned ribbons. With a sudden harsh tug, she pulled him onto her, and then pressed his head down.

"You heard him," she said, her voice raspy with pleasure. "Get to work, pretty boy."

Cook's frozen bread dough had defrosted and risen overnight. Robert was given the task of punching it back down, separating it into even loaves, and then making braids. Cook showed him once how to use a sharp knife to do the dividing, how to roll out even strips, and then the simple method of braiding and tucking the ends in. Then she turned away from him to begin making up her shopping lists.

Robert did as he was instructed. It really was as easy as she had said, he reflected, neatly slicing through the pounded down dough. Just slice, slice, and then roll, roll, and before you knew it, three even strands. Then one over the other, from end to end, and neatly pinch the ends together before you tuck them under. His first loaf was almost identical to hers. He moved it onto the wooden tray where it would rise one more time, and draped a damp linen cloth over it.

"Very good," Alexandra said.

He jumped up from his seat, dropping the next ball of pounded dough. It fell with a dull thud against the table and landed in a misshapen heap.

"Oh! I'm dreadfully sorry!" Robert tried to pick up the dough, and his fingers sank into it. He pushed it together and awkwardly threw it back into the bowl. He shifted nervously back and forth and then finally came to rest facing Alexandra, his head down and his hands clutched behind his back.

Alexandra studied him.

"Where on earth did you get the idea that this is how you should greet me?" she asked.

"Wh-what? Um. I don't know, ma'am. I'm sorry. I ... I ..."

Alexandra hushed him. "You've been reading too much into some of the more formal instructions in the behavioral guide. Robert, how many times do I have to tell you to listen to what you've been told, and follow *my* instructions first? I know you're trying to be good, but you're also making a fool out of yourself—and proving that you have difficulty following direct orders."

He whimpered and his lower lip trembled.

"And stop that whining! I swear, you're worse than Claudia!"

He sniffed hard. The sight of him trying to control himself was almost as comical as his outbursts. Alexandra kept what she hoped was a fairly neutral look on her face. It was important that he get firmness, not amusement. But he was damn silly.

She turned her attention back to the table. "Now as I was saying—sit down, Robert, sit down—that was a good job you did on that loaf. Have you ever baked before?"

"Not, um, before I came here, ma'am," he said. His voice was terrible. Whenever he tried to avoid slipping into his falsetto, he sounded like he was trying to imitate an adolescent boy at the time of a voice change. It was grating.

"Well, get back to work. I'm not here to disturb you." She directed his attention back to the bread, but didn't move from where she was standing.

The dough stuck to the bowl, despite the dusting of flour on the sides. It fell from his hands and wouldn't roll out neatly. His strips were raggedly cut, and he had to do them again. The second time, they came out with a distinct curve, narrowing to shapes vaguely reminiscent of a child's drawing of a quarter-moon.

He tried not to look over his shoulder. Sweat broke out in the middle of his back and along his hairline. Desperately, he rolled out three lumpy, uneven strips and braided them with trembling fingers. Pinching one end, he ended up breaking three pieces off.

The finished product looked like a Play-Doh approximation of what a braided loaf of bread might look like to a visually-impaired four-year-old. He heard Alexandra's thoughtful "tsking" behind him, and he began to sob.

"I'll see you this afternoon, Robert. Let's hope you regain your composure and your dexterity by then."

Alex met Grendel in the hallway. He looked at her compassionately.

"Headache already?" he asked.

"I think we might have made a mistake with him," Alex said, rubbing her temples.

"Here, let me do that." Grendel got behind her and, applying his fingertips to the area below her hairline, began to gently massage. "Don't write him off so fast; it's only the first day."

"I know that. It's just hard to see him as a sex object when he's blubbering over a mound of bread dough. How do I reach the real Robert? Somewhere in there is a man who cared enough about his body to work it in high school and college. A man who played and coached football." She smiled and leaned back. "Mmmm. That's good."

"I'm glad. And, if there's any way to find that man under the maid's uniform, you'll find it. You're the best." He kissed the back of her neck, and she chuckled. "Listen, I'm going out to the stable to check on darling Sharon. Care for some entertainment?"

"No, I don't think so. I'm going to work Claudia, and the contrast is just too jarring. But thanks for the offer, and the vote of confidence. I'll return the favor when you're ready to give up on Brian."

He stopped massaging and laughed. "That's a good point. Well, I'll leave you to Missy Perfection while I get her evil sister. At least *you* get laid."

"Ha! Don't count on it," Alex turned around and smiled back. "See you later, my dear." She kissed him gently and they went their separate ways.

"Are you out of your fucking mind?!" Sharon screamed.

Jack blinked and mimed wiping spittle from his face. "I asked for th' news, not the bleedin' weather," he said laconically. He tossed the rake over to her and turned away to get something else off the wall.

Sharon saw the rake coming and leapt gingerly out of the way. "You're crazy if you think I'm doing this shit!" she continued to yell. "You go and get Grendel right now, and tell him this is just out of the fucking question!"

"'Ere's a coverall, you'll be wantin' that, and there's muckin' boots in the nor' shed. They may be a bit large for your feet, but you can always wrap a bit o' tape about the tops to keep 'em on. If it works for the 'orses, it'll work for you." He tossed the plain denim coverall at her, and she reached out to catch it.

"Did you hear me?" she asked, clutching the garment in front of her. "I'm *not* doing it."

"Aye, I got you. But you've got to realize something, model." Jack grinned, showing a mouth full of strong white teeth. "You'll be doin' what I say, or you'll be packin' your bags for 'ome, and that's for damn sure. Y'see, Mr. Elliot and Mr. Parker told me all about you and your fancy ways. Yet, 'ere you are. So put the cover on like a good little model an' go an' get your booties and we'll 'ave a nice lesson in muckin' to start the day."

Sharon looked at him in a state of incredulous horror. He smiled again and snapped his fingers. "Go to it, lass! You won't be liking what 'appens if you waste my precious time!"

"Look," the beautiful young woman said, trying to stall for time. "You don't understand."

"Oh aye?" Jack leaned on a stall post and folded his powerful, sinewy arms. "Educate me. Elucidate my boggled mind."

"I ... I ... don't know how to do this," Sharon began, pointing at the fallen rake. "And ... I'm allergic to animals, OK? And ... and ..."

"And?" He looked interested.

"And look," Sharon dropped the coverall away from the front of her body. She spread her arms out slowly and then lowered them in front of her in a coy, practiced gesture. Her skin was the color of warm honey, save for a gently contrasting triangle of white between her thighs. In the cool of the morning, her nipples were erect, and pointed slightly upward. Her lips parted in a sweet, childish pout.

"Do I look like I was made to work in a stable?"

"Naw, y' surely don't."

"Then, *please* speak to Grendel about this? I'm sure it was all, like, a mistake." She smiled back at him. "I'll wait right here, if you want."

Jack sucked in a short breath and nodded. He turned away from her and walked to the far end of the stable, toward the tack room.

I don't believe this, Sharon thought to herself, looking around. I mean, what do I have to do to get through to these people?

She had come to the stable, carefully picking her way over damp patches of ground and wrinkling her nose at the smell of horses and horseshit, thinking that she was going to be taught how to ride a horse. Not clean up after one! After all, horseback riding was one of the things that Grendel mentioned good slaves should be able to do. Wasn't it?

She felt itchy. The pathway in front of the empty

stalls was dirt and straw on top of concrete, and there was no clean place to stand. She stepped on top of the discarded coverall and wiped her feet against it. There, that was better. She turned around looking out the wide side door, into the paddock. The horses were out there somewhere, probably eating their oats or grass or whatever they ate for breakfast. Maybe she would get a really pretty one, like all white, or maybe a big black one with a white star on its forehead? And she could wear those totally cool clothes, all those suits and top hats and stuff. Or was that for fox hunting? Never mind, the tight pants would look good on her, and so would those shiny black boots. Or would she look too dykey?

Lost in her reverie, she didn't hear Jack's return.

Suddenly, an incredibly strong hand grasped her left wrist and looped something around it. As she screamed her surprise, Jack jerked her body around and caught her right wrist in a neat cross-tie. In an instant, the loops were pulled tight, and her hands were bound together. In another instant, she was rudely kneed into an adjoining stall, and the end of the rein was threaded through a ring set at the highest point Jack could comfortably reach. He pulled it taut and tied it off, chuckling while he did it.

It had taken less than thirty seconds. Sharon's protest, one long screech of outrage, ended when she ran out of breath, and she pulled ineffectually against her bondage. The loops of leather were strong, and her efforts pulled them tighter around her wrists.

"You're some package, model," Jack choked out. He was still laughing. "Y' don't know 'ow. You're allergic to *animals*." He mimicked her whining cadence. "You're too much of a precious bleedin' little mama's girl that y' can't get your pretty little 'ands dirty, that's what y'are!" He tilted his head back and roared. "You're too bleedin' much!"

"What ... what are you doing? What are you going to do? Let me go, this hurts!" Sharon, not having learned her lesson the first time, pulled at her bonds again.

"It 'urts!" Jack gasped out. "You silly git, it's supposed to! Now, take your med'cine like a good girl!"

Trying to control his hilarity, he took a sweat scraper out of his back pocket and palmed it. It was a piece of aluminum fourteen inches long, curved and shaped to be pulled along a horse's body, pushing rivers of sweat or bathwater before it. It was bent somewhat like a shepherd's crook, to be able to get into narrow spaces as well as along the broad flanks and back of the animal. He took hold of the straight end, and tapped the back of the tool experimentally against Sharon's butt. Faint marks from previous beatings were still discernible on her skin.

He grinned.

With one easy, powerful backswing, he brought the length of the scraper smacking across Sharon's ass. She screamed as it hit. The lightweight metal cut through the air faster than Chris's heavy strap, and the narrow hitting surface intensified the pain of the blow.

"Be a brave girl, now!" Jack laughed as he swung again. This time, he aimed slightly higher, and the spot he managed to get made Sharon gasp for breath. Her hands were already pounding. She wailed as he drew his arm back and began a slow, orderly, excruciatingly thorough beating of her rear end. He moved the aim of the scraper up and down, careful to cover every inch, and then began to strike at the backs of her thighs.

Her screams went up in scale, and she began to choke on them. There wasn't enough time between blows to adequately catch her breath. Desperate to get away from the steady, burning bites of the tool, she began to twist and squirm in her bonds.

"Damn you!" she gasped out, throwing her hip to one side. "Stop! Please! Ow! Stoppit!!"

Jack pushed one arm against her back and thrust her against the stall to hold her still.

"Not until you say you're sorry, lass!" The blows continued.

"I'm sorry! I'm sorry!" she screamed back.

"Aye? For what?" Jack laughed again and picked up the tempo. Sharon's answer was taken over by her breathless cries of anguish, which lasted several seconds after Jack stopped beating her. She gasped for breath, and sobbed, and then wailed.

"We're not finished with you yet, my pretty model," Jack announced, pulling his hand from her back. "We're just finished with this side!" He turned her around without bothering to adjust her bonds, and she stumbled against them. Her hands seemed to be two balls of pins and needles. Before she could even begin to form words, Jack kicked her thighs apart and pushed her back against the wall.

He reached out with one hand and took hold of her right nipple. Catching it between his fingers, he put light pressure on it and then began to smack heavily at the insides of her thighs with the scraper.

The first time she tried to pull her legs together,

he gave her nipple a vicious twist. "You should know to be a good girl by now, model," he said, giving her an extra hard smack. "You 'old yourself still and open for Jack, an' I won't 'ave to get nasty with you, understand?"

She sniffed and winced, and yelped when he smacked her again, this one directly over her shaven pussy lips. "I b'lieve I asked you a question, model. An' I sure as 'ell didn't get an answer!"

"Wha?" Sharon opened her eyes in confusion. Her arms, her ass, her thighs, everything was a blur of pain. "Yes! Whatever! Yes!"

"Oh, you are a treasure, model, that you are!" Jack resumed his beating, covering the delta between her legs with dozens of stinging swats. And despite his grip on her nipple, she twisted and contorted her body to escape the blows. Her cries changed both tempo and timbre as genuine pain replaced shame, shock, and discomfort. Finally, she slumped against the reins, unable to stand against his steady assault.

Instantly, Jack slipped the scraper back into his pocket and boosted her back onto her feet. He pushed her against the wall and reached over to untie the rein. She fell down, her knees buckling, and slid to the floor of the stall, nestled among the bedding. Flies buzzed, and she cried, unable even to shoo them away.

"I don't believe you're doing this!" she wailed.

"Y' got off easy this mornin'," Jack said, standing over her. "Now listen to me proper. You're 'ere to learn the proper care and feedin' of the denizens o' this stable. You'll do as I say, when I say, and 'ow I say, or you'll get that, an' worse. You don't impress me, model. I've 'ad prettier ones, and nicer ones than you." He casually opened the top button of his sturdy jeans and beckoned to her. "Now get over 'ere and thank me right."

Sharon flexed her fingers back and forth to get some life into them and openly gaped at the stableman. Standing there, cool as could be, his blond hair damp with sweat and his hands tucked into the sides of his leather suspenders, he looked like he was showing off a prize calf at a state fair. She glanced at his waist and registered the open trouser button, and then looked back up at him. Surely, he couldn't mean ...?

"Do as you're told, girl!"

She sniffed and crawled forward to him, the straw and sawdust sticking to her sweaty body. She sneezed heavily and sobbed at the indignity of it all. When she got to him and pulled herself up, she eyed the bulge in his pants with nothing but despair. She shook her head and sank back on her heels.

"I'm sorry, I can't," she whimpered. "I just can't ... not here, not like this ... I have to pull myself together, OK?"

Jack stared down at her in sheer confusion for a moment, and then unhooked his fingers from his suspenders. With a well-practiced move, he tore open the buttons on his fly and pulled his cock out. It was thick, uncut, and hard. Grabbing a handful of her hair, he jerked her up between his legs and shoved his cock violently into her mouth.

She gasped as the fleshy intrusion passed her lips and slammed against the back of her throat. A sound like a strangled, muffled scream came from her, and tears sprang from her eyes as she choked and gagged. Jack pulled her head back, away from his cock.

"Y' don't use that word with me, model. There isn't a damn bloody thing you *can't* do! You do as you're told, an' you do it good!" She gasped for breath as he aimed and thrust forward again. His sweat was sweetly salty, the smell of him was of old leather and horses. He filled her mouth and drew back, dragging her spit out, making her drool down her chin.

Sharon's inarticulate cries continued as Jack began to methodically rape her mouth. She wanted it, oh, she wanted it so bad! But not like this! His relentlessly calm motions dragged her back and forth, making her choke on him over and over again, until he pulled her head back in disgust.

"You 'aven't got the sucking talent God gave a mosquito," he said. "Do it right, will you? Get in there, before I lose it."

Sharon stared up at him and her mouth gaped open in disbelief. "No!" she shrieked, pulling back. "Leave me alone! I don't want to!"

Jack leaned forward and laughed at her. "Still with th' mouth?" With a smile still on his face, he calmly drew his hand back and cuffed her across her full lips. Then, as she fell over and tried to get away from him by crawling through the straw, he followed her. Her panicked movements and her lack of direction got her into the far corner in moments, and Jack stood in front of her. As he reached down for her, she screamed.

"What the hell is going on here?"

Jack turned toward Grendel and stood up

straight. He ducked his head in a brief nod before speaking.

"Sorry to bother you, Mr. Elliot. New fluff's actin' up a bit, but she'll come along."

Grendel looked down at Sharon. She was a pitiful sight. Sweaty, dusty, and covered with small scratches and smudgy marks, she crouched in the corner of the stall, her hair a tangled mess around her shoulders. She was out of breath, gulping air in between sobs.

"What's the problem?" Grendel asked, leaning one elbow against the partition.

"She's got a bit o' spunk in 'er, that's all," Jack grinned. He casually tucked his cock back into his heavy jeans. "Or not enough, maybe." He laughed at his own joke.

"Spunk, Sharon, hardly becomes a pleasure slave," Grendel sighed. "Don't put that away yet, Jack, keep it busy. Sharon wants to take care of you. Don't you Sharon?"

As Jack took hold of his cock and began to work it back into a full erection, the young woman raised her head to look at the master of the house and sneezed. "I can't," she whimpered. "I … it's too dirty … can't we go somewhere else?"

"Get on your knees in front of Jack right now." Grendel's voice was low, but the note of command was unmistakable.

Sharon shivered in disgust, but quickly picked her way through the straw to the spot Grendel had indicated. Jack's hand was still stroking his cock, pulling the foreskin back with every stroke and cupping his rough fingers around the head.

"Now, lean forward and let him feel your breath

on his cock. No, don't grab him! I didn't tell you to do anything with your hands. Keep them down! Just listen and do exactly what I tell you." Grendel remained standing by the stall gate, his body casually leaning against it. But his voice was clear and hard.

Sharon followed his orders, Jack's cock bobbing directly in front of her mouth.

"How does it feel?"

"Oh, not too bad, Mr. Elliot, not too bad. She's not got the talent I bet the boy does, though." The stableman's hand never stopped. A drop of glistening fluid appeared at the tip of his cock and he quickly wiped it across Sharon's cheek.

"You're probably right," Grendel admitted. "I'll let you have some time with him and you can give me a report. Sharon, now move forward and gently lick around the head. Just the ridge, and just your tongue."

Sharon moved forward with an open mouth, but Jack caught her and tapped the sensuously shaped ridge defining the head of his cock. "Just around 'ere, girl."

She flicked her tongue out and began licking.

"You're like magic for the girl, Mr. Elliot, that's f'sure!"

"That's because she knows she's always ten minutes away from a train station, Jack. In the future, if she ever gives you a really hard time, just send her to Chris and he'll pack her up."

Sharon moaned, even as she licked. She heard a familiar crackling, tearing sound.

"Here, Jack. Catch."

Jack reached up and easily caught the foil package Grendel had pulled out of his pocket. "What's your pleasure then, Mr. Elliot? Y' want her to finish me off like this, then?"

"No. She claims she's a great fuck, so why don't you investigate? But first, let's see if that mouth has any practical use at all."

"Take this, model," Jack said, passing the condom down. "Get it on my ol' cock like a good backstreet whore does. Slip it right on with them pretty lips, an' make it nice an' slow."

Sharon tore the little package open with trembling hands. Was it possible that only an hour ago, her hands had been soft and clean, her nails glistening and shining? She produced the condom and placed it on the head of Jack's cock. He immediately cuffed her again, and she yelped.

"With your mouth, girl! Do you not hear me?"

Frantically, she pushed the condom between her lips and then spent a hellishly long minute struggling to get it over his pulled-back foreskin and then down the length of the shaft. By the time she was finished, her lips felt bruised and swollen. And still, there was more.

She was pushed onto her hands and knees, her face pressed close to the stall floor, while Jack casually knelt behind her. While Grendel watched, a vaguely bored look on his face, Jack entered the kneeling woman in one strong thrust, his powerful hands wrapped around her upper thighs.

Sharon rose up at his entry—her back arched, and she yowled like a cat in heat. She was open and wet with excitement, despite her horrible circumstances, and Jack chuckled as he slipped all the way in.

"Oh, she's a ripe 'un, Mr. Elliot," he grunted,

pulling out to thrust back in again. "For all 'er words and tears, she's randy as a bitch."

"But is she good?"

Jack pressed himself deep into the woman and shifted his hips comfortably. "Not bad, not bad."

"Good. Let me know if she improves by Thursday. I may want to take Skipper out later; you'll see he's ready, won't you?"

"Oh, yessir, Mr. Elliot. See you later, then!"

While the men exchanged words, Sharon cradled her head in her arms and emitted a steady, breathless stream of moans. Jack never missed a stroke as he casually chatted with Grendel. But as soon as the master left, Jack pressed in hard and fast, gripping Sharon tightly against him.

With no sounds but the rustling of the straw beneath them and Sharon's punctuating gasps and whimpers, he continued to use her, his pace quickening. Sharon began to whine, and then to pound her fists against the floor, raising small clouds of dust and getting strands of straw tangled in her hair. She bucked back at him, taking him all, wanting more.

"Don't even think o' coming," Jack growled, slapping her red ass cheek. "You take my spunk like a good girl and then you'll be gettin' your tail to work, bitch-model. You hear me?"

"Y-yes! Yes!" She squirmed and thrust back just the same, and Jack forced her still.

"You know you're mine now, don't you, model? Mr. Elliot just gave you to me, every day 'til Thursday next, didja know that?"

Sharon moaned.

"So," Jack panted, pushing harder and harder

against her, "you might just get yourself accustomed to this, model. When you work the stables in
this 'ouse, you get to work with old Jack." With a
final series of steady, fast grinding pumps, Jack let
himself go, spurting his come while enveloped by
her hot pussy. He sighed and growled alternately,
and then abruptly pulled out of her. She whimpered
and wailed out her frustration.

"Aahhh, that was not bad, Sharon girl. Not bad.
But you'll be a bit more cooperative tomorrow, or
we'll be doin' this in a stall a bit more, eh, funky,
than this 'un." He stripped the condom off and
tossed it next to her. "When you clean this up, don't
forget that, right?"

Sharon made distinct sobbing noises, which Jack
cheerfully ignored.

"Oh, and 'ere's your coverall—ah, look, someone's gone and stepped on it! Well, too bad." He
buttoned his fly and picked the stained coverall up
and examined it. "Aye, too bad. I don't 'ave another
one, you'll 'ave to make do today." He tossed it into
the stall.

"The boots are in the back," he said, stepping
away from her. "I'll be back after I 'ave a smoke to
show you the fine art o' muckin'. Be dressed proper,
or you'll do it in your skin."

After his footsteps faded away, Sharon drew the
stained and slightly grubby coverall to her body
and pulled it over her trembling limbs.

Chapter Nine

Alexandra patiently waited for Claudia to dry her eyes and pull herself together. Chris wordlessly took the handkerchief back from the naked slave girl and then stepped away from her.

Little Claudia took it better than I thought she would, Alex reflected. I thought she was going to break down in hysterics, or faint, or something suitably proper for a frail little femme to do when she finds out that her beloved mistress no longer wants her.

It was a difficult decision to make, and Madeleine had been resistant. But Claudia's training couldn't go a step forward unless she really understood what was at stake. And unfortunately for her, Madeleine was very, very disappointed in the initial report that Alexandra had tendered.

166

"Well," the elegant mistress had asked, "what do you think she would fetch at a good auction?"

"Are you absolutely sure?" Alexandra pressed. "She is a treasure, Madeleine. I've never seen someone more devoted to a role before. Why don't you just add someone new to the household and keep her as a fancy?"

"Alex honey, I'm not that rich. No, if I'm going to have a maid, she'd better be interesting and fun in bed. Besides, Carl is complaining that we don't have any regular boys around the house, so that's one major purchase for next year already."

Alex nodded, mentally noting the possibility of a referral. "Well, then I suppose we can shape her up a little and look for a good offering. Do you have preferences for her?"

Madeleine paused. It was obviously hard for her to consider. "Just ... just make sure she goes someplace nice," she said finally. "I'll write up a reference."

And then it fell to Alexandra to explain this to the shivering young woman who stood before her in the warm solarium.

"Is there any chance?" Claudia asked, after she got some of her bearing back. "Could ... could I learn to be what Mistress wants? Can't you teach me? I'll try! I'll do anything you say!"

"Claudia darling, your greatest problem is that you can't seem to do anything we say." Alexandra spoke firmly, but with compassion. "Chris reports that when given a task you find displeasurable, your attention wanders, you waste time crying or staring at it, or you do it so badly it becomes necessary to give you another assignment. You resist all attempts to bring out your sexual side, at least any-where beyond giving you a nice spanking and fin-gering you until you come. You're afraid of Grendel—to the point that you become incoherent when he asks you questions—you fall apart at the slightest chastisement, and the less reality matches your concept of what must be, the more unhappy you get. And the more unhappy you are, the more easily you fall into bad behavior. Frankly, you seem dedicated to your role as a French maid, and your mistress has given us permission to market you as such."

The handsome woman leaned back and gazed at Claudia with a thoughtful expression on her face. "And that's not bad," she said after moment. "There is a strong market for fancy slaves, people trained in one specific task or role, and little else. It's not usu-ally what we like to deal in, but we have contacts all over the world. You could go to England or France, for example. There's also a strong interest for slaves like you in Brazil and in the Far East. Not that you have much of a choice," she added, "but your future certainly won't be dull."

Claudia nodded, her face forlorn. "I ... thank you, ma'am. But I want to stay with my mistress. Please, please ... I'll do better! I'll be the best girl you ever had here."

"Claudia, it took you almost four days to clean a pile of silver that could have been done in two."

"Please, ma'am, I know I haven't been good," Claudia said, desperation growing in her voice. "I was so unhappy! And I didn't know why I was here! I thought that Mistress was punishing me for something!" The words began to spill out in a rush.

"And ... and I didn't want to think about anything else, because I thought that—oh, I didn't know what I thought! Maybe Mistress just wanted me to be ... better. And I want to! I can be whatever she wants me to be!"

"Claudia, you burst into tears as soon as Chris takes his strap off his belt."

"I'll be braver! I won't cry any more! I'll never cry, if only I have a chance to go back to Mistress!" Her voice scaled up.

Alexandra pulled at one curl, longer than the others, and twirled it through her fingers. Claudia was actually beginning to change, although only in subtle, barely noticeable ways. There was some sincerity behind the note of desperation in her voice. Maybe there was some potential there after all. Maybe it had been a mistake to hide the depth of Madeleine's disappointment from the little slave? It would be a shame to deprive them both of such quality.

"So what do you think I should do," Alexandra asked carefully, "to encourage proper behavior from you? Supposing that I decided to allow you to try to change, what do you think you should be doing to break out of your role?"

Claudia swallowed hard. Normally, she had been trained to answer any question that began with "What do you think...?" with, "Please do as you think best, Mistress." Last week, during her interviews, that answer had been denied to her. Here, they really wanted to know what you thought. It was unnerving.

"Perhaps you could give me more work to do, ma'am," Claudia suggested, trying to think quickly.

"And...?"

"And, maybe, I mean, should you decide to use me, ma'am, I could be trained to do the things that Mistress wanted me to do."

"Name them," Alexandra snapped back. "Be specific. You'll have to learn to talk about them before you're able to do them comfortably."

"Oh!" Claudia squirmed. "To ... to play with myself ma'am?"

"And...?"

"To be, to be ... to take ma'am's, um, to be ..."

"To be fucked, Claudia?"

She blushed a deep red. "Yes, ma'am."

"Then say it!" Alexandra's calm voice was edged with impatience.

"To be fucked, ma'am." Claudia's blush deepened.

"And you know that it wouldn't be just me who will use you, Claudia." Alexandra stood, a study in strength and determination. As she walked toward Claudia, her eyes bore into the younger woman and held her still. "If I choose, anyone in this house might want to try a taste of you. Certainly Grendel might be interested. Perhaps even Chris would. I might even decide to turn you over to one of your fellow slaves. Do you understand that?"

Claudia trembled but held her ground. "Yes, ma'am!"

"And there's a lot more in life than fucking and sucking, Claudia. You *do* understand that sucking is a part of this?"

Claudia nodded. "Y-yes ma'am."

Alexandra paused in front of the slave and studied her from up close. Yes, there was definitely something new here. And a secret, as well. She studied the guarded look in the slave's eyes, and put the information away for further speculation. Perhaps she could salvage this situation after all. There were other things happening as well, once you got into the poor girl's face. Her breath was getting more shallow and coming faster. And beyond the embarrassed blush from having to use a forbidden obscenity was a growing sensual flush. Her nipples were wrinkled little knobs of flesh.

"Chris," Alexandra said softly. "Come here and take her in hand, will you?"

"With pleasure, ma'am."

As Chris approached, Alexandra smiled. "Hm," she said out loud, "it seems that Chris is more interested than I thought." Claudia made a slight whimpering sound, but cut it off quickly. "Good girl," Alexandra noted.

Chris came behind Claudia and firmly pulled her arms behind her back. She gasped at the unexpected move, but submitted. He held her wrists together in one hand and reached around her body, pulling her so that she half rested on his bent knee, which he pressed between her legs. Her thighs parted, and she lost her balance and fell against him. But he stood firm.

Alexandra stepped back a little. Claudia stared up at her, her breath coming in pants now, her body shaking. Chris felt solid behind her back, but her position seemed dangerously unsteady.

"Stroke her," Alexandra said, going back to her chair. "Let's see what she's got."

Chris took his free hand and slowly let it drift up Claudia's body, from her waist to her throat. She

shivered and gave a little moan. Gently, the major-
domo began to run the tips of his fingers across her
body, making little swirls around her nipples, and
then gentle rubbing motions on her belly. She
sighed.

"Good. Now get more specific," Alexandra
prompted.

Chris made more determined motions, circling
Claudia's erect nipples with rough fingers and
squeezing them. She gasped, but didn't protest or
try to squirm away. From there, he stroked her hip
with ever smaller circles until he moved inward,
toward her belly, and then down to the mound
above her delta. There, he pressed and rubbed until
she squirmed, just a little bit. At that moment, his
fingers darted down to the area so recently shaven
white and pressed her lips together.

She moaned! After a week of self-denial and
shame, the security and the pleasure was nearly
overwhelming. This was so right, this was so good.
Held securely, explored with skill and gentleness,
and then teased to a climax, oh it was heaven! She
sighed and settled deeper against him as his fingers
opened her gently and explored. She thought warmly, he knows what he is doing, and closed her eyes.

Chris's fingers stroked her outer lips until her
moisture began to gather, and then gently pried
them apart. They opened like the proverbial petals
of a flower, and he easily located that elusive center
of pleasure, which he gave but one soft touch before
returning his attention to her lips. The soft, glistening folds of her inner lips almost throbbed with the
intensity of her arousal. Alexandra smiled as she
watched.

She might be a lot of fun once she gets into this, the mistress thought. Should I give her an easy one, for encouragement? No, I don't think so. She makes it now, or she realizes that she hasn't got what she needs. Either way, we know, once and for all.

Claudia was beginning to shift against Chris. Her breath came in a rhythmic pattern, and Alexandra nodded. "That's enough, Chris."

Claudia's eyes snapped open. Chris took his hand away and brought his fingers up to Claudia's mouth. Even as she moaned her frustration, she licked them clean of her juices.

"Finish yourself off, Claudia," Alexandra said, when Chris pulled his hand away.

Claudia bit her lip, fighting back an instinctive protest. Chris released her right arm, but maintained a strong hold on her left, and kept his knee firmly between her legs. Claudia let her hand hang loosely for a moment and looked flustered, but then started to bring it up to her mouth. She stopped herself before it got there and looked up at Alexandra, her eyes wide.

Alex nodded. "Get them good and wet," she said softly. "Do whatever you have to do to get yourself off for me. Make it good. Get me interested. Show me how much you need this."

Claudia gulped and placed her own fingers in her mouth to moisten them. Then she let her hand seek that place she knew so well, and her eyes closed as she began the familiar series of touches that until now had been her private pleasures.

Alexandra gave a moment's thought to telling the girl to open her eyes, but decided that this time, she would let Claudia have the comfort of that sense of privacy. Next time, it would be different.

Held tightly against Chris's compact body, Claudia began to shift against him, responding to the steady pulsing that was building between her legs. She couldn't squeeze her legs together the way she would have if she were alone, but a week of frustration and confusing desperation had done some remarkable work on her psyche. She needed this so bad! Her fingers began to fly as she dipped into herself for more of her sweet wetness, bringing it up to that little center of heat. She began to gasp and then pant.

"That's it," Alex coaxed. "That's a good girl. Let's hear you come now. Let's see how good you can be. Let it out for me. Let it all out."

"Ahh!" Claudia moaned, twisting and squirming back onto Chris's leg. "Ah, yesss!"

Alexandra smiled and moved in closer. "Do it now! Come!"

Claudia gave a long, uneven moan of pleasure and stiffened in Chris's embrace. Her hips jerked upward, as though she were rising to meet the thrusts of a dynamic lover. Gritting her teeth, she collapsed back into Chris's arms, shuddering and crooning, and gulping air in between erotic shivers.

When she opened her eyes, she knew that her entire face was flushed with the humiliation of displaying such passion before a mistress, but Alexandra seemed very pleased.

"You may release her," Alexandra said with a nod. "And go call Madeleine. Tell her we may have something to work with."

Grendel met Chris in the hallway in the late afternoon, just before dinner. The sounds of table-setting and the clattering of the kitchen were faint in the background, and no one was near them. Chris had nodded, and was about to pass Grendel by, but the master of the house put out one hand to stay the major-domo.

"I hear you're interested in Claudia," Grendel said.

Chris's eyes matched Grendel's for a long moment, and then he dropped them. A tiny smile touched his lips. "I'm eager to aid in their training, sir."

"Oh, I see." Grendel moved in closer and carefully took a firm grip on Chris's shirt front, grasping it and the tie in one fist. Chris let loose an involuntary gasp and looked up, keeping his eyes open and locked as Grendel pulled him closer, and then higher, until the heels of the man's boots lifted off the floor.

"Wise-ass," Grendel said fondly. He didn't relax his grip. "That's the epicure in you; you always go for the ones with the best pedigree. Has Alex said you can have the girl?"

"No, sir." Chris's breath came in short, paced inhalations. When Grendel lowered his fist and began propelling Chris backward until his back touched the wall, Chris took two long, ragged breaths and shifted his eyes to the right.

"They'll either come and see you like this or they won't," Grendel said. "Keep your eyes on me, boy."

"Yes, sir."

"That would be something, wouldn't it? To let them know right now that we can make you shake and tremble the way they do? That one touch can make you lose your cool? That might do something to the effectiveness of your discipline, don't you think?" Grendel continued to speak softly, his voice just above a whisper, slow and almost hypnotic. Chris pushed his head against the wall to better be able to look up into Grendel's eyes.

"They obey you, sir," he said. There was now a raspy quality to his voice, and he gave a little cough to try to clear it. "I'm just a tool."

Grendel shook his clenched fist, digging his fingers into the hollow under Chris's throat. "Don't pull that false modesty on me too often," he warned. "I don't like being buried in your bullshit, boy. The fact is that you still wish you were in their place. Every morning, you wake up and you go to them and you hate their guts because they've got what you never had. And they'll get more this year than you'll ever dream of getting. That's why you want them, the best of them."

Chris swallowed hard and replied, "As you say, sir."

Grendel smiled, but kept his grip. "When was the last time you were fucked, boy?"

"Two months ago, sir. And a few days."

"Ha! Good, you're pretending that you don't know the exact number of days; that's good. You might sound desperate and petulant if you did that. Well, let me tell you this," Grendel reinforced his words with a rocking motion of his hand. "You might get yours when they start to break, and not one minute before. And we'll see which of them you'll get to handle when they start to show the signs of your teaching. There's one thing for sure, boy." He released his hold and smoothed down the crumpled shirt front, and carefully straightened Chris's tie. "You *won't* get Claudia." Chris nodded and closed his eyes, and Grendel gave him a gentle pat on the head. "You'd better go," Grendel said, looking over his shoulder. "Dinner's almost ready."

That night, the four slaves sheepishly eyed each others' marks and badges. Claudia looked terrified, but strangely determined. Sharon was a mass of red marks, faint bruises, scratches, and smudges. And Brian couldn't even hold his head up. His body was still decorated with various ribbons and bows, and marked in several places with reddened areas that looked almost angry in their intensity. Only Robert seemed to have survived the day without something traumatic happening to him—at least as far as anyone could tell.

Back in their room, they retreated to their beds in silence. Once again, none of them had been chosen to accompany either the master or the mistress of the house for the evening, and Chris told them to just go and sit on their beds until lights out and think about what they could do to remedy that situation. Before dismissing them, he took Brian's decorations off and took them away without saying a word.

They sat in silence for about one minute.

"How ... how did everyone do today?" Robert asked. Groans from three directions was his response. The four looked up at each other, and a ripple of hesitant snickers and giggles swept through the room.

"That bad, huh?" Robert said, leaning back. "Well, at least you all are getting some attention. I think

Mistress Alexandra is so disgusted with me that she just wishes I'd go away." He said it lightly, but the look on his face was very serious.

"Aww, you don't know that," Brian said, waving a hand at the big man. "It could be just another psyche-out game they're playing with you." They nodded in agreement and then fell back into silence.

"It's not just games," Claudia announced suddenly. "If ... if Mistress Alexandra didn't tell me something today, I might have ... I might have made the biggest mistake of my entire life!"

"Oh yeah? What did she say?" Brian asked.

Claudia gently bit her lip, considering. "I think I'd rather not say, Brian," she said finally. "But I did learn something frightening! Chris ... *wants* me."

"Really?" Brian and Robert echoed each other.

"Yes! While Mistress Alexandra was ... um ... training me ... he held me. And I *felt* him, behind my back. His ... you know." She blushed slightly.

Robert looked down in embarrassment. Brian stroked the place where his mustache had been and wondered if he should share his little piece of important information. He coughed and said, "Actually, Claudia, there's something you should know about that little bastard. The first day I was here—"

"Could all of you just *shut up*?" Sharon interrupted with a snarl. "We're supposed to be quiet!"

The three reacted to her outburst with raised eyebrows, plus one snicker from Brian. "Oh dear, look who's turned out to be the new Miss Goody-Two-Shoes. Reading that manual and reciting it every night has brainwashed you, hasn't it, sweetie? Or was it your refreshing experiences in the outdoors today?"

Sharon looked like she was going to retort, but turned away from all of them with a jerky twist of her body. Without another word, she wrapped the thin covers over her body and put her head to the pillow. Brian shrugged, and then turned back to Claudia.

"You might as well spill it, Claudia. It looks like we'll be in this for a while. Why don't we get back to telling our life stories again? Wanna start the next chapter?"

"Oh no, I don't think I can," Claudia said soberly. "Not tonight, anyway. Why don't you go, Robert?"

Robert shifted on the mattress and thought it over for a minute. "All right," he finally said. "But it's not very interesting, I'm afraid."

"Trust us, we're a captive audience," Brian sighed.

And with the rapt attention of at least two of his comrades, Robert began his tale.

Chapter Five

Robert's Story

I guess I had everything a man could want these days. I had a good job, a wife, two kids, a house in the suburbs, the works. We even had a dog, this mutt we picked out from the shelter. The kids went to camp in the summer, we even took them to DisneyWorld one year. We had it real good, and we knew it.

Angie, my wife, was … is … the best. She was a well-known sociologist. She wrote this series of papers on the effects of violence on kids, and they were published all over the world. She was invited to speak in northern Ireland, and we all went. I was so proud of her.

And in the meantime, I went to the city every day in my suit and tie, and I … well, I basically sold toys to overage kids. You know, you've probably seen catalogs from my company. Gyroscopes made from space-age metals. Computerized bar guides. Neon artwork. Hand-carved desk accessories from some country where workers only get paid thirty-five cents an hour. We targeted those catalogs to households in the richest neighborhoods, and we sponsored expensive research into gentrification so we could find all the yuppies in any given town within five days of their signing a mortgage. As senior vice president in charge of marketing, I had my finger on the pulse of every American man who was earning three times as much as the government thought a family of four should live comfortably on.

At home, I tried to be active in my family's life. I went to school plays and softball games. I even went to PTA meetings for a while. I ... we ... always tried to do things with the kids on the weekends, and I always remembered birthdays and special days. And I had my own stuff, my hobbies. I played a little football in school, so I coached the local teenage team. I went to the gym.

And I was the unhappiest man in the world. Because I had the biggest, dirtiest secret. I had a mistress.

And it wasn't like all the other guys, either. I mean, they had lovers on the side. Women who worked with them, or women they met at bars after work, or even their own babysitters! But I had a real mistress. A *mistress*. And ... and I paid her. To see me. Once a week, every week for over two years.

Don't get me wrong. I ... loved her. But she was just too important to be able to see everyone who wanted to see her. I mean, she was famous. Really, if

I told you her name, you would recognize it immediately. She's even been on TV. And she didn't have
a job, so she would charge men for what they needed. I never thought of it as a fee, really. It was more
like tribute. To my empress, my goddess. The
money didn't mean a thing. But what she did to me
was worth all the money in the world.

I guess I'm starting in the middle, aren't I? Well,
my life wasn't very interesting until then, I guess.
Except for this huge secret I had, that was always
there. I can remember being thirteen years old, and
smuggling this dirty magazine into my room and
jerking off to a picture of this woman in thigh-high
leather boots. But I never talked to anyone about it.
Never! Until I met my first mistress.

What had happened was I went to this chic party
in one of those trendy clubs, some remodeled
church or something. I can't even remember what it
was for, but my company had these tickets because
we sponsored the appearance of one of our boy-
genius inventors or designers or something. My
wife had actually gone to a few of these things with
me, but she opted out of this one because she said it
sounded loud and obnoxious. I guess it was one of
the few mistakes she made in her entire life.

Because she didn't go, I spent most of the night
just kind of standing by the bar and watching
things. You see, if she had been there, we would
have walked around a lot, talking to people.
Everyone liked to talk to her. But by myself, I could
just fade into the background, drink until the room
got fuzzy, and then try to sober up enough to get
home by myself. Instead, there I was by the bar all
night. And that's how I saw them.

This guy kept coming to the bar and buying one drink. He was dressed a little warmly for the night, with a turtleneck sweater and a jacket, I remember. He'd buy the drink and almost dash back into the crowd, like a linebacker who has the ball. And then he'd give the drink to this blonde woman and stand next to her. He never had a drink of his own. And he never spoke to her. She would be talking to someone else, turn to him, and off he'd go for another drink. He would light her cigarettes, too, but he didn't smoke himself.

They were so obvious, I couldn't bring myself to believe it for at least two hours. Instead, I watched them. I watched him, the way he stood behind, but next to, her, attentive to her every gesture. I watched the way she flicked ashes onto the floor, carelessly close to his leg sometimes, and how he never moved out of the way. People would sometimes greet them, and he'd shake their hands, but never really participate in the conversation.

By the end of the evening, I knew I had to meet her. I wandered close to them, close enough to eavesdrop on more than one conversation. By the time I was very close, my palms were wet. I had to keep rubbing them against my pants leg. I was so nervous! What I was going to say became a kind of cruel game my mind was playing. People passed me by and I couldn't say who they were, or even whether or not they said hello to me. It was like the whole room had shrunk to me, that woman, and her male companion.

Finally, I was close enough to actually look like I was interested in the conversation. And this I remember well. She was talking about a fashion show she had gone to, where the models were dressed in fantasy clothing, like leather and lace and rubber. The people around her were amused and titillated. I thought my heart was going to pound its way out of my chest in another second. When a break in the conversation came, I stuck my hand out and said, "Hi! I'm Robert. Sounds like you go interesting places!"

I'm sure I must have had the sickest-looking fake grin on my face. Even as the words left me, I felt weak in the knees. I must have looked and sounded like the worst kind of moron.

And do you know what she did? She looked down at my hand, and put her cigarette to her lips. I thought she was going to leave it there and shake with me, but instead, she took a long draw and put her hand back down. I was left holding my hand out like an idiot.

"Not as interesting as the places you should be going," she said calmly.

I could have died. To the snickers of the people around me, I put my hand down, and tried to match them with a laugh of my own. But it was useless. I was already beaten. I couldn't stay, but I couldn't walk away.

I didn't try to engage her in conversation anymore. I just faded slightly into the background and continued to watch her, this time from up close. It may sound strange, but I was happy just to be like that. I felt like I was orbiting her. And then, suddenly, she made some kind of gesture to the man next to her, and he passed me her card. Before she left for the night, she said to me, "Call me on Monday evening at 6 P.M."

I went home feeling like I had cheated on Angie. But I couldn't bring myself to throw the card away. I opened the window of my car while I drove up the expressway, and I actually held it outside for a while, letting the rushing air blow against it, but I was really helpless. I put it in my business card case.

I stayed awake all night, next to the body of my faithful, loving wife. The mother of my two great kids, and the woman I had promised to love, honor, and cherish for the rest of my life.

You see, even when we had gotten married, I still had fantasies of powerful, controlling women. Even on our wedding day, as I stood in front of the minister, I thought, wouldn't it be wonderful if I could take the vow to *obey* her as well? Wouldn't it be great to have her put a gold collar on me instead of a gold ring? But Angie was … is … a strong believer in individual strength. She could never have stood for the kind of man I really am.

I called the mistress on Monday, from my desk at work, promptly at six. She told me to come to a certain address by seven, and hung up.

I called home and told Angie some story about late meetings. She took it in stride. Business was going through the roof, and I was an important man.

Two hours later, I was crawling naked across a bathroom floor, begging to lick the rim of a toilet seat.

I know what you're thinking, and you're right. I was a heel. A jerk. A bad husband and a poor father. But how can I possibly explain how fulfilled I felt when this woman, who I had only met two days before, put a chain around my neck and told me what a weakling I was? How can I put words to it? It was so right! I was really home! This was what I should have been doing all along. I was perpetrating a huge fraud on the world, masquerading as a good man, a husband and father and hard worker. Deep inside, I knew, and she knew—I was nothing but a weakling. A pathetic shadow of a man.

I made time for her every week. I told Angie that I was spearheading a special program for accelerated training for regional managers, or something like that. And every Monday night, I would go to her East Side home. I'd take off all my clothing in the hallway and crawl into her presence. Then, after a while, she would recognize my presence and begin my training.

It was all designed to make me suffer for my audacity. You see, according to my mistress, this charade of mine was insulting to every woman who lived, and I deserved to be punished for it. I agreed, and I looked forward to every correction she offered. When she beat me, I cowered and shrank onto the floor. When she had me shackled and tormented with tiny metal clamps all over my body, I cried like a four-year-old who lost his parents at the mall. I was shameless. Sometimes she would have some other slave present to watch what was happening to me. I used to think that those times were the worst, because she would be even more vicious and cruel. But I was still ignorant and selfish then. I didn't know what true suffering was.

She would assign me books to read, and then quiz me on their contents the following week. That was hell, because I didn't have anywhere I could hide them except for my office. I began locking my filing cabinet, and my secretary became annoyed. But I had no choice. I couldn't bring them home, could I? Finally, I bought a cabinet just for the things my mistress made me accumulate, and started a collection of pornography, sadomasochistic literature, and sex toys. And I kept everything right in my office, right under all the framed pictures of me with famous people, my diplomas, and my community recognition awards. I was an even bigger sham than before.

After she got to know me, my mistress began to slowly change my training. I was still going to be punished regularly, but now she was going to begin to make something out of me. I was so happy! At last, I was going to be molded, trained, and fashioned for a woman's pleasure! I was eager to receive this training. I was so hungry for it, I didn't realize what it might mean until it was much too late.

One of the first things she did to teach me my place was fuck me. Oh, how she drew out the act! First, she beat my ass until it was so tender I cried when she just tapped on it. Then, she brought out her collection of ... dildos, I guess, fake cocks of all kinds. And she made me kiss all of them. And, and ... lick them. And then she asked me to choose the one that would take my virginity the way men had ripped it from women for thousands of years. The first three I picked were all unsuitable. For the first one, she put heavy clamps on my nipples. For the second, she put a leather parachute around my balls. It hurt like hell! It had little pointy studs lining the inside. For the third, she put a terrible black hood over my head. It had a removable gag and blindfold, which she put on the side. But even without them, it felt like my head was in a tight cage. Finally, I chose one she approved of.

Then she sent me into the bathroom to clean myself out. She never watched. Doing it for the first time, with a hood on, and the parachute swinging between my legs and those clamps on my nipples, was a terrible, terrible experience. She had to send me back. I didn't know the first thing about how long I had to wait, how much water I should use, or anything. She was very, very angry with me. When I finally came out, she told me that because I was so inept, she wasn't going to fuck me at all. I had to grovel for over thirty minutes, begging her to do it, before she relented. I must have looked like a great big shaggy dog, whining and squirming on the floor with my ass high in the air, waiting for her to open it. By the time she got ready, I was crying a river of tears.

She put the blindfold on me, snapping it onto the hood with loud snaps. Then, she produced the gag that went with it. I couldn't see it, of course, but she told me all about it. It was shaped like a cockhead. She told me that she was going to use my mouth after my ass-pussy, so I better get used to having it filled. And then she pushed it into my mouth, and snapped it on. Thank god I could breathe through my nose, because that thing stretched my mouth so wide, I could barely breathe around it.

And then, she beat me again. When my ass was so sore that the flicking touch of one of her nails made me screech into the gag like a cat in heat, she opened the cheeks of my ass and slammed her cock into me.

It was then that I came to the greatest understanding I will ever receive in my entire life. For all the agony men have caused women through the ages, for all the rapes, the wedding-night horrors, and the terror we inflicted on them just because we saw them as weaker, men like me deserved to suffer. Even as I screamed a muffled cry of anguish and pain, I cried for all the women I had possibly harmed in my life.

Including poor Angie.

Angie noticed that I seemed sore the morning after my mistress used me sexually. She expressed concern. Did I have a back problem? Was I getting a cold? I told her that I pulled some muscles out of whack in a tougher than usual gym routine, and she seemed to believe it. I had taken care not to be naked in any well-lit room with her for the past several weeks, so I thought she probably didn't suspect that I had any marks to hide. And actually, I would have never had the kinds of marks she would have understood.

How wrong I was. She found blood spots on the sheet, probably about the same time I found them when I happened to look down in my elegant executive washroom. When I came home that night, she confronted me about them. Bleeding hemorrhoids? she asked, her face full of concern. Did I see a doctor? Why didn't I tell her?

That night, I realized I couldn't lie to her any more. I took her aside, in private, and began to tell her what kind of a man she had really married.

The divorce came shortly after that. Not only didn't I contest it, but I insisted that she get everything. The house, the car, everything. After all, nothing I could give her could ever erase the shame of having been married to a wimp, to have thought you loved him, that he was a good, strong man. I didn't even argue when she had her lawyer tell me that she didn't want me to have unsupervised visits with the kids. It hurt, sure. It hurt like hell. But I could see her reasoning. Who would want a pervert to have access to their kids? She was a great mom, very wise. Very strong. Why should her kids be subjected to me?

But it still hurts. I go see them when I can, and I send them cards and presents all the time. And Angie agreed not to tell them what I really am. She and I tell them that we just had grown-up disagreements, and that we still love each other and that we both still love them very much. That's the right thing to do, I guess.

I moved into a studio in the city, near where my mistress lived. I told her that she could have greater freedom to do as she wished with me. The first thing she did was order me to shave off all my body hair. And the next time I arrived and stripped, she had an outfit ready for me. It was black and white, with a short little skirt and a white ruffled apron. It was French maid's uniform, made for a man like me. When I put it on, I felt like I was putting on my real clothes. From there, I went to high-heeled shoes, makeup, and cock-and-ball restraints under everything. I even wore them to work. She had a locking belt that held them on, and sometime she would lock me into it for a few days at a time. While I wore it, I couldn't piss standing up. I had to sit down, like a woman. And then there were the days when a belt locked a buttplug in me, and I had to call her to get permission to remove it to, well, you know. There'd be times when I was leading a big, important business meeting with a fat plug up my ass and my cock locked in a little steel cage, and no one there had any way of knowing.

Then she began to invite her friends over to laugh at me, and help with my training. She loaned me out from time to time, to different women, all mistresses like her, who would torture me and laugh. She would take me to strange, underground clubs, I guess like the ones that Sharon used to go to, and she'd show me off. Sometimes, she'd make me lie on the floor, and she and her friends would flick their cigarette ashes onto my body and dig their heels into my flesh while they talked and gossiped.

Of course, she still had a lot of other slaves, who each had their own special times with her. If our rivalry became too obvious, she would set up sessions with the offending slaves and make them do awful things. Once, she thought I was not understanding enough of her time constraints, so she set up a session with another one of her big sissies. She made us oil ourselves up and wrestle for her entertainment. Anytime it looked like one of us was winning, she would stand over the dominant one and beat him with a carriage whip until he cried out and relaxed his hold. The match seemed to go on forever! I remember feeling so exhausted that I couldn't fight one more second, and then the other slave pressed me down. Because he won, he got to ... my mistress told him to ... use me.

While he did, she stood over me and told me how much of a woman I really was, how much I enjoyed being used like one. And I knew she was right. Before he was finished, I had made a mess on her floor.

She made me lick it up. And then she used me too, first in my mouth and then in my ass-pussy.

Before too long, I didn't know who or what I was any more. Was I a man, or a woman? Did I have a life of freedom and responsibility, or was I a slave? I couldn't quit my job, because then I couldn't afford to buy my mistress the trinkets and clothing she liked, and I couldn't afford to bring her tribute. But at the same time, it got harder and harder to concentrate on my job. All I wanted was to be with her. Or just to be near her! Finally, one night, I begged her to decide for me. What should I do?

She told me that if I wanted to be with her full-time, I would have to give up the thing that made me so repulsive to her. My cock. My nasty-thing, as I had learned to call it.

At first I recoiled, and tried to tell myself that there had to be easier ways to find a mistress. But the more I thought about it, the more I realized that sooner or later, balancing between being a free man and being her abject slave was going to drop me on one side or another. Slowly, I began to investigate how it could be done.

It's not easy! You just can't go to a doctor and say, "Lop it off, I don't want it any more!" If you do, they'll lock you up. They have programs for people who feel that they're born into the wrong bodies, though, so I started looking into those. I figured maybe I could find a psychiatrist who could help me out.

Instead, I found Mistress Allison. Mistress Allison is ... well, she was ... she's very different. A very special kind of lady. She saw me at one of these meetings, and she knew I didn't belong. I was just trying to masquerade through this the way I did through the rest of my life. She knew I really didn't want to actually be a woman. I'm not good enough to be a woman! When she explained it all to me, I just cried and cried. Now, I had no hope at all. I couldn't keep on faking a real life forever, and my mistress wouldn't take me as long as I had a nasty-thing between my legs.

Mistress Allison took pity on me. She went to see my mistress, several times, in fact, and my mistress tried her best to show me in a good light. But I am just a big, clumsy idiot, no matter how much training I have, and I'm afraid I made my mistress ashamed of me. Within two weeks, she gave me to Mistress Allison. And Mistress Allison told me about the Marketplace.

I quit my job just two weeks ago. And I came here hoping that I could finally find a mistress who wants me for what I am. Instead, I'm realizing that I'm not much of anything. And everyone knows it.

Chapter Eleven

Grendel and Alexandra met after dinner one night, having sent the four applicants off to bed for the fifth night in a row without taking any of them for the evening. Chris was doing a wonderful job of constantly reminding them how disgusting it was that in a week, none of them had polished themselves enough to be considered as even of minimal entertainment or use to the owners of the house. And from all observable signs, the four slaves were suffering from their perceived rejection. Every chance they got, they tried to impress Grendel and Alex in any way possible. They always seemed to fail.

"Of course," Grendel noted, "suffering is good for the soul."

"And who would know better than you?" Alex

teased back. She was very pleased with the way Claudia was shaping up. For all the disappointment that Robert engendered, Claudia was getting stronger every day, and more willing to do things she had balked at before. Alex had spent a lot of time with the girl discussing the relative merits of tears, and how a good slave should shed them, and Claudia was responding like a true champion.

In contrast, Grendel was not doing too well with his brace of failures, as he called them. The two of them are so superficial, he had noted one day, that repeated washing would no doubt make them vanish into nothing. Sharon, at least, was getting the benefits of real labor and the joy of getting one's hands dirty on a daily basis. At the very least, it would help build character. Fortunately, Jack was a horny bastard who could be every bit as sadistic a taskmaster as Chris could. The hours Sharon spent in the stable were hours that Grendel didn't have to think about her, which was just fine. As for the rest of the day, when she was training with him, he had learned to have aspirin handy. She was abysmally ignorant of the most basic things. Grendel smiled, remembering something Chris had reported.

"Did you hear what Sharon's first question to Chris was?" he asked, pouring himself a brandy, since Chris was still upstairs yelling at the slaves.

Alex looked up and frowned. "No, I don't think so."

"The first night, before anyone else could even think of something to ask, Sharon pipes up, 'Why am I stuck working in that disgusting stable?' Chris replied, 'To teach you humility and dignity in labor.'"

"That sounds like Chris, all right," Alex laughed. "He can be so pompous sometimes."

"Oh, but that's not the funny part. The funny part is that Sharon stood up and said back to him, 'All right, so I'm *really* humiliated, OK?' or something like that. Chris admitted that he almost lost it."

"Oh god. And she meant it too, didn't she?"

"Of course. Chris sent her down to the library and told her not to come back until she could use the word 'humility' in three different sentences and explain the meaning. I guess it might be easy to think that they mean the same thing, but really." Grendel sighed and took a sip of the brandy.

They had instituted a custom for their house, allowing the slaves to each ask one question a week of Grendel, Alex, and Chris. Those three questions, the slaves had been warned, would be the extent that their curiosity would be indulged beyond simple questions about how to perform their assigned tasks. They had also been told that the mark of a good slave was not asking any questions at all. Only Claudia had followed the not-so-subtle warning thus far, although the two men had showed admirable restraint both in the subject matter and in the pacing of their questions.

"Well, at least we're educating her. Shall we get down to business?" At Grendel's nod, she folded her own hands around her steaming cup of tea and began. "I've found out what Robert's two biggest problems are. The first is his role confusion, obviously. He still has very inappropriate responses to situations where there is any stress whatsoever, whether it's as simple as answering a question or as difficult as taking a good strapping from Chris. It doesn't do much good to punish him, by the way, at least not in the ways we've been trying so far. He seems to think that the more stress he's undergoing, the greater license he has to behave like a stereotype of a helpless, clumsy serving wench. We're working on that, both with the insistence on his growing back all the hair on his body and with assigning him some good outdoor work. He's not happy about the hair, especially the beard he's growing now. But he does surprisingly well on various heavy jobs. Chris says that Robert could be of some use in maintaining the cars, so I suggest we start him driving at the same time."

"Good idea." Grendel nodded. "He'd make an impressive chauffeur."

"My thought exactly. But his second problem has to be dealt with before he can be an impressive anything."

"Oh? What is it?"

"Stage fright."

Grendel nodded again. The oldest handicap in the world, and the one guaranteed to end any sort of career in the Marketplace. For never is a person more on display as when they are placed up for bid. And never is a possession more exhibited than when you've paid a lot of money and want to show off what you can get and train.

"So," Alex continued, "I'm going to start a series of confidence-building exercises for him. I know, confidence-builders for slaves, what a concept. But he really is dedicated, and I think he'll be a gem once we break him of those two training wheels." She paused again, tapping her weekly schedule book. "But it is so hard to reconcile the clumsy, inept man I see when I meet with him with the same man who managed to catch a full plate of cookies off a falling tray without dropping one. He's got a terrific sense of balance and a keen eye. He just can't seem to use them when anyone is watching!"

"Well, he's still looking a little bit better than he did last week. I think I have an idea about how to discipline him without pushing him into full retreat, by the way. I'll talk to you about it tomorrow, or maybe Sunday. I just want to see a little more of him before I trust my instinct on it."

"Tease!"

"And you love it," he retorted. "Actually, though, you sound like you've got things going OK." Grendel drank a little more brandy before starting his own report. "I wish I could say the same. Brian hates the bows and rhinestones Chris keeps coming up with, and Rachel says that he's able, but not wonderfully eager, to please. Rachel may be a little severe, but she's hardly unattractive. That says suspicious things about his supposed bisexuality, I think. He may be a Kinsey true-type, which makes it difficult to figure out what to do with him. Are you sure you don't want to try him out?"

"Positive. I have my hands full. Why don't you just play with him a little and see how he responds? You can judge his reactions to you versus his reactions to Rachel, and go on from there."

"I was planning to, but I think Paul and I have too much in common. He might be responding to someone he sees as just another leather daddy. I was thinking of letting Chris have a go at him, but Chris seems unwilling."

Alex's eyebrow inched up. "That's odd."

Grendel shrugged. "If I press the issue, he'll do it. But right now, I think he's too effective playing drill sergeant. You're probably right, though. I'll take Brian personally in hand this weekend. Now, getting back to my problems, there's Sharon. She's proving to be capable of memorizing things rather well, but her retention skills don't seem to carry over to actually *using* the information she's memorized. Also, despite her lessons in 'humiliation,' it's so clear that she's putting on an act that it's embarrassing to be with her. Maybe I did make a mistake there."

"Well, if you did, it's not a terrible one. Let's start with her roughest spots. Can we do anything to educate her further without enrolling her in a local university?" Alex wasn't exactly joking. They had done just that on several occasions before.

"I have an idea, actually. Robert seems to have a lot of background in seminars and coaching. Perhaps we can combine his need for confidence-building with her need to not be so stupid. What do you think?"

"That just might work," Alex admitted. She glanced at the weekly schedule and began to make notes. "In fact, that might fit in with what I had in mind! OK, that's one rough spot. Next?"

"Jack tells me that although she does well in pleasing him sexually, she seems to have a definitely class-based prejudicial attitude about it. Apparently, she's got it into her head that only the master will do, and she resents any other circumstance. You know what I want to do about that, no doubt."

"You've got my approval. Except for one thing. I

still haven't had Robert to myself for some practical examination of that substantial tool between his legs. Let me see what I can do with him over the weekend, and I'll give him instructions on Monday morning."

Grendel nodded. "So the boys get a workout, huh? Well, Claudia needs a little more time finding herself. And after Monday, Sharon will wonder why she ever complained." He made some notes on his own schedule and looked across the small table at Alex, who was finishing her tea. "I miss you," he said casually.

She mimed a kiss at him, and he grinned. "Your dungeon or mine?" she asked, getting up to leave.

"Since you ask, why, yours, of course."

Four exhausted, beaten, and bleary-eyed slaves stood in the garden awaiting their dismissal. Throughout the week, their bodies and minds had been worked constantly, from early morning until late evening when they collapsed into their beds with groans and a desire to curl up and sleep for the next two days.

Their trials showed on their bodies as an endless array of red and white lines, light bruises, and various cuts and scrapes gotten in assorted labor. But the reaction in their minds and souls came out in the way they bore themselves and how they dealt with new insanities and new demands. Robert, despite claims that he was trying his best to behave the way Alexandra wanted him too, was a constant mess, fluttering between panicked gibberish and impassioned begging and pleading for mercy. Claudia, on the other hand, in less than one week, was begin-

ning to hold herself with a new kind of quiet dignity. Although she still couldn't bear to be punished
publicly and cried more often than not, her tears
came in silence now, trickling down her face in a
glistening shower. Brian stumbled more, and his
speech became less cocky, and less stylized. Every
day, he endured some new trinket or adornment
that Chris got from god-knows-where, and his head
sank down into his chest when people giggled at
them. He was starting to become slightly sullen.

And Sharon showed her stress by fluctuating
between a stubborn and resentful dedication to her
duties and outright surliness to her comrades. They
spoke less and less to her, even in jest, and no one
helped her out in the bathroom. Full-time training
was turning out to be a little more harsh than anyone had expected.

That evening out in the garden, Chris paused
before sending them off to bed and said, "Claudia
and Sharon, you are dismissed."

The four looked at him and then at each other. He
repeated himself, "You are dismissed, girls.
Go—to—bed." His fingers jerked toward the strap,
and Claudia turned and fled. Sharon opened her
mouth for a moment, and then thought better of it
and followed her better-behaved sister.

"Robert and Brian, you have thirty minutes to
make yourselves fully presentable. Then you, Brian,
will report to Master Grendel, and Robert to
Mistress Alexandra. You both remember where their
suites are?"

He was answered with two mute nods. "Good,"
Chris said, glancing at his watch. "You have thirty
minutes starting from now." The two men took off

at a run, and Chris strolled casually into the house
after them, whistling a show tune.

Robert was so used to being naked that walking
through the hallways was no big deal. But somehow,
when he reached the doors to Mistress Alexandra's
suite, he trembled and felt the weight of the chain
around his neck. He was also dreadfully conscious of
the amount of body hair that was now almost in full
pelt all over his frame. Next to the smooth-shaven
bodies of the other three, he felt obscenely dirty, like
his body was covered in moss or mud. When he was
allowed to ask his questions, he asked why he wasn't
permitted to go shorn like everyone else. Chris had
answered, "Because you prize being shorn. You must
learn that no pleasure belongs to you, only to your
owners."

Which made sense, actually. But now, standing
before the doorway that might very well lead him to
the nearest railroad station, he felt dirty. Despite the
vigorous washing he had just given himself.

As the clock downstairs began to chime the hour,
he knocked. And at Alexandra's invitation, he
entered her sanctum, a place he had only seen
before in bright daylight. Now, with only small
table lamps lit, it was a sensuous series of caverns.
An outer room, with tables and chairs and a comfortable couch, for receiving visitors. A large master
bedroom, with a walk-in closet and a bathroom that
had a shower and a personal-sized jacuzzi. And a
small antechamber on the other end, with a big
comfortable chair and a reading lamp and a magnif-
icent view of the garden. It was her private world,
all done in clean, plain lines, with shelves of trea-

sured books, cabinets of souvenirs and *objets d'art*, and no televisions or radios to distract her from the tranquility of the design. She was waiting for him in the outer chamber, dressed in a light summer blouse and casual, form-fitting slacks.

He had never seen his mistress in New York in regular clothing. Not after the first night he met her. Yet somehow, Alexandra's casual dress and manner was very alluring. It spoke of a power that didn't need costumes or amulets to work. And for all the hours he spent bound and gagged in a room hung with red and black drapes, with heavy wood furniture upholstered in black leather with gleaming silver buckles and snaps, such a decor had never made him shiver the way he did now when he stepped onto the softness of the Oriental rug in the middle of her floor and inclined his head in what she had taught him was a proper bow.

"Good. You're on time," Alexandra noted. "Let's go inside, I want to get a good look at you." He followed her obediently into the bedroom, where his shivering turned into trembling.

"That's it," Alexandra said, stopping in front of him. "Right in the middle of the carpet here. Now, lace your fingers behind your neck and stand straight." He obeyed, and she took a walk around him, like she had the first time she examined him. Only this time, she was much closer to him.

"I think your workouts are too easy for you, Robert," she said, her voice directly behind his left shoulder. "I see by your charts that you finish them early most of the time. You should have told me."

"Y-yes, ma'am," Robert managed to croak out. His voice always started up high. He always needed to a moment to gain control of it and drag it down. He waited for her to appear within his peripheral vision again, but she stayed where she was.

"I know of a master," she said softly, "who tattoos his slaves here, on the shoulder, with an intricate rose pattern." She touched Robert's shoulder up high, tracing the area she was speaking about. "He actually cuts the design into them, with a surgeon's tool, and then rubs colored inks into the raw cut, so that it looks like a regular tattoo."

Robert's back actually rippled in a shudder.

"Yes, it sounds painful, doesn't it? He puts theirs on the left shoulder, which a few people have wondered about. What is the significance of that placement, Robert?" She neither moved nor took her hand away. In fact, she began to run her fingers lightly across his back.

"Um, um," Robert strangled on the words. "Ma'am, uh ..."

"Gather yourself before you speak, Robert."

"Yes, ma'am." The big man took a deep breath. "In the gay culture, ma'am, the custom of, um, placing keys on the left means that you're a master, and on the right means that you're a slave." Somehow, despite her maddeningly erotic touch, he managed to spew out that simple fact. He felt like he had just finished a wrestling bout. Answering questions while he was like this was so hard!

"That's correct, Robert. Yet this master places his mark left. Can you imagine why?"

"N-no, ma'am."

"Work on your imagination, then. I will tell you this, though. It is rumored that the master has a rose tattooed on his *right* shoulder. Isn't that a delicious piece of gossip? Doesn't it suggest a longer tale?"

"Yes, ma'am."

Alex left off her explorations of his back and cupped one hand around a firm cheek. "You have quite a good-looking body," she said, caressing him. "Do you realize that?"

Robert colored, deeply and suddenly. He coughed and tried to lower his head, but couldn't without disturbing the position he was in. "N-no, ma'am!"

"Are you suggesting that I'm wrong, or do you think I'm lying to you?" Alex asked, a little smile on her face. She patted his ass lightly. "Spread your legs wider apart."

He did so, awkwardly. "No, no, ma'am!" he said, trying to maintain his balance. "Of course not!"

"Then pay attention. One of the best things you have right now is your body, Robert. Your training is shoddy and your deportment is a mess. But you should thank god every night that you look like a nice piece of meat." She walked back around to face him.

"When was the last time you sexually pleased a woman, Robert?"

"Um ... oh, dear," Robert squirmed a little, avoiding her eyes. "Over two years ago, ma'am," he finally squeaked out. "My ... my mistress never ... she wouldn't ever let me...."

Alex stroked his left nipple until his stammering dissolved into a moaning whimper. "And how are you at massage?" she asked.

"Oh, I'm very good at foot massage, ma'am!" Robert's face brightened. Finally, something he did well! "I used to do it for all of my mistress' friends!"

"OK," Alex said, nodding. She walked over to a chair by a window and sat down. "Show me what you can do."

In no time, Robert had Alex sighing in relaxation. His large, worn hands cradled her feet in a firm, warm grip, and his fingers, so clumsy in so many other things, kneaded their way to nerves and muscles until she felt like purring. He certainly was good, past the skill level of an attentive and caring lover. And once he was seated on the floor, working diligently on a task he was eager to do, some of the confidence that had given him the strength to be a successful man in mundane society seemed to peek through his self-erected barriers.

"How are you on the rest of the body?" Alex asked, looking forward to an all-over massage.

Robert looked up in panic. His hands stopped working. "T-the rest?" he said. "But ma'am would have to ... I mean, I never ..."

"Yes, I think I'd like that very much," Alex said, pulling her foot from his hands. "You'll find some oils in my bathroom. Pick something soothing and bring it here with a few towels. If you run the bottle under hot water for a little while, it will make the oil nice and warm." Robert looked slightly helpless, and he was slow to get up, so Alex leaned over and cupped his chin in her hand. "If you can give a near-professional massage, now it would be worth our while to get you to a professional level and make it part of your qualifications, Robert. It's a very popular item, especially among women. So do as you're told."

She was ready for him, wearing nothing but a loose robe by the time he returned. She told him how to lay out the towels and how much oil to use, and then stood away from him. "Now come and remove my robe. Drape it nicely over the arm of the chair. I want every move to be graceful."

Of course it wasn't. His hands fumbled at her belt, and she could feel him trembling as he eased the silk over her shoulders. Since he turned away from her to lay the robe down, she could only hear the ragged inhalation of breath that sounded almost like a sob. She ignored it and made herself comfortable on the bed, her head resting on her forearms.

"You may begin, Robert."

He took a few more seconds than he should have to actually approach her. She was so ready for that first touch that she sighed at the heat of his palms. He began by gently rubbing the slightly warmed oil into her shoulders and across the blades. The rough tips of his fingers were like delicate abrasions. She made a satisfied humming sound and settled down into the bed, more relaxed than she had been before.

Robert worked diligently at spreading a thin layer of the expensive, lush-smelling oil, and then began to press his hands down, pushing against the muscles and beginning to grip with his fingers. He alternated each wave across or down her back with light scratching motions, which she seemed to like very much. The more she liked it, the bolder he became. His hands worked steadily in increasing pressure, working knots out of her muscles and encouraging blood flow. Gently, he eased her arms out from under her head and worked his magic on them, even to her fingertips, before letting her have them back. Then he worked his way across her neck and down her spine to her lower back.

Alexandra was in heaven. Good sex was always nice (mediocre sex wasn't all that bad either, when you got down to it), but a good massage was ecstasy! And damn, if Robert didn't know what he was doing! No doubt, he'd blossom with just a few sessions with Julio, their regular masseur. And since he didn't feel that she was actually watching him, he seemed fully capable of doing his genuine best.

He paused, and she stopped her reverie to wonder why. Oh, yes, he had reached her ass. She smiled against her pillow and then lifted her head to order him to continue. As he did, his hands light again, their trembling discernible as he pressed them against her, she praised him and let her head drop back down. It took barely a minute for him to regain his ability and work on her with the excellence he had shown on her back.

By the time he was finished, she was sleepy and awash with a delicious languor. She turned her head and ordered him to clean up and get out. When he did so quickly and in absolute silence, she smiled again. Ah, she thought, reaching for the switch on the lamp beside her bed, there's hope for him yet!

"So you don't like Chris's little ribbons and bows?"

"No, sir!"

"Well, that's just too bad, isn't it?" Grendel smiled a narrow but feral smile. His eyes fixed squarely on Brian's, his face close enough to be in that danger area that would make most people back away. But Brian would not, could not, retreat from it. If he did, he would find himself back in the little dorm room. So he had been warned.

"I ... I guess so, sir."

"Try again."

"Yes, sir."

Grendel nodded and swept a hand across Brian's chest and belly. The expanse of his taut skin was clean of stubble, the shaving job was very nice. Of course, it would be. Brian's obsession with his looks had allowed him to achieve a supreme level of leather clonedom. Oddly, it failed when it came to less black-cowhide-stereotyped body and dress modes.

"Do you know why you're here tonight?" Grendel asked, walking away.

"No, sir."

"Can you guess?"

"To serve you, sir?"

"That's a good guess. A safe one, but a good one." Grendel reached his destination, a chest of drawers that stood next to his glass balcony doors. He opened the top drawer and took out a few items, laying them to one side.

Like Alexandra's rooms, Grendel's reflected a soul that loved a sense of clean, luxurious privacy. He favored a heavy, almost industrial look, with solid bases and shining surfaces, bare of showy ornamentation but stylish just the same. Artifacts of a nautical nature hung on the walls or stood with sedate grace on a series of high shelves, and with the windows open, the slight breeze almost seemed to carry a tang.

"Yes," Grendel said, as he turned back toward Brian, "you are here to serve. But tonight, my purpose is more direct than that. I'll be perfectly frank. Rachel has given me some disappointing reports about you. Alexandra is so discouraged, she won't even agree to do a session with you. I want to know why you're not shaping up. I thought you were supposed to be working your ass off to make Paul proud. Instead, you're mostly sitting on it or getting it strapped into black-and-blue lines because your snotty attitude won't stop. Am I making myself clear?"

"Yes, sir!"

"Then explain to me why you're not doing well."

Brian found himself at a loss for words. As far as he was concerned, he wasn't causing any problems! He did as he was told. He bore the various frilly badges of shame that marked him every day. What else was wanted of him? The position he was in, ramrod straight, with his hands at his side and his feet together, also made him very uncomfortable. He was used to a wider stance.

"I don't know what to say, sir," he finally muttered, lowering his head. His thick hair was still damp from the shower.

"What a shame," Grendel said. "I'm sure you'll figure out something, eventually. In the meantime, let's see what kind of a toy you can be." He pointed at a sturdy writing desk along one wall. "Go over there and bend forward, bracing your arms. While you're thinking, I might as well have a little fun with you."

When Brian did as he was told, he braced himself for the sting and wallop of a strap. Of course he was going to be punished again. But this time, for Master's pleasure. Well, that was OK. Maybe Grendel had a different way of handling things than Chris did. Maybe this would be a nice, ass-blistering beating, the way other men had given Brian a little pleasure.

Instead, Grendel casually and lightly examined and stroked Brian's ass and the backs of his legs. Brian's legs were pushed wider apart, so that his cock and balls hung straight down, bare even of stubble and free for the older man's touch. Grendel paid them minimal attention. Then, after a brief absence of touch, Grendel's hands returned, and one of them pushed into the cleft between Brian's cheeks. A smooth finger, slippery with a cool dollop of lube, pressed against the rim of Brian's asshole, and then invaded it. Brian moaned and shifted back.

"Like it?" Grendel asked.

"Oh, yes, sir," Brian replied, sighing. "Very much, sir!"

"Good. You're staying in this position until I get an answer to my question." Grendel gently fucked the finger in and out, and added more lube. Brian bit the inside of his cheek. The fit would be tighter without so much wet stuff. But he didn't say a word. He wasn't going to foul up the best chance he had for a scene with the master. No way. He couldn't wait to be properly fucked.

But wait. What was that about staying in position? Until he answered what question? He gasped as another finger worked its way in beside the first, and remembered. Well, fine. What was he supposed to say? Nothing, certainly, until this fuck was over. Then he'd think of something. But only after he was good and reamed.

The fingers pulled out suddenly, making him sway and grasp the desk to keep from falling. Had he really closed his eyes, and so soon? He opened them and waited for the return of the pressure. It didn't come.

"You're very accessible," Grendel commented, wiping his hand off on a small towel. "You open up very nicely. Unfortunately, that's the one part of you we could have easily trained. Do you have an answer yet? No? Well, keep thinking."

The heavy carpeting kept Brian from hearing any footsteps, but he could definitely feel the lack of a person near him. Light shuffling sounds seemed magnified beyond belief, right along with his own heartbeat, which pounded in his ears. He waited with what he felt was great patience for the next sensation. Would it be a strap? A paddle? Or ... please, please, he thought, perhaps Grendel might actually bring himself to just push Brian to the floor and make him prove the boast uttered so long ago in Grendel's office?

None of those things happened. In fact, nothing happened at all. Brian's arms began to feel stiff; he was holding them too tightly. He relaxed a little but maintained the position. He wanted to raise his head and find out where Grendel was, but at the same time, he dared not. He tried to keep his exhalations from sounding out his growing frustration.

Just as he debated stretching his legs a little bit, he heard the sound of a shower running. Carefully, he twisted his neck and looked around. The bathroom door was open, and Grendel was indeed taking a shower. The master of the house had just left Brian in position and gone off to bathe.

Now what? Brian asked himself. Do I get up? Should I leave? Or do I have to stay where I am, bent over like this? He lifted and shook out each leg and stretched as well as he could without actually standing up. Obviously, I have to stay where I am, he decided. Then, when he gets back, he'll praise me and we'll go on from there. No sweat. He'll see—but wait. Was Grendel really waiting for an answer to that question? How the hell should I know why I'm not working out the way they want, was his first bitter thought. I didn't write the frigging rules here!

But as the water continued to run in that smaller room off to the side, Brian's dread grew. Maybe he did have to come up with an answer. Maybe Grendel would come back, turn on the news or something and then just go to bed, and leave Brian like this all night!

Get a grip, he scolded himself. Just come up with something plausible and we can get back on the case here. He devoted the next several minutes to seriously thinking about it, his thoughts broken only by the sound of someone entering the room, passing him without even a pause, and putting down something that clinked on one of the bedside tables. That person left again without comment, closing the door. For some reason, the entire moment made Brian more acutely conscious of his submissive vulnerability than he had even been. That other person, and it could have been Rachel, or maybe even Chris, didn't even seem to notice he was there.

I can't stand it! Brian's entire body shook in a mixture of humiliation, anxiety, and confusion. I don't understand what's going on! All I want is to be owned, is that so hard? All I want is for some master to take me away and just tell me what to do. To his horror, a tear crept from behind one eyelid and trailed down the side of his nose. He raised one hand to wipe it hurriedly away, but then realized that the water had stopped running. He stayed in position, and felt another tear escape. He opened his eyes wide to try to make them dry quickly. But his courage was fading fast, and he had so little control left.

Again, he felt rather than witnessed Grendel's movements through the room. The scrape of porcelain made it clear that someone had brought the older man a cup of something hot, and that he was silently drinking it, across the room from Brian. Nothing was said. The silence grew more and more oppressive as Brian fought to control the raging turmoil of his conflicting emotions. He tried to turn his attention back to the question, but his fears and worries kept getting in the way.

After a while, his lower back and the backs of his calves began to ache.

He had no idea how long he had been there, bent over in silence, before a sudden cramp in one leg forced him off balance. It seemed that Grendel was at his side in a second.

"You could have told me at any time that you were experiencing weakness," Grendel said, as he helped Brian lower himself to the floor. "This was not intended to be an endurance contest. Or did you forget what it was you were supposed to be doing?" He was wearing a summer-weight robe now, carelessly belted low around his waist. Black hair showed in a coarse profusion across his naked chest. Brian saw it and lusted to touch it, grab it in one hand and hold on tightly, and his mind felt like it was spinning into a long reel. He finally felt the carpet beneath his hands, and groped for his calf to begin massaging it.

"I'm sorry, sir," he said, surprised at the hoarseness of his voice. The wave of sensual need passed through him again, and he was aware that his cock was jutting upward between his legs, despite the pain from the cramp and the humiliation of the stumble out of position. "I'm sorry," he repeated helplessly.

"Yes, I'm sure you are. But for what? For failing to become a piece of still life, or for failing to answer my question?" Grendel went back to his table to get the cup that still had a little coffee, now cool, in the bottom. Brining it back to Brian, he gestured for the younger man to open his mouth, and made him drink the dregs. To Brian, who had not had coffee in two weeks, the strong and cold stuff was like ambrosia. He drank it eagerly, not even minding when Grendel slapped his offer of a hand to hold the cup.

"Now you have two questions to answer, Brian," Grendel said, taking the cup away.

"Yes," Brian said, savoring the bitterness and still rubbing his leg. "Yes, sir. I'm sorry I couldn't come up with an answer to your question, sir. I don't know why I'm not doing well." He lowered his head and his hands fell away from his leg. It wasn't so bad now, and the intensity of having felt Grendel's strength and that unexpected boon of a sip of coffee suddenly seemed overwhelming. His eyes filled with tears again. "I-I'm sorry, sir," he said yet again.

"Yes, I can see that," Grendel said softly. There was a new, thoughtful tone in his voice. "Well, admitting that you don't know will be enough of an answer tonight. You may go now."

Brian looked up in confusion. "G-go? But, aren't … don't you want to …"

"What?"

"Please sir," Brian pleaded, "won't you let me show you how … good I can be? I'll show you what I was trained to do, sir, you'll see, I can …"

"No, I'm not interested, Brian," Grendel said, the thoughtful tone gone again. "I gave you a chance to do that and you fucked up. So get your ass out of here before I have to tell you twice."

Brian struggled to his feet and gave the simple, nodding bow he had been taught to make when exiting, and escaped out to the hall before tears began to flood his cheeks. He paid a visit to the slaves' bathroom before going to bed, and washed his face over and over again, his head pounding from confusion and pain. When he got back and realized that Robert hadn't returned, he had to bite into his pillow to keep from cursing aloud.

What did I do wrong? he screamed internally. What did I do wrong?

He was awake enough when Robert did return to smile in a nasty triumph. If I didn't do too well, he thought, then the big sissy must have been a total flop. Oh god, was his next immediate thought. I'm getting as bad as Sharon. Robert never did anything to me, he's a nice guy. He hugged his pillow to his chest and curled around it, the way he used to do when he was a child. What should I do? he asked himself as he dropped off to sleep. What should I do?

Chapter Twelve

The added dimension of being required to serve after traditional lights-out time became something none of the slaves was adequately prepared for, even though several of them had longed for it. Grendel and Alexandra seemed to be distant apparitions during the day. Even the private sessions they had with the new slaves were more teaching instruments than personal episodes of dominance, submission, and erotic slavery. The daylight and the intrusion of meals and chores served to make the day seem more like a working or learning environment. Somehow, at night though, the mystique deepened. The slaves were allowed into rooms where beds suddenly became the center of attention. They were admitted into a shadowy world of privacy and intensity, with no interruptions or time limits. It was frightening and thrilling and stressful. And it produced a new element into their relationships with each other. Real jealousy.

The first weekend, Robert and Brian were called twice, and both were sent back to their own beds each time. Claudia noticed and did her best to remain silent, but Sharon was simply livid! How dare the owners call the fairy and the sissy when they had a fully trained, eager and *more than willing* pleasure slave at their beck and call? Why was she giving blowjobs and getting screwed by the filthy *stableboy*, for crissakes, while these two half-men get called up to the luxurious bedrooms? She expressed her anger and indignation to Claudia whenever she had a chance, until Claudia learned to ignore the sounds of Sharon's voice.

Come Monday morning, all four were barely speaking to each other. It wasn't because of fights they had. Fighting, as Chris would put it, was unacceptable behavior. But unspoken protests, accusations, apologies, and sheer gloating made all of them wary of what they were saying. After breakfast, Chris came to give them their week's worth of assignments, and kept them a little later for a "special announcement."

"This week starts a new phase in your training," the short man began. He was dressed up today, in a jacket and tie. The jacket emphasized the blockiness of his shoulders and body. So far, even in the summer's heat, they had never seen him in anything as casual as a polo shirt.

"Starting this morning, some of your instruction and duties will include a newer, more intense level of sensual interaction with Mr. Elliot, Ms. Selador, or myself. That does not change your habits in regard to the servants at all. In fact, your eager submission to them is very important this week, as most of them will be taking a vacation after this weekend.

"What this means for *you* is that you must strive to be pleasing not only in your deportment and in the tasks you have been assigned to do, but in being constantly available, in mind and body, to serve whatever function you may be called upon for. This is not a reward, but a new responsibility. Fail to please, and you will be punished severely. Fail to show proper submission and an outstanding will-ingness to perform, and you will be denied the opportunity to show what few skills you may have." He glanced at his notes.

"Starting this morning, Sharon will offer to per-form oral sex on the other three of you until orgasm. Keep in mind, however, the boys must withdraw and deposit their come on her body, or in a recepta-cle suitable for such disposal, and *not* in her mouth. That style of service is reserved. Anyone wanting to take advantage of her offers may do so at any free time during the day, providing that they are not late for any appointment or in completing an assigned chore."

Sharon gasped and her mouth dropped open in shock. Claudia echoed her and blushed. Robert coughed out a piece of apple that tried to go down the wrong way and covered his face, trying not to look at Sharon as she reacted to this pronounce-ment. Brian raised an eyebrow and grinned.

"Brian will begin afternoon outdoor work under Jack, the stableman. Robert, you will now begin to work more with me, but in the afternoon, you and Sharon will have some special training sessions with either of the owners. And Claudia, you will work with Ms. Rachel in the afternoon. The new schedules are printed up, and one will be posted in your room.

"Did you have a question, Sharon?" Chris asked innocently.

"I have to ask the other slaves if they want...?" Sharon shook her beautiful head in confusion. "Did you say...?"

"Every morning, you are to go to each of your companions, and in some mannerly and inviting way offer your oral services to them. That means offering the boys fellatio and offering Claudia cunnilingus. If they accept, you will arrange with them the time and place, so that neither you nor they are inconvenienced, and then you will preform to the best of your abilities until they are satisfied. This duty begins today—now, as a matter of fact. Is that clearer?"

Sharon's mouth worked silently. There was a long moment when everyone waited for her outburst, but it didn't come. Instead, she nodded, her teeth tightly clenched.

"Then we are settled. You three," he cast his cold eyes on the others, "are not obligated to receive Sharon's service or to reject it. But I will remind you that you are still forbidden any other form of sexual release, and choosing this may provide you with an allowable pleasure. If any of you choose to accept the attention, you may be expected to critique her skills, either to me or to the owners. Do you all understand this?"

Three nods answered him.

"Good. You have twenty minutes if you choose to begin this new ritual. If there isn't enough time for Sharon to grant the favors she offers, you may always make an appointment for later in the day, such as during or after lunch, or just before lights out. As soon as everything is worked out, Sharon and Brian are to report directly to Mr. Elliot, who is out near the south paddock; Robert, you come find me; and Claudia, I believe you have a workout waiting. You are all dismissed!"

As he left, three heads turned back to look at Sharon, who was licking her lips nervously. Robert looked away quickly.

"Well, let's hear it, sweetie," Brian taunted.

"OK, wiseass," Sharon snapped back in a rush of bravado. "You wanna blowjob?"

Brian hooted his derision. "Wow, with a come-on like that, no wonder you always had guys fighting over you! Hey, don't do me any favors, gorgeous. I'll have the whole rest of the week to think about when you're gonna suck my big fat one." He waggled the spoken-of member at her. "And I can't wait to see this big lad put it to you nicely. Let's see what sultry, seductive language she lays on you, huh Robert?"

Robert immediately rushed the door and fumbled for the knob. "I-I ... you don't have to ask, Sharon. I'm not ... I mean, you're lovely, but I can't ... I wouldn't ... why won't this damn door open! Ah!" He pulled it open in a flourish and dashed away.

Sharon smirked at his retreating back and turned to Claudia, her voice heavy with sweet sarcasm.

"Oh, Miss Goody-Two-Shoes, do you want me to lap your cunt until you come like a little alley cat being gang-banged by a bunch of stud cats?"

Claudia didn't say a word. She just turned and fled. Sharon laughed after the retreats of her companions and sat down to finish off a particularly ripe peach. This was turning out to be easier than she had thought. She looked up at Brian, who seemed lost in thought and bit into the soft fruit and let the juices run over her chin. It was kind of obvious, wasn't it? He was so queer, he didn't think he could keep it up if she played music on his hairless pipe there. So, he toughs it out, leaving empty threats. Meanwhile, Wimp One and Wimp Two run for their lives.

Sometimes, Sharon thought, licking her fingers, being a slave can be awfully easy! She walked to the bathroom casually and cleaned herself up for this new session time with Grendel. She was so happy to be out of the stable for a while, she even sang to herself.

Robert escaped the impossible situation in the servant's dining room with nothing but a wholehearted sense of terror. If beautiful Sharon (the bitch, he reminded himself) could be put to such use, what could possibly happen to him? And how embarrassing, to have to ask everyone else if they wanted you! He fretted over his refusal. Surely Sharon wouldn't see it as a rejection, would she? She couldn't possibly want to do … that … for him, could she? The big man shook his head and went to find Chris.

"'So, wiseass, wanna blowjob?' That was her invitation this morning?" Grendel sat on the top rail of the paddock fence, one leg swinging. "Tell me, Sharon, have you had much success with that particular line? Or were you intending to do something to get you punished so severely that you'd wish you had died before this day started?"

Sharon fumed, glared at Brian, and then looked back at Grendel. "No one said I had to, like, ask any special way, OK?" she complained. "I did ask!"

"That's not entirely true, Sharon. I wrote out Chris's instructions last night, and they included the phrase, 'mannerly and inviting.' Now, I *know* that Chris obeys me. He's rather good at being literal. Are you suggesting that he forgot to say those words?"

Sharon bit her lip, considering. Did the little bastard say something like that? Probably. She dropped her head down a little. "No," she mumbled.

"OK. Why do you think you were given this particular assignment, Sharon?"

"Uh, because you wanted to—I don't know!" Next to her, Brian winced. Grendel sighed and kicked his free leg back and forth. He casually pulled a length of braided leather out of his pocket and began to unbraid it.

"Sharon, ever since you've gotten here, you've bitched and moaned and bragged about what you think you should be doing. You're supposed to be a pleasure slave, correct? Well, I've decided that you haven't done enough pleasing around here. As to how you were supposed to ask, you're supposed to ask and perform like the slave you supposedly want to be, regardless of who is receiving the dubious pleasures you offer. So, since you neatly scared away everyone this morning, I think it's only fair that you give them all a second chance. You'll start with Brian right now." He gestured for them to face each other. In the distance, they could hear the horses calling to each other as Jack brought them out for the morning sun.

Sharon clenched her teeth. Why did it have to be *him*? she asked herself, staring back into Brian's teasing, insolent eyes. She drew a deep breath and stopped herself before she started to talk in a higher pitch than usual. She coughed to cover up her error and concentrated, closing her eyes and imagining that it was one of her former masters standing in front of her instead. "Would you like me to suck your cock?" she asked finally. She liked the sound. Her voice was low and throaty, and when she actually said it, her body made a sensual movement like a slight twist. She kept her mouth slightly open at the end of the question and ran her tongue along her upper lip. What man could resist her?

Apparently, Brian could. "Sorry, not today, sweetie," he answered lightly. "But thanks for the offer."

"Dull and unimaginative, but serviceable," Grendel admitted. "You'll have to come up with lines more original than that, Sharon. Brian, put your hands behind your back. And you, too, Sharon." He jumped down from the fence and quickly passed a leather loop around first Brian's and then Sharon's wrists, binding them in place. The two slaves stood facing each other, their wrists now tightly held behind their backs.

"Put a little more creativity in the actual deed," Grendel suggested, looking at Sharon. "Get down there and start working."

"But sir," Brian said, shifting nervously. "I said no...."

"To *her*, Brian. Not to *me*. There's a big difference. Remind me to punish you later. And I did give you an order, Sharon."

Sharon dropped to her knees on the grass, and was faced with Brian's entirely uninterested cock. It hung limply, framed by a long, pale ball sac, the area smooth and very clean. At least it was better than Jack, who rarely wore underwear and worked with horses all day. His crotch often smelled more of horse than of man. This one was, at the very least, soft and clean. She moistened her lips and moved in.

Brian hissed a breath through his teeth as she slurped the entire length of his cock into her mouth and began to work it with strong sucking movements and a fast whipping of her tongue. His toes curled into the ground and his body actually shook. She was good! No, correct that, she was great! His cock went from slumber to attention in record time, and he arched his back to give her better access to him.

"So you might not have been lying outright," Grendel commented, flicking his last strand of leather at Sharon's shoulder. It stung her lightly. "You can get a man who's been sexually frustrated for two weeks to pay attention to you. No, don't stop, keep going. I'm going to want to see all of your techniques by the time we're through. And Brian," another flick, and a sting to Brian's chest, "you will not do me the discourtesy of coming without permission, will you?"

Brian moaned, "No, sir!"

"You should have taken her up on her offer, Brian," Grendel teased, hitting Brian again. "If you had, you could have been assured of a nice orgasm this morning. Now, it's entirely in my hands."

Brian began to breathe more regularly and nodded. "Yes, sir. As it should be, sir, if you'll excuse my saying it." He planted his feet more firmly in place and closed his eyes.

"I will this time," Grendel said idly. He looked down at Sharon, who was moving her head back and forth to stroke Brian's cock with her tongue. It was a nice move, but nothing impressive. "Get your mouth on his balls," he said, punctuating his words with more flicks. "Let me see how you treat a pair of nuts."

Sharon obediently swept her mouth off of Brian's cock and twisted her shoulders to get underneath it. Despite the fact that it kept slipping across her face, she managed to start licking at at the spheres in question. Brian sighed.

Grendel made a little slipknot in one end of the strip of leather he held and looped it neatly behind the curved head of Brian's cock. Then, he tugged up, raising the cock so that it was flat against the man's belly. He pushed Brian's head down a little and put the tether end of the cock leash into his mouth, and then stepped back.

Oh yes, much better. Brian stood, his feet planted far apart, his hands behind his back, and his head bent forward. His cock was stiff, up against his belly, and his balls were exposed for Sharon's ministrations. And Sharon took advantage of the opportunity. She lavished attention on them, licking them up and down and back and forth. Then, she gently sucked one into her mouth and ran her tongue around it. The same treatment went to its twin. The result of this was Brian's making several sharp sounds between his clenched jaws. Sounds very much like whimpers.

Sharon suppressed a nasty grin and extended her tongue up behind his balls, as far as she could. That always got them going! And it worked on Brian, too. Wadda you know, she thought, feeling him jerk and tasting new sweat on him. He's not as queer as he acts. So where's his snottiness now, huh? He's nothing but another guy, crying like a baby because someone knows what to do with his precious cock! She nibbled on the loose flesh around his balls, enjoying the sounds he continued to make around the piece of leather clenched in his teeth.

Grendel was, despite his reservations concerning Sharon, mildly impressed. If nothing else, she seemed to be a good cocksucker. He reached in and freed Brian's cock. Brian made a gasping sound as the tension was taken away, and moaned out the air when Sharon instinctively brought his cock back between her lips and massaged the head with pressure from her tongue.

"Oh, my god, oh sir!" Brian's back arched even further and his hips thrust forward. "Oh please, I can't hold it, sir!"

"But you will," Grendel said sternly. "This is only the beginning."

Brian groaned and tried to think of the multiplication tables, the subway schedules, the number of colored handkerchiefs in the hanky code. Anything but what was happening to him! It was just amazing how good this crass, ignorant piece of stuck-up girl was! As she pulled back, drawing her tight, wet lips along his shaft, he began to pant.

Don't fuck up now! a nagging voice in his head screamed. Think of nasty things, hotdogs with ketchup, liver with onions, pastrami with mayo! Think of cold things, like popsicles and ice cubes, on your crotch, where there was now enough heat to ...

"Arrgh!" he finally yelled out, twisting and pulling away from her. His cock slipped out of her mouth and her eyes opened wide in surprise. Glistening wet and stiffly jerking in front of his body, his cock flopped up and down, the very motion a hellish erotic wave.

Grendel stepped closer and pushed Brian violently forward, spearing Sharon's mouth with that cock once more. Sharon yelped and tried to keep her balance, but she fell back and then onto her side in the grass. Brian stumbled to his knees next to her.

"Looks like we're going to have to try that again," Grendel said. He gazed down at the two of them and reached into a pocket. Then, he tossed a strip of six wrapped condoms onto the grass between them.

"Between the two of you, I want one of these separated from the others, opened, and on Brian's stiff cock in—" he took a quick glance at his watch—"two minutes. Starting now!"

They scrambled for the strip of safes, bumping into each other as their heads dived for them. Grendel sighed. "And you'd better figure out a good way to achieve this," he added, watching them fumble and fight. "We'll have five more to go through by the end of this session."

Robert found Chris in the library, picking through a

stack of binders and books on one of the tables. "There is a special assignment for you, Robert," the major-domo said, beckoning the man forward. "These"—he shoved a small stack of paperbacks to one side—"are books of soliloquies and famous speeches. Several are marked off. You are to begin to memorize them in preparation for a recital every other day."

Robert swallowed hard. Did he really hear that? He blinked and nodded, to let Chris continue.

"These"—Chris shoved over a pile of binders—"are lesson plans. You are to familiarize yourself with them as well, in preparation for some tutoring that Mistress Alexandra wants done."

"T-tutoring?" Robert echoed. "In what? Um, who? Please, Chris, I never …"

"Don't be silly, Robert, of course you've taught. I've seen your résumé. You've conducted seminars in very high level marketing strategies and product placement and mail order catalog design. These lessons are in subjects far easier than the ones you've been successful in, and you'll be providing a service for the house." Chris seemed to be much more encouraging than he usually was, and Robert was taken aback by the man's apparent friendliness and helpfulness. He stared and then nodded helplessly.

"You'll find some clothing in a box under your bed, and hanging on the back of the door of the dorm. Put these books neatly by that box, and then get dressed and meet me by the garage. Ms. Selador has a few errands to run, and you will be driving. Your license is in the jacket pocket. Please strive for speed, we'd like to get this done early today."

Robert was at the door when he remembered something and turned back. "Please, Chris," he said earnestly, "if I may ask … who will I be tutoring?"

A bit of the familiar, nasty Chris showed up in a wide grin. "Sharon, of course. With speed, Robert, with speed!"

Claudia climbed off the stepping machine and wiped the sweat off of her forehead with a clean, soft towel. She had nothing against strenuous activity every once in a while, but sweating was so … so … unladylike. She dutifully recorded her progress on her chart and padded over to the bar for a drink of water. When she turned back, she was surprised to see Rachel standing in the doorway.

"Oh!" the little slave gasped. She set her glass down carefully. "I'm sorry, miss, you just startled me."

Rachel smiled. "That's all right," she purred, moving into the room. "It's good to be startled. I see you're assigned to me today, Claudia baby."

Claudia nodded.

"That's nice," Rachel said. "Because I don't have much to do this afternoon. So I can afford to spend a lot of time paying attention to you."

Claudia gulped and nodded again, afraid to do anything else. Rachel had never behaved like this before! Despite the way she reportedly terrorized poor Brian, neither Claudia nor Robert had ever been even harshly disciplined by her. The times that Claudia had worked with the second-floor housekeeper had been spent in sweeping, cleaning, and making beds, or folding laundry. Now, however, the look in Rachel's eyes suggested something far more personal. She waved one hand casually at Claudia. "Go on, finish your exercise," she suggested. "I'll just watch for a little while."

And so Rachel did, staying through Claudia's stretching and low-impact aerobics, and then through the cool-down yoga as well. When Claudia opened her eyes after her tenth deep breath cycle, the housekeeper was gone.

Chapter Thirteen

Brian limped off to the stable, bruised and sore and streaked with grimy bands of sweat and dust. Grass stains marked his knees and thighs and the sides of his arms, and smudged dirt covered his body. Anywhere that wasn't covered with the marks of a man who had just spent almost two hours rolling around in a field was slashed with a series of thin, angry, red lines, which stung and glowed with heat.

Individual strands of grass and leaves were still stuck in his hair, although he had spent a few minutes trying to pull them out by combing his fingers through. It hadn't worked very well. And he was hungry. No lunch today, Grendel had announced. They had wasted too much time trying to do a simple exercise, and there was no sense in giving them more time to be lazy. Brian would proceed to the stable and begin working, and Sharon would clean herself up in time to ask Robert and Claudia if they wanted the oral services she was supposed to have properly offered them that morning. He was, he told them, extremely disappointed. During the entire morning, they had only managed the feat once.

First, they squabbled over who should pick up the strip of packages. Then, tearing the whole thing in half with their teeth, they were each stuck with three wrapped ones and nothing loose. With no hands to hold the packages, there was nothing to do but crawl to each other, grasp one pack together, and rip it open.

Of course, they couldn't relinquish the three that each of them already had, though. Each one wanted the other to drop theirs. Each one growled and cursed at the other through teeth clenched around the edges of these little gold-and-white packages.

Grendel called the two-minute time limit and picked up a rod he had left lying on the top fence rail. It was white, and some kind of plastic, and it had a short handle on one end. To Brian, it looked like a comically long conductor's baton. Grendel slashed it a couple of times through the air, allowing the two slaves to hear the whistle of its passage, and then proceeded to whip the two of them almost to tears. Then he told them to start over. And over. And over. They began to drool around the soft squares of metallic plastic, and when they finally tore one open, it kept dropping out of Sharon's mouth, and she had to keep dropping onto her belly to retrieve it. And never mind that *she* dropped it—they were both punished.

By the time Sharon finally had one properly positioned in her mouth, the state of Brian's cock was not up to being covered in latex. She tried, oh, she tried, but she could not arouse it while holding the rolled latex. Another beating, this time accompanied by tears and cries, and then she started again from the beginning. They ended up tearing open four of the six packages, ripping holes in three of the four condoms, and then finally getting one, just one, over the head of Brian's not-quite-as-hard cock.

Then Grendel untied the two of them, gave them their instructions, and dismissed them. Oh, and he told Brian to pick up the shredded detritus of the morning's wrestling and throw it away. Which was why Brian had a handful of torn plastic and latex in one hand, and grass and dirt in his hair. He found a large trash container and tossed everything into it, and then ruffled his hair, causing more bits and pieces to fall out. He looked down at the assorted trash and sighed heavily. What a glorious future I face, he mused. What made me think this was going to be like some hot story out of a gay porn magazine? I spend hours and hours trying to please a woman who is insatiable, my own cock is so neglected it jumps up whenever a breeze hits it, and the most exercise I get is wrestling with another woman while my dick does pushups. I'm never going to get off again. I think I made a mistake.

"'Ere now, it's th' pretty boy 'imself come to work wi' th' commoners," Jack drawled out, watching him. "You look like you've 'ad a bit o' wrestlin' action this mornin', y' do."

Brian looked up with a wearily and shrugged. "I'm here to work with you," he said sullenly.

"Oh, yes, Mr. Elliot said you'd be by," Jack admitted. "But I didn't think you'd be lookin' like somethin' the bleedin' cat dragged in!" He chuckled. "Well, no matter! You'll do for what purposes I've got t'day. C'mon, I'll show you th' tack, an' teach you t' clean it proper."

Brian followed the stableman to a shed that adjoined the stable, and breathed in the rich, enveloping scent of expensive, well-kept leather. English-style saddles and bridles and working gear hung from gleaming brass hooks and sat on polished wooden racks. The floor was a burnished blond wood, and the late morning sun streamed in through the opened side door. The windows of the shed were of colored glass, creating muted shadows inside. Brian could have gladly lived in this room. He breathed the smell in deeply.

"Aye, it's nice, ennit?" Jack asked idly. "This 'ere's the finest gear you'll find, pretty boy. All quality stuff, so mind me when I show you somethin', and don't muck around wi' what y' don't know 'ow t' do. Got that?"

Brian nodded, and Jack pulled a worn blanket from a shelf and tossed it on the floor. "You'll work down there. You've got saddle soap ..." Patiently, the stableman explained the cleaning and finishing process and showed Brian where everything was. When Brian could repeat all of it back, the Aussie nodded and motioned outside.

"Then y' better wash off this mud 'n such, boy. You'll find th' water out 'round to your right. Come on back when you're nice n' clean!"

Brian found the water. It was a regular garden hose and the water was cold. But he splashed and rubbed and tried to stand in the sun. He gasped when he saw the the thick pattern of lash marks that Grendel had given him—it covered his body from the tops of his shoulders almost to his knees. His arms were especially bad. Shivering, he shook like a wet dog and went back around to where Jack was still waiting. But Jack had something new in his hand—something Sharon had gotten used to seeing daily, but Brian had not seen before. Brian stopped, looked down, and then back up at Jack's dancing eyes.

"Y' know," Jack said slowly, working his hand back and forth, "I b'lieve I've got one more thing t' teach you, pretty boy. Come on inside."

Brian walked forward, a dazed look in his eyes. Now? Here? Like this?! When he entered the tack room, he saw that Jack had tossed a long nylon strap up through two of the internal crossbeams. Each end of the strap was a loop, about three feet off the ground. They were about four feet apart. The blanket was folded underneath them.

As he stared at this strange arrangement, Jack took him by one shoulder, threw him down onto the floor, and kicked him to position himself so that his shoulders were on the blanket. The swiftness of the attack and the pain in his body dulled Brian into a kind of shock, but he paid attention as Jack caught one ankle, placed it into one of the open loops, and tightened the strap around it. Now Brian's leg was pulled up and out, forcing his shoulders and back against the floor. He groaned, but offered no resistance as Jack fastened the other leg as well, leaving both his legs up in the air.

"That's a nice boy," Jack crooned. "Nice an' open,

aren't you?" Brian could only whimper as Jack positioned himself comfortably, his cock level with Brian's butthole.

His body wracked with shivers and tremors of anticipation, Brian screamed out and pounded his fists against the floor when Jack finally plunged in with one sharp thrust. Yes! Yes! Do it! Somewhere, he heard himself actually saying these things, but the only sound in the hot little room was Jack's satisfied grunting and Brian's groans of pleasure and agony. His much abused cock rose yet again, and Jack started to play with it!

"Y' know, pretty boy," the stableman said, pulling out to plunge in again, "you're not allowed to shoot y' spunk."

But Brian did anyway, screaming his frustration and ecstasy while Jack laughed and finished him off.

Brian suddenly remembered why he had wanted to become a slave.

Claudia followed Ms. Rachel up to the floor with the servants' quarters and worked at changing sheets. She had never been in these rooms before, and she marveled at how well they were appointed and furnished. The household servants lived much better than the slaves. They had television sets and VCRs. In a large recreation room, there was even a pinball machine, and a magazine rack held what looked like all the latest media and entertainment guides. Rachel had Claudia clean up a table of empty cups and a bowl that held popcorn, but shooed her out of the room when Claudia's eyes lingered too long on the cover of a women's magazine.

As Claudia carried the tray down to the kitchen, she thought, that's another strange thing about being here. At my mistress' house, I watched TV and movies with her and Carl. We always had a lot of newspapers and magazines, and I could read them if I wanted to. Now I don't know anything that's going on in the world. I don't know what's happening on my favorite shows, or even if there has been any big, important news that everyone is talking about. My entire world is here.

When she came back upstairs, Rachel met her at the head of the stairs and directed her to one of the servant's rooms. As they crossed the threshold, Rachel reached out and took a tight handful of Claudia's hair and shook her head gently. Claudia froze.

"Now it's my turn," the housekeeper said, pushing the slave into the room and maintaining the grip in her hair. "Your friend with the black hair is all right, but I think you'll be better."

"Oh!" Claudia whimpered. "Oh, my...."

"Hush now, little girl. No need to talk. You want this, and you want it bad. I heard you turned down the pretty one at lunch time. That was probably a good choice. She looks like she could turn a wrestle in the sheets into something that's as much fun as humping a rock." Rachel spoke softly, her voice pitched almost in a whisper. "But you want a girl, don't you? A real girl, not an overgrown Barbie doll. So when I turn you loose, you're going to turn around and undress me, and then I'm going to make you scream, little girl. And you're going to love every minute of it and thank me sweet, like the good little kitten you are."

Claudia's breath was already coming in gasps. She moaned as Rachel gave her head one more shake. "And what's more, my kitten, you're not going to get to come today. And you'll still thank me."

Claudia's hands trembled as she unfastened the buttons and zippers of Rachel's plain but well-made uniform. As it was shed and neatly hung up, piece by piece, Rachel was revealed to be a woman with a few secrets under her dark, forbidding garb. Gold rings pierced her thick, dark nipples, and a tattoo of a winged cat with long claws and exposed fangs curled around her upper right arm, reaching to the top of her shoulder. Claudia swallowed hard. She had seen such decoration on various guests at Mistress' parties, but never so closely. And never under similar circumstances.

"Do you like them?" Rachel asked, touching her breasts. The rings sparkled and danced as she cupped her breasts and lifted them. "Kiss them. Show me that you appreciate how beautiful they are."

Claudia bent her head and placed her soft lips carefully on one nipple. They are beautiful, she thought, pressing harder. Her eyes closed in the proper way to worship. Why hadn't Brian mentioned them?

"Good kitten. Now finish."

The skirt was removed, displaying another tattoo, this one in the small of Rachel's back. It was a work of art. A winged disk rested in the center, just above the arch of her buttocks, and from it radiated black and purple feathers changing at the tips to blue licks of flame, which ended at her hips.

Claudia gasped and dropped to her knees. Without being asked to, she kissed the center of the disk.

"Oh, you are hungry," Rachel said with a chuckle. "Now, if I were one of the owners, you'd be in trouble! But I like that, kitten, so why don't you just keep on doing it?"

Claudia eagerly ran her lips over the design, giving loving kisses to every inch, following the top of Rachel's ass to both sides of her body. Rachel sighed and played with her nipple rings for a while, stopping Claudia only after the girl had made three passes over the entire tattoo.

"Now you get to do that all over me," she sighed. And she stretched out on her bed, putting her arms comfortably behind her head and nodded to the kneeling girl.

Claudia threw herself into the task, licking and kissing every inch of Rachel's torso, and then following Rachel's directive to skip the delta between her legs and just continue at the thighs and work down to the feet. Claudia followed every direction with a speed and joy that amazed her. Surely the room couldn't be as warm as Claudia felt? Surely this ... this ... *maid* wasn't making Claudia's body squirm and thrust with such eager passion?

Ah, but it was. Claudia kissed every toe on each foot, and sucked on them when Rachel suggested that such a service might feel very nice. And then, when Rachel finally sat up, grabbed Claudia by the hair once again and dragged her mouth into her triangle of dark hair, Claudia let out a moaning cry of joy. Rachel laughed with erotic satisfaction as Claudia writhed and clutched and tried so pathetically and preciously to please.

Claudia felt Rachel tremble and shake and tasted the sharp nectar of a woman's ecstasy. But Rachel was in no way sated. Her hand pulled Claudia tighter to her and Claudia mewed and continued. It hadn't been that long ago when her mistress had commanded such service, but her hunger and her joy in finding someone so easy to please were as powerful as Rachel's lust. When Rachel pulled Claudia up and put her on her back, Claudia whimpered and thrust up to Rachel's cruel fingers, making sounds that she had never made before. She was far too hot to remember to be embarrassed. Each pinch of a nipple, each thrust into her own sex, and every biting kiss was sensual agony and an explosion of bliss.

As Rachel finally fell back to take several long breaths and stretch out, Claudia felt like an old rag—limp, soaking wet, and worn to a frazzle. The taste and feel of the other woman was coating her, covering her in a cloak of the familiar, and making her body tingle with need, desire, and the torment of being unfulfilled.

"Ah, you're not bad, kitten," Rachel finally said.

"Thank you, miss," Claudia whispered. "You ... you're wonderful." And so beautiful, she thought, looking at the decorated woman's body. No one would ever know that such a strong, tough lady was under those dark, plain clothes. She wished she could hear Rachel's story.

But Rachel only laughed and pushed herself up on one elbow. "You think so? Well, wait until you've been done by Alex! Or even Grendel." She gave the slave a push off the bed. "Now get out, I'm sure Chris has got something for you to do for a while.

I'll see you in two hours or so."

With Rachel's chuckles following her, Claudia left the room, suddenly supremely conscious of the red bite marks on her small breasts, and probably on her thighs as well, the sticky wetness between her legs, and the flush of color all over her body. In the cool hallway, her nipples tightened and sprang back erect, and she moaned at the sensation.

Wait until she was "done" by Alexandra?

Oh, oh, dear. Claudia had to stop and hug herself to keep from sinking to the floor. If she was so shameless with a woman who was a servant in this household, how would she behave with the mistress? And Grendel?

She shivered suddenly and ran to the shower room. There she stood under hot water until the shivering stopped, knowing full well that it wasn't the temperature in the hall that had caused it. But she couldn't think about … that other thing. Not now, and maybe not at all. She went to find Chris, praying that he had something intense and mindlessly difficult for her to do.

"You did well for a first day," Chris said, after Robert backed the car into the garage. "Your driving is acceptable, and your ability to concentrate on what you're doing is very good. But you must work on your ability to respond to your passengers more naturally. And you have to learn when it's proper to apologize and when it's proper to just keep your mouth shut."

"Yes, Chris, you're right," Robert admitted. He felt very strange, sitting in a car, dressed in normal clothes. The light wool blend scratched against his bruises and cuts, and his nasty-thing had stayed at half-mast throughout the trip. Chris got out, and Robert followed him, passing the keys back.

"And you have to keep in mind that a good driver has to see everything outside the car and nothing inside of it. That might be the hardest thing for you, actually. We'll work on it another day. For now, I think Mr. Elliot has something in mind for you."

"What—?" Robert started to ask. Then he turned around to see Grendel, pushing Sharon ahead of him, heading for the garage. Out of the corner of his eye, he saw Chris make a slight, formal movement that almost looked like a bow. Robert aped the movement, but instinctively performed it deeper.

Grendel beckoned the two of them away from the garage, and they obediently met him halfway. Sharon was a mess. Her body was covered with little bruises and many red stripes, and although she wasn't dirty, there was a look of dishevelment about her. Oh, Robert realized, as he looked closer, her hair isn't combed or brushed at all. Amazing how that can make someone look so ... slovenly. Even when they are so beautiful.

"Robert, get those clothes off immediately," Grendel snapped. "You've been told that you should no longer wear clothing on this property."

"Uh ... y-yes, yes sir," Robert stammered out, reaching for the tie. "B-but I was ... d-driving M-mistress...."

"You *were*, Robert! Were. Now you're *back*." The owner's voice was very harsh. There was something wrong here, but Robert was too flustered to be interested in finding out what. He stripped off his tie and tore open the buttons of his shirt.

"I'm sorry, sir," he dimly heard Chris say.

"Yes, well, I'll have to talk with you later, boy," Grendel said. "Take his clothes and get inside." Robert gasped and whimpered. Never had anyone spoken so harshly to Chris in the presence of one of the slaves. He pulled the shirt off with the jacket, leaving them entangled, kicked off his shoes, and dropped his pants. Chris calmly and mutely gathered the pieces, and with another short bow, walked back toward the side entrance to the house.

When Robert was naked, Grendel pushed Sharon forward. "Sharon has something to offer you," he said.

Robert could only stand there in confusion as Sharon shot him a glance that was pure anger and snarling hatred, and then said in a sweet voice, "Please Robert, would you like me to suck your big, juicy cock?"

Robert's mouth opened and he gaped. Her pose, her voice, even the way she lightly licked at her full lips (were they a little bit cut and bruised?) were so pulsatingly lusty and explosive, it was hard to believe that this was the same woman who had made catty remarks about him and called him a sissy. Yet there she was, offering him this incredible service, and so sweetly!

"Very common," Grendel noted. "I want to hear more originality, missy." She sighed. Grendel looked at Robert and asked, impatiently, "Well? Do you want it today? I understand she wasn't very gracious this morning, and she is very, very eager to make up for it, aren't you?"

"Yes, sir," she answered. Her tone was almost right, but that look crept back into her eyes. Robert gulped.

"Oh, oh dear, no," he gasped. His voice had scaled up again, without his thinking about it.

"Why not?" Grendel asked, pushing Sharon down to her knees. She adopted a position that was totally open and inviting, her knees spread wide and her shoulders thrown back. "She's apparently not too bad, according to two accounts. And you do like to have your cock sucked, don't you?"

Robert blushed, and his hands flew down to cover his nasty-thing before he remembered that he wasn't supposed to do that anymore. Grendel's eyes narrowed in anger.

"Get your ass inside, you idiot," he growled, pulling Sharon up and pushing her back to the house. His voice was low, and his words came out in a slow, metered pace; but fury burned in them. "How *dare* you try to cover yourself in front of me? How dare you fall into that pattern Alexandra has told you a hundred times not to act out?"

Robert fled ahead of the master of the house, tears filling his eyes. Each angry word and question forced them out, and by the time he passed the door frame, he was sobbing. Grendel stepped in last and slammed the door behind him. "Chris!" he called out, his deep voice echoing in the main hallway. "Get over here! You—" he gestured toward Sharon, "are dismissed. Get back to the stable and do some real work for a change." She ran, passing Chris in the same doorway. Grendel put his hand out.

"Give me your strap," he said. And as Chris unhooked it and passed it over, Grendel's eyes caught Claudia coming down the stairs. He looked over at Robert, who was crying freely and shivering, and then back at Claudia, standing stock still on the stairs.

"Claudia, front and center," he said quietly, pointing to a spot before him. As she approached, he gestured to Chris. "Hold him on the side, so he has a good view."

Chris pulled Robert by the arm over to the side of the hallway, against the wall, and gestured for him to kneel. As Robert obeyed, Chris pulled his right arm up high behind his back and grasped a handful of hair, keeping Robert's head up. Robert whined.

"Present," Grendel said softly. Claudia was positioned so that the dainty curves of her ass were presented to Robert in their fullest glory. She braced herself against a table on the opposite side of the hall. Grendel stepped into position and brought Chris's strap across her asscheeks in a perfectly straight line, bisecting them. The sound seemed deafening. It echoed in a series of cracks, and Robert cried out an inarticulate scream that was louder than Claudia's.

Claudia heard her voice and Robert's mingle. Her confusion and fear were at their zenith. Why was this happening? Had Rachel complained about something? What did she do wrong? And why was Robert forced to watch her being punished like this? She wailed as the blows of the strap built up. If Chris was accurate with his tool, Grendel was deadly. And his blows were harder, each one pushing her forward. Her arms trembled with every new crack. She could hear Robert sobbing and carrying on behind her in between the kisses of the strap.

And then, as suddenly as it had started, the beating ended. She sank to her knees, tears streaming down her cheeks, and kissed the leather when it was presented to her lips. Grendel carried the gesture further and pressed it to her cheeks to gather the moisture before passing it back to Chris.

"Give these worthless people something to do," he snapped, as Chris let go of Robert to take his strap. "And then come see me. Obviously, you've been lax in some basic training matters." Without waiting for Chris to acknowledge him, he turned and strode up the stairs.

"Yes, sir," Chris said softly. The major-domo turned back to the two slaves kneeling in the hallway and fixed the harshest, most intimidating glare they had ever seen upon them.

"You," he whispered, with all the displeasure any human being could lodge in a single word, "you ... will both report to Shaw, right now. Tell him that I think it's time to turn the compost. Tell him that I think it will benefit from being done with bare hands. And be grateful I didn't say with your teeth."

Robert and Claudia fled as though demons were on their heels. Even if they had been familiar with the filthy, odorous job they had just been assigned, they would have run just as fast.

Chris mounted the stairs holding his strap in one hand. It glistened with Claudia's tears.

Long, hot showers were the order of the day when the four slaves wearily returned to the house after their assorted afternoon chores. Claudia and Robert in particular stank of rotten foliage and old garbage, and looked about as dejected as two self-proclaimed dainties could be when covered with slime and muck. Brian, pungent with the richer smells of a stable, looked as though he had accumulated the most

248 / *Sara Adamson*

damage in one day. His body was a battlefield of marks, and his every move advertised an assortment of aches. After they finished drying, they all noticed that Sharon no longer had a comb or a brush in her bathing kit. She struggled to pull the tangles out of her hair with her fingers, but didn't ask any of them for a loan. No one offered one either.

Claudia was serving dinner in the main dining room, under the supervision of Cook and Chris, so the other three ate without her. It was another gloomy meal, with no chatting and no complaining, and very little eating. For their own reasons, each of them had lost much of their appetites, even though Brian and Sharon hadn't eaten since breakfast. When Chris came into the room with Claudia, they sat up with a combination of relief and dread.

"Tonight," the major-domo said, "Robert starts his studies in the library. Brian and Sharon, you are being punished for her ill manners and the failure to obey orders that both of you demonstrated today, and you will go right to bed. Claudia, you missed an opportunity for study this afternoon, so I suggest that you join Robert in the library, or you may also go to bed." He handed Claudia a paperback book, with erotic-looking cover art. "You may find this work of particular interest. Mistress Alexandra recommend that you read a little every day. As soon as you are all finished eating, you may consider yourselves dismissed."

They looked at each other in confusion when he left. No lectures? No nasty comments? No sarcasm? Even the tone of his voice was much softer than usual, barely edged with his usual cool. Robert wondered what had happened after he and Claudia scampered away to their afternoon of wallowing in filth. What had Grendel said? What did he do?

"Who is he?" Robert gulped when he realized that his thought had managed to sneak out of his mouth.

"A fucking nasty bastard," Sharon said, toying with a piece of whole wheat bread.

"Oh, very perceptive," Brian shot back. "What do you mean, Rob?"

"I mean, well, who is he around here?" Robert kept his voice low. "The first day I was here, I thought he was a master. But he's not really."

"He's the major-domo," Claudia said, putting some vegetables on her plate. "It's like a butler. It means house manager or something like that."

"Hmph." Sharon shrugged. "More like overseer, if you ask me, OK? Like in the Old South. Yassuh, Mr. Big Shot, I'll keep the slaves in line fo' y'all!"

"No, no, it's not like that," Robert insisted, his tone still soft. "He may seem like an overseer, but overseers were free men. I think Chris is their slave. Alexandra's and Grendel's, I mean."

Claudia turned to look over one shoulder, as if she expected the man to return. "I don't know, Robert," she said in between chews. "He doesn't wear a collar. But on the other hand, the way he answers them is very deferential. And the way Master Grendel spoke to him today was very frightening!"

"Oh, yeah?" Brian asked. "Tell me."

Claudia and Robert shared their story, with Sharon dropping in to add that, indeed, Grendel seemed more than a little pissed today. She, of course, had no idea why. Brian exchanged glances with her, and they both kept mum about their early-morning adventures.

"So the little guy gets a taste of what we live with every fucking day? Awww, too bad," Sharon finally remarked.

"So you think he's a slave?" Robert asked. "Do you think Grendel ... punished him? The way we are?"

They sat in silence for a minute, considering what little they knew. Finally Brian decided that now was a good time to expose the delicious piece of gossip he had been hoarding about the man, and he leaned forward to share it. "I don't exactly know what he is," he began, his eyes dancing suddenly in the joy of spreading a juicy bit of news, "but I do know something special about the guy. The first day I was here, Paul was telling Grendel what a good cocksucker I was. And then Grendel told Chris to get into the office, and—"

The door opened suddenly, and the four slaves, who had all leaned forward on their elbows to hear what Brian was saying, jumped up in their seats. Plates and mugs clattered against the table and chair legs squeaked across the tile floor.

Chris stood in the doorway, and four hearts pounded faster than four hunted hounds.

"I believe you've had enough time to eat," the major-domo said evenly. "Get going!"

They fled. They didn't notice that no one was called to serve that night until they were all in bed. Robert and Claudia returned at the usual lights-out time, and found Brian and Sharon in bed but not sleeping. They got into their beds with the usual creaks and moans, and lay there, staring at the faint shadows on the ceiling.

"All right," Robert said, breaking the silence first. "Who's turn is it next?"

"Huh?" Sharon asked.

"To tell their story. You told yours, I told mine. How about you, Brian?"

Brian groaned. "Oh god, not tonight. I can't even think tonight. You wanna tell us all about your life and loves, Claudia?"

Claudia sat up, clutching her pillow. "Well," she said, considering, "it's not very interesting, I'm afraid. What you see is what I've always been."

"Yeah, but there's more," Robert said encouragingly. "How did you end up here? I mean, you're so good! Why would—oh!" He blushed suddenly. "I-I'm sorry, Claudia. I'll shut up now. You don't have to say anything."

"Why not?" Sharon demanded. "We did! We agreed that everyone was going to tell their story, right? Well, I wanna know how you got here, Miss Goody-Two-Shoes."

"Now wait—" Brian began.

"No, Brian, it's all right," Claudia said. "Sharon is right. We did agree. I'll try to make it short."

Chapter Fourteen

Claudia's Story

I was nothing before I realized what my true purpose in life was. I know that sounds odd, but it's true. I lived a dull, ordinary, nothing life. My father was a big, scary man, who worked at constructing big office buildings, and my mother was a nice lady who perhaps drank more than she should have. I was a middle child. I wasn't oldest, or youngest, or a boy, so I lived like a little nothing.

It was very nice, sometimes, being nothing. People never expected anything from me, except that I stay out of the way and stay quiet. And I was a good child, I think. I tried not to bother anyone.

When I was in school, thinking about going to college, I had a boyfriend. He was kind to me and very gentle. We would take long walks together, and I wrote poems to him. It was like one of those romances you read about in those cheap books with the pretty covers, the ones that sell millions of copies to secretaries and housewives. It was ... sweet. Yes, that's it. Sweet. We were sweethearts.

But one day, all of that changed. He became very—well—obsessed, with one thing. If I loved him, he told me, I would, um, sleep with him. All the other kids were doing it, he said. And besides, if I didn't want to, it meant that there would be no future for us as a couple. Grown-up men and women have sex, he kept telling me. When would I grow up?

I guess he was right, really. Everyone was doing it. And he was never forceful with me! No, he was just insistent until I firmly said no, and then he'd sigh and start the car and we'd go home. It was just that even though I really liked him, maybe even loved him, I didn't want to ... do that ... with him. It didn't seem right.

So that year, I thought maybe there was something wrong with me. All the other girls I knew were interested in boys and sex. They talked about it all the time. And the teachers at school spent so much time telling us not to do it, I knew it must be wonderful! But I was never interested in anyone enough to investigate it. I was a good student, and I acted and danced in plays, and I had a busy life. I guess I didn't miss it much.

But I guess I also always knew that something was different about me. I found out what it was the day I walked into my first part-time job and I fell in love with my boss. You see, my boss was a woman. A very sexy, powerful woman, with short hair and a long stride and a way about her that made men afraid of her. And there I was, a little invisible nothing, loving her and wanting to be with her. So I thought I was gay.

Which was fine. You see, gay women are just like bigger nothings! No one notices them at all. When people talk about why they don't like gay people, they're really thinking of gay men. Even in big crowds, almost no one ever notices the women. So it was kind of natural for me to find a place where women I thought were like me hung out, and it was easy to start seeing a woman, and it was easy to go to bed with her. No one noticed, no one was hurt, and I guess everyone just thought that we were best friends. The only trouble with this was that it wasn't very interesting. She was nice, and I guess I loved her the best I could, but I always thought something was missing.

I could never figure out what it was, though. We would lie together in bed, touching each other's bodies so softly and so gently, and I would just purr like ... like a kitten. She was very good to me, she always made sure that I was, well, satisfied. She taught me how to please a woman, and we lived together for three years before we realized that somehow we had stopped having sex at all. It had gotten to be something routine. So we said sad good-byes and kissed each other and moved apart again.

I tried to find another girlfriend right away. It took a little while, but I found this nice, cute butch who wore leather jackets and was very political. She was very smart, too. She could talk about anything, for as long as you'd want. She liked me to wear sexy little black dresses and big jewelry, and she liked to hold my hand when we walked in the streets. It was scary and wonderful—for a while.

I thought she was all right in bed, but I was a little disappointed, too. Again, I couldn't explain why. Again, I thought that there must be something dreadfully wrong with me.

I finally found out what was so wrong because of this woman's politics. One day I went with her to a demonstration. There were these women there who were saying things about pornography and women, powerful, nasty things about exploitation and pain and degradation. I started to look at the pictures they had, and suddenly I knew what was so different about me.

I wasn't straight or gay. I was submissive. All those pictures they had, of women in sexy costumes, all tied up and gagged, I wanted *that*. I even remember seeing one picture of a woman lying on the floor, all bound in yards and yards of rope, and this other woman was resting her feet on her. They both wore high-heeled shoes, so high I could never imagine walking in them! But the thing that stopped me cold was a picture of a sexy lady in a little skirt way up on her thighs, a little white lace apron, and a little lacy cap on her head. She was holding a tray in her hands and giving the warmest, most inviting smile! And this made me ... well, it turned me on. More than anything ever had before. And I knew all this while standing in the middle of hundreds of women chanting slogans and waving signs *against* it.

So I started reading about it, mostly in men's magazines. No one notices when women buy them, you know. I thought that someone would, and he would make a comment about it, but no one ever did. I read the ads, and started to send away for books and tapes. I still lived alone, so I hid everything way back under my bed. In time, my butch girlfriend went on to find someone more her style, and we parted as friends.

I couldn't figure out how to meet anybody new, though. Now that I really knew what I wanted, it seemed it should be easy to find someone. But it wasn't! There were no clubs for people like me where I came from. But just in case I did meet someone, I started to practice. I bought high heels and learned to walk in them. I read the books out loud, and said the words that the slaves said, over and over, until I got the sounds right. I even read books about being a waitress, making good tea, and the history of teatime! I finally knew what I wanted—I wanted to be a sexy maid, just like in the pictures, carrying hot drinks and being ever so embarrassed when people could see my legs or my … my chest, or anything! It was a delicious fantasy.

Then, one night, I was reading the personals in one of these magazines, and there was an ad for Mistress Madeleine. She was looking for a new house slave, and being a French Maid was going to be part of her requirements. It took me a long time just to get the nerve to write to her. I tore the advertisement out and read it every day, having the most naughty thoughts about what she might be like, and what she might want from me. Finally, my fantasies grew to be too much, and I poured my thoughts out in a letter and sent it to the box number in the advertisement.

And that was it, really. I answered it, and she

invited me to go out and meet her, and four months later, I quit my job and went to live with her.

Well, I guess it was more than that. Mistress was more used to men than women, and she was surprised that I answered her ad. She later told me that there weren't a lot of women who actually liked the fantasy, that it was considered very degrading and something that only men really like. So she was looking for a pretty blond man to serve tea to all her lady friends. I explained to her that men or women didn't make a difference to me, I just wanted to be submissive, and to be in that kind of role. And if that was degrading, then I loved to be degraded. So she agreed to kind of try me out for a few days, and see if she liked me. She called it playing, but I was never more serious in my life.

She's ... she's beautiful. Tall, and dark, and clever and ... she's just perfect. The minute I saw her in her leather clothing and her high boots, holding a whip in one hand, I wanted nothing more than to crawl to her and do anything she said. Oh, how she played with me those first days! She tied me up, she spanked me, she told me what a naughty girl I was. She dressed me up to please her, in short, short skirts and stockings and little bodices that pushed me in and up. I wore stiff collars with shiny studs all over them, and sometimes she would even put me on a leash, and I would crawl after her like a dog.

I knew right away that that was where I belonged. I would do anything to live that kind of a life. I offered myself to Mistress every weekend, and she would say, "Not yet, not yet." I think she wanted to make sure I was serious. So I would try even harder to please her. When she permitted me to ... to ... worship her body and please her in sensual ways, I cried with joy. This was what had been missing from the relationships I had before! I never had the security of being held by my lover, being told what to do, and having no real choice. I cried in her arms when she began to love me, and I swore I'd never love anyone else the way I worshiped her.

It was Mistress who made me into a maid. She ordered my custom outfits and gave them to me to wear. She began to take tea every day, just to watch me. Every move I made, I had her eyes on me, watching that my hands never shook, and that my posture was perfect. Then, when I was good enough, she would have real tea parties and invite her friends over to socialize.

Before long, everyone knew that I was her little French maid slave girl. I had my own little room, with pink curtains and a fluffy bed with pure, white sheets and big pillows. She bought me a closet full of clothes, little uniforms in different colors, and special costumes for holidays and parties, and for when I was being very, very good. Every day, she would tell me what to wear, and I would put it on with a big smile.

Dainty shoes with tall, spiked heels; heavy, thick velvet ribbons in my hair and around my throat; lacy gloves and stockings; the thin gold chains she would attach to my cuffs; the jeweled earrings; and even starched white aprons—I loved every piece of my wardrobe. I always tried to look my best for her.

My life was very simple. I did a little dusting and cleaning, but not too heavy, because she had a regular cleaning woman come in for that, or had one of

her male slaves do it. I served coffee at breakfast, tea
in the afternoon and sometimes in the evening. I
would carry some of the lighter trays of canapés
during a party, and generally fetch and carry things
around the house whenever Mistress was there. I
had a lot of free time, and Mistress encouraged me
to read.

The best times were when she would command
me directly and continue my training. I was a very
clumsy girl, and I needed correction all the time.
Mistress was very, very patient. But she was also
very harsh. I was caned a lot, and I had to learn to
kiss the cane every time. It was so hard to do that!
But I did, and even though I cried, Mistress would
be pleased and she would forgive me, and we
would go on to the next lesson. Sometimes the
marks would last for days, and oh, how dreadful it
was when she would ask me to show them to someone! But I always did, sliding my skirt up around
my hips and bending forward to make them easy to
see. Just the thought of it makes me shiver. Those
were some of the times when I felt most like a slave.

Sometimes, Mistress wanted me to do things I
didn't know how to do ... well, that's not right. She
wouldn't have done that, and it wasn't nice of me to
say it. She wanted me to do things I didn't want to
do, and I would find a way not to do them! It's true!
I was very stubborn, and stupid. I didn't realize it
then, but now I do.

I ... I was always very shy about my own ... my
own pleasure. Do you understand that? I knew I
needed to serve, and that was my greatest pleasure.
But ... touching ... myself ... was something else. It
was pleasure that never seemed to belong to the

other thing I wanted. So I just pushed it away in my mind, and didn't really think about it. I suppose I thought that all of my pleasures belonged to Mistress now, so I shouldn't do it anymore. Or at least that's what I kept telling myself when the time came for me to figure out how I really felt.

Because when she told me to ... do it ... in front of her, I just couldn't. I disobeyed my Mistress! I don't believe I did that! And she was so good to me, so patient and kind, and she loved me so ... but I couldn't let go of my fears and my silly embarrassment, and she was very unhappy with me.

At first, she thought I was just a little shy. So she would try to get me to do things a little at a time. I never objected when she touched me, of course, so she would take my hand in hers and guide it over my body. But something strange would happen inside my head and I would just freeze. I wouldn't ever fight her, or say no to her, but my body would do things or not do things without me even thinking about it. And I would go all cold on her, and then I'd cry, because I couldn't stop it, and then she would get angry, and then ...

And then she would hold me until I wasn't afraid any more and I would sleep in her arms and hope that she forgave me. And that was only one thing that I couldn't do for her. There were others, too, but they're more complicated. The simple fact is that when I thought I was submitting to her, I was really only doing the things I wanted to do.

No wonder she didn't want me any more.

I always knew about the Marketplace. I even met Alexandra and Grendel before. They would come, once in a while, to Mistress' parties. Mistress

Alexandra even came to tea! Mistress had a lot of friends who had slaves from the Marketplace. In fact, one of the reasons why she waited four months to invite me to stay with her and be her girl was because she had intended to get a girl from the Marketplace and not have to train her. I guess she must feel like she made the wrong decision, because when I couldn't be what she wanted, she sent me here.

She didn't tell me why I was coming here. She just told me that I was to obey Grendel and Alexandra and that they would tell me what was happening and why, and when I could go back. I cried and cried, because I thought that I was being punished for being such a bad girl. But now I know that Mistress didn't want to punish me. She wanted to give me a chance to change and become the kind of girl she really wants. Or give me the opportunity to be a good slave to some other person somewhere else.

Except that there's no happiness for me without my place at Mistress' feet. And I will fight as hard as anyone to get back there and make her proud of me. Because I love her—more than life itself. So I'm here to learn how to get back home.

Chapter Fifteen

The worst thing about being a slave, Brian reflected as he tossed more dirty straw into the wheelbarrow, is not the pain of the punishments, the degradation of the usage, or the sheer hard labor that they can demand of you. It's not being sexually deprived, or sexually used, and it's not even being tortured for the sheer pleasure of it. It's the enforced ignorance.

He leaned on the pitchfork, admiring the phrase. Yes, that's it, enforced ignorance. No one knows why things are happening, at all.

Take for example, Sharon. The body of a fashion model, the face of an angel, and the brains of a fruit fly. Do they fuck her brains out and make her prance around in lacy nothings? No, they make her memorize pages of rules and recite them, and then stick her in private tutoring sessions with a sissy

262

salesman. Learning grammar, for crying out loud!

And Claudia. She arrives already perfect. So what do they do? They give her things to do that she doesn't have the slightest knowledge about, like some kind of accounting or record keeping or something like that, and treat her like she was the world's biggest clumsy idiot. Cute as a button and eager to serve, and she spends a lot of time crying her little eyes out.

And then there's Robert. Bad slave material to begin with, right? But Chris practically dotes on him, giving him private advice, encouragement, and light duties so he has more time to study. And what is the salesman studying? Speeches and poems. Very strange.

Of course, Brian mused, scanning the stall for leftover bits, there's little old me. Prime slave material, good-looking, neat and fit, knows how to speak to a master, knows how to suck a golf ball through a garden hose, and can lick a mean boot. And what do we do with this lad? We put him out with the dumb horses, picking up their horse balls and cleaning up their messes and getting screwed by the one man on the estate who did seem to like to fuck.

Which wouldn't be too bad, if they hadn't made sure that no "accidents" happened like the one that had happened the first time he came out here. He looked glumly down the front of the loose coverall to the glint of steel between his legs. A little metal cage was closed around his soft cock, bending it and pressing it against his balls. The whole thing was attached to a belt that went around him like a jock strap. The contraption didn't have a lock, and it was dutifully taken off when he had to take a piss; the leather and steel was dutifully cleaned by him every night.

They hadn't given him this new adornment until the second time he came without permission, again while under Jack's tender care. He had thought he could control it. Hadn't he had two mornings of nice orgasms when Sharon asked him sweetly if he would like one and he said yes right away? And oh, how that bitch could work a dick! He had joyfully spurted out two wonderful, thrilling, and extraordinarily satisfying comes, one right against her beautiful tits, the other into her hair. (She wasn't speaking to him at all any more. It was a wonderful bonus.)

But when Jack mounted him from behind, like a stallion, Brian just lost control. It was terrible and wonderful all at once. And definitely not worth the two days of extra chores and extra beatings and early bedtimes. And then came the cock cage.

Which was another oddity. Ever since that first day, when a huge gag was strapped into his mouth for speaking out of turn, he hadn't seen a single piece of fetish gear. Everything from peach switches to real riding crops to sweat-scrapers, rulers, and whatever was at hand, had been used at one time or another on the slaves. But the only piece of leather had been Chris's well-worn strap. Until this piece. And then Claudia had whispered one night after lights out that Alexandra had used a leather blindfold on her during one of their increasingly intimate encounters, and how it felt like she was going home. The other slaves had all shivered in empathic agreement. Slowly, some toys were coming out. But from where? No one had seen, in their visits to the master bedrooms, any cases of equipment, any racks in closets or behind doors. They speculated about Grendel's workshop, a place he retreated to for a little while every day. Was that actually a dungeon?

Brian smoothed the straw out and went on to the next stall, brushing flies away as he walked, and pondering the mysteries of his life. Regardless of his distaste for her personally, he had to feel sorry for Sharon. The woman was sexually used like she was a box of Kleenex, take one and pass the box. Jack used her, Rachel had taken to dragging her off every once in a while, and even the visiting masseur, Jose or Julio or whatever, dipped into her when he was in. She had to go through the motions of asking her fellow slaves if they wanted to get some, and whenever no one said yes, Chris had taken to just assigning someone at random to receive her attentions. Eventually Brian just automatically said yes each time Sharon asked, and that was fine until Grendel decided that Brian should not be allowed even *that* pleasure, and now Sharon alternated between Robert and Claudia. And every time Sharon failed to please, not only was she punished in the regular way, with beatings and deprivations, but Chris would take something out of her bathing kit, like her hairbrush, or her shampoo, or even her soap. Brian wasn't quite sure if he understood how Sharon felt about having to appear looking messy or dirty, or even smelling of sex and sweat, but he figured it must be pretty awful. He knew he would hate it.

The only people who hadn't used her were Grendel and Alexandra. In fact, she still hadn't even been invited to see them after dinner. She was the only one. And she didn't like that one bit. When the week turned and she had a chance to ask her questions again, she demanded to know why she hadn't been chosen to serve the owners in their bedrooms.

"Because you're not good enough," was Chris's quick, dispassionate response.

"Well, what do I have to do to get good enough?" she had immediately asked.

"You'll have to ask Ms. Selador or Mr. Elliot about that, Sharon."

Brian didn't know what her answers had been when she did, but it was two days after the questions had been asked, and she still hadn't been called out of the evening lineup to freshen up and see either the mistress or the master.

And what was going on with Robert? Not only was Chris treating him so nicely, but his punishments were down to practically nothing! Instead, every time Robert messed up and lapsed into his little-girl behavior or whimpered when he should have moaned, or cried when there wasn't a reason, Chris grabbed whoever else was nearby and beat the hell out of them! And there was no avoiding this; everyone had to pass someone while they did their work. Many of these proxy punishments happened during one of their lineups, when everyone was there, ready to be chosen, seemingly at random. Brian had already caught two strappings for Robert's bad behavior. And no one could think of anything to do about it but learn to hate poor Robert, who was clueless over the whole thing.

We are all being messed with, he finally decided. There's a huge scam going, and Alexandra and Grendel are just playing these big games with our minds. He remembered a cartoon he had seen once.

A hand was spreading toothpaste on a figure of a smiling man. The caption read, "God brushes his teeth with our minds twice a day." Somehow, that applied here.

He heard the sound of people approaching and looked up in surprise. It was amazing how more than one set of shod feet had become such an alien sound. And the kind of casual chatting and laughter that accompanied the approach was also foreign. He shuddered. He was getting farther and farther away from the real world.

"So where are the horses? Are they still out?"

"Looks like it."

The first voice was unfamiliar, a man. The second was Alexandra's. Brian felt oddly panicked.

"Oh, but you do have something interesting in the stable," the man said with a laugh.

"It's just another of their new toys," said a woman's voice behind his.

Alexandra led the two strangers into the pathway between the stalls and looked casually over at Brian, who stood up straight and then bowed his shoulders respectfully. He was getting better and better at such moves; they all were.

"No, that's not a toy," Alexandra said. "That's Brian, one of our applicants. Would you like to see him?"

"Sure," the man said. He was tall and slender, and dressed in tight blue jeans and leather cowboy boots. His hair, a light chestnut color, spilled over his ears and a little down his back, and his eyes were hidden by mirrored sunglasses. Brian could easily imagine him at a country and western dance, doing a two-step, his thumbs loose in his belt, the boots flashing as they twisted and turned to the music.

"Brian, come out here and show yourself," Alexandra ordered, pointing. Brian leaned the pitchfork against the wall, and listened to the sound of his heart pounding against his eardrums. "Show yourself," Chris had said, "is one of the common commands in the Marketplace. It means, generally, to divest yourself of any clothing or covering, and then perform three moves...."

Brian dropped the coverall to his ankles (very easy to do, since it was as loose as a blanket), and stepped out of the stall, hoping that the cock-cage didn't count as "covering." He walked carefully into the middle of the aisle and lifted his arms and locked them behind his neck, pulling his body up straight and spreading his legs in a wide stance. He waited several seconds while a droplet of sweat rolled down from his forehead to the side of his nose, and blinked it away from his eyelid. Flies buzzed around him.

The man nodded. Next to him, a woman with piercing eyes and a pert, fashionable haircut sniffed. "You've had better," she said to Alexandra.

"Much better," Alexandra agreed. "Turn."

Brian executed the turn with a smooth movement that satisfied him, and resumed the same position. And when Alexandra said, "Over," he bent forward and braced his hands on his knees. Finally, after an interminably long silence, she said, "Down!" and he turned back to face them and dropped to his widespread knees, placing his hands behind his back, bowing his head, and keeping his back straight.

"He does the moves very well," the man commented. "What is he?"

"Common male slave. No specialty, which is good. Jack says he's slightly more than adequate in cocksucking, but he's not as dedicated in anything else. And he's got a very poor grasp on the concept of controlling his own body. Thus," Alexandra waved a hand at the belt, "the cage."

"Don't you ever get anyone who's good at women?" the other woman asked. Brian tried not to look up at her—did she look lesbian? Her clothing had been brightly colored and well suited to her body, he remembered the flowing burgundy of her skirt, and matching stones in the sparkling choker she wore. Was she standing close to the man in the cowboy boots? Were they together? And what was Alexandra doing, outlining all his faults to them? Weren't they buyers? More sweat dripped down his face, and trickled down his back.

"In this bunch, everyone else is more than adequate. I'll take you around to see them, if you want, and after lunch, you can take your pick. But you wanted to see the horses, right? They're probably out back."

"Alexandra, wait a minute. Why don't you take Nancy to find the others. I'll try this one out right here; he's ripe for it," the man hitched a thumb into his belt. "And we'll see the horses later. I'd just as soon wait for Gren and go for a ride together anyway."

"Your choice," Alexandra said lightly.

"OK, I'll see you in a little while, honey," the woman said. And she and Alexandra left the stable, heading for the house. Brian found that his posture and the amount of sweat on his body was beginning to make him tingle all over. When he heard the sound of a zipper coming down, he almost cried with relief.

Ten minutes later, his face and mouth battered to bruising, he cried tears of frustration and pain, bent over in a crouch by the side of a stall. The sounds that came from his assaulted throat were harsh and ugly, and when Jack found him, the stableman just nodded and walked away.

That was the start of yet another new phase in their training. After the house servants left for vacation at the end of the week, Alexandra and Grendel would have regular visits from various friends, of varied tastes and proclivities. These friends would be offered the use of any slave not being punished, and their opinions taken down for possible inclusion in the slaves' folders. "So we shouldn't be bored when the maids leave town," Brian said sarcastically one night.

It would hardly make a difference, in his opinion, except that Rachel would be one less demand on his time. The woman was absolutely insatiable, he often thought. But since she had started playing with Claudia, she had apparently taken a special liking to her and came after him less and less. Good riddance. Shaw, although he was quick to anger and would take a swat at you with his huge open hand if you didn't move fast enough or dig deep enough or pull up enough weeds, didn't use any of them sexually. Rachel had a part-time woman who took the dry-cleaning and handled special errands and did some heavy cleaning when there wasn't a handy slave to do it; she ignored the slaves. There was also a mysterious handyman who came in a few times a week to make small repairs and maintain the various machinery on the property, but so far only Sharon had seen him, and he only used her once. An alternate driver, who got a blowjob from Brian while waiting for Alexandra's guests to leave one afternoon, was also rarely seen. So what was the big deal? It certainly wouldn't take a lot of people to replace the steady use they got from the servants who were taking vacations. And very early on, it seemed clear that the visitors had very strong preferences for what kind of a slave they wanted to try out. They almost all wanted a piece of Sharon.

On that first day, Sharon found herself serving the desires of the woman named Nancy not once, but four times, before the day was over. The first was just as Nancy's lover, Lawrence, was busy abusing Brian in the stable. Nancy took one look at Sharon's body and immediately pointed at her and nodded. Alexandra commanded Sharon through the same set of moves as Brian, and Sharon performed them perfectly, ending up on her knees, her face buried under Nancy's flowing skirt until Nancy sighed and purred with pleasure.

Sharon found herself in similar positions at lunchtime, and after the four people took an afternoon ride, and again after Alexandra and Nancy had enjoyed a dip in the big jacuzzi.

By the end of the day, Sharon looked like she had been the biggest grosser at the county fair kissing booth. And she felt like she had run her mouth over about thirty acres of carpeting. She had never met a woman with sexual appetites that matched her own.

She fell asleep soundly and instantly that night and woke up with her hand in her crotch. It took all of her will power not to continue what the dream had started.

I can't believe this, Sharon thought, getting up one more time to stretch. How can people remember all this shit? I mean, English is English, and no one's ever had any problem understanding me!

"It's just not proper to use the word 'totally' to indicate that something is exaggerated," Robert explained. "Totally great means the same thing as great."

"No it doesn't," Sharon shot back, exasperated. "*Totally great* is better than just great. Like these lessons are *totally* stupid, OK?"

"And don't end your sentences or declarations with OK?, OK?" Robert moaned and rubbed his temple. "Oh god, now I'm doing it."

"Jeeze, I don't know what the fuss it about," Sharon said. "It's only words. No one is going to care how I talk."

"How you *speak*. And they will care if they want a pleasure slave they can take to Europe," Robert replied. "Don't you want to be able to go to Paris, or Geneva? Europeans hate Americans with accents and speech patterns like yours. They think that people who speak like that are rubes."

"Huh?" Oh shit, here comes another lecture. Sharon twirled a finger through her hair as Robert the Sissy explained what a stupid rube was. Like, who cared? She felt the softness of her hair with satisfaction. Since she had shown those two guys such a good time yesterday, Chris had actually sent her a little bottle of some very nice conditioning rinse.

I'm not doing too bad, she thought, nodding her head so that Robert would keep talking. I thought I was in deep shit because the head honchos weren't fucking me, but they're letting all their friends at me. And I know what they're saying, too. That I'm the hottest babe they've ever had. Sooner or later, one of them, Alexandra or Grendel—and I don't care which—is going to have to give in and take a roll with me, and that will end all this bullshit once and for all.

"So you want to change the way you speak, so it will improve your value," Robert finished. "You also want to do it because you've been ordered to, and we'll both be punished if you don't!"

"No, we won't," Sharon snapped, her eyes narrowing. "*I'll* be punished. *You'll* get some more sweet talk from your pal Chris. C'mon, sissy, what's the deal there? You giving him blowjobs on the side or something?"

Robert blushed. He was trying his best to control that reaction, but Sharon seemed to be very capable of bringing it out in him.

"I mean," she continued, "you can't keep it up even when *I* suck you off, so you must be queer. Worse than pretty-boy Brian, even. He could give me a good workout, if they ever let him. But you? Like, you're all steak and no sizzle!"

He winced. "Actually," he said, his voice beginning to waver, "the phrase is 'all sizzle and no—'"

"I don't give a fuck!" Sharon reached over and pushed all of Robert's books and folders and papers to the floor. "I don't care what anything means! I don't care how you say anything! This is all stupid! *Totally* fucking stupid!"

"Sharon!" Robert hurriedly put a finger to his lips, and then dived for the floor to pick up the books. "Shh!" He gathered up one binder and moaned when he saw that it had opened, and papers were strewn all over the floor. "Don't shout, you'll—"

"Well, I don't care," Sharon said, although she looked toward the closed library door, and did lower her voice, shifting her tone from angry to petulant. She watched Robert pick up the things she had dumped to the floor, but didn't help him.

Stupid asshole, she thought. It's his own damn fault. Who does he think he is, trying to pretend he's my teacher or something? Everyone's got some reason to think they're better than me. Even Good-Girl Claudia. Ever since she and that hyper-bitch Rachel have been running off together, she thinks she's Miss High and Mighty! Just look at her, walking around with a clipboard, taking notes, and even talking about how to make up our schedules! I mean, the servants are only going away on vacation; it's not like she's going to have a real job or anything. And besides, Rachel's not that hot, and she's only a freaking maid. With biker tattoos! So I don't know why little Claudia thinks she's on the way to a better life around here.

And I can't stand the way she flaunts it when Alexandra takes her after dinner. I mean, it's not like she was spending the night or anything! And besides, Alexandra and Claudia's mistress are old buddies. Alexandra is probably just being nice.

Throwing herself back down on the couch,

Sharon examined her nails and sighed. Chris had hinted that manicures might start after she had reached the final stage of training, whatever that was. No one told them anything around here, even with the magic three questions and shit. Huh. That was cute. They give you three questions, but they don't guarantee a good answer. And if you ask the question wrong, bang, you're outta there! What a racket.

She glanced at Robert, busily putting his papers back in order. I don't get you, sissy, she thought. You've got a dick that could choke a horse or something, but you can't keep it going. You're pretty educated and everything, but you open your mouth and stupid stuff comes out. And now, its like you're just dipped in gold around here—*we* get your punishments. Hey, maybe I'll ask about that next week. How would I say it? How come we get punished whenever Robert screws up? That's clear, isn't it?

"D-do you want to continue?" Robert asked, smoothing out a crinkle on a page. "We were discussing how to keep yourself from using unnecessary words."

"I'm tired," Sharon said with a yawn to demonstrate. "Let's quit for the night, OK?"

"We can't." Robert looked up at the clock. "We have another hour to go."

Sharon scowled. "I hate this shit!"

Robert sighed and agreed with all his heart.

Robert was genuinely confused at the change in the way he was treated. Chris had reverted to the cold but kindly man that Robert had met the first day he was here, and almost no one beat him any more. Instead, they made him watch while they beat everyone else, which in a way was much worse. And the harder he cried for them, or the louder he wailed, the more they were beaten.

Oh, he got his share of beatings at the evening lineup, for small infractions and such, but his body didn't bear the constant bands of pink and the series of light bruisings that everyone else lived with every day. And the more he got out, to drive the cars or to mow the lawn with the small tractor, or even to carry the grocery boxes in from the delivery van, the more he was aware of the amount of time he spent clothed. If you didn't count the coveralls that Jack gave his stable workers, no one else ever got any clothing. Of course, Robert was very careful to strip as soon as possible after finishing whatever needed to be done while covered.

What are they doing with me? he often wondered. When Alexandra or Grendel brought their friends around to look at the four slaves, they spent less time with him than any of the others. And the guests almost never chose him to play with or use. Only once had someone decided to try him out; he had gotten a very light spanking from a woman who seemed to be doing it for the first time. Compared to Sharon, he was a virgin. Clearly, no one wanted him, which was just as well. Because his sessions with Mistress Alexandra weren't exactly going the way she wanted them to.

Oh, I'm getting very good at massage, he reminded himself. A wiry man with iron-gray hair and a densely muscled body had started to come by every other day to teach him how to do a professional massage. He had learned quite a bit, actually, about anatomy and different styles of massage like shiatsu and reflexology. He was even studying acupuncture. And according to Alexandra, who fairly purred and sang when he practiced on her, he was adding something priceless to his folder, a skill that many people wanted in a house slave.

Unfortunately, that's about the only thing I do well, he thought. Every time she touches me, I get all hard and then I go limp again, and she doesn't like that, not one bit. She wants me to be able to get hard and stay hard, but I don't know how to manage that! And every time she mentions Grendel, I just get scared, and I can't perform well. And that's not fair, because he might be a very nice man. But I'm scared—of him and of other men. I just can't help it.

Poor Brian. Other men use him all the time now, and he's got his nast—I mean, his *cock*—in that little steel cage. It's almost as bad as the one I used to have to wear. And he goes to see Grendel and always comes back early. Well, at least I'm not the only one who's scared of Grendel. So is Claudia, although she doesn't say why. I think it's because she's gay, and maybe she doesn't like men at all.

I'm worried about what's going to happen when the servants go away. It's clear that Claudia will replace Rachel (who, thank god, has never shown the slightest interest in me!), and I think that I'll be driving and doing some of the kitchen work. But that leaves a lot of cleaning and washing and folding and, oh, all sorts of stuff. It's going to be hard to do all those things and our other chores and try to be good slaves at the same time.

And I start my recitals tomorrow, he remembered. He felt a familiar sensation in the pit of his stomach. I know I'm going to mess up, he thought miserably. How am I supposed to deliver it? In front of whom? Will the other slaves be there? They'll all laugh, and I won't be able to keep my cool, and I'll cry, and then something terrible will happen.

"Maybe you're right," he said out loud, shaking Sharon from her own thoughts. "Why don't you go to bed? I have some studying to do anyway."

Claudia sponged some more of the floral-scented bubbles over Alex's back, and then rinsed them away. Her movements were becoming more assured every day, and not a drop of water spilled over the side of the high tub. Alex hit the drain and stood, allowing Claudia to rinse Alex's body off with the flexible shower head. Claudia put it back in the ring with ease and hurried to fetch a large, fluffy, warmed towel, which she wrapped around Alex's body.

Serving in the bath was a little like serving tea, she thought, suppressing a smile. You have to be well balanced, know what ingredients have to be offered first, know how to pour, and pick things up and put them down again. But afterward, you have a pretty, naked woman instead of a table of dirty dishes and cups. She widened her eyes at her disrespectful thought, and tried to concentrate on drying Alex's body. But a little smile played across her lips all the same.

"Would you like me to send for something to drink, ma'am?" she asked, turning to put the bottles of oils and gels away.

"No, Claudia. Just turn down the bed and lower the lights, will you?"

"Yes, ma'am."

That was swiftly done, the lamps adjusted so that Alex could put them out with a simple touch. Claudia drew the curtains and plumped up the pillows before Alex came into the room.

"Good," the mistress of the house murmured. "You're coming along very well, Claudia. Come here and let me look at you."

Claudia approached and stood for Alex to examine her, turning her body at the lightest touch, bending when pushed, raising her arms when they were tapped. Her responses were excellent.

Alex tapped Claudia's lips with her fingers, and Claudia took two of them into her mouth, encircling them softly and wetting them. She sighed as Alex trailed them down her throat and then returned to get them remoistened. Several motions like that ran a trail of moisture from Claudia's throat across her nipples, which immediately sprang erect, and down to her belly. She sighed.

Alex walked over to her bed and leaned back against the pillows. "Come here and please me," she said simply. Claudia turned and eagerly joined the mistress, poising herself comfortably above her. "Start up here," Alex said as she stroked her own throat, and Claudia leaned forward to kiss it.

She pressed her lips gently to the places that Alex liked, and then slowly warmed to the task, giving little nibbles and flicks of her tongue. Alex encouraged her, guiding her head and then bringing one of Claudia's hands up to start stroking the sides of her breast. Claudia whimpered a little at the move, but changed her position and did as she was directed. She waved her fingers lightly over Alex's body, not quite teasing and never rough, and passed her kisses down one shoulder. Alex brought one of her hands up and cupped Claudia's left breast, compressing her nipple and making her moan.

"You want this, don't you?" she prompted.

"Oh, yes, yes, ma'am," Claudia said breathlessly.

"And you love it. Say it."

"I love it, ma'am! I love every touch, I love pleasing you!"

Alex smiled and brought Claudia's head up. "Good girl. Turn around and show me how wet you are. Tell me about it—that's it—put your head down against the bed. Spread your legs apart. Wider. That's it. I can see how much you need this, Claudia, did you know that?" Claudia moaned in humiliation, but maintained her position. She folded her arms to act as a cradle for her head, and straddled Alex's legs, facing away. At the center of the inverted V of her spread thighs, her hairless pussy was open, the sides lustrous with her moisture.

"Tell me," Alex said again. The mistress sat up a little more for a better view, and casually touched herself as Claudia began to speak.

"I ... I am wet, ma'am," Claudia began. It was so hard to talk about these things, especially when she was like this! But the potential rewards outweighed any embarrassment, so she plunged onward. "I was when I first came to see you tonight. I always am when I'm with you! And ... and I want your touch, ma'am, oh, I need it! Please, please, let me serve you, let me make you happy...."

"Get off the bed," Alex said gently, "and crawl across the room. Behind the door in the next room are two things I would like you to bring back here. You may not carry them in your hands, so think carefully before coming back. Go."

Claudia unfolded herself and climbed off the bed. How surprising! She had been positive that Alexandra would keep her there longer, making her say these things until she ran out of words. She scampered across the floor in an adorable crawl, and found her way into the next room.

Behind the door, sitting on a square of black silk, was a leather gag and a small brown leather paddle. She stopped and stared at them. How long had it been since she had seen toys like these? A new rush of warmth spread through her, and she touched them with one careful finger. Now—how to carry them? She could probably put the strap of the gag in her mouth, and then one side of the paddle, but that would keep her mouth open wide, and it would look very unaesthetic. But there seemed no other way, so she positioned them both carefully and started the long crawl back. Of course, Alexandra was lying on the edge of the bed, watching her every step of the trip. She tried to concentrate on not dropping the items or biting them hard enough to put marks in them.

Alexandra was silent as she took them from Claudia's mouth, examined them, and then carefully buckled the gag on. It had a soft rubber mouthpiece, and it wrapped firmly around the girl's lips. It emphasized the pleading quality in her eyes, and despite the fact that Alex didn't much like gags, she had to admit that Claudia looked particularly helpless and cute in this one. Sitting back in a comfortable position, she patted her lap, and watched as Claudia climbed up, trying not to show her eagerness.

The paddle was made of good, thick leather, and the sounds it made were not as startling as the sounds that Chris's strap produced. But Alex wasn't interested in punishment. She took time to rub the leather against Claudia's body, patting her thighs and her back with it, and then lightly swatting at her sex. Each change in tactic evoked new, muffled sounds of pleasure from the girl, who was squirming delightfully in no time. She even did that well, managing to move sensuously without losing her balance or giving the impression that she was trying to get away.

Alex picked up the tempo slowly, building up a warm, glowing sensation on Claudia's rounded cheeks and taking a lot of time to continue her relentless tantalizing, stroking and patting and occasionally running her fingernails along sensitive places on Claudia's body. Claudia's cries became more frantic as Alex circled closer and closer to her sex.

"You want to come for me tonight," Alex said. It wasn't a question, because there didn't need to be an answer. "And you will, if ..."

Claudia raised her head, her nostrils flaring around the gag.

"If ... you're a very good girl and promise to scream as loud as you can when you do. That's why the gag is there, Claudia. I want you to be able to scream into it loud enough to shake the windows. I want you to thrash around and arch and bend and let everything go until the last vestiges of pleasure are simply screamed out and there's nothing left but exhaustion."

Claudia trembled.

"If you can't promise me that, then we'll just keep going like this for a while, and then you'll go to bed. If you promise, nod your head."

Claudia's head pounded with the weight of the decision. I want to come, she whimpered to herself. Oh, I want it so bad! But I couldn't ... I never ... She shook all over as Alexandra trailed her long cool fingers down her back, and to her delighted dismay, she raised her head higher and nodded. Oh, what's happened to me? she thought, moaning into the gag again. I'm becoming nothing but a slut!

"That's a good girl," Alexandra crooned, as though to counter Claudia's thoughts. "Then let's get on with it, shall we?"

And the seduction/torment continued, with spanks that awakened fire in Claudia's loins and strokes that made her twist, until Alexandra took hold of Claudia's right hand and guided it under her body. "You did realize," Alexandra whispered, "that you would bring yourself off, didn't you?"

And Claudia screamed! Behind the soft leather of the gag, her mouth opened around the rubber mouthpiece, and she screeched out the first of a series of yelps of pleasure. Her fingers had automatically slipped into the most perfect spot, and Alexandra's soft voice and firm hold were all that were needed to spark the explosion. Each wave of pleasure wrenched out another yelp, and when Alexandra's voice came to her again, urging her to do it "Again!" and then "Again!" Claudia could only obey, her body thrusting against her hand and Alexandra's lap, her head shaking up and down with a frenetic fury, and even her pretty little feet rising up to kick at the empty air.

By the time Alexandra let her slump to the floor, she was a sodden, wasted wreck of a lovely young women, still shaking from the aftereffects of her orgasms, covered in sweat, tears, and the abundant moisture from between her thighs. Alex bent down and took off the gag, and Claudia made a sobbing sound as it was drawn from her mouth. Her jaw hurt, her throat was sore, her ass felt like it glowed; she was positively raw, and she was absolutely happy. She rolled over onto her belly to cover Alex's feet with grateful, wet kisses.

And for the first time, one of the slaves did not return to the dorm to sleep.

Chapter Sixteen

"... And finally, Claudia, Sharon, and Brian will meet with me after dinner and we will proceed to the main dining room to hear Robert's first presentation. Is everyone clear on their assignments today?"

Three nods, accompanied by "Yes, Chris," in perfect unison, and one choking sound answered him. He locked his gaze onto Robert, who somehow found a way to fumble the simple act of holding a fork.

"I hope your voice is in better form tonight," Chris said with a slight smile. "You are all dismissed."

The first day without Rachel to control her portion of the household, and without the temporary help that walked in and out of the house like industrious shadows, was a day of barely missed disasters. Claudia, constantly referring to her pages of handwritten notes on what had to be done and in what order, got lost and frightened and panicked. In mid-afternoon, Chris took her aside, organized her notes for her and, curiously, did not beat the living daylights out of her. Claudia was too relieved to wonder why. After the wondrous night she had spent with Alexandra, the hustle of the new day was almost unbearable.

Brian began to think that he was living the life of a schizophrenic. He started out working in the stable in the morning, where Jack was his usual unintelligible horny self, and then after lunch found himself being decked out in peach-colored lace bows, including one that he had to thread through the wire cage around his cock. Thus attired, he vacuumed and carried things under Claudia's cautious and apologetic direction. Since she was unsure of how to actually tell him what to do and he was unaware of what had to be done next, they often found themselves hiding from one another, avoiding the inevitable time when they would have to make believe they knew what was going on.

Sharon endured yet another lesson with a very distracted Robert, and then found herself scrubbing the kitchen floor, dusting the rooms on the first floor, and then putting stamps on a pile of letters that Grendel had in his office. In the afternoon, dying of boredom, she found herself having to spend a good chunk of time going down on Claudia while Alexandra watched. Since this event took place in the middle of the second floor landing, right by the rail overlooking the main hallway, it was a little different than usual. And Claudia, a girl Sharon had decided was just plain frigid, seemed more than willing to let it all hang out today, which did make it more fun than usual. But after that, it was back to work, this time slicing potatoes for a dinner salad. It was all Sharon could do to keep from screaming.

As for Robert, the entire day passed in a blur of varied intensity, until he found himself unable to eat anything at dinner and shaking like a leaf when Chris came in to dismiss them. The major-domo took the other three away, and told Robert to go directly to the main dining room and wait. Robert sat in the large room, his knees together, running his memorized poem through his head over and over again. Oh, why did he have to do it in front of them? And why did Alexandra choose this poem for him to do first?

I can't cry, he thought, closing his eyes. They'll all be there, and I just couldn't stand it if any of them took a beating for me again. What if they decided to beat Claudia? I'd just die. I have to stay calm. I have to be manly. I have to be ... dignified. Maybe I can just pretend that I'm talking to all those men in suits. I used to be able to sell them electric *apple slicers*, for godssake, I can just say this stupid poem and get it over with—can't I?

Chris came in and snapped his fingers, and Robert shot up. Together they set up the dining room chairs, three front and center, two off to the side. And then Chris gave Robert a little lopsided smile and left again. When he returned, Alexandra and Grendel walked in with him, and took the two seats over to the side. Alexandra said, "Turn around, Robert. Since we don't have a curtain, you'll have to turn to face the audience when we're all assembled."

He did as she said, and heard the sounds of his companions entering the room and taking their three seats. It seemed kind of odd to him—why weren't the slaves on the floor? And why wasn't there a seat for Chris? And how—

Chris's voice cut through Robert's wonderings. "Applicants, tonight Robert will entertain us with a dramatic reading of a classic poem. Robert, you may now turn around and begin."

Robert took a deep breath. Stay calm! Stay calm! Carefully, trying to be as fluid and elegant as Alexandra said he could be, he turned around and opened his eyes. And after a moment of sheer confusion, tried his damnedest to keep from bursting out into laughter.

Because arrayed before him in three chairs, were his three companions, their faces touched with light blushes and, at least in Brian's case, barely disguised mirth.

Brian was sitting in his chair dressed in a white lace apron, with a lace cap on his head and little strings of pearls dangling between his nipple rings. Heavy ropes of more pearls hung around his neck, and Victorian-style earrings danced and dangled from his ears. Helping out and exaggerating the natural color on his cheeks were bright circles of paint that could only have accompanied a clown costume.

Claudia was wearing a pair of loud, plaid boxer shorts much too big for her, and men's socks with old-fashioned garters. A pair of suspenders held the shorts up, with a smiley-face button attached to the right suspender and a McGovern campaign button on the left. Her hair was in pigtails.

And Sharon—well, Sharon was dressed in something that looked like it came out of the latest rock video or an old science fiction pulp magazine cover. Her breasts were covered with demonically pointed golden cones attached with strands of chain, and a skintight pair of Lycra leggings in a tasteful gold lamé covering her from ankles to hips. Her feet were encased in fluffy, pink bunny slippers, and a pair of gold antennae bounced above her ears.

Robert stared in shock. He could see that Brian was struggling not to laugh, and the young man was losing the battle. Finally, Brian folded his arms over his chest, hiding the pearls, and looked down at the floor. Claudia was in a kind of shock herself. She seemed not to know what to make of the entire affair, except that it was silly and maybe a little bit embarrassing and she tried not to look at Robert for fear of distracting him, knowing full well that he couldn't help being distracted.

And Sharon? Well, she simply blazed with her uncomprehending anger. The look on her face was hostile, and Robert couldn't tell if she was angry at him, or Chris, or Alexandra, or what! But somehow, the tit-cones and the bunny slippers made her seem terribly ridiculous, and Robert had to struggle to control the twitching at the side of his mouth. He glanced over at Alexandra, and felt a droplet of sweat run down the back of his neck. Alexandra, seemingly unaffected by the oddly dressed slaves, waved her hand for him to start. Grendel was hiding his amused mouth behind one hand. Chris was standing behind the two of them, his hands behind his back and an entirely uninterested look on his face.

Robert swallowed, cleared his throat, and tried to focus his eyes on the air above everyone's head. He must not stammer. He must not speak in a high-pitched tone of voice. He must sound impressive and clear.

Sharon's antennae bounced into his peripheral vision.

Laughter spurted up within him, growing in his belly and chest, and he fought it back down. Carefully, trying to keep his voice steady, he put his hands behind his back and began, "'Twas brillig, and the slithy toves, did gyre and gimble in the wabe ...,'" and collapsed into peals of laughter. It was infectious. Brian burst out into loud guffaws, actually slapping his knee, and Claudia snickered and giggled until tears formed in her eyes. Their laughter rose in intensity every time they looked at each other. Sharon looked confused for a moment and looked around, unable to figure out what to do. Finally, she allowed a snicker to escape, and reinforced it by staring at the bouncing pearls on Brian's chest. In no time, the four slaves were laughing so hard that tears trickled down their cheeks and they had to gasp for breath.

Alexandra hid a smile but maintained her composure. It was her show, after all. But Grendel threw back his head and grinned at Chris, the only one in the room still struggling to keep a neutral look on his face.

"That's quite enough!" the major-domo said sternly. "Pull yourselves together!" Claudia managed to obey first, by staring at the floor and physically holding her mouth closed. Brian and Sharon took an extra minute, their shoulders shaking almost uncontrollably. And Robert, wiping the tears out of his own eyes, cleared his throat again and looked over to Alex, who nodded for him to begin again.

Words that, only moments before, had threatened to come out in chunks of strangled sound flowed from Robert's lips like the well-known phrases of a liturgy. The barely constrained hilarity of the moment was a perfect tonic, and even as the lines of the nonsense poem rolled out in a smooth—although not very dramatic—cadence, Robert found himself amazed at the ease of his delivery. Having the three sitting directly in front of him in their funny costumes was only one part of what made it easy. The other part was the subtle encouragement he felt from them. Hints of giggles and snickers rose during some of the stranger linguistic jumbles, but everyone managed to maintain some form of composure until the end.

He finished with a slightly halting final line, afraid to add any flourishes. He looked at Alexandra for a moment, and then cast his eyes down quickly.

"You need some dramatic coaching, but that was very good for a first-time effort, Robert," she said as she rose. "Follow me." She turned to leave after giving Grendel a covert wink, and walked toward the door. Robert looked up after her, gazed around in one moment of insecurity, and then dashed past his fellow slaves to catch up.

"All right, get up, strip down, and put these chairs back," Chris barked at the three. "You've served your purpose; let's get back into proper roles here!"

Grendel got up and patted Chris lightly on one shoulder. "Carry on," he said lightly.

"Would you like any of the others sent to you tonight, sir?"

The tall man looked over at the three, still divesting themselves of the bits of old Halloween costumes that Chris had dug out of storage. "No," he said, driving a spike of shame through each of them. "I don't think so."

"You did very well," Alexandra said as she led Robert away from the dining room. "I'm pleased."

"Oh, thank—" Robert stopped himself and coughed. Out of habit, his voice had been an octave higher. "I mean, thank you, ma'am."

"I also like the fact that you're giving more thought to how you sound and act. So I'm going to reward you." Grace led him past the staircase, and he looked back at it in confusion. They were headed toward her "studio," one of the rooms the slaves had been forbidden to enter. His heart began to pound.

"Oh. Oh my," he murmured.

"Don't ruin things, Robert." Alex stopped at the door and looked back at him. "My rules for your new behavior don't end at this doorway."

"No, ma'am!"

"Then let's get on with it." She pushed the door open and flicked a light switch. And Robert, whose sole experience with the term "dungeon" meant cheap, heavy black leather with silver studs adorning heavy, pseudo-medieval furniture all lit by black lights and candles, blinked in amazement and wonder at what he could see from the doorway.

Just as Alex's taste in bedrooms was light, airy, and elegant, so was her flavor of playroom. Although the lighting was not bright enough to read fine print by, the L-shaped room was washed in muted colored lights that illuminated the decor rather than cast it in shadows. The furnishings were varied and well spaced out, including a large square frame that looked like it was made of a well-varnished and-polished mahogany, fitted with rigging gear of a contrasting metallic hue, and several well-padded pieces of equipment that looked intriguingly designed to be delightfully adjustable and support a human body in a number of positions. Everything seemed to be custom-made to Alex's tastes, including plenty of soft fabrics and a scattered array of thick rugs and large pillows that could serve as platforms or bolsters for all sorts of activities, or provide a comfortable seating area for voyeurs.

"It-it's wonderful, ma'am," Robert gasped, stepping into the room to follow her. His bare feet sank into the carpeting.

"Yes," she agreed. "That's why you're generally not allowed here." Without any further explanation, she walked around the perimeter of the room, considering her options. Robert felt that he was to stop following her and stood by the door. When she gestured, he closed it behind him.

"Go into the other part of the studio," Alex said finally. "Bring me back two things you'd like me to use on you." She pointed and he ran.

The other side of the room, out of direct sight of the door, held her collection of toys. Robert gasped again, struck with absolute amazement at the wonder that was arrayed before him. Neatly put away in glossy cubicles or hanging from brass-colored racks were cuffs in heavy canvas and soft leather, bondage arrays designed for women and men and either gender, blindfolds with fat layers of sheepskin or soft linings of silk, a whole row of paddles, straps, and canes, a line of whips ranging from the smallest, most viciously cutting, knotted and twisted rubber to huge, luxuriously thick, electric blue deerskin, as soft as velvet. Coils of rope lay in nautical precision on one shelf next to a rack of metal devices that would make the most dedicated torturer cry with envy. Cockrings, with snaps, studs, or little tormenting teeth on the inside; long, narrow silver clamps attached by chains; assorted cock-and-ball harnesses; labia stretchers; tit clamps. A small chest full of plain wooden clothespins; dispensers, jars, and tubes of lotions, creams, and lubricants, and a very eclectic assortment of dildos, buttplugs, cock-shaped vibrators, and other objects for delving into one orifice or another. There were also harnesses to keep such devices in, or to harness one to a woman's loins.

Robert felt a wave of dizziness pass through him. He had never seen such an assortment of SM gear before, not ever. Not even at the shops he went to when he bought tribute for Mistress. Sure, they had a lot of inventory, but it was never so varied, never so colorful, so inviting, and so, so sexy! And the way everything was stored or displayed was so friendly! He wanted to touch the tresses of the whips and feel their weight upon his hands. He wanted to open the clamps and see how they worked, and play with the pile of soft things, the fur and the feathers, and he wanted to smell the rich leather on the straps that looked so soft and well worn! Robert trembled. It was intoxicating. It was bewildering.

And Alexandra was waiting! Quickly, he shifted his gaze back and forth, chewing on his lower lip. What did she say? Two things? Was a pair of cuffs one thing or two? He reached out for something soft and furry-looking and then jerked his hand back as if it were burned. What kind of things? Surely not these sensuous-looking lover toys?

He stuck his hand out and encountered a thick paddle, and took it, and then looked over at the whips. His trained instinct told him to get one that was knotted and rough-looking, but the colors confused him and were far too compelling. He choose a red one, with a thick bundle of heavy tresses, and scurried back into the other side of the studio. Trying not to rise up on his toes when he walked, he padded over to Alexandra, who was sitting patiently on top of a spanking bench, and knelt in front of her. It was a move suggested in one of the behavior manuals, and he copied it exactly, holding the whip and paddle above him as he lowered his head.

Alex took the paddle first and turned it over in her hands. It had two different textures on it, a gleaming rubber side and a softer, leather-covered side. Then she took the whip, and ran her fingers through the soft tresses.

"You have good taste," she said, stroking the whip. "This is one of my favorites. We'll save it for last. Right now, I want you bent over this bench." She hopped down and patted it.

When Robert positioned himself, he realized that the curved cushioning of the top of the bench provided a very secure place to rest his body. He closed his eyes and sighed. After so many days of standing while braced against tables and doors, or crouching on all fours, or being bent over fences, rails and the side of a car, the sensation of being on a piece of equipment actually designed for this purpose was absolutely decadent.

Alex used the leather side of the paddle, and started lightly on Robert's mostly unbruised ass. He tensed and relaxed under her as she smacked him, using mostly the same pattern she had used so successfully on Claudia. But when he started to squirm, she stopped, allowed him to rest, and then started up again, each time picking up force and tempo. Soon, he started to whimper.

"Don't you like this?" she asked, pausing.

"Oh! Yes, ma'am!"

"Then why do you sound like I'm hurting you?"

Robert's eyes snapped open. What an odd question! He tried to gather his thoughts and failed, and tried again. Alexandra stopped beating him, which made it easier to think.

"D-don't you want me to react this way, ma'am?" he finally asked.

"Not particularly," Alex replied. "This is supposed to be a reward. Perhaps instead of sounding like you're enduring this for me, you should try to offer me some forms of gratitude."

"Ma'am?" Robert's voice did scale up a bit, and he coughed before he could continue. "How shall I thank you, ma'am?"

"By saying so!" Alex drew her arm back and

delivered one sharp smack under his asscheeks, driving him upward an inch or two, and he yelped.

"Oh! Ah! Thank you, ma'am!" he cried out, as she began to paddle him with vigor. "Yes! Thank you!"

"Now we're getting somewhere," Alex said with satisfaction. She covered his ass with a band of solid pink, concentrating on the curves below the middle of his ass, and bringing her strokes in underhand to provide that "lift" as they hit. In no time at all, Robert had fallen into a litany of gratitude, and was putting his ass out for more.

"Good boy," Alex declared, putting the paddle down. She ran her fingers over the spanked area with satisfaction, making Robert hiss with intense pleasure. "Are you ready for the whip?"

"Yes, ma'am!"

He took his lashes kneeling on a low platform, so that his back was at exactly the level Alex needed. She positioned him with his fingers laced behind his neck, and started his beating with dozens of light blows delivered slowly so that the soft tresses could drape over his back and caress his muscles, trailing down to his waist. He shivered in appreciation, and after one or two false starts, began to thank her again.

"You're so kind to me," he moaned, arching his shoulders out to meet the whip. "Thank you, thank you, ma'am!"

Alex smiled to herself and began giving the heavy whip a bit more speed on each round of blows. The ends of the tresses landed with precision on his shoulders and on the big muscles of his back. They began to make noise, a nice, muted thump, and as she moved to allow more or less of the whip to hit him, they sounded louder and louder.

Across his shoulders, down each side of his back, it was a leather rain that fell with a steady, heartbeat rhythm, which Robert matched with moans of pleasure. His fat cock, already tumescent from the paddling, rose stiffly between his legs and he trembled with near ecstasy. When Alexandra moved around to face him and used the whip on his chest, he closed his eyes, but his lips parted in a series of inarticulate cries, mixed in with sincere, simple thanks.

Alex stopped when his chest was about the same color as his ass, and she looked critically at him. The body is very nice, she mused, just the way it is. I'm not going to bulk him up, there are plenty of bodybuilders out there. And he can take a nice thumping indeed, when he realizes that he's supposed to react naturally. We know he can overreact, but it's good to note that he can be sensual, too. Will he ever be able to take it stoically?

Never mind, now's not the time to test it. Reward desired behavior sparingly but with encouragement, that was the pattern. She dropped the whip down in front of him, and he opened his eyes with a start.

"Put the toys away and bring me a leather cock-ring that will fit you," Alex told him. When he did, his hand shaking as he presented it to her, she approved of it and told him to put it on. When he finished wrapping it around the base of his balls, he fastened it tight enough to make his cock seem even heavier and thicker, and adjusted the snaps so that they were out of sight.

Oh yeah, Alex thought, admiring the package.

We are including one photo of that in his folder. She touched it, stroking the side of his cock, and he trembled. "This looks very nice," she mused. "Have you been behaving? Have you come at all since you've been here?"

"No, ma'am," he choked out.

"Would you like to?"

"Ah! Oh, no—I mean … if it would please you, ma'am!"

Alexandra cupped the shaft, holding it from the bottom as if she were weighing it. "It might," she said. "I definitely have plans for it. But perhaps you've had enough stress for one evening."

She let it drop, and Robert fought the urge to draw his knees together and squirm until the burning need went away. But he maintained his posture in front of her, and watched her movements for clues about what he should do next.

"Would you like to sleep at the foot of my bed tonight?" she asked suddenly.

"Oh, yes, please ma'am!" His voice broke, and he blushed, and tried to control himself. "It—it would be an honor!"

"Yes, it would," she admitted. But the look in her eyes had suddenly lost its approval. "But it's an honor we'll have save for the next time I feel like rewarding you. Watch your voice, Robert, it's your greatest fault. You may return to your studies or go to bed; I'll see you in two days. Keep the ring on until you go to bed and put it back on after you shower in the morning."

She called to him as he walked quietly toward the door. "Oh, Robert? I suggest—not command, but *suggest*—that you strongly consider taking advantage of what Sharon offers you every day."

He choked, and then said, "Yes, ma'am" and got out of the room with a spinning head and a throbbing hard-on.

Chris reviewed Claudia's first day on the job and ran his finger down a checklist. At least half the items he had listed did not have checks next to them. Claudia and Brian, both comfortably naked again, were kneeling by his desk. They had never been in Chris's office before, and they struggled not to twist and turn their heads to look around and get a better feel for the somber major-domo. What they did know was that he had computers and a lot of framed documents and photographs, and piles of papers and files everywhere. Unlike the offices/studies of the owners, his workspace did have items of fetish interest. Hanging from an antique coat rack was a heavy motorcycle-style jacket, its epaulets hung with silver rings and strands of chain, for example. Brian's eyes widened as he snuck peeks at it. It would have fit in at any leather bar on any given Saturday night, and he just could not imagine Chris wearing it.

What caught Claudia's eyes was an umbrella stand in which nothing was held that could have kept rain off. But there were several glossy canes protruding from the top, one with a curved crook, the others with banded or woven handles. After feeling the weight and pain of his ever-present strap, she was astonished to see such civilized pieces of paraphernalia in his private space. The canes shared their container with an assortment of riding crops, a thin rod that would have been painfully familiar to Sharon and Brian, and two or three long dressage-style whips.

And even from across the room, they could see that several books on a tall set of shelves had very familiar spines. Chris, it seemed, had a collection of the very books that they had searched the library for so many times. Between the two of them, they spotted several classic SM novels, and two notorious trilogies.

"This is distressing," Chris commented, pushing the list away. "You've both had plenty of time to learn what has to be done in this house on a daily basis. Claudia, you in particular have been given no regular assignments outside the house, and Rachel had taken you under strict supervision all this week."

"I'm sorry, Chris," she said softly. "I know it's my fault, I promise to do better tomorrow!"

"So you say. However, it's clear that many of these things should have been done by Brian, as directed by you. Are you having trouble managing him? Has he been unavailable or slow?"

Claudia shot a glance at Brian, who felt a trickle of nervousness grow up his spine. Had he been avoiding her today? Yes, he had, after she stared at him helplessly for the third time or so. He had just taken more time to do some simple things, assuming that when she was ready to let him know what had to be done, she'd find him. He prayed that she wouldn't betray him. I swear, he tried to communicate with his eyes, I swear it'll be different tomorrow! Don't mess me up, girl!

"Uh, it's all my fault, Chris," Claudia stammered out. "Please don't blame Brian."

Chris nodded and turned his attention to the relieved slave. "Do you agree with that assessment, Brian? That you did well, and this report reflects badly on Claudia?"

"Um." Brian cleared his throat. He hadn't expected that he would be placed in this position! He glanced back at Claudia, who suddenly looked about as panicked as he felt, and then he looked back at Chris. "I ... I did my best, sir, I mean, Chris ... but maybe I can share part of the blame. It was only our first day...."

"You still talk too much," Chris said, cutting him off. "And you still think you can lie to us and your lies aren't as transparent as plastic wrap." He didn't sound angry, but he was more than annoyed. "Claudia didn't get many of these things done because she wasn't willing to stay on you as you did them, and neither was she willing to go looking for you while you dawdled and wasted your time. That much is her fault, and we'll be working on it. The rest is yours, however, and seeing as you didn't have the honesty or the courage to own up to them, I have no alternative but to punish you severely."

Brian dropped his head and his entire body tingled with dread.

"For the next three days, unless your work requires that you stand, I want you to fulfill the posture and speech requirements of a pet, Brian. Do you remember reading about them?"

Brian nodded, and his guts twisted inside him. Pets, he remembered, don't use furniture. They crawl, all the time. They carry things in their mouths, but gently, so as not to leave teeth marks. And they do not talk, but whine, whimper, mew, bark, or whatever is appropriate for the kind of pet they are.

"Perhaps in that time, you'll learn that when humans are slaves, they retain some of their humanity. That part should include honesty and integrity. And while you snuffle and whine your way around the house, maybe you'll remember that your answers to questions should be brief, to the point, and simply phrased, without dissembling or hedging or flattery. You may find it slightly more difficult to lie without being able to talk, I think."

Claudia looked at Chris in horror. She couldn't imagine a worse sentence for the talkative, teasing Brian.

"Claudia, before I dismiss you, I have something for you." Chris got up and walked over to the umbrella stand. Claudia's eyes widened as he drew out a short, flexible cane with a wrapped leather handle. He beckoned and she rose and walked over to him, her eyes on the varnished rod.

"This," Chris said thoughtfully, "is an excellent style of cane. It is made from imported rattan, and it passes the circle test." To demonstrate, he swiftly bent it in a tight arc so that the two ends came close to touching. "I have selected it for use on Brian."

She looked up at him in confusion. Brian's head shot up as well.

"You are familiar with the principles of using one, I assume?" Chris handed it to her.

She took it gingerly, holding it with the deep respect she felt. "Please, Chris ... I am familiar, but never ... I only ..."

"Yes, well if you are ever given a position of authority over other slaves, you will be expected to know when and how to express it. The strap requires a little more upper arm strength than you have to be effective, but your hand-eye coordination is excellent. If you're unsure, we'll have a lesson right now." Chris took it back and snapped his fingers. "Up, boy. I want you bent at the waist, your hands around your ankles!"

As Brian got into position, Claudia felt suddenly warm in the small room. "Please, please," she said desperately. "I can't ... I mean, I won't be able to do it well, Chris. I'm really just a slave, I can't be in charge of anyone!"

"But you will be," Chris answered sternly. "This is part of your training. Now pay attention."

He walked over to stand at an appropriate distance and angle from Brian's upturned posterior, and showed Claudia how to bring the cane across in a straight line, keeping the wrist firm. After showing her the movement in slow motion, tapping Brian each time, he sped it up and delivered a whistling strike exactly across the middle of Brian's ass. Brian yelped in pain, and gripped his ankles harder, gritting his teeth. The cane left a line that went from white to red in an instant, and Chris called Claudia over to look at it.

Three more demonstration strikes, each one getting another cry of pain, and then Chris took Claudia's arm and guided her through the swinging motion, looking for all the world like a golf pro. Claudia's first practice swings were bouncy waves of the punishment instrument, but with Chris's arm over hers, she helped add a fifth and sixth mark to Brian's ass.

"You'll get better with practice," Chris promised.

"By the end of the week, I want you to be able to judge when one of your strikes will mark and when it will draw blood. Keep it clean and dry, and never leave it lying on the floor where someone can step on it. Down, boy, we're finished with you. Go sit in the corner." Chris pointed and Brian crawled.

"Tomorrow and for the next three days, I will advise you when to use it, but after that, you will be expected to figure that out by yourself. And Claudia, I'll give you this warning only once." He wrapped his fingers through the chain that was her collar and pulled her close to him. She could smell mint on his breath and see the faint lines of a scar on his cheek. "If I find out that you are being more lenient than the situation demands, or that you have decided suddenly that Brian never needs correction, you can find yourself changing places with Sharon very quickly. I'm sure she'd love to give up stablework for housework, and serving you for supervising Brian. Am I very clear?" Chris released her and she stumbled back.

"Yes, yes, Chris," she answered quickly. "I understand!"

"Then you may go."

She backed away from him, and with one last glance at Brian, she left the room. Chris waited until the door was closed, and then turned to Brian, who crouched in the corner, four good stripes on his ass and two already getting faint. The major-domo walked slowly back to his desk and put things away for a while, shuffling papers and shutting the computer down. Brian remained where he was, in silence.

"You know," Chris said, leaning back in his chair,

"you're probably the worst one here. You really think that we're fooled by your 'successful slave' attitude, and that all the things you once heard about 'bottom pride' and 'tops disease' apply here. You and Sharon have read far too much, both fiction and theory, and you've never really lived any of it."

Brian bit his lip, but didn't move.

"Go to bed, Brian," Chris sighed. "Claudia will explain to the others why you can't join them in their usual sarcastic, antagonistic, or mindless remarks. And if she doesn't, you'll just have to endure their questions about why you've curled up on the floor next to your bed. Sleep well, little pet."

Chapter Seventeen

Claudia did indeed explain Brian's silence and his strange sleeping habit to the other slaves when they met at lights out, and his predicament sobered them all. The morning was even worse, when he crawled to the bathroom as they walked, crawled to the dining room where they took breakfast, and ate on the floor, from a round bowl that Cook had laid for him.

Of course, there wasn't a lot of time to give him sympathy. Breakfast had to be served to the owners, and the dishes cleared away, and by the time he crawled out of the back door to head for the stables, everyone was too busy with work or assignments of their own to give him much thought. And besides, the cane that Claudia suddenly carried around was far more mysterious and disconcerting. She had refused to say anything about it. And just as new

308 / *Sara Adamson*

but slightly less frightening was Robert's new cock-ring, which made him look bigger and more impressive. He, too, refused to elaborate on where it came from.

When Sharon went through her halfhearted invitations for oral sex, both Robert and Claudia demurred as usual, and Chris didn't push the issue for a change. The only thing he did was give one short glance in Robert's direction, which for some reason made the big man blush. But then he just shrugged and dismissed them to their chores and assignments.

By early afternoon, Brian's silence seemed to fall on all of them. His presence back in the house was a constant reminder of the kind of behavior any one of them could be ordered to emulate, or worse, live by. When Chris put little yellow ribbons in Brian's hair, situated approximately where one would decorate a poodle or other show dog, the other three blushed for him. And when Claudia was ordered to give Brian her first six stripes, for failing to empty bedroom trash bins fast enough, she cried even as she swung the rattan. Chris wasn't satisfied and had her give Brian another six.

On the second day of his sentence, a dance instructor arrived, and Sharon started formal training in several different styles of dance. She was paired with Robert for practice, and was told that she would be expected to be excellent at following leads and mastering the art of looking like it was all effortless. One pair of heels was returned to her to dance in, plus a pair of boots to practice Country Western styles. When she asked why, without thinking, Chris smiled and told her that the Marketplace had a lot of buyers from Texas and the American Southwest, and that was her question for the week.

Brian didn't get any questions that week. But on his second afternoon of being a pet, he got a long, cigar-shaped plug inserted into his rear, with a profusion of ribbons extending from the other end, suggesting a curly, metallic, purple tail. It matched the little purple bells that Chris had hung from his nipple rings, which tinkled and rang with every breath. They shook like hell, giving off a constant jingling sound when Claudia screwed up her courage and placed six "real" stripes on his ass while Chris watched. She had missed with one of them and cut him terribly across the soft part of his leg where the thigh touches the bottom of the ass, but Chris shrugged and told her to just do that one again. When she was finished, Chris told her to reinsert the "tail," which she did with much reluctance and more than a little distaste.

The bad stripe, the lowest one, hurt the most. It was also the first one that drew blood. As Claudia cleaned the cane, she cried again, but softly, so no one would hear.

"Actually, I'm enjoying this," Sharon said cruelly, looking directly at Brian, who was already curled up in his blanket on the floor. "It's a lot quieter in here with the fairy motor-mouth being a good little puppy dog." She made little barking noises at him and he pulled the blanket tighter around his shoulders.

"Aww, the little puppy doesn't have any wiseass stuff to say," she mocked. "Isn't it just too bad, he can't tell us all what to do!"

"Why don't you leave him alone?" Robert asked, annoyed. "Don't you think he has a hard enough time as it is?"

"Oh, shut up, sissy boy," she snapped back at him. "I don't have to listen to you. Just because you're licking Chris's butthole so deep your, like, nose is as brown as dirt doesn't mean a thing to me, OK? You're nothing but a big, fat wimp. Even Claudia can whip your ass, and see if she doesn't start to next week!"

Robert glared back at her. "You know, I'm tired of your insults," he said. His voice was so strong that Brian poked his head out of the blanket to watch. "You're not exactly the best of show here, you know. You work out in the damn stable, for crying out loud! Even Brian didn't start out there his first week! And they've never bothered to rotate you inside, like the rest of us. And Master Grendel and Mistress Alexandra don't even see you privately except to test you on how much you're learning or to lend you to someone else! I even have to teach you how to talk like a normal human being! So I don't know where you get off insulting any of us!" He swept his arm around the room.

Sharon stared at him in partial amazement. She wasn't the only one. Claudia, who, lacking anywhere else to put it at night, was tying the cane to the steel frame of the bed, silently cheered him.

But Sharon recovered quickly. "Don't try to pull this bullshit with me, you, you, *eunuch*!" She spat out the word triumphantly. "That's what you are, you know. That's all you're good for, because no one needs straight guy slaves, OK? No one! So you're looking at a life of being big and stupid and ... and you'll be lucky if they cut your dick off, because it doesn't work anyway!"

He glared at her for another moment, and then dropped his head and turned away. He shot a glance of sympathy in Brian's direction, only to see Brian give him a thumbs-up sign and a wink, and then they both drew covers around themselves.

I don't need this, Robert thought, snuggling down. I was so thrown by what happened to Brian, I was a mess tonight, even thought it was only Mistress Alexandra who could hear me. Maybe I need to have people to laugh at before I can say anything right. He snickered a little at the thought of trotting out his fellow slaves in assorted costumes just so he could release some tension before performing. Then he sighed and rubbed his bearded cheek against the pillow.

Funny, he thought, as he got comfortable, I feel a lot better now that I've told her off. Maybe she'll leave me alone now. Oh, no such luck; I'll have to deal with her in the morning, when she ...

"Please let me lick your big, fat balls and nibble on your cock," Sharon begged, her eyes lost in a sea of boredom. Chris stood by, noting down her exact words for Grendel to review.

"Hmmm," Robert said, spreading his legs. He was still seated at the breakfast table. Since it had been his turn to serve the owners, he was eating last. He peeled an orange and took a slice to eat, and then looked down at his lap. Then he looked down at Sharon, who had issued her offer/request from a kneeling position. "Well, since you asked so nicely, how can I refuse?"

Sharon nodded and started to rise before what he said got through her. She stared at him, her mouth opening in shock.

"Good," Chris murmured. "Sharon, go to it."

Sharon drew in one hissing breath and let it out in a hot rush over Robert's cock. It felt great! He slid down further in the seat and spread his legs wider. As he watched the beautiful woman bend her neck and begin to lick at him, the tendrils of pleasure ran all the way through his body, down to his toes! Now tell me what a sissy I am, he thought, relaxing as she washed the flat of her tongue over his shaft. Now tell me anything, you selfish little harridan!

She licked around the bulbous head, and then took it into her mouth, opening wide to receive it, and he lifted his hips to stuff more in. He hadn't felt anything like this since the early months of his marriage, when he and his wife were trying so hard to fulfill each other's perceived fantasies. He sighed as she pushed herself forward as far as she could and her throat contracted around the head. Now say anything, my little spoiled slave girl, he thought vindictively. Where the hell did you get off acting like you were my mistress? I don't have to listen to you anymore!

And then, his thoughts of mean-spiritedness faded away under the onslaught of her lips and tongue. She was so good! How could he not have appreciated this before? As she pulled away and stuck her tongue up, between his balls and his cock, making them press around the constricting band of the leather cockring, he swelled almost painfully, and moaned his pleasure.

Brian, from his vantage place on the floor, was

staring in open-mouthed amazement. Robert's cock, engorged and bound by the cockring, was all of his wet dreams come true. Fat and limp, it had held promise; but in its glory, it was nothing less than art. His mouth watered and he had to look away.

Sharon returned to the cock and took it back in her mouth and began to suck in earnest. She was having a little difficulty, which seemed to amuse Chris, but she kept with it, wetting her lips down with kittenish licks from her pink tongue, and then diving in again for another taste. The cockring became genuinely uncomfortable, but its pressure provided a kind of pain that Robert enjoyed, and he gasped, throwing his head back.

"On her!" Chris warned.

Robert heard and reached out to grasp Sharon's bobbing head. As his orgasm gathered up in him, he pulled her back away from him and grabbed his cock with the other hand. He came in heavy, fast spurts that shot directly into Sharon's face, against her cheeks and mouth, and then against her chin and down her throat. She grimaced, but couldn't pull away from him as he milked his cock of its last fluids and shook it at her, sending a few more drops to land on her breasts and belly.

Brian felt like applauding. Claudia didn't know whether to be horrified or amused. Sharon dragged a napkin down from the table to wipe herself off.

Chris calmly turned his attention back to the schedule, and the day began. Although she was hostile and glared at him all through her lesson, Sharon didn't say a cross word to Robert all day. Unfortunately, his euphoria was not as long-lived as he would have liked. In the late afternoon,

Alexandra called upon him to report to her and
Grendel about how the lessons with Sharon were
going. Robert was reluctant to tell them that he
thought Sharon was a lost cause, so he hesitated and
stammered, and lost track of what he was saying,
and made a fool of himself. Worst of all, his voice
scaled up and he called Alexandra "mistress."
Grendel stepped into the hall and grabbed Brian,
who was crawling by on his way to see if the towels
in the laundry were dry, and kicked him into the
library, where he took a very nasty beating that
Robert had to watch.

The only sounds that Brian could make were ani-
mal-like whines and whimpers. Robert fought back
tears, and wanted to crawl out of the room himself,
but he left with only a warning to behave better.

That evening, Brian crawled on his hands and knees
into the kitchen where he was told Chris was waiting for him. Chris was alone, and it was late. The
smell of freshly brewed coffee competed with the
scent of the night-blooming flowers planted in the
rear gardens. Chris had the back door open, and
there was an open newspaper on the kitchen work
table. He beckoned to Brian and pointed at the floor
in front of him, and Brian moved to the correct spot
and waited.

Chris finished turning the pages and casually
dropped one hand to rub Brian on the side of his
head, near his ear. Brian shook at the caress, and a
whimper came from his throat.

"I thought you might like that," Chris said. "You
hate living this way, but you also love it, don't
you?"

Brian felt a rush of heat and lowered his head,

but Chris followed the movement with his hand. "You'd love nothing more right now than to be able to lie down on the floor and fall asleep, just like a faithful dog. Am I right?"

Brian nodded, his eyes closed.

"So listen very carefully, Brian. This may be the best advice you will ever get from me. Remember this feeling every waking moment. Think of it before you open your mouth to speak, think of it when you're doing some unpleasant chore, and think of it when you're being punished. Because this is real, Brian: your body and mind attuned to one thing, to being the loyal and loving pet of a master or mistress whose feet you yearn to sleep at." Chris stood up and stretched. "Your punishment is lifted. You have, how-ever, lost whatever status you had. As far as we are concerned, you're starting back at the beginning. Don't ever try to lie or dissemble again. Or you'll be sent away."

Brian cleared his throat but didn't get up. He spoke his first words in three days. "Thank you, Chris."

"You're very welcome, boy," Chris patted his head and shooed him out.

Brian was the last one in when he got back to the dorm. He want over to Robert and kissed him full on the mouth. Robert snapped open his eyes and looked at him suspiciously.

"That was a thank-you for your standing up to her," he said with a grin. "It was the best thing I heard in the three days!"

Robert smiled and Sharon scowled.

"I'm glad they lifted your sentence," Robert said,

sitting up. "It was getting kind of quiet in here. And … I'm sorry about today."

Brian shrugged. "Hey, at least I got a beating from the big guy himself. As far as I'm concerned, that's something."

"Well, I'm sick and tired of getting beat on because he fucked up," Sharon complained. "It might be OK for you, but when I don't do anything wrong, I wanna know what I'm being kicked around for. It's not fair. He doesn't get beat when we fuck up."

"It's not my fault," Robert said softly. "They won't even let me ask about it because it has to do with my training. I'm so sorry. Really."

"You mean you don't get it?" Brian asked. He sat gingerly on his own bed, amazed at the sensation of sitting down, with his knees bent and his feet on the floor. "I thought you knew but you just couldn't control it."

"What do you mean?"

"They're beating on us whenever you act, well, sissy. If you mess up any other way, Chris just wades in with the strap, right? Like the time you knocked over the pile of trays in the kitchen?"

Robert nodded.

"But any time you put yourself up on tiptoes or you start to talk in that funny voice, wham, one of us gets it." Brian spread his arms. "I think we're supposed to be encouraging you not to do it any-more."

"So stop doing it!" Sharon interjected.

"Oh." Robert thought about it for a moment. "I don't know, Brian, or maybe I just don't understand. How is beating you supposed to make me behave better? I can't change so easily! This was the way I was taught everything! I ... I have to think about it. Maybe I asked the wrong question. I'm sorry. I'm really sorry." And he turned to go to sleep.

Claudia found herself caught in all sorts of difficult positions.

First of all, her ability to relate to and please Mistress Alexandra was improving, which was good. Oddly though, she still hadn't been in Alexandra's playroom, something that only Robert had seen. Now, speculations about Grendel's "workshop" had reached the point of accepted truth. So there were dungeons here! It's just that they were reserved for special uses. They all prayed nightly that they would soon see the inside of one or the other. But the bad thing about Claudia's getting better at sensual exercises was that Alexandra kept talking about it being time for Claudia to have more experiences with men. She tried not to look unhappy whenever the topic came up, hoping that her casual acceptance of the possibility would be taken as enough of an effort.

Secondly, her new job as housekeeper was an endless array of headaches. Despite copious notes and assurances from Rachel (whom she missed) that the job really was very simple, there was just not enough time in the day to make sure everything got done. And even though Brian didn't exactly hide from her anymore, neither was he much of a self-starter. He really did need her to tell him where things went, and he needed her to check things after they were cleaned. And if she didn't, then Chris might just come along and notice things weren't going well, and she'd have to take that cane to Brian again! Housekeeping was generally bad.

But she threw herself into the work with energy and dedication, amazed at the sheer diversity of skills and knowledge a good housekeeper had to have. And she found out things that no one knew before, like where Chris slept (he had a suite of rooms on the third floor), and how they housed overnight guests who had slaves.

"We never assume anything about someone's bedding requirements," Chris explained, showing her a special storage closet. "Here you'll find pallets for the side or foot of the bed, and even bedding for them. They should be placed on the folding rack by the bathroom in each guest room, so that they can make their own arrangements. If you find the pallet on the floor in the morning, replace it after the regular cleaning and treat it as you would a bed. Of course, some guests may have special preferences or needs, but most of them know to approach me with them."

How endlessly interesting.

When Brian was summoned to go to Alexandra's sunny workroom, he thought it might be for some menial task that Robert was unavailable for. Instead, he found himself standing with his hands behind his back while Claudia worked his body over with her fingers and her mouth. It was excruciatingly pleasurable, especially when he got a hard-on and it thrummed with painful intensity against the narrow bars of the steel cage he still wore about his cock.

"Yes, that's it," Alex said encouragingly. "Go ahead and get your mouth on the nipples, the rings are old, you don't have to worry about special sensitivity. Of course, if you are working on a top, you may have to make sure before you begin how they feel about your even touching body modifications such as piercings."

"Yes, ma'am," Claudia whispered. And trying not to look up into Brian's eyes, she put her lips to each of his nipples in turn and flicked the rings up and down with her tongue.

"When you leave them, use your fingers on them, and let your mouth trail down the center of his chest, that's it. Now you're working your way down to his belly, so let the nipples go and put your hands around his hips. Good. Nice. Now like you did on me, across his abdomen, just like that. See how effective it is?"

Claudia could see how effective she was, and hear it, and even, oh, god, smell it. She was blushing again, too, partly from doing this to poor Brian, who was forbidden to come at all, and partly from Alexandra's casual references to what Claudia had done with her in Alex's bedroom on a number of nights. It was disconcerting to hear of those intensely private times being discussed as though these were things done while shopping at the mall.

"Very good. Now go around to his back and start at the back of his neck."

Brian moaned but stayed still as the young woman pressed her lips to that sensitive spot he loved so much. It was all the more agonizing when Claudia was told to remove his belt and cage and kiss and lick at his cock. He bit his tongue and squirmed, and somehow managed to keep himself from coming. It was truly a Herculean effort.

Although she lacked Sharon's raw expertise, Claudia was talented, and her attentions, amateur as they were, had a charm to them that was refreshing and undeniably hot. By the time Alexandra called the end of the session, Brian had a hard-on that just wouldn't quit, and there was no way it was going back into the cage. Alex eyed it, sighed, and gave it a brisk backhand slap.

Brian howled! And his knees came together as he doubled over in shock and pain. He literally saw stars.

"Well, at least we know he doesn't get off on that," Alex commented to Claudia as she ushered the girl out of the room. "Get the cage back on and get to work, Brian!" she called over her shoulder.

Grendel was watching as Chris taught the basic information about wine. It was such a huge topic that they could really only touch on it, so all four slaves had been gathered to learn together. They heard about types of wines, and how to drink them, and with what. They learned how to decant, and what letting wine "breathe" meant. Chris showed them how to identify good crystal and then how to pour it and let Claudia explain how to listen for the ringing sound that liquid made as it filled a glass; they were all impressed at her skill at hearing it and using the sound as a tool to help her handle the wine better.

They each took turns at pouring, and tried to listen, and then practiced different ways of presenting glasses, bottles, and trays. It would have just been another one of their useful lessons on a specialized topic if Robert hadn't noticed Alexandra coming in with a riding crop in one hand (she had just been out riding), and allowed his eye to wander from the tray he was holding. The tray survived, very well in fact. He whirled to catch it, although it wasn't falling, and bumped his shoulder into Brian, who was leaning over a glass that Claudia was slowly filling so that he could hear the ring. He fell into Claudia, who tried to save the bottle, and did so with some admirable grace before landing on her rump. Brian's glass spilled, sending red wine spreading all over the tabletop and splashing onto the floor.

And in one moment of supreme panic and confusion, Robert simply lost it.

"Oh dear! Oh no! Oh, please, let me help—oh, I'm so sorry!" His voice was an unrestrained falsetto, rising and falling in intensity as he wavered back and forth between steadying the glasses on the table and trying to help Brian and Claudia. He bent down to give Claudia a hand up and hit Brian, who was trying to keep his balance, and Brian gave up the second time and just fell. Sharon, for once out of the way of things, barely managed to stifle a giggle, and she quickly moved out of the tangle of bodies to grab one of the towels from a tray and use it to wipe up some of the spilled wine.

Chris stood off to the side. He looked toward Grendel and then to Alexandra as he unfastened the strap from his belt loop, but didn't move as Alex approached him. She pointed to the knot of slaves. "Bring Robert and Claudia to my playroom, right now."

He nodded and waded in, pulling at arms and hanks of hair until the three were disentangled.

Grendel just shook his head and left the room with Alex.

In the hall, as he caught up with her, he asked, "Now?"

"Oh, yes," she smiled back at him. "Now."

"Oh, goody. Can I watch?"

"Hell, yes. You can help!"

Robert finally managed to contain his wailing when his knees hit the hallway carpeting. That was also when the enormity of the situation hit him. He had behaved like that in front of everyone! There could have been no worse time to lapse into that role. He stumbled trying to get up, and Chris's strap caught him neatly at the back of one thigh.

"Crawl there, you idiot," Chris snarled. "After that performance, you'll be lucky if you get the privilege to walk out of this house! And for godssake, keep your mouth shut! Claudia, move! Follow the ungrateful asshole." He pointed down the hall and turned back to the dining room. "And you two, clean up and get back to work!"

He followed Robert and Claudia down the hall and around the corner through the wing to the door to the playroom. Without knocking, he opened it and pushed them in, Claudia with his hand, Robert with a well-placed kick. And when Alex caught his eye and pointed, he dragged Robert across the room by his hair, and then pulled him to his feet. A pair of heavy cuffs were suspended from a rigging set into the wooden frame Robert remembered from the last time he was in this room. While he bit into his lip to avoid whimpering, Chris wrapped the cuffs around his wrists and locked them on. When Chris walked away, he hit a wall switch and a gear mechanism drew the cuffs, and Robert, upward. The motion didn't stop until Robert was balanced on the balls of his feet.

Claudia was given the same treatment, her body placed opposite Robert's, facing him. When they were bound, they were about five feet apart, with perfect views of each other.

"You've been warned," Alexandra said, coming forward. In one hand, she had one of the whips that Robert had been afraid of when he saw her collection. In the other, she held a fat buttplug. She passed it to Chris, and he came back over to Robert, and held it up to the man's mouth.

"Get it wet," he growled. "As wet as you can, because it'll be easier on you."

With a sob, Robert opened his mouth and took in as much of the silicon plug as he could. His jaw stretched and he slobbered over it, watching as Alex took a swing with the whip. It whistled. It wasn't very thick, and it seemed to be made of some kind of harsh cord. When Chris took the plug away from his mouth, he tried to speak, to beg, but no sounds came out. And when Chris vanished behind him and went to work, what came out of his mouth was not articulate.

"Ahhh! Oh, oh, pl-pl-eeese...!" He arched his back, taking the weight of his body on his arms as Chris kicked his legs farther apart and pushed the fat plug into him.

"Better," Alexandra commented to Grendel. "At least his voice is normal."

"Even if his asshole is tight. I think I might want a piece of that."

"Oh, you'll get it. But first, this situation." Alex

stepped into a good position to flog Claudia and cocked her arm back.

Robert panted and moaned, and struggled to bring his legs under him. When Chris's hands left him, all that was left was a huge throbbing pain in his rear, and the fear and knowledge of what was coming next. Tears were on his face; he had no idea when they had appeared. Again, he tried to speak, but now there was no moisture in his mouth, and his tongue felt thick. He tasted, dimly, as through anesthesia, blood in his mouth. He had bitten his tongue during that awful penetration.

Then he heard Claudia scream! Alexandra was just as good with the lighter, faster, meaner whip as she was with the luxurious one Robert had felt not so long ago. And each lash that fell on Claudia's body left long, red lines, like heavy scratches.

Poor Claudia had no idea what do to. She had never felt anything like it in her entire life! She attempted to take it quietly, but no one told her she had to, and she ended up screaming at each burning lash.

Robert sobbed, heavily, hanging his head between his upstretched arms. An internal litany of "I'm sorry, I'm sorry," played in his head, and his lips mumbled the words, but he vaguely knew that he wasn't shouting. Claudia's screams were echoing through his brain, stabbing into him like gut punches. He closed his eyes, and then Chris was there again, pulling his head up and back by a handful of hair, making him watch, making him see what was in front of him. A beautiful young woman, writhing in pain, crying out her anguish, and it was all his fault, all his fault, all his fault, all his fault...!

"Stop it!" he yelled, his voice as hoarse as it would have been had he been shouting instead of her. "Stop it, please, please, beat me, it's my fault, she didn't do anything!"

Alexandra paused, but then let another stripe land, sharp and biting. Claudia wailed and tears flowed down her cheeks.

"Please, ma'am," Robert pleaded. "Please, it's my fault, I'll take the punishment, any punishment you want, please don't ... please ..." He sobbed again, his voice low and breaking.

Alex tossed the whip to Grendel, who had already rolled up one sleeve. "Get out of there, boy," he said, gesturing to Chris. As Chris got out of the way, Grendel stepped into position and laid a line of fire across Robert's shoulders.

If this was what Claudia had been taking, Robert felt a renewed surge of guilt. He gasped in agony, barely able to take another breath before the second razor-sharp slash landed, and then the third and then the fourth.

"Good," Grendel murmured, his mouth suddenly right next to Robert's ear. "Very good! Take it like this until I'm finished!" And then he stepped back, before Robert could even begin to protest that his silence was only because he couldn't gather the energy to scream. As Grendel continued, Robert groaned and gasped his way through the twelve unspeakably painful slashes, finally slumping forward in his cuffs, dizzy and more than a little nauseated. Dimly he heard Grendel order Chris to go do something, heard Claudia whimper as they let her down, saw her fall into a little ball under her side of the frame.

And then Grendel and Alex left. He just blinked and they were gone. He winced as sweat ran into his eyes, and shook his head to get the droplets away. It took concentration just to breathe. In, out, pull yourself together man, stand up! Shifting and wincing as he did, he gasped when the real pain of the cuts on his back reached him. For they were cuts—and he knew, somehow, that all of the trickles on his back were not coming from sweat. He opened his eyes and looked at Claudia, and mouthed yet again, "I'm sorry." It came out as a croak.

Claudia sighed and looked up. Although there were several deep red lines on her back, she was not damaged by her beating. She gazed at him and wiped her eyes, and then looked around. They were alone in the room. Slowly, she pushed herself up, first on her knees, and then up on her feet. Steadying herself, she walked over to him, stood on tiptoes, and kissed him gently on the lips. They both bore the marks of the recent assault on their own mouths, so she moved down to kiss his throat, as she had been taught, and then his nipples, and then she trailed her mouth down his belly.

Suddenly, Robert was again aware of the plug filling his tight asshole, as he twitched and his insides constricted with pleasure when she touched him. He moaned, low and long, as her hands wrapped around his hips, holding onto him softly, and then her mouth descended to touch his cock, driven to softness by the beating and now miraculously awakened by her breath. He sighed, the combination of pain and discomfort and the restriction of bondage mixing with the incredible pleasure of her ministrations. When she carefully took the fat head into her mouth, letting her breath wash over it, he cried out and arched his back, not caring that it pulled at the lines of fire that decorated it.

And then her mouth was gone. He heard her shriek, and opened his eyes.

Chris had pulled her away. He smiled and grabbed her by the scruff of her neck. "Get back to work, girl," he said as he pushed her toward the door.

Much later, Robert found himself spread-eagled on one of the low tables, a folded towel under his back. He had no idea why he was back in the playroom.

The slaves had returned to their usual routine after the beatings. Robert had not been excused from dinner or from finishing his tasks, so when Chris had finally let him down, he had staggered off to get back to work as soon as he could. The others were all impressed by the marks on his back, and when he had been told to freshen up after evening duties, he had looked at himself in the mirror and gasped.

And then he had reported back to Chris, who delivered him here, secured him, blindfolded him, and left, all without a word. Am I going to sleep here tonight? he asked himself. Is this more punishment?

He heard the door, but the thick carpeting muffled all other sounds except for some vague clinking that came from far away. He was only aware of someone next to him when his hand was touched. He jumped, as far as he could in bondage, and gasped.

"Good evening, Robert," Alexandra said.

"G-good evening, ma'am," he managed to reply. Her cool fingers traced the outline of his arm, and she walked around him, checking his bondage.

"I'm going to do something very different with you tonight," she said, her voice now coming from the direction of his feet. "There will be no protests from you, and you will strive to please me in all ways. Those are your only instructions."

"Yes, ma'am!"

She began by putting wide, flat clamps on his nipples, compressing them into little erections on his chest. A line of clips led from each one, trailing down his chest and across his stomach. He drew in harsh breaths whenever she added a new one, and lost count at about thirty. They began to appear on his arms and legs, and one line of them was planted just above his hairline, digging into the flesh above his groin. The last set was buried around his cock and balls, with five of them gathering up the loose flesh on the underside of his cock.

The pinching sensation was unfamiliar but not frightening. Although he reacted to each placement, most of them were quite bearable, at least until the line of five on his cock. He shook when she put them in place.

"You could fit eight or nine," was her only comment. Robert could only nod and say, "Yes, ma'am," and then shut up.

She began to touch the pins, one at a time, alternating from one side of his body to another, first just tapping them, and then actually bending or twisting them. He moaned as she played with him, his fingers stretching out and then clenching into fists again, sighing when she left troublesome pins alone, grinding his teeth when she pinched them to make them tighter. Her tormenting was methodical in pace, but random in target site, and he squirmed a little. He gasped and jumped when she started to take them off.

"That's my big fella," Alex said, giving one pin on his belly a hard twist as she pulled it off. "I like the way you're taking this. Do you like the way it feels?"

"Yes, ma'am!"

"Good." She continued to pluck them off. "Do you know how many you took, Robert?"

"No, ma'am. Ah!" She had pulled off two at the same time.

"Tsk, tsk. That's not very attentive of you. I put fifty-five pins on you, and because you didn't count them, I'm going to hit you fifty-five times when they're off." Two more, on his thigh, came off, and he moaned.

It seemed that last on/last off was the rule of the day, and the final five came off slowly, making blood rush into his cock at dizzying speed. He thanked her, profusely, the same words over and over, stopping only when something light smacked against his tingling left nipple.

"Fifty-five, Robert; keep count. By counting backwards." She smacked him with the short, light whip one more time, and he cried out more in shock than in pain.

In a low voice, he said, "Fifty-four, ma'am."

The whip had to be short—she seemed to be standing very close to him. It was tressed in leather that smacked with an almost elastic quality against his body. Even as he counted and she worked it over his torso and the fronts of his thighs, he felt his cock beginning to stand up again, and he gasped when she took casual swipes at it.

"And how many are left?" she asked him from time to time.

"Thirty-one, ma'am," he answered, and then "Thirty" when she landed one on his belly, and then later, "Twenty, ma'am!" and so on.

The whip left no marks on his body, but the ritual and the feeling of being beaten without the true sense of getting hurt, had worked magic on the bound man. His back was just a memory, lines of minor aching he dismissed at will. The bonds on his wrists and ankles were security for him; his mistress would not let him go; he was all hers. And as he finished the count, each magical number-word was a countdown to something, if only his excellent completion of it at her command. The final blow, as he tremblingly voiced, "One, ma'am!" was gently draped across his face, the tresses trailing by his mouth so he could breathe in the rich, smoky scent of them and kiss them as they moved across his cheeks.

In the short silence that followed, he tried to find a better way of saying "thank you."

Then he felt movement above him, things around him being adjusted. A pillow was placed under his head, tilting his neck a little more than he thought would be comfortable, but he kept silent. His silence was met with a rustling sound, and then a slight creak as Alex joined him on the table. She made herself comfortable, and his first realization of what she was doing hit him like the rush of good cocaine.

She was kneeling above him, right above his face. Her pubic hair tickled his chin as she made herself more comfortable, and then rose up to offer her pussy to his lips.

"Do what will please me," she said softly. "Get in there and work at it, show me how much you want to make me happy."

A long, body-length shiver of anticipation ran through Robert's body, and he licked his lips. Gently, he kissed her, allowing his mouth to learn exactly where she was, how close, how far, and how open. To his searching mouth, she revealed that she, too, had enjoyed the session with the pins, and he thanked her with warm, loving kisses at her center of pleasure, daring to lick carefully at the edges. Encouraged by her shifting agreeably, he began to explore her with his tongue and lips together, wetting her down and tasting her wetness. He could barely hear her sigh above him, but what he heard was encouragement enough. He moved his head even closer, cursing his bonds for the first time, and then blessing them.

He would have never had the courage to do this without them.

Carefully, he took her pussy lips and bathed them with his tongue, and then dipped deeper into her to taste her again. Back and forth he went, until her juices and his melded and mixed all over her pussy and all over his mouth and chin. He extended his tongue farther out to touch the hooded spot near the top of her cleft, and when she dipped lower, he concentrated there for a long time, washing it over with rhythmic strokes that made her fairly purr.

That's my man, she thought, arching up away

from him and then settling back down. Oh, yes, that's it. Nice and open, nice and wet, nice and easy. Oh, you know the secret here, big guy, just stick with what works and do it over and over again, until—ah, yes, that's it! And that's enough of that for now. Nearing her own pleasure, she denied it to him and pulled away. There was something else she had her eye on, and now was the time to get it.

Robert gulped air, and moaned. But he didn't know if he was moaning because of the sudden deprivation, or because of deep, sincere gratitude. He managed to gasp out, "Thank you, ma'am! Thank you so much!"

"Oh, but it's not over yet," Alex assured him. He felt her touch the head of his cock and put something on it. Was it another torture device? He felt her fingers along the sides, rubbing him, no, pushing something down....

She was covering his cock with a rubber. He began to shake, and she squeezed his erection in her hands she unrolled the condom all the way to the base of his cock.

"You're going to keep it up until I get mine," she said, maintaining her soft voice. "No protests, no failures."

And with that, she turned around, made herself comfortable again, and guided herself onto him. As she predicted when she first saw it, his big, handsome cock filled her nicely, and sinking onto it made her feel like she was sitting on a fat, warm pole. She shifted for comfort and rose to accommodate more of him.

Robert felt as though he could die, right then, of pleasure. It had been ages since his cock was in a woman like this, and he had almost forgotten what it felt like. The images and sensations that barreled into each other in his brain were of hot honey and velvet walls, smooth creams and warm towels. He shuddered and lifted his hips to meet her, and she rode him easily, shifting to give herself more pleasure and a better position to ride in.

Before long, he was giving out little cries as she rose and fell, and those cries gave way to harsh gasps of breath when she rocked back and forth. Alexandra stroked herself, very turned on by the body and the thick cock of the man beneath her, and sighed as her body settled into a rhythm that would take her over the top.

"That's it," she murmured, thrusting her hips forward, "that's it, such a good boy, keep it nice and hard, nice and fat, while I ride...."

"Yes, ma'am," he wrenched out, pulling against all his bonds now. "Oh, yes ma'am! Use me, ma'am!"

Alex took one deep, rasping breath and then began to come. It started out feeling mild, the way it usually did, but she rode it until her hips thrust back into and onto him, and her entire body shook with the need for that final pleasure. Her breaths came in gasps, shaking her body from head to toe, as the quake of sensation erupted between her legs. She rode him as the steady contractions subsided a little, and noticed that he was still hard!

He had not come.

"Good boy," she breathed softly, stroking his chest. Carefully, she rose off of him, hissing a little when he slid out of her, and then she got down from the table. As she stretched and looked at him, she saw that his teeth were still clenched tightly shut, probably his mechanism to keep from coming. Good boy, she thought. *Very* good.

She hit the cuffs one after the other, releasing them. "When you've put the cuffs away and cleaned this place up a little, come to my room. If I'm already asleep, you'll find your place at the foot of my bed."

"Yes, ma'am," he whispered finally, not evening knowing if she was still in the room. "Thank you, ma'am."

Chapter Eighteen

Days passed, merging with each other. Sharon and Brian became obsessed with Grendel's refusal to either use them sexually or even call them to serve him in the evening. Claudia and Robert tried to downplay their increased activities with Alexandra, so that they wouldn't cause undue stress for their companions, but their repeated absences from the dorm made that impossible.

It was even worse when Alexandra told both of her slave trainees that she expected to loan them to Grendel for some training of a different sort. They both kept that nugget of information to themselves.

Brian recovered from his days as a pet and threw himself wholeheartedly into being a good slave. He finished his tasks quickly and ran to Claudia for instructions for the next one. He kept his body

336 / *Sara Adamson*

scrupulously clean, and began to practice certain
bows, genuflections, and postures when he was in
the bathroom, so he could execute them in the best
way. When he was with Jack, he concentrated on
giving nothing but world-class blowjobs, and eagerly assumed whatever strange position Jack dreamt
up for him. One day, after a particularly long session involving spurs and a rubber bit, Jack laconically admitted that "You an' th' model are about neck
'n' neck at th' line for 'oo gives the best nut bathin',
but you're a sweet one t' fuck, m' boy!"

Claudia admitted that she really had no complaints about his performance and Chris could find
nothing glaringly disappointing. When they took
away his cage and belt, he thought, "Now, maybe
now!" And still nothing happened.

One late night, he got out of bed to use the bathroom, padding down the hall in the dim light cast
by various hallway fixtures. When he heard something clinking in the direction of the main hallway,
he froze. At first, he thought he was hearing things.
Who the hell would be walking around at some
ungodly hour in this house? The owners were both
early risers, and Chris, well, that guy just never
slept....

At that thought, Brian turned and went the other
way down the hall, toward the big staircase and the
main hall. He slipped down the stairs, toward the
sound, and stopped cold when he almost ran into it.
Or him. Because it was indeed Chris. A Chris he
could never have imagined.

The stocky major-domo was decked out in what
the boys called "full leathers." His regular work
boots had been replaced with gleaming black engi-

neer boots, one with a simple silver chain around the left ankle. Leather jeans rode on the boots, ending right above the ankle. Under the motorcycle jacket Brian remembered from Chris's office, the man was wearing a crisp black shirt, crossed by a Sam Browne belt. Tight at his throat was a narrow black tie. Jammed on top of his short, thick hair was a black officer's cap, the brim gleaming silver.

Brian's mouth went dry just before Chris caught him by the throat and pushed him violently against the wall.

"Why the fuck are you out of bed?" he demanded, his voice low. "What the hell are you doing down here?"

"Please!" Brian choked. He clutched at the hands holding him.

"Tell me!" Chris demanded, loosening his grip slightly.

"I heard ... heard you from upstairs," Brian said, after a cough. "I was going to the bathroom. I thought it might be ... I thought I should invest——"

"Who did you think it might be?" Chris pushed. "A burglar?"

"No!" Brian shook his head. "I thought it might be you."

Chris let him go. "Idiot," he spat. "Well, it's me. Now go back to bed."

"But ... wait ..." Brian reached out and touched Chris's jacket lightly. "Please ... it's been so long. Please, let me, just let me look...."

Chris shook his head. "Why don't you understand?" he asked, taking his cap off. He ran his fingers through his matted hair. "This isn't real, Brian.

This is just costumes. You're lusting for something that doesn't exist."

"But you wear it. You live it!" Brian insisted. "This is you!"

"No, Brian. This isn't me, it's just a skin I wear. I live this!" The major-domo reached out and thumped the bannister of the staircase. "And I live this!" he stamped one boot against the floor. "This house, and its owners, are my life."

"I do this when I go hunting." He spread his hands, showing off the outfit.

"Hunting for what?" Brian asked, knowing the answer.

"For little lost boys like you, who don't know enough to be in their own beds in the middle of the night." Chris tucked his cap under one arm in a gesture Brian had seen thousands of times. "Go back to sleep."

"Please," Brian begged. "Please tell me one thing."

"What, Brian, what? I don't have all night!"

"Grendel not using me ... does it have something to do with the way I ... with how I messed up that first day? Does anyone else know? Do you hate me? Do you know how sorry I am?" His words came out in a rush, questions he never could have asked in front of the others, perhaps one of the reasons he had never really remembered to share his gossip with them.

Chris sighed. "That's not my business," he said gently. "Yes, some people know, but not most. I'm not sensitive about it. No, I don't hate you. I have never asked for an apology because Mr. Elliot didn't seem to think that one was necessary, and I am generally guided by him in these things. But if it will make you sleep easier, I accept your apology. Now get back to bed before I beat you the hell up those stairs." And with that, he gave one good swat at Brian and sent him up the stairs and back toward the bathroom.

In the morning, the whole episode almost seemed like a dream.

"Tonight you go to Grendel," Alexandra told Claudia when she arrived. "You might as well go now; he's waiting. And don't disappoint me, girl."

"Yes, ma'am," Claudia responded automatically. And then she walked around the inner balcony to the other wing and came to a stop in front of Grendel's door. She found herself inside before she even realized that she had gone. There was a dreadful, heavy feeling in the pit of her stomach. The time had come.

I must be brave, she thought, pouring his coffee and delivering it to him while he soaked in his jacuzzi. She placed the cup and saucer down gingerly on the little carved wooden stool next to his headrest, and retreated to the spot he told her to kneel on, across the room, where he could see her fully. By the time she got there and settled down, he had opened his eyes and was sitting up a little more to get the drink.

"So," Grendel said, after drinking for a while. "Alex thinks you're coming along very well. What do you think?"

"I hope I'm doing well enough to make my mistress consider taking me back, sir," she replied honestly. "I'm doing my best."

"Well, complaints about you have been very scant," he admitted. "You've even improved dramatically in your organizational skills."

"Thank you, sir."

He nodded. "Of course, there is the little matter of what you're so terrified about tonight."

She blushed suddenly and ducked her head. "Was it that obvious, sir?"

"It was obvious to Alex when she first casually mentioned that she might like to loan you to me. It's obvious in the way you talk to me, and it's also obvious in the way you've approached certain facts of life around here. So why don't we cut to the chase, and you tell me exactly what you think the problem is."

Claudia shifted nervously and lowered her eyes again. Grendel's voice was so nice and friendly right now, surely he'd understand! But how could she explain that she ... that she ...

"I'm a virgin," she blurted out.

"Yes, I know," Grendel nodded and finished his coffee.

"What?" Claudia's head bounced back up, and she looked into Grendel's amused eyes. "But ... but how...?"

"I'll explain. But first, fetch me a towel, and then get my robe, please." She rushed to do as he said, and he continued to speak while she attended to him.

"It was really simple. Alex was the one who put it all together. First, you as much as told us so in your personal bio, when you mentioned that you broke up with your first boyfriend when he became insistent over the issue of sex, and then you never mentioned a sexual experience with a man or dildo-wielding dyke lover," he ticked off one finger. "Second, Madeleine suspected something of the sort." He held up another finger. "And third, Alex thought that you felt resistant on a number of occasions when she wanted to get more than slightly *penetrative* with you. Now each of these alone would not have been enough. But all three, plus your thinly disguised fear of being sexually used by men, did indicate a certain something that needed resolution."

She bowed her head again. "I'm sorry, sir."

"Nothing to be sorry about," he said lightly. "It's a common condition, we all have it at one time or another. Of course, you should have realized that this was the kind of thing that should have been brought to someone's attention. You should have told Madeleine, and you should have told us. There are some people who actually think that your state of being sexually aware and functional while still being 'intact' is of special value. Personally, I think the whole concept of valuing something everyone is born with but only half the population can evidence is barbaric."

She dried his back and held the robe for him. "I thought it was a problem, sir," she said, backing away. He belted the robe and pointed into the bedroom and she preceded him.

"It is. But the problem is not specifically your virginity. The problem is what to do about it. We normally don't have to deal with something like this. I can honestly count the number of intact virgins I've seen over the years, and it's not many. Virginity isn't prized as much as someone who knows what

they're doing. At least not in the market we serve."
At his gesture, she poured him another cup of coffee, and sat at his feet when he pointed.

"I, for one, have no interest in being your first,"
he said seriously. Her eyes widened in amazement.
"It's no insult, believe me. But I happen to feel that
first times, no matter what the social standing of the
person, should be by choice, not by circumstance. If
I believed that you lusted wildly after me, that
might be different. But we won't even pretend that
this is so, and that puts us right back to the question
of what to do.

"I would like to send you back to Madeleine the
way you are, but of course we're not sure what her
plans are going to be. I can tell you that fucking you
is certainly one of her interests. Going through a
drama with you over the issue might not be. Alex
feels much the same—willing but not especially
eager. And you have to understand, Claudia, *it's not
you*. It's just that you've managed to build up this
fear and shame around the issue. I—we—would
prefer it if we were sure that you had made some
sort of personal decision about what you want to
do. If it's unsuitable for this house, we'll leave you
as is, and it just won't be an issue for us."

He stretched out his legs comfortably. "Enjoy the
time you take to make the decision. This is probably
only the third time we've presented such an issue to
an applicant here, and this is the least unpleasant
circumstance."

"Sir? I'm not sure what my choices are," Claudia
said finally.

"Well, you can choose to leave yourself vaginally
virginal, whatever that means to a woman who has

been in several lesbian relationships and survived the experience with the ability to have multiple orgasms. Or you can ask that Alex deal with this and you in a more mistress-to-slave fashion. For that matter, you could still try to convince me that I should be your first penetrator. Or, if there is some-one else here who you might have naturally chosen, we can explore that possibility."

"Someone else," she mused, putting her head down. After a moment, she looked back up. "I know what I want," she said finally. And she told him. He thought about it for a moment and then nodded.

"I don't see why not. I'll speak to Alex in the morning. Of course, by doing this, you're placing control of the event in our hands." He looked down at her with hard eyes. "I think I might like to watch that, for example."

She gulped, but didn't waver. "I think ... that might make me feel safer, sir," she answered.

"Ha! Good answer. Come on, turn out the lights and lie next to me in bed. Alex tells me you've got some nice moves. Now that the scary part is over, you can get back to your training."

"Sir? May I ask a favor please?"

Grendel looked interested. "I'll listen to your request."

"It—it's not for me, sir. It's for Sharon, and Brian." She lowered her eyes, knowing that she was over-stepping.

"OK. I'm still listening."

She raise her head hopefully. "Sir, they want to be good slaves, I know it. But they're confused, and scared, and I think they want your attention very much, but they don't know what they should be doing. Please sir, is there some way you can give them a hint, or provide them with more direction? I'm sure they'll be excellent once they're given a chance, sir."

Grendel nodded while she spoke and waited until she was finished. Then, he said, "I'm sure you know how inappropriate that request was."

Claudia nodded, her face falling.

"Your concern is touching, but your interference in matters of training is not allowed. However, you approached it properly, and I'm not angry with you. In fact, I'll take your comments into consideration. But you're not to mention that you made this request, or that I responded to it, do you understand?"

"Oh, yes sir! Thank you, sir!"

"Then come on up here." He lay back and spread out one arm, and she curled up next to him. He touched her and explored her, and directed her to him, and she found herself enjoying it. When he turned and moved her with him, she sighed, liking the warmth of his body and the security of his size and strength. When he released her without any demands on her, she went to the cool pallet on the floor and thought, why he's very nice. That thought kept her awake for many long minutes. *I was so afraid of him, and he's so nice.*

"Robert, this is Sensei Chen." Chris performed the introductions. The sensei, in sweat pants and a cut off T-shirt, looked like a college student at a track meet. He nodded to Robert, who was now used to people not reacting to his nakedness.

"The sensei is here to start a new series of lessons for you. He is an expert in the technique of Go-Ju, a Chinese form of karate. For the next three weeks, you will see him every day for one hour, and three hours on Wednesdays. Practice time is your own to schedule, but you will be responsible for keeping up with his outlined goals." Chris bowed formally to the sensei, who grinned and bowed back, and Chris left without another word.

Robert blinked and looked down at the young man. This new twist was totally confusing. Dancing, and karate. He resigned himself to realizing that nothing was ever going to make sense here.

"Hiya, Robert. You're a big guy, huh? We're gonna have to get you a jockstrap, I think. Well, let's go out back and see what you're made of, and then we'll see what I can teach you, huh?" The sensei led Robert into a clear area of grass out near the garage.

"Is this going to hurt?" Robert asked.

"Oh, not more than you can take," the sensei said with a grin.

"Great," the big man sighed.

One night, Sharon found herself called to see Grendel. She went after dinner, walking proudly through the halls, confident that her time had come at last.

But when she got there, he didn't do anything. He didn't tie her up, or play with her, or even take a freaking bath and have her wash his back, something that little airhead Claudia seemed to think was such a hot thing to do. Instead, he posed her on this little mat-thing by the door, and left her kneeling there for, well, a long, long time. It felt like hours. And he made some phone calls, and he read for a while, and Chris came in with some coffee, and nothing happened at all!

And then finally, when she was about to just die from the boredom and the itchy feeling in her legs, he looked over at her and said, "You may spend the night."

"Thank you, sir!" she purred at him. "May I get up?" When he nodded, she gave herself a mental pat on the back. Oh, she knew all the tricks now. Don't move a muscle until you get permission, that was a good one. Now, she rose and stretched, careful not to leave the spot she was in. Oh yeah, some sex was going to feel really good right now. She wondered if he was going to make her start with a blowjob. She really wanted to get fucked. Blowjobs are OK, but when I'm horny, oh, I want it bad, she thought, twisting around.

"May I come to you, sir?" she asked, when she was ready.

Grendel looked up from his book, as though he was surprised that she was still there. "If you like," he said, putting the book down. She walked across the room slowly, making it her most sensuous stride, and sank to her knees gracefully at the edge of the bed.

"Very nice," Grendel admitted. He reached out and stroked her hair for a moment. "You may go to sleep now. I'll turn out the lights."

Sharon felt confusion building. She looked up at him and started to get up. "Um." She stopped and then gathered her thoughts before the word "like" got out. "Sir ... I thought ... didn't you want to, um, use me, sir?"

"No, not really." Grendel smiled gently. "But you can stay anyway."

"Oh." Sharon tried to keep the scowl from her face, and she sighed prettily. "Yes, sir," she said, keeping her voice light. And then she tried to get into bed. He stopped her with one hand.

"Where do you think you're going?" he asked.

"T-to, um, sleep?"

"There's a pallet down there with a blanket," Grendel pointed to the foot of the bed. "That's where you sleep, girl. It's in the book."

Oh damn, was it? Oh yeah, something about sleeping at the foot of the bed unless other arrangements were made. But Sharon looked down at the end and saw the little futon-like thing that was down on the floor and then back at Grendel. I thought it meant that you slept at the bottom of the mattress, she thought, this time allowing the frown to escape.

"You don't like it?"

She should have been warned by the light, friendly tone of his voice.

"Sir, don't you think … wouldn't you rather I was up here with you?" Sharon tried offering good stuff instead of complaining. Maybe that was the way to go.

"What's wrong?" Grendel asked. He got up and looked at the pallet. "Don't you like it?"

"Well, sure, sir," she said, sliding up to him. "But don't you think I belong closer to you than on the floor? If I'm really good, don't I deserve to be somewhere special?"

Grendel nodded and stroked his beard. "You have a point," he said with a nod. He walked back to the his table and hit the intercom button on the phone. "Chris, could you come to my room, please?"

"You know, you've really given me something to think about," he said, as the two of them stood in the middle of the room. Sharon smiled sweetly, wondering what Chris was for. She entertained a brief fantasy that Grendel was going to yell at the little guy, telling him to never put one of these pallet things on the floor when Sharon was going to be here. She smiled even sweeter.

"Chris, Sharon isn't satisfied with the sleeping arrangements here," Grendel said. "She seems to believe that her special needs call for special accommodations. I'm sure you can find her something appropriate?"

"Wait," Sharon started to say.

"You made your choice, Sharon, and I'm respecting it. Good night." As the two of them left, Grendel allowed himself a laugh. Well, Claudia, he thought, going back to his book, there's one!

When Chris grabbed her by the arm and marched her out, Sharon's mouth opened in shock. Well! Of all the goddamn nerve! What did she do wrong? She was so outraged and obsessed with this weird situation, she didn't notice that they weren't heading toward the dorm room.

"Wait," she said again, pulling back a little. "Where are we going?"

"To find you a more appropriate place to sleep. Shut your mouth, you ungrateful little mink." Chris grasped her arm more firmly, and propelled her into the kitchen, where he let her go for a moment while he went into one of the storage rooms. When he came out, he was holding a large flashlight and a bag that clanked. She was grasped again, and pushed out the back door and along the path to the stables. Halfway there, she started to struggle, and he had to threaten to use his strap on her to get her to walk. Then she tried pleading, begging, and finally screaming, which he cut off by calling her attention to the many unpleasant things that she could be gagged with if she disturbed the horses.

She ended up in an empty stall, a chain around one ankle, locked to the sliding bar that held all the stalls closed. "It will open automatically in case of fire," Chris explained. "Here is your bedding," he kicked up some straw around her, "and here is your coverlet." He tossed in a horse blanket made of heavy netting. "There's water in the bucket, and if you can't wait until morning, you'll find that straw can be very moisture-absorbing. I hope these accommodations are more to your liking."

"Chris, Chris," she moaned, clutching the blanket to her body. "Please don't leave me like this! I swear, I didn't mean anything! I didn't know! I didn't remember! I'm sorry! I'll never do it again!"

"You little fool," Chris scolded, gathering up his flashlight. "Many slaves wish that they had the honor of sleeping at the foot of their master's bed. You knew. You read all about it. But you thought it didn't apply to you. Sleep well."

He turned out the light when he left. The oppressive heat made wrapping herself up in the blanket unadvisable, but the straw was scratchy against her skin, and she was afraid of bugs, so she did it anyway. And she sobbed until the tears just couldn't come any more, and she was afraid that she might wake the stupid horses and get into more trouble. Sharon spent a long, uncomfortable night, sure that her life could not get worse, not in a million years. She was so very wrong.

Just one day later, Alexandra had Sharon show herself to a pair of men wearing expensive European suits and carrying small, exquisitely designed briefcases. The men were alike enough to be brothers, spare and economical in movement and bearing themselves as though they were diamond merchants looking at decidedly inferior merchandise. Conferring with each other in fluid Italian, they prodded her and issued curt commands in lightly accented English.

"She does not look healthy," the man in the light suit commented to Alex. "Do you have her medical files?"

"Of course."

"Turn—no—slowly! Lift your arm up, that's it, higher, higher...." The other man stroked the inside of her arm, and she giggled. He drew his hand away immediately and slapped her, hard, across the breast. Sharon gasped and yelped, and her arm came down. She ground her teeth together in the incredible effort not to demand what the hell this guy was doing! And he turned away from her with a look on his face that was more eloquent than any verbal exchange.

The man in the dark suit shook his head. "No, Alexandra, I don't think so. She's not even ready to enter our training program. But we thank you for allowing us to look at her first."

"Your house is always welcome to place advance

bids here," Alex said, rising. "When we heard you were looking for her type ..."

"Yes, and we appreciate it. She would be adequate for out needs if she had better training. Not to suggest that you have not done splendid work with her!" Light suit hurried to correct himself. "But perhaps when she has completed her training, we can come out and take another look at her. Six more weeks? Eight, perhaps?"

"Maybe you have something else to show us?" dark suit suggested. "We have the new catalogs from Los Angeles and Stockholm, and they are very disappointing." He opened his case and pulled out several bound documents, placing them on her desk. "I think the market will like to see some fresh faces from New York this year."

"Thanks," Alex said, flipping through one. "I'll show you the others if you like, but I'm afraid I don't have anything else like her right now. Why don't we meet with Grendel; he wanted to ask you about the possibility of creating a kind of foreign exchange program to foster a more marketable linguistic base for some specialty merchandise."

"Good idea! Excellent!" Dark suit nodded, and they let Alex precede them. On the way out, Alex gestured a dismissal to Sharon, who slumped into a pouting position as soon as they left.

Are they staging all this stuff for me, she asked herself. I mean, what is this shit? They don't like me because I'm, like, ticklish!? I don't believe it, I mean, what am I supposed to do? She was going to leave, but then the glossy covers of the catalogs caught her eye. She walked over to the desk, and contrary to everything she had been warned not to do, picked up the top one. As she flipped through the pages, her eyes widened and she licked her lips.

They were catalogs of slaves! One of them, with elegant gold-bordered pages, showed photos and numbers only, but the photos were astounding. Each slave was shown in several poses, full frontal, kneeling with legs spread, rear, and head shot. They all wore chain collars around their necks, with numbered tags. Many of them sported piercings, through nipples, labia, clit hood, and even through the head of a cock or two. Some had tattoos. Since the photos were in color, she could see that almost all of them had experienced recent beatings.

They were male and female, terribly young and well into middle age. They were white, mostly, but an elegant Asian woman with sensual lips gazed out from one page, and a muscular black man with a shaved head and several rings along the bottom of his cock posed on another. There were at least fifty people in the catalog, identified only by a number.

Oh god, Sharon thought, flipping through the book. Some of these guys are fucking gorgeous! So hot! The men looked good enough to grovel to, their bodies hard and sculpted, their poses placing them at angles to show off biceps and asses, cocks and heavy balls. And some of the women made the world's top models look plastic and one-dimensional. Not all of them, Sharon noted with satisfaction. I'd be no dog in this group. In fact, as she flipped back and forth, she noticed that mixed in with the cuties were a couple of perfectly ordinary looking guys and girls. But even their pictures showed a sense of erotic aestheticism, like even they were seen as objects of desire and people to be possessed.

She looked in vain for information about these people, their names and how old they were and where they came from, but didn't find any. The other catalog was the same way, only there were more people of color in it, and more exotic-looking slaves.

I could be in these, Sharon mused. In a minute. I don't know why they're doing this to me, but they're not being fair.

By the time she left the room, the two Italian agents had already met with Grendel and they all shook hands on the start of a new program between their houses. As a courtesy, Alex made them an offer, and to show her that they didn't mean any insult to her house, they asked for Sharon. She sent Sharon to them in the largest guest room, with her compliments.

"She thinks she's worth something to us because she is a skinny American girl with big eyes and a hunger for sex," Dark suit said, pinching her nipples sharply. "She's a fool."

"There are a million girls like her," Light suit added, pulling a pair of nipple clamps out of the top drawer of the dresser. "And they are smarter, they know more languages, and they know how to behave when they are being examined. Or they can be taught."

Sharon winced and whimpered as Dark suit started to twist her nipples back and forth. Why were they talking about her like she wasn't there?

"She, on the other hand, seems to have a talent for not learning," Light suit continued. He passed the clamps to his companion, who attached them quickly, making her cry out. "When we saw her photograph, we thought she might be worthwhile. Now, we are sure that she is not. Which is a shame for this house. Don't you agree, Michael?"

"Yes, of course," Michael said, tugging on the chain. "But we will have success with them in the winter. For now, let's see if this girl has any potential at all. There are places where the brains don't matter."

Sharon started to open her mouth to say something, anything, but all that came out was a little scream when Michael dragged her down to her knees by the chain that linked her nipples. Light suit got behind her and pushed her head down with his foot, pressing her face into Michael's narrow, polished walking boot. "Lick!" he shouted down at her. "Show us what a slave you are!"

Quickly she lapped her tongue out, running across shiny smooth leather while the man behind her smashed his hand into her again and again, hitting her thighs and the sides of her upturned ass, places where it hurt a lot. Sharon moaned and cried out, and her mouth was pressed even harder against the man's boots.

"She's useless!" The man behind her said. He switched to a torrent of Italian, and while he was speaking thrust two fingers into her, twisting them around as if to determine her size and depth. He found her wet, despite her obvious discomfort, and his announcement of that fact led to her being pushed around until her lips were on his boots, so that Michael could explore her too.

"What a pity she's such a ... difficult case," Michael said, wiping his fingers across her back. He took his belt off and doubled it in one hand. "Let's see if she can run. Run, little doggy, around the room!" He swung the belt fast and hard, and when it connected, she sprang forward, practically into the other man's legs. Sharon howled like a dog as Michael kept up a steady rhythm of heavy, biting smacks. She tried to get up, and he beat her back down, and then she understood that he wanted her to crawl around the room.

He chased her three times around the room, until bruises began to show faintly on the backs of her thighs. His companion cheered them on lustily, and when they got back to him for the third time, he thrust his hard cock directly into her gasping mouth, before she had a chance to gasp for air. Laughing, he clamped his hands onto her head and held her to him, cutting off her air until her struggles became frantic, and then he pushed her away. With one quick move, he caught her shoulder and arm and spun her around so that Michael could spear her mouth for a while.

Between the two of them, she never caught a full breath. The only time they let her breathe was when they were turning her back and forth, from one to the other. Sharon became dizzy, and started to cry, and one of them, she wasn't sure who, slapped her, hard, across the face. They began to speak exclusively in Italian to each other, and they laughed when she stumbled or choked. They just cuffed her when she gagged.

When it seemed that they had enough of that, the one in the light suit took a turn chasing her around the room, using a heavy wooden paddle to encourage her. Then he tossed things across the room, and made her fetch them in her teeth. The first was a thick, heavy dildo. When she brought it back, he shoved it deeply into her, and warned her to keep it in while she went after things like another pair of nipple clamps (which he then put on her, replacing the first pair), a pair of handcuffs (which also went on, locking her hands behind her), and finally a strip of condoms.

They used her in tandem, Michael in her mouth and the other up her tight ass. She screamed against the cock in her mouth, the pressure from the dildo and the anal intrusion almost too much for her to take. Light suit, whose presence in her asshole was so terrible and so good, reached under her and began to play with the dildo, pulling it out when he was in, pushing it in when he pulled out, and when Michael picked up the chain attached to her nipple clamps and tugged on it to bring her mouth up against his pubic bone, she screamed again, a sound well muffled and barely heeded.

They switched places after a while.

And then again.

They never spoke to her, other than to yell a command to change positions. And every time she seemed to come close to actually enjoying what they were doing, they stopped, and brought out more items of torture to play with. They both beat her with riding crops, making her race from one side of the room to the other. They clamped the lips of her cunt and beat the clamps off, and then made her clean them off in her mouth. They put the clamps on her tongue for a while, fucking her mouth with the handles of their crops, before they put her back on her chest and knees for them to take turns in whatever hole suited them.

Sharon didn't know who was fucking her any-more. They had blindfolded her at one time or another, and now, she was positive that they were both in her at once, one up her cunt and the other in her ass. A thick gag with a mouthpiece shaped like a cockhead spread her jaws open. The sounds she made might have been pleas, or they might have been sounds of pain or joy. When the two men final-ly finished with her, she wasn't sure what she was hearing or saying. She only knew that she would do anything to make them stop. When the gag came out, she eagerly kissed whatever was offered to her, an ass, a foot, a cock, a hand, a dildo, anything....

"Shall we visit Anderson and see what she has this year?" Michael said in English as they dressed. Sharon lay between them, her hands still behind her back, the blindfold still on, the dildo sticking half out of her ass. Assorted nipple clamps and paddles and riding crops lay scattered on the floor beside her.

"We can give her a call from here and see if she's receiving," the other man said. "I would hate to just, as they say, barge in on her."

"Good. Let's go see Alexandra again, and then we'll get on our way."

Sharon panted and sobbed, and her voice broke as she shifted around, trying to get into a position where the pain wasn't so bad. Her cries faded into hiccups, and she kicked weakly, unable to summon the energy to get up on her knees. She didn't know how long she lay there until someone touched her. She jerked, her whole body tensing.

"Be still," Chris said, unlocking the cuffs. "It's me." He removed them carefully, and massaged her

358 / *Sara Adamson*

wrists for a moment before removing the dildo from her, and then the blindfold.

"Oh, god," she sobbed, bringing her hands around to shield her eyes. "God, that was fucked up."

"Remember your language," Chris warned. He gestured toward the scattered toys. "Clean these things up and bring them downstairs. You can give them to Claudia to put away after you've washed the appropriate items."

Sharon gazed up at him in amazement. He didn't have the least sympathy for her condition. "You ... please, Chris," she swallowed bile. "Can't you see? I'm ... I think I'm hurt. I can't do anything now! How could you ... do you know what they did?!"

"They used you," Grendel said. She snapped her head up. She hadn't seen him standing in the doorway!

"They used you like a piece of property can be used, Sharon." He leaned against the jamb, and looked down at her with the patience of a good teacher. "They broke no rule or code of conduct that we apply in this house, and they stayed within the parameters you set yourself."

"What do you mean?" Sharon asked, her voice almost a shriek. "That this was just a test?"

"Don't you dare take that tone with me, missy!" Grendel drew himself up. "That was no test, my dear, it was just Alex being generous and hospitable to two business associates. And before I go and let Chris get on with the punishment you just earned yourself, I'll let you in on something interesting. Both Michael and Jules are single men. Either of them would be eligible for the special rider in your contract."

Sharon pushed herself up on her hands. "At least punish me yourself, you son of a bi——!" she screamed. Chris cut her off with a vicious backhand slap, which threw her back to the floor.

Grendel stopped without turning back. He said, "Double it!" and left.

That night, Sharon had to be helped up the stairs. Her ass and the backs of her thighs were black and blue, and her back was tender up through her shoulders. She whimpered when anything touched her nipples, and couldn't find a position to lie in without leaning on something that hurt.

Her condition was sobering. Even the cuts on Robert's back hadn't been that bad. He had been able to walk away, go back to work, and even sleep on his back without much of a problem. But Sharon had been beaten methodically, heavily, and with the sole purpose of causing her pain she would never forget. Claudia whispered to Robert that she had seen Chris carrying several rubber implements back to Grendel's side of the house when he had finished with Sharon. Rubber, they both knew, hurt more and marked less. Whatever had marked poor Sharon had probably been nightmarish. She, of course, refused to talk about it.

Chris had drawn their attention to Sharon and her condition when she didn't appear for dinner. "Sharon is being severely disciplined," he had said. "I would advise you all to give the condition of her body some serious consideration. What has been done to her is something none of you may escape. For your edification, the reason for the severity was clear and profound disrespect for Master Grendel, in the form of her address toward him and her demands for his attention. I hope you will all learn from her example."

They looked at her and they all did learn. To the pits of their stomachs and curling through their sex, it hammered home one thing for sure. That could have been any of them.

While Sharon groaned and shifted to find some way to lie comfortably, Robert sighed with her. Finally, he got up and walked over to her bed, carrying his pillow. "Sharon," he said softly. "Here. Sit up a little, and let me show you how to do it."

Sharon shifted up on one elbow and looked at him. Her eyes looked black from all her crying, and her lip was swollen.

"Listen," Robert said. "I used to come home like that a lot. You have to give yourself different places to support your body." He showed her how to fold his pillow up and lean against it, her body on its side, the pillow raising her belly just a little bit, so she could wrap herself around it. When he was finished, she did actually feel a little more comfortable. She whispered "Thank you," as he went back to his bed.

"You're a good guy," Brian said, leaning back on his arms.

Robert shook his head. "I've never seen anyone work a woman like that."

"Hey. Equal opportunity slave-training," Brian said lightly. "They'll beat and fuck us all to death, regardless of gender, race, creed, color, or sexual orientation."

"Let's not talk about that," Claudia said, sitting up. "I think it's about time you told us your story, Brian."

"Yeah," Robert agreed. "If it's as long and boring as you've made it out to be, maybe it'll help Sharon fall asleep."

"Hmm. More likely give her nightmares," Brian quipped. But he looked at his fellow slaves, and saw that they were serious, so he pulled himself up to sit cross-legged, and thought about it for a little while. Then he began to speak.

Chapter Nineteen

Brian's Story

I suppose that my story begins back when I was a kid. I grew up in Brooklyn, in this nice neighborhood with lots of kids and trees. Very residential, very middle class. I was best pals with a kid named Nick, and we played together for, hell, years and years. Up to high school, I guess. When we were about ten or something, we got into comic books, like all kids do for a while. But we liked the weird stuff. Not the pumped-up guys in their Danskins, no, that was for the regular sissies. Everyone read those. No, we went for the different ones, like war comics and horror magazines with pictures of vampires and gore on the covers. And Westerns. Can't forget the Westerns, because that's where I first saw this hero.

He wasn't even like any of the others. Cowboy gun-slingers were pretty standard. They were all waspy-looking, fresh-faced pretty guys who wore neatly pressed jeans and chaps and had names like "The Something Kid." But there was this one book that was about an Indian hero. *Thunder, Native Warrior*, was the name of the comic and his name. And he was so hot. He was taller than the other Indians and bigger. He could run faster, outfight a whole battalion of cavalry, and then saunter into town to beat up the rednecks in the local saloon. He had this drop-dead gorgeous Indian maiden who was really hot for him, and every couple of issues, some white girl would fall for him and cause some plot twist, but he didn't have any time for them. He was always out with the guys, hunting, or discovering hidden treasures before some greedy white guy took it all, or saving innocent people from cattle stampedes or some other happy shit. And without fail, every issue, he'd be on the cover in one of two poses.

Either he'd be standing triumphant over a fallen enemy, gazing off into the distance, or he'd be in some kind of weird bondage with some filthy, leering cowboy holding a whip or a branding iron that looked like it was aiming for a tit or for his loin-cloth.

He was the ultimate switch. He was either stomping heads and getting them to beg for mercy, or he was getting beaten up by a gang of clod-busters. And all of this dressed in nothing more than this decorated strip of leather between his legs and a pair of high lace-up boots. I guess he got me as hot as a little kid can get. Nick and I would fool around sometimes, and I'd play the evil Nazi to his

Captain Victory, and he'd be the mad scientist to my monster or werewolf, and then I'd get to be Thunder while he was a raging horde of cowboys with yards of clothesline and sticks that we pretended were branding irons.

Now, I figure if you grow up with memories like this, you gotta know what you want when your body tells you to go out and find it. I sure did. I just didn't exactly know how to get it. So for a lot of years, I played around, dating girls, reading cheap porn, trading dirty stories with the guys, you know, typical stuff. When I was working full-time, I found a girlfriend who was willing to be a little kinky with me, and we had fun for a while. She and I would buy these dirty magazines and read these fake letters to each other, or we'd rent X-rated videos, and then we'd decide what we wanted to do. If we liked it, we'd do it again.

Soon, we had a regular menu of kinky sex scenes. We'd say, "Oh, let's do the teenage virgin scene tonight" or maybe "the jailhouse scene." It didn't take her too long to figure out what got my engine going. The thing I liked best was "new man in the cellblock," where she'd tie me to the bed, or over the back of her couch, and use her vibrator to fuck the hell out of my ass, telling me how many men were raping me in one night. Sometimes I'd come without even knowing it! In the beginning, she thought it was really hot. I mean, all her girlfriends had these jerk, asshole boyfriends who had too much macho and slapped them around or treated them like dirt. But she had a guy who was so open-minded; he liked to have her fuck him up the ass. She seemed to get off on it, and I always tried my best to satisfy her fantasies when she wanted them.

I can't say that anything exactly went bad with our relationship, except that we both might have wanted something different and were killing some pretty pleasurable time with each other. I don't think we were ever in love, but we were sure in lust! I noticed that she was getting a little bored before she did, and I started looking for something else to do. We both started seeing other people, and we just kind of drifted apart. The best thing about it was that we remained friends. I'd always call her when my night went well, and we even did phone sex for a while. She still calls me when she wants to chat.

After her, I just hung out and wandered around for a while. The memories of the sex we had kept gnawing away at me, though. The image of a real man fucking me became a regular part of my jerk-off fantasies. Sometimes he would be dark and have long black hair, just like Thunder. It was only a matter of time before I hit my first gay bar.

New York is heaven for a gay guy. You can find anything in the community there. I hit bars for dancers, for cross-dressers, for young punks, and for latino boys. I shook it down with the party crowd, went to after-hours clubs, and stood for hours in crowded, smoky bars with older guys in leather and denim. It didn't take me long at all to figure out where I belonged.

At first, I was totally lost. I didn't know a thing about keys, hankies, tops and bottoms, or anything. Let's face it, my entire education came out of magazines designed for straight, middle-aged white men. So I just shut my mouth and drank and listened and watched. It was at one of these bars, The Shaft, I think it was, that I met Ron. Ron was my first master. He was older than me, about forty, I guess, and a real old-guard leatherman. I am so glad I couldn't afford a leather jacket that year, because he once told me that if I had been wearing one, he would have never taken me seriously. You see, the way he was taught, bottoms had to earn their leather. And I was the lowest of the low, inexperienced and raw, and if I was wearing some stuff I just bought off the rack because it looked good, I would only be good enough to play around with.

The way I figure it, whether he was right or wrong, he wore his leathers like he was born in them. And never all shiny and gaudy with studs, like every Mr. Leather Whatever who figures he's big and tough. No, Ron dressed plainly but with style. Black chaps that were custom-made a long time ago. Black T-shirts when he wore shirts, skin tight over his nicely developed chest. The man had pecs that would knock your eyes out! Levi 501s, always. A plain bar vest with no colors or club pins on it, and maybe an armband across his left bicep. Black motorcycle boots, no chains and no spurs or shit like that. And when it was cool enough, his leather jacket.

Some guys called him plain. What he was, though, was austere. Dignified. He didn't need twenty pounds of silver studs to let you know he was a topman. When I asked him if I could buy him a drink, the line I had used to some success on other men, he declined. I was a little confused then, because they always took a free drink, so I tried to think of something else I could offer. Finally, I said, "Is there anything I can get for you?"

"Sure," he said back. "Your ass, over that bar stool."

I guess I fell in love with him that minute. It was so hot, getting spanked by him in that crowded bar, other men laughing and making comments, or just standing around watching intently. And when he pulled me up to face him and breathed smoke in my face, I realized that I had actually cried. He gripped the front of my shirt tight in one hand, and told me that if I wanted more, I'd have to get down and kiss his boots and follow him out without another word.

It was a long way to the door on my hands and knees. I lost sight of his legs in a sea of black leather, and men parted for me so I could catch up. The bouncer laughed as I passed him, but I didn't care. When I got out onto the sidewalk, he pulled me up again and said, softly, "Piss."

And without thinking, I let go, and my hot piss streamed down my pants legs, covering the tops of my boots and dripping gradually onto the ground.

That was the first time I saw him smile. "You've got potential, boy," he said. And then he dragged me home and fucked me silly.

Now, I didn't move in with him or anything. I had a full-time job, and I was taking civil service exams, and I had a life I just couldn't leave behind. But that was OK, because Ron had a lot of other boys he played with, and one special one that I guess was his favorite, so he didn't need me around day and night. But any chance I could, I'd see him and he'd put me through my paces. He was the one who insisted that I join a gym, and he was the one who pierced my nipples. That was an incredible thing, let me tell you. I screamed like a drag queen who missed a sale at Bloomingdale's! But he liked the way they looked, so I kept them. In time, the pain went away, and now they're just hot decorations. A lot of men like them.

One of Ron's friends thought I had a good chance to win this leather contest, and started telling me about them. It seemed like a great deal. You strut around in sexy clothes, make a speech, and wave your dick at the judges, and if you win, they send you on trips to bigger contests, and lots of guys want to fuck you. And if you lose, at least a couple of hundred guys saw you on stage and got to check out the goods. So I signed up to be a contestant.

As far as Ron went, that was a big mistake. When he heard that, the first thing he did was call me up and tell me to get out of it. I wanted to know why. What was the big deal? Well, Ron had this thing about leather contests. He thought they were full of what he called "Naugahyde Nellies," guys who dressed up in new or borrowed leather and faked their interest and dedication to the leather lifestyle. The way Ron saw it, he was living a leather lifestyle, not these guys in fancy sashes, and he resented their automatic role as community leaders.

Well, I have to admit I didn't see it that way. To me, that was all just politics. I figured that Ron just had something against contests or contestants, and that he was trying to pull his topman stuff on me in something he thought mattered to me just to see if I would listen to him. So I argued with him. I told him I was just doing it for fun, and that the world wouldn't end if I just danced around in my underwear a little bit. And then, he told me that if I competed, I could never be his boy.

Now, you gotta understand that I thought I already *was* his boy. Sort of. I mean, we never made it formal or anything, but I called him sir, and he was my man, and I thought of myself as his boy. So I got real hurt, and we yelled at each other, and then he just hung up on me. I was so pissed, I didn't call back. And I entered the damn contest and I came in second place.

That night, it seemed that every guy who didn't sleep with the winner wanted to sleep with me. For weeks, I had my pick. But they were never what I really needed. They weren't tough enough, or top enough, or caring enough. I would go home with them, even spend a weekend with them, and then not miss them when the next weekend came around.

I floated around like that for a while, and even dated another woman for a few months. I found two guys who I thought I could call master, but neither one of them worked out. One of them wanted a slave who was more of a muscle-guy, and the other was really a bottom himself, and he hoped he could bring out my top side. Then I heard about another contest, and signed up for that one. I hadn't talked to Ron in almost a year. I avoided The Shaft on nights when he used to go.

During the second contest I competed in, suddenly I knew I wasn't going to win this time either. First of all, there were only four contestants. One was sponsored by this local gym, and he was a walking statue, man, just perfect. Muscles on his muscles, and a jock that was so stuffed with meat, you could have sliced it for lunch. The other guy was all hairy, and kind of older-looking and short, but the last guy, the only other contestant, was the producer's lover, or boy, or whatever. And two of the judges had just spent the week sightseeing with the guy. I mean, what a set-up. I went through it feeling like the world's biggest asshole. When I came in third, I wanted to shove the cheap plastic trophy up the producer's nose, and the long-stemmed rose up his boy's ass, and get the hell out of the contest world, the scene, and the leather life.

What I didn't know when I stomped off to get my clothes was that this guy named Paul saw me from the audience. He came looking for me after-ward. While I was pulling on jeans and thinking of how soon I could move out of New York, he asked me if I was seeing anyone right now. I thought he was just another star fucker so I figured, maybe I'll get laid tonight and feel better in the morning. So I told him I was single. And then he smiled. He told me that he knew what I needed, and that if I did, I could find him outside where the air was cleaner.

He reminded me of Ron, even though he was smaller and had a beard. I didn't have anything to lose, so I met him outside. He had a motorcycle and a spare helmet, and I went back to his place with him.

I guess I sound easy. I'm not, really. It's just that some kinds of men make me ready to give up every-thing for them. And Paul, like Ron, was real. I had enough of prancing around in my underwear. I lost Ron, and I didn't intend to lose Paul.

What I didn't know about Paul was that he was a spotter, or an agent, for the Marketplace. He told me that he was personally responsible for over thirty people entering the system. He had no slaves of his own, at least not in the apartment he was living in when he met me, and he wasn't interested in them. What he liked, he told me, was finding good merchandise, testing it out, and sending it on. Would I like to be tested?

At that point, I was so hot, I would have agreed to be sold away, lock, stock, and barrel! And so for a couple of weeks, he beat me, tied me up, trained me to talk in certain ways, and fucked me standing, kneeling, sitting, bent over, upside down, on my belly, on my back, and every which way but out the door. And he told me he liked what he saw. But if I was serious, he said, I'd need to quit my job and move in with him, to see if I could live it full-time.

It took a lot of thought, but I decided I'd give it a try. And those weeks were the best weeks I ever had in my entire life. I was his total slave. He used me any way he wanted to, any time he wanted to. He stopped dealing with me like a human being and made sure I could take it. And I kept on doing my best to please him. Once I made the commitment to leave my job, I had to. I had no where else to go. So I kept asking him when I could go to the Marketplace. Over and over again, until he finally said I was probably as ready as I'd ever be, and he called his old pal Grendel. And that is how I ended up here.

Chapter Twenty

It took several days for Sharon to really recover, but her work still had to be done or they all suffered. Whatever she couldn't do, the others chipped in to help with, warning her that they couldn't keep up that kind of pace forever. Sharon wisely held her tongue and tried to do as much as she could, and no one had to be beaten much more than usual.

It was disturbing, however, when Robert was called out to the field behind the paddock, and ordered to do something that just didn't compute. Sharon was lying on the grass, still damp from the hosing that Jack gave her before she went back to the house. Alexandra was there, waiting for Jack to bring out her favorite gelding, and she just pointed at Sharon and told Robert to "Fuck her."

"Ma'am?" Robert said, hesitantly. He had just bid

farewell to his sensei, and his jockstrap was still knotted into a little ball in one hand.

"Don't make me repeat myself, Robert. Just do it. I want to watch. Do you need some help?"

Robert swallowed hard and looked down. He certainly did. Sharon was told to get to work, and when her now-familiar lips caressed him, he sighed and moaned until she drew back from a healthy erection. She affixed a condom neatly on him, covering it with her mouth in one smooth motion. She was so good, he barely noticed what she was doing. With a nod from Alex, she lay back down, gingerly, because of the bruises still on her rear.

"Please, ma'am," Robert said, kneeling down, "I don't mean to be disrespectful, but shall we try another position? I don't want to hurt her."

"How considerate," Alex agreed. "Very well, try it this way."

Facing each other, Robert helped her wrap one leg up around his hip. Like animals in the field, he suddenly flashed, the image burning through his soul.

"Oh, yeah," Sharon sighed, as he slipped into her. "Oh, yeah, fill me up!"

Robert closed his eyes. The fantasy of being a beast mating before an amused owner, a performing animal doing tricks out in the field, slaves together, wrestling for mistress' amusement and titillation …

He trembled and began to stroke back and forth, holding onto Sharon, holding her up at one point. He heard Alexandra call out to him to lift her up, and he did, turning onto his own back, keeping himself inside her and giving her time to adjust her balance on him. As she rose above him, he closed his eyes again, and remembered how this was the way his mistress had used him; with several long, shuddering thrusts upward, he drew close to coming.

"Ma'am!" He cried out. "Oh, ma'am, please, please, I'm ... shall I hold it, ma'am?" He barely knew if he could. The heat of the sun, the sensuous feel of the grass, and the steady, hungry rocking of the woman above him were overwhelming. He groaned, almost drowning out Alex's reply.

"No, don't hold it, Robert," Alex said, smiling. "Finish well. And then get back to work." She took the reins from Jack and mounted her horse, and watched Robert and Sharon rock and thrust their way to pleasure.

It was all preparation for a very special entertainment coming up soon.

"What?" Robert was so flustered that he lost control of his role. But Alex was pleased to note that his voice remained consistent with his normal one. He no longer scaled it up when he was surprised or in pain.

"Claudia has asked for you to be her first male partner in typical heterosexual-style intercourse," Alex repeated. "And, after a consultation with her mistress and several days of making sure that you could serve properly and that she was not really that much afraid of the process, we've decided to allow her this boon. We're doing it tomorrow night."

"Um, ma'am?" Robert said. "Please ... *we* are doing it tomorrow night?"

"Yep." Alex leaned back in her chair and smiled.

"Grendel had an idea that he'd like to watch. I agree; it's something we don't have a chance to witness every day. So we will be present when the deed it done, and we expect a certain amount of entertainment from it. When Sharon asks if you'd like a blowjob tomorrow, I think you should turn her down; save yourself for Claudia. In fact"—she leaned forward and jotted down a note—"I'll tell Claudia the same thing. Sharon will think she's getting a day off! Well, that's it for tonight, Robert; you may go now."

"Yes, ma'am. Thank you, ma'am." In a daze, Robert stood, bowed, and left.

"Are you sure?" Robert whispered. He and Claudia were alone in the bathroom, but he felt a foolish compulsion to keep his voice down, if only for her modesty. "You can do so much better! Surely Grendel—"

Claudia shook her head firmly. "He doesn't really want to, Robert, and ... well, he's very nice, and I'm sure he would be gentle, but ... I like you. You're kind, and smart, and you're always nice to everyone. Even to Sharon, who calls you names and makes fun of you all the time. If we weren't slaves, I'd, um ..." She blushed. "I'd like to be your friend. I think you could be a lot of fun. And I know you'll try to make me happy."

Robert was taken aback by her simple honesty, and he had to sit on the only seat available. He clasped his hands together and sighed, and looked so comical that Claudia giggled. When he realized what she was laughing at, he stood back up and faced her.

"I'd never want to hurt you," he said firmly. "And if this is what you want, I'll do it. I hope I'm good enough for you, Claudia. I'll ... I'll be the best I can."

She ran to him and hugged him, the first hug he'd felt in months. Together, they stood on the cool tile, breathing into each other and relaxing in each other's arms.

It was truly an event. Claudia and Robert were even sent to different ends of the house to clean up after dinner, and Sharon was told to prepare herself for some use. Neither Brian nor Sharon was told exactly what was happening.

Brian was summoned to Alexandra's playroom slightly ahead of time, where he was met by Chris. Chris examined him, and then buckled restraints on his wrists and ankles.

"I didn't realize that I was going to be part of what's happening tonight," Brian said.

"You're not really," Chris replied. "And sadly, you still talk too much. Open." A gag was stuffed into Brian's mouth, and buckled around his head. A half-hood, with a blindfold, followed it, and then Brian was pressed down onto all fours. He grunted into the gag as a buttplug invaded his asshole.

His ankles were linked together, and something pushed under his belly. It felt like a block of some kind. He bent over it perfectly, his hands and knees touching the carpet on either side. Chris attached the wrist cuffs, and then wrapped lengths of leather strap around his forearms, running the straps alongside the box to wrap around Brian's upper thighs. Straps buckled over his shoulders and waist. As

Chris checked each binding, Brian tested them, trying not to move much. It wasn't difficult. The arrangement held him immobile, half-kneeling, half-supported, bound to the box that supported him and strapped into a position he could not stretch in.

He breathed slowly, through his nose, and wondered when the torture would begin. Would he be beaten? His ass was exposed. Would it be hot wax? Yes, he could hear the hiss of a match! He tensed, but nothing fell on him. Instead, he heard matches being lit further away from him. Maybe the whole room was going to be lit by candles. Very romantic, but I can't tell, not with this blindfold on.

Then something did touch his back. He tried to figure out what it was. It wasn't hot or cool, and it just rested, right between his shoulder blades. And then another something joined it. And he was left alone again.

Jeeze, he thought, shifting just a little bit. You'd think I was just a ...

I'm a table, he realized. He tied me up tight so I could stay here for a long time, and he put things on my back. I'm a table. The realization sent a shiver through his body, and he resisted the urge to fight the bondage. It's OK, he tried to tell himself. It's OK. I can handle this. It's not that bad. Maybe it's just for a little while. And in the darkness and silence, he waited for the others to show up.

He didn't know that Sharon was also being blindfolded and bound in the same room. But instead of binding her to something, Chris just cuffed her hands loosely in front of her. He positioned her a few feet away from Brian, kneeling, and put a leash onto her collar, letting it trail between her breasts.

Neither of Grendel's slaves saw the owners enter, dressed in loose robes and carrying drinks. The cushions that Chris had arranged in front of Brian were there for the owners' comfort. They sank down on them with accustomed ease, rearranging them for convenience. Their drinks went onto the coasters thoughtfully placed on Brian's back.

Robert and Claudia came in together, following Chris. As they were told, they bowed to Alex and Grendel, and then went to the platform of mats made for them on Alex's low table. Chris had told them that there would be supplies handy. Robert noted the presence of lubricant and condoms, and he fought the continual blushing that had come over him when Claudia slipped her hand in his and gave him a quick kiss outside the door.

The room was mostly shadowed, with light coming from flickering candles placed on shelves and on the corners of equipment. Claudia was grateful that it seemed the owners could see her better than she could see them. Thinking of this day, this time, had given her a sense of romance and naughtiness at the same time. How terrible to make love in front of people, like you were doing some kind of sex show! And how wonderful to do it for the pleasure of a mistress, with someone who is kind and loving, in a room designed for the most exotic sensual encounters. She turned and kissed Robert again, full on the mouth, surprising him.

In the shadows, Grendel smiled. He reached over to his right and found Sharon's leash, and tugged. Carefully, he guided her to his lap, bending her

head down to his groin. Alex gave him a brief
glance and drank some more. She would wait until
something interesting was happening in front of
them. She replaced her glass on Brian's back and
turned her attention back to the two slaves.

It took Robert a moment to respond, but when he
realized that the time had come, he took Claudia
into his arms and kissed her back, passionately. She
felt good in his arms, small and strong, all curves
and curls, smelling of soap and flowers. He ran one
gentle hand through her hair, and then started running kisses over her throat and then across her
shoulders. She tried to do the same for him, but he
was taller and more insistent, and she relaxed in his
arms and let him do as he pleased.

"Very nice," Grendel muttered. Alex wasn't sure
if he was referring to what he was watching or what
he was feeling, and she smiled again.

Robert slid down to his knees, sinking into the
soft mats, and began to kiss and lick at Claudia's
belly, moving his mouth down the way Alex had
taught him. This time, Grendel smiled. He pulled
Sharon away from him and passed her leash to
Alexandra, who reeled her in. Watching Robert perform as he was taught and feeling Sharon perform
as *she* was taught was a nice rush. Alex leaned back
and spread her legs wider, so she was more comfortable.

Robert was eager to please Claudia. And she was
more than eager to be pleased. He tasted her arousal
as soon as he dipped his mouth to the pink mound
between her legs, and they both moaned together.
She pressed his head to her, and he responded by
doing what he did when Alex did the same. He

aimed for the places that she liked best and fastened onto them with a steady, long washing of his tongue, pulling slightly with his lips, and never with his teeth, until she squirmed and moved her hips to meet him.

"Nice," Alex sighed, and then smiled broadly, because she wasn't sure if it was what she was watching or Sharon's excellent services. She waited a few more moments and then passed Sharon back to Gren. This was certainly the right way to watch an erotic performance, even one as vanilla as this one.

Claudia and Robert ended up lying down, with Robert continuing to work between her legs. Her gasps and moans provided the only soundtrack needed, and Grendel and Alex found themselves enjoying the sight. For all their shyness when they had arrived, the two "French maids" were certainly behaving like a couple of horny kids on a hot date, with hands everywhere and moans and sighs every minute. When Claudia pulled herself away and turned to Robert and went down on him in one smooth motion, taking a great deal of his fat cock into her little mouth, Alex reached out and dragged Sharon off of Grendel and back to her. Grendel chuckled and picked up his neglected drink.

It took a while for Robert to realize that he had something he had to do. Trading oral attentions with Claudia was something he could keep doing all night, with or without an audience! But their eyes met, bleary with pleasure and hunger, and she nodded. He reached for the rubber and put it on himself. And despite the copious natural lubrication which had made little wet spots all over the mats, he added more to the head of his cock, and carefully lowered himself into place. He rubbed the head against her lips, and up against the hood over her clit, and she thrust her hips up to meet him over and over again. Finally, she lifted one leg up behind his back, and put a hand between them to guide him into her.

"Now!" she gasped, pushing up toward him.

"Oh, yes!" he hissed back, meeting her. It was easy and slow, and she cried out as she was filled, a cry of pleasure and raw lust. He gasped at her intense heat, the feeling of being inside her, and his hips thrust all the way down, pinning her and pressing into her, trapping her hand between them, where her fingers touched her clit.

"Yes," Alex sighed, leaning back again. "Good girl." She didn't protest as Grendel pulled Sharon back.

"Oh yes," Robert's brain echoed over and over. So good! So hot, so nice! Ah, Claudia, I love you, I'll always love you.... He opened his eyes, kissed her, and fell into a slow, steady thrusting, bringing his weight off of her, and easing back. When she realized what he was doing, she shifted comfortably, so he could put his arms underneath her. They rolled together, and while they were on their sides, she felt a familiar tremor growing, and clasped her leg tighter around him.

"Do it, do it!" she begged, not knowing what to say.

But Robert guessed, and he pulled her closer to him, rocking faster and stronger. In no time, she came, throwing her head back and banging her hips against him. Her curls flew back and forth as her body shuddered, and he groaned as he felt the contractions of her walls around him. But he stayed hard, stayed even and strong, and as she gasped for breath and started to recover, he twisted and pulled her along with him so that she was now on top.

When she realized that she was in control now, she braced herself on his chest and moved her hips around, leaning forward. The pressure and the slow circles drove Robert mad, and he clutched at the edges of the mats to keep himself from grabbing her. When he felt that he could control it, he lifted his hands and lightly, very lightly, brushed his fingers across her nipples. She responded by sighing and grinding down into him.

"Harder," Alexandra softly urged. She didn't say it very loud, but Robert's fingers closed into little pincers, and he pinched Claudia's nipples, making her moan in pleasure. Alex smiled and reached one hand out. Grendel sighed and passed Sharon back.

It didn't take long for Claudia to reach her second orgasm, and then her third followed quickly. By that time, Robert was more than ready to come himself. He knew he didn't have to ask permission. His instructions were to get Claudia off and do it well, and then to take care of himself. When the tremors and contractions of her third orgasm subsided, he concentrated on thrusting up at her, surprising her but making her smile. When he couldn't take it any more, he pulled her down to him and hugged her body to his, cupping her asscheeks as he shot his come, holding onto her like she was the best lover he would ever have, knowing that this would be a memory seared into him for life. His hips thrust until every drop of come in him was gone, and when he slipped out of her, they both exchanged sad, loving glances.

"Excellently done," Grendel said softly. "Very good."

"Thank you, sir" came wearily from the two slaves. Grendel stood and rebelted his robe. "A very nice evening. See you tomorrow, Alex."

"Good night," Alex said, waving. She had already pushed Sharon away, and magically, Chris was there to take her. "All right, you two, you've earned a reward. Come on up with me."

Two matching smiles.

Chris waited until they were gone to untie Sharon and remove her blindfold, and then he went to unfasten Brian. They were both in tears, and Chris walked them back to their room in silence.

They lay on their beds, rubbing wrists and ankles and stretching and wiping their tears away with harsh, jerky motions.

"I hate this," Sharon said, shivering. She wrapped her blanket around her body. "I hate not being sent for and I hate being blindfolded and not knowing who the hell I'm doing, and I hate the whole fucking system!"

"Well, how do you think I feel?" Brian demanded. "At least you're being fucked! You weren't a goddamned table!"

"Is that what you were?" she asked in amazement.

"Didn't you notice? Oh, yeah, you were blindfolded. Well, meet Brian, the human end table." He spread his arms. "What did you end up doing?"

"I'm pretty sure that Grendel and Alex passed me back and forth," she admitted. "I think it was them. It wasn't Claudia for sure, and it wasn't Robert, and it didn't smell like Jack, and there's no other women here, so I guess I'm right."

"So? At least they used you. I haven't even seen Grendel's cock, and Alexandra won't touch me." Brian lowered his head in a rush of self-pity. "The only guy who has ever treated me even halfway human is Chris, and he can't stand me. I can't blame him, actually."

"Now you sound like Robert!" Sharon declared.

"No, really. I did something to him, the first day we were here. And I guess he hasn't forgotten it."

"Oh yeah? What didja do?" Sharon sat up, wrapped in her blanket.

Brian considered telling her. Chris did say that some people knew, didn't he? And that he wasn't sensitive about it? Be honest, Brian told himself. You're pissed off, and the little bastard isn't helping. You might as well get some kind of kick by blowing his cover.

"Chris ... he's not like a regular guy," he said cautiously.

"What do you mean? Is he deformed or something?"

"I guess. Kind of. You see, when I was in Grendel's office for the first time, he told me to suck Chris's cock. And I said, sure, no problem, because I figured, little guy, little cock, and I get to look good. So I was totally surprised when Chris starts hauling this monster out of his pants. And it was big, all right. But there was something a little wrong with it...."

It wasn't real.

It was beautiful, though. Highly detailed and custom-

formed, it even had wisps of black, curly hair matted at the base, and the hint of balls underneath it. The head was pleasingly plum-shaped, and there was even a slight circumcision scar behind it. The texture looked soft, but the heft and curve looked solid enough for fucking. A connoisseur's cock, to be sure.

Brian had never seen a dildo that obviously had such attention paid to its design. But even as his mind registered that, he had recoiled from it, words spilling thoughtlessly from his mouth.

"It's not real!"

"And that's when I knew I fucked up, big time. I wanted to stuff those words right back down my throat, but I said them, and they wouldn't let me have another chance. And that's why I figure he hates me, and why Grendel won't even throw me a mercy fuck."

Sharon stared. "You mean the little bastard doesn't have a dick?"

"Well, he's got one, it's just not attached to his body." Brian shrugged. "Who knows why."

"Maybe he's a freak," Sharon suggested. "Like he was born without one."

"Or maybe he had it cut off," Brian suggested. "In an accident." He winced.

"Maybe he was gonna be a woman once and changed his mind too late," Sharon mused. "Like the way Robert wanted to have his dick cut off for his mistress."

"No, if that was true, he'd have tits, and he would have done hormones and everything," Brian explained. "It's like Robert said, you can't just go in and ask them to carve your dick off; you've got to go through therapy and stuff. I don't know why he hasn't got one, but he doesn't. And that's why I'm in the doghouse."

Sharon nodded, but was lost in her own thoughts. She knew people who wore fake dicks. And they were all ...

"Hey!" she said suddenly. "Do you think Chris is a dyke?"

"Huh?" Brian looked at her as if she were crazy. "What the hell do you mean? Of course he's not a dyke, he's a guy!"

"Yeah, but how do you know?" Sharon asked, warming to her theory. "I mean, he could just be a dyke with a real short haircut who doesn't have real big tits. Did you ever see his chest? No, right? And does he have a mustache or a beard? No, right?"

"He can grow one," Robert said, waving one hand at her. "I don't have a mustache and I'm not a dyke. Besides, I've known some dykes with huge—"

"Yeah, but what about his chest, huh? And what about the fact that he's so short? He'd be an average woman, right? But he's a short guy! He's a dyke in drag!"

"Sharon, you're nuts," Brian insisted. "I saw him dressed up for a leather bar, OK? I've been close enough to him to smell him, and he's a guy. He's just a short guy without a dick, that's all. I mean, who knows? He might have a real dick under there, but it's real small. Or maybe he was wearing the fake one just for show, to freak me out. It's no big deal, it was just my theory for why he hates me."

"Where did you say his room was?" Sharon asked.

"On Grendel's side, third floor ... hey, where are you going?"

"Oh," Sharon said, standing up, "the bathroom. I gotta pee."

"Sharon," Brian warned. "You can get into a lot of trouble if you do this. You know the rules."

"I'm just going to the bathroom," she insisted. "Go to sleep, OK?"

It wasn't hard to find, actually. She saw the light under one door, and paused outside of it, listening carefully. There were faint sounds like tapping, which she finally realized was the sound of typing. Hearing it, she smiled and continued down the hall. Claudia had said "suite," and in this house, suites had at least two doors. The next one was unlocked, and she turned the handle and opened it. It was dark inside, a little light coming in from the first room, the outer room, where Chris was still working.

Keep typing, my butch pal, Sharon said to herself. And she tiptoed carefully into this room, the bedroom, following the wall, until she found another door. She was in luck; she had found the bathroom! She went inside and turned on the light after she closed the door behind her. I've got you now, she thought, cheerfully. There's nothing a real butch dyke likes more than a fem type who just loves her big cock!

Now, for evidence. There are things that every woman has to have, no matter how butch, she thought with a smile. She checked under the sink, and in the medicine cabinet. Deodorant, some major national brand. Shampoo, but no conditioner. No facial supplies, either. No birth control pills, no diaphragm, just a pile of condoms and some little tubes of lube. One toothbrush. A steel razor rested on a shelf, and it had a few very short black hairs caught in it. Chris also apparently used the same shaving gel the slaves used. There was an enema bag under the sink.

There were no pads, no tampons, no douche bag, no hairspray, not even the slightest hint that a woman ever used this bathroom. In fact, the magazine that sat on the counter with one page turned back was about motorcycles.

Well, maybe he—she—keeps the stuff hidden, Sharon thought. If I was going in drag all the time, maybe I would hide it, just in case anyone would kind of casually find something and say "Oh-oh!" and get me. She sighed. Well, maybe tomorrow, I can—

The door flew open, and Sharon screamed. Chris stood there, his eyes blazing behind his glasses. When he saw who was standing there, he reached in and grabbed her by the collar and slapped her across the face, hard. Her head snapped back, and he tightened his hold on the chain.

"You idiot!" He shouted at her. "You brazen, stupid, asshole! I could have cut your imbecilic throat!"

That's when Sharon's eyes focussed on the hand holding onto her collar. Chris was holding a big knife in his hand, the steel edge just barely touching her skin. She whimpered and flinched, but he held her.

"What the hell are you doing out of your room? And what are you doing in *my* room?" Chris continued to shout, his hoarse voice echoing in the tiled room.

"Please!" Sharon coughed. "Please ... too ... tight ..."

Chris shook her and loosened his hold. He took the knife out of his clenched hand and put it down on the counter. "Talk!"

"I'm ... I'm sorry," Sharon gasped out. "I just wanted to know ... I wanted you to know ..."

"What?"

"I know about you!" she blurted out. "I know what you are! And I want to be with you!"

Chris let her go entirely and stepped back. The look on his face was anger mixing slowly with confusion. For the first time, she could see what he was wearing. It was the first time she had seen the major-domo only partially dressed. He had on a crisp, white T-shirt that showed off his clearly plain, barrel-shaped chest. The definite shape of a man's chest, with well-spaced nipples, which were noticeable. Sharon felt her belly make little flip-flops.

He was also wearing an open man's robe in a dark red plaid, the type of robe thousands of men get for Christmas gifts. The belt hung down low, almost to his knees. And he was wearing pajama bottoms in a matching pattern.

Someone bought him the set, Sharon thought weirdly. They're always on sale.

"Get inside," Chris said, gesturing. "I think I need to hear this." He picked up the knife and pulled her into his bedroom. There, with the only light coming from the bathroom, he pushed her down to her knees next to his bed, and sat down on the edge.

"Talk," he demanded. "Now."

But she wasn't sure any more! Sharon clenched

her fists and considered. Then, she began to talk. "I ... I know about you," she repeated, hesitantly.

"*What* do you know about me?"

"That ... that you ... that you're not what you look like," she finished lamely.

"Is that so? And what exactly made you break a house rule near the last phase of your training to come and sneak around in my bathroom?"

Sharon moved a little closer to the bed. "Because even though ... I know ... it makes me hot," she said, lowering her voice seductively. "It's all right with me. And ... and it makes you special to me." She leaned forward and gently kissed his knee. "I wanted to be with you."

"Your wants vanished after the first week, Sharon," Chris said, pushing her head away. "And you disobeyed a direct instruction. Grendel will be very displeased. Go back to your room, and we'll deal with this in the morning."

"But wait!" Sharon protested. "Please! Please, Chris, I'll make you happy! I know how, I swear! And I'll never tell anyone!" She threw herself forward, folding her arms around his legs. "Please don't send me back! Give me a chance to please you, you'll see; I mean what I say!"

"Sharon, you haven't made any sense since you came in here!" Chris pried her off him again. "What is this big secret you think you know about me?"

"That you're really a woman!" Sharon blurted out.

"Oh?" Chris sounded amused. "How interesting. Someone will have to tell my mother."

"But you are!" Sharon said, frustrated. "You don't have ... I mean, everyone knows that you've got ... and you're short, and you don't ..." Her arguments—the most telling one an account by a man who admitted that it could have all been a hoax—vanished. She slumped forward and put her head down to the floor. "Oh god, oh god, I just know!" she wailed.

Chris reached out and grasped a handful of her hair and twisted her head up.

"You just know," he savagely mocked. "You just know. So you break rules, you sneak into my rooms, you babble your pitiful stories to me, and you place your entire future on the line in the hopes that I'll be so overwhelmed by your charity that I'll treat you kinder and make your way easier!"

"No!" she gasped.

"Oh yes," Chris insisted. "Well, you just might get more than you bargained for, little Sharon." He pulled up, and she followed his hand, wailing. He pushed her face-first over the edge of the bed and jerked her wrists together up in the small of her back. Standing up behind her, he reached into his crotch and moved in close. His legs pushed hers apart as his hands pushed her body onto the bed.

"So you think I'm a woman," he said, resting against her. "You think I'll like what you have to offer me. Well, here's a taste of what I like, Sharon. Open wide for me. Get your butt up! Higher!"

His fingers thrust into her, three at first, and then four. She groaned and cried into the bed as he rammed them in and out of her brutally, spreading her open and working her until it hurt, it hurt, it hurt!

"Have you ever been fisted, Sharon? I like fisting."

"No!" Sharon howled. "Please, please, no, please!"

"No? Then I guess you wouldn't be too good at making me happy, would you?" The fingers were jerked out, and he let go of her arms. She pulled them to her sides, tried to put them under her to brace herself, but he was on top of her in a second. She felt two things nudging into her. A heavy bulge near her leg that could only be the cock that Brian described, and the cold steel edge of the knife Chris had brought with him. It was against the back of her throat.

"I also like knives," Chris hissed into her ear. "I like to cut people a little bit, watch them bleed, let them taste their own blood off the blade when I'm through. I cut pretty designs into their bodies, and they love it. They come back for my special designs, and some of them actually beg to serve me so that they can have the honor of being marked. Shall I do that to you, Sharon?"

"No," she whimpered. "Please, I don't want to be marked, I can't, please, I'll do ... I'll go...."

"Then that's another way we can't have fun, Sharon!" Chris pulled the knife away. "It looks like you're only good for one thing that I like, girl." There was the familiar rustle of a small package being torn open. "And that's fucking. But I don't like it the way you probably do. And that's too fucking bad, because I need it now, and you're handy."

He tore into her asshole with one savage thrust that made her scream. He pushed her face down into the bed, muffling her cries, and began to mercilessly saw back and forth. The small amount of lube on the rubber wasn't nearly enough, and Sharon wailed a continuous stream of promises, pleases, and inarticulate sounds of pain. Finally, he pulled out and dragged her off the bed.

"Aren't you happy to be pleasing me?" he asked, throwing her down on the floor.

"Yes!" she cried. "Yes, anything!"

"Put your head down! Get your ass up! Crawl back to the bathroom, you moron, and keep your face to the floor! Let's finish this where you started it!" He dragged her there, her arms and legs trembling, and as she laid her cheek on the cool tiles, she could hear him opening the medicine chest. She was so grateful for the snapping sound of the bottle of lube opening that she kissed his bare foot near her.

"I didn't say you could do that!" he snapped. "Put those lips on the fucking floor! That's it, kiss it! Lick it! And stay there!"

His reentry was smoother, but not that much less painful. Under his steady, harsh pounding, she kept her tongue to the floor, washing the same space of tile with her tongue, dripping tears and spit on it, making incoherent cries. Finally, with several long, swift strokes that made her feel like he was going to burst through her body in another second, he shuddered against her, and she could swear that she felt the heat of his cock as his throat made a series of deep growls. He ground his hips into her, and then jerked the cock out all at once, before it ... softened?

Sharon cried. She was exhausted, humiliated, afraid, and now confused. When he got up and walked away, she just slumped down on the floor and shivered and moaned until he came back. He bent down to examine her, and then stood back. He watched her sob for a while.

"Get up," he finally said, nudging her. She needed his help, and he escorted her through the halls and back to her room. Brian was awake, his eyes open when Chris walked in, and he didn't even try to pretend he had been asleep. Chris put Sharon in her bed and walked out without saying a word. Brian listened to the sobs for a while, and then rolled over and put his arm over his ear. He didn't want to know.

In another wing of the house, Alex slept, with one slave on either side of her, their bodies curled toward her. It was the first time any of them had actually shared a bed with an owner.

Chapter Twenty-One

When the servants came back, the slaves were so used to doing almost everything that it took a day or two to readjust to the revised schedules. They had all officially entered the last phases of their basic training, and now came the specific lessons in formal behavior and in all the knowledge a slave has to have before entering the Marketplace. It wasn't all about how and when to bow, either. They had to learn the hierarchy of the system, and how to deal with it, how to make contact with it if they were lost, how to treat people from the Marketplace in mixed situations, and which rules must be obeyed in which circumstances. Their questions were rapidly used up on items of history and fact about the system they were—hopefully—about to enter. And they learned what happens when someone betrays that system.

"To be shunned by the Marketplace is to be sure that the rest of your life is spent doing the very things you four are all escaping from," Chris explained one afternoon. "Little organizations of dilettantes, shallow displays of crude imitations of the real thing, purveyors of pornography for idiots, and casual players who have no concept that people actually live this life. To be shunned is to be forever barred from our meetings, our social events, the sales and the trades, the parties and the resorts...."

"The resorts are real?" Sharon had asked, eagerly.

"Oh, yes," Chris assured her. "Not exactly as portrayed in those trashy novels you like so much, but they do exist. Mr. Elliot and Ms. Selador often like to spend a winter vacation one in the Caribbean."

"Wait," Brian said with a laugh, "why should they want to go? They've got it all right here."

"They go to get away from stupid novices," Chris replied smoothly.

Then there were the intensified lessons in anything that hadn't caught on in the early training. Sharon spent more and more time talking to herself, trying out words and phrases and learning little mental tricks to slow down her speaking rhythms so that she could get words such as "like" and phrases such as "I mean" and "you know?" out of her vocabulary. It was a slow process, combined with her ongoing education about all things that could be called fun.

"Bridge!" she complained one day, drying dishes while Robert washed. "I, uh ... who plays bridge anyway, except for middle-class ladies with nothing else to do?" She had caught that "I mean," and was pleased.

"Millionaires play bridge," Robert told her. "They bet on it, or they pay off in points. Some of them actually become professional bridge players."

"No shit," Sharon said without thinking. "I mean … uh … no kidding?"

Claudia began an intense study of the art of managing a household. Between Chris and Rachel, she got advice and details on everything from building additions to contracting outside labor, from planning weekly schedules to writing out a yearly budget, from researching the soup to buying bulk nuts.

"You keep the file like this, making notes on everyone your owners have on their guest lists. You mark down important things like what you know they're allergic to, what their favorite brandy is, and whether they like cigars after a meal. Make sure to remember to put down their religion!" Rachel showed the slave the space for it on their customized guest cards.

"Religion? Why?"

"Because you can't serve pork or shellfish to Jews and Muslims, that's why. You can ruin an entire evening just by serving the wrong appetizer." Rachel grinned. "The stories I could tell you! Just be sure to know your guests. That's one headache you can take away from your mistress. If she can trust you to plan an evening and not offend anyone or send them puking out the door, you'll have another feather in your cap."

"Thank you, miss," Claudia said sincerely. Her eyes shone whenever she looked at Rachel these days. She was very happy to have her back.

Guests appeared regularly, and the slaves were often examined under less than optimal circumstances. Interrupting them during workouts in the gym was common, as was finding them at some messy or difficult task. But each time, they were expected to pull themselves together and present themselves with grace and style, ready to answer questions, perform movements, or submit to pain or arousal at the guests' whims. Robert's skill as a masseur, Sharon's skills in raw sensuality, Claudia's quick mind, clever tongue, wonderful manners, and her ability to take a very nice beating, and even Brian's eagerness to please, were all becoming strong points for them. They were coached to emphasize these points, and worked harder on the subjects they were weaker in. They could all see the end of the training period approaching, and as their dreams and nightmares melded and mixed, they worked themselves as hard as Chris drove them. None of them could afford to fail.

Brian continued to be the least used and least worked slave of the four. He had plenty of work to do, and spent plenty of time suffering for the same kinds of mistakes and flaws his fellow slaves suffered for, but even Robert had gotten to spend a night with Grendel, and Brian never had. After her major faux pas, Sharon wasn't invited back either, but that was different.

I never did anything wrong! Brian thought. And no matter how he searched his heart, he couldn't see when he possibly could have. If the matter about Chris was of any weight, he surely suffered no more or less after Sharon's ill-advised late night visit to the major-domo. So maybe Chris was right, and it had nothing to do with anything. Sharon certainly never shed any light on the subject, and Brian didn't pursue it.

Brian was, however, the first to see Grendel's workshop. Unlike Alex's studio, which everyone now referred to as her playroom, Grendel's space never changed its name. It was still a workshop, and when Brian was taken there to be worked, it was only to be used as an adjunct to someone else's session. He was central, as a matter of fact, to teaching Robert how to suck cock, something the man had only done once to a real live one. But when Grendel was ready to test Robert's skill, Brian was dismissed. Brian never even got to *see* his master's cock. He began to dream about it.

As the other slaves seemed guided to certain ends and goals, Brian fell further and further into a gray area of no clear definition. It became clear, for example, that Robert, with his football-trained body, his sharp sense of balance and instinct, and his elegant manners, was being set up as a kind of bodyguard/companion. He practiced driving a lot, learning to handle a stretch limo, and studied basic self-defense and several cute disarming tricks with sensei Chen. He studied a little with Chris in matters of deportment, and started escorting Alexandra when she went on short trips. He looked very good in the sharply tailored suit Alex chose for him, his chest filling out the jacket nicely. With a cap on, he looked the very image of a wealthy person's loyal chauffeur: handsome, polite, slightly scholarly, and almost formidable. Brian had to admit that it suited the man perfectly. Robert had gained new confidence that showed in his firm, slow voice, honed by sessions of dramatic and humorous reading of everything from children's poems to famous speeches of Martin Luther King. And when the clothing was off, his firm, trim body was covered with a tangle of fine hairs, nicely masculine yet not overpowering. He had also turned into an accomplished masseur, and a skillful bodyslave, happy to serve in any way commanded, honored to sleep across the threshold when night fell.

Not bad for a six-foot French maid who lisped and whined.

And Claudia, who had wanted nothing more than to go back home, was slowly turning into a manager in her own right. Deeply concerned with appearances, she used that concern and transferred it to caring for how her mistress appeared—and found that planning and managing weren't as hard as they had seemed three weeks ago. Once afraid to raise her voice at all, Brian overheard her yelling at the butcher who sent a less-than-acceptable quality of beef. Her indignation was fierce, her determination amazing, and her ability to demand proper action—and get it!—was nothing short of miraculous. And if her blushes meant anything, her ability to be fun in bed had increased tenfold in the few weeks she had been here. Brian regretted that he couldn't see the night she and Robert did their thing in front of Alex and Gren. He still didn't understand everything that night was about, but he knew that it was something special by the way the two of them still exchanged glances when it was mentioned. He also knew that Grendel had now spent several nights with Claudia, and the way she avoided talking about it suggested that they did more than just talk.

Even Sharon was better. Her attention to improving her language skills was starting to pay off, and she seemed to be able to grasp the essentials of the many entertainment activities she was introduced to. Guests picked her most often to try out, and her looks were definitely going to be an asset for her potential sale. Brian knew she wasn't going to be voice-trained, no way, but still, she was a hot babe with a long list of fun things she could do. And thanks to her many lessons with Robert, she had gained a very limited but still better-than-usual appreciation for the arts like opera and serious theater. She might never be able to engage a master in a game of chess, but she could be counted on to know how to behave in a theater and when to cry at the opera. And she could dance. Who knows? For the right man, she might be perfect.

But I'm going nowhere, Brian realized. And the more he thought about it, the more it scraped away his nerves and his confidence. He had no way of knowing what was going to happen to him, either as a slave in this house, or even as Brian Cohen, the man who gave up his life to live a fantasy. Each night, noticing who was with him and who was kept by one of the owners, he curled into a neat fetal position and cradled his aching stomach, knowing that the pain was really in his head. Each morning, he woke up with a hard-on so bad it hurt, and each indignity or punishment seemed to magnify it until he thought he was going to burst. And each evening, he prayed that his name would be announced by Chris, and he died a little when he didn't hear it.

It wasn't exactly a conscious act when he

watched Claudia cheerfully follow Alex into the house one night, and he found himself on his belly in front of Grendel, begging for a touch. And surely, it wasn't *him* who continued to beg, sincerely, tearfully, and steadily, even while Chris laid the strap on. It wasn't any Brian he knew who begged, not for mercy, but for sir to please, please, just watch, please favor him with a glance. And when the beating stopped, he knew it wasn't *him* who begged for it to continue, if sir so desired, and then begged to be allowed to thank his tormenter. Nor was it *him* who kissed the strap with such passion, and bowed his head to the ground by Grendel's feet, begging forgiveness in words that didn't sound at all like he had gotten them out of a book.

"Well," Grendel said to Chris, who was putting the strap back in its place. "It looks like we've found Brian. Bring him to the workshop." Chris grinned when he bent down to pull the broken man to his feet.

The other three almost needed introductions to the new Brian, a person Chris called "the real Brian" with some measure of satisfaction. The new Brian had lost a great deal of his sarcastic edge, and some of his cynicism. He was tearfully, almost embarrassingly eager to serve, and the difference between the way he managed himself before and now defied language when they tried to explain it. Yes, he was willing and eager before. But it had always seemed that he was doing things because he wanted something—they were all means to an end.

Now, he seemed to take joy in doing anything from clearing the table to sitting on the floor studying while Alex wrote or taking a message to Jack from Grendel.

Rachel tried out the new Brian and pronounced him a major improvement on the old. One rainy afternoon, she took him and Claudia into Grendel's workshop and put them both through their paces, directing them to make love to each other for her amusement, and then to her for her satisfaction, and then back to each other just to see how far they could go. As a consequence, a lot of work didn't get done that day, and Chris's strap was busy that night; but no one regretted it.

Grendel kept his distance, knowing that it had been the key to breaking down Brian's façade of slavery and by doing so, he kept the boy hungry. Slowly he brought him closer and closer, first by watching as Brian serviced Sharon and Robert, then by exhibiting Brian to visiting friends, and then one one night by using Robert in front of Brian, while Brian crouched on the floor in full sight of the scene. When he told Robert to stay and dismissed Brian, the boy crawled over to him and thanked him tearfully for the chance to see him in such a way.

"So you *may* have been right, boy," Grendel said to Chris the next day. "Don't get cocky!"

"Never, sir," Chris assured him.

That night, Grendel took Brian in hand and finally let him show off the skills that Paul had boasted about a month ago. And judging by the way Brian reacted, from Grendel's first touch to the moment when the owner closed his eyes and felt his come bursting out almost painfully in the hot channel of Brian's ass, dammit, Chris was right.

They had some real slave material on their hands here.

The following week, Alexandra and Grendel met to discuss how to proceed.

"Claudia will go home, there's no doubt about it," Alex said. "I think Madeleine will be thrilled, and I think we can expect some major referrals from her in the future, as well as a standing invitation to go to all her parties."

"I'd call Claudia a success," Grendel agreed.

"And I think Robert's good enough to go to general auction."

"Really?" Grendel checked the calendar. "There is one soon, we could probably get him in, if we call now. But I was thinking, why don't we ask Madame to ask around her friends and see if someone we know might be interested?"

"Well, if you want to make the call," Alex said.

"Sure." Grendel jotted down a note. "I'd hesitate to do the same with Sharon, though. I'd just as soon make sure no one thinks we're passing on very good merchandise here."

"On the other hand, there is the question of that clause in her contract," Alex reminded him. "I'll tell you what. Since you're doing the mistress circuit, I'll see if I can scrape up some potential bids for our showpiece."

"More than fair. Now ... about Brian." Grendel leaned back. "I think we should keep him for another month and refine him some more. By the end of the summer, he'll double in value, easily."

Alex whistled. "Are you serious?"

"Absolutely. He's raw material now; it's like handling nitro. I think we can mold him into our nice little plastique package and move him out as an all-purpose slave, ready for any master's wishes." Grendel let his hand fall to his side, where it brushed Chris's hair. "Besides, it gives us a little more time with him. He could be fun. Regret pointing him out, boy?"

"No, sir. He will bring honor to the house."

"Oh, shut up." Grendel pointedly ignored the slight snicker from beside his chair and looked directly at Alex. "Well? What do you think?"

"I think you're *both* full of yourselves," Alex announced. "Send me your prodigy tomorrow night, and I'll tell you what I think."

Two mornings later, Alexandra initialed her approval of entering Brian into the next level of training when he completed this one.

"This week marks the end of the basic training period," Chris announced one morning. The four slaves looked up from their breakfast. "In the month and a week you've been here, you have all progressed, and the owners are now determining which step you will take next. For the first three days of this week, the people who come here are all potential buyers. I know I don't need to remind you how to behave. Do not disgrace this house in any way."

"There's more to it than that," Grendel said, entering the room. The slaves rose, as they had been placed on formal behavior for the week, and he waved them back down. Alex joined him, and they addressed the slaves from the head of the table.

"The people you meet this week may desire you and want to possess you," Grendel continued.

"This is the purpose for which you have been trained. Every move you make, every gesture and sound, has a value in their decision-making process. If you follow directions and behave the way you've been taught, you can guarantee that they will take you at face value. If you mess up, you aren't just making us look bad, you're making yourself look stupid."

"These buyers are familiar with this house, our track record, and our training methods," Alex said. "They know what to expect, and they'll know immediately if a fault of yours was something we neglected or something you just refused to correct. You are novices. These people are buyers. Don't insult their intelligence."

"Yes, ma'am" came a chorus of voices.

"Then let's begin this final week."

The buyers came in trickles and they came in groups. Some of them had been by before, as visitors during the earlier phase in training, and most of them were eager to see any changes in the slaves they had tried out the last time. Sharon was kept busy, and Claudia was excused from most showings because of her unique status. But she was often kept nearby for serving drinks and fetching things like writing tablets. To separate her from the slaves that were being offered, she was given a plain black dress, much like the one Rachel sometimes wore.

Each day, the slaves found themselves showing themselves, posing, answering questions, and being touched, invaded, and tormented by a variety of people. And for the nights, when all the showings were over and they had had a chance to eat, they were all sent immediately to bed in order to be fresh for the following morning.

It was delightfully maddening, frustrating, and horrible. They talked about their dream owners every night and slept like children.

When the showings were finally over, Alex and Grendel had enough interest to actually auction off Sharon and Robert, and they set Friday as the night it would be done. They summoned Brian and told him that they wanted to keep him on for further training, and Brian thanked them so effusively and well that it was almost impossible to believe that this was the same man they had met almost six weeks ago. When he left, Grendel turned to Alex and said, "You know I need to deal with Chris a little bit."

She waved a hand at him. "Go right ahead. I'm not going to be able to relax until the sale is over anyway."

With the sale and the arrival of Mistress Madeleine (who the other three slaves wanted desperately to see) only one day away, the slaves were just beside themselves with anxiety and excitement. No one had been able to eat dinner, even with the pleadings of Cook, who had made some special foods to say good-bye. They had nibbled politely, but left most of it alone.

The early bedtime worked against them now. They were all wide awake and overwrought, and far too excited to sleep. When Grendel actually walked into the room with Chris, they were astonished but eager for whatever was coming next. They scrambled out of their beds and knelt, and Grendel suppressed a smile. New slaves were so alike. He nodded a release, and they returned to where they had been.

"Since this will probably be your last night here," Grendel began, "I've decided to do something special. While you've been here, you've been limited as to how much curiosity you could indulge. In the past two weeks, you've all done well in controlling it, which is the mark of a good slave. However, right now, before you go to sleep, I'm offering you a chance to ask any final questions about this house, our methods, or staff. I'm not promising that I'll reveal anything sensitive or things you have no business knowing, but I'm sure there are some questions you've been burning to settle. If you have no questions, I'm also prepared to hear comments."

And Claudia, the little darling, did just as he instructed her to.

"Sir?" she asked, raising her hand shyly. "If it's permitted, I have one question. What is Chris, in the hierarchy of this house?"

Grendel looked at Chris, who looked startled, and said, "I think I'll leave that to Chris to answer."

"Well," Chris said with a slight frown, "I'm the major-domo, which means the chief of the house. A steward, perhaps, or a butler."

Robert said, "But you're more than that, Chris, aren't you? I think what Claudia meant was, how do you fit in? We're slaves. Ms. Rachel and Jack and Cook and Mr. Shaw are employees. Are you an employee of the house?"

Chris looked a little uncomfortable and glanced at Grendel, whose gaze was suddenly hard. "Answer."

"I am … not exactly an employee," Chris finally said. "Although my needs are met quite adequately."

"Tell them exactly what you are," Grendel prompted. A shift occurred in the room, and all the slaves felt it. There was something happening that was scary and wonderful. The power they felt was odd, and rich, and Brian actually shivered in pleasure. Even Sharon felt it, and in her mind, she knew, *this is real*.

Chris lowered his head for a moment. "I am an adjunct to this house," he said after some thought. "I am not a slave, as you understand the term. I have no contract and wear no collar. I work here of my own free will, and of that will, I subject myself to the will and whims of Mr. Elliot and Ms. Selador."

"But … " Brian said, haltingly, "I don't understand. If you're submitting to them, why…?" He looked up at Grendel. "I'm sorry, sir, I withdraw my comments."

Grendel shrugged. "It's a fair question. You want to know why we don't accept him as a slave, since he obviously is one in all but name. The reason is that we, Alex and I, don't own slaves. In our line of work, it seems far easier to hire experienced people who will not be prone to feelings of abandonment, jealousy, or insecurity every time we go through a new group of novices. But we found that we couldn't send him away because he provides the perfect solution to our household needs as well as makes a generally agreeable companion. We know that he hates not being able to be what he desires most, but at the same time, our refusal to accept him is a sublime torture that no amount of scenes could ever match. You, Brian, are now aware of the unique type of pain rejection and the withholding of a desired place can be."

"Yes, sir," Brian whispered. Chris's face was a mask of controlled emotion, but it was clear that he was more than slightly humiliated by Grendel's explanations.

"Sir," Robert said, clearing his throat, "I'm a little confused. If Chris ... if all he wants is to be ... what we are, why is he in charge of the new slaves? Wouldn't someone who is a top be more appropriate?"

Grendel laughed. "Go ahead, Chris, tell them."

Chris colored a little. A very little. And remained silent.

"No? Then I will. Chris *is* a top, Robert, as if you didn't have first-hand knowledge of that. When we first met Chris, he was teaching tops. In fact, Chris has had offers from slaves, and Chris has been mentioned many times as a very promising trainer within the Marketplace. Even the legendary Anderson has mentioned him in her reports. That's something quite special." Grendel watched the slaves carefully, and saw some levels of comprehension dawning.

Brian remembered Chris in full leathers, pounding the bannister and the floor, saying "This is me!" He blushed for the major-domo, and felt in his gut a sympathetic twinge of pain.

Grendel went on. "Chris *created* the program you've just been through, my new slaves. Hoping that someone would put him through it one day, no doubt. Would you agree to that, boy?"

Chris looked up. "That would be pointless now,

sir," he answered. His voice had an edge to it, sharp but still polite.

"Yes, I suppose it would," Grendel agreed. "And that's the reason why he's so damn useful around here. He takes care of the administrative side of the training so that Alex and I get to go directly to the roots of things and do what we handle best." He smiled, his work done. "Any other questions?"

After that, they asked nice, predictable questions about how long the house had been operating, and how often they went to the resorts, and which of the books was closest to the truth, and other nonsense. When the questions petered out, Grendel tapped Chris on one shoulder and sent him out to the hall, and said good-night for the last time to the four slaves. He hit the lights as he left.

In the hallway, he reached for a handful of Chris's hair and clenched it. Chris drew in a sharp breath and straightened up.

"You handled that well, boy," Grendel said, holding tight. "I love to see you under pressure like that. You look good when you squirm."

"It's my pleasure to serve you, sir," Chris said, closing his eyes. He opened them again when Grendel gave him a shake.

"Yes, so you've told me. You did very well in general this time around, especially in spotting the potential in Brian. So naturally, I'm putting you in charge of him when the others leave."

"Yes, sir." Between clenched teeth.

"Now, now, don't sulk. You saw him, you insisted we keep him, now he's going to be your problem for a few more weeks. Tonight was just to remind you that your status here is precarious. You may be valuable, but you're ours as long as you need us." His words were harsh, but his voice was kind, and Chris closed his eyes again. Grendel let Chris go. "Go to bed. There will be a lot of people expecting to see you tomorrow, and I want you looking sharp."

"Yes, sir. I'll try to improve myself, sir."

Grendel walked away without comment, thinking: goddamn perfectionist!

Chapter
Twenty-Two

Many pictures have been painted of the sales within the Marketplace. Bright lights and stages, glass cages and mirrored tables, golden chains and liveried waiters serving up trays of paddles have all appeared from time to time. Some of those elements have even appeared in the actual events as well as the books supposedly written about them.

But one thing is true: In the pages of fiction and on the bidding tables of the Marketplace, the auctions take place silently, with numbers entered on computers or written down in leather folios or passed to special couriers in sealed envelopes. It would never do for a slave to know what their value is. Or to see their potential owners fighting among themselves. No, it's best that they are forced to wait in silence, enduring the pain of the mystery, until a hand comes to snap shut that open lock that hangs from their simple chain collars.

The procedure is simple at our house. Each slave is mounted on a special pedestal, a number on a tag around their neck. An open padlock joins the two ends of the collar, and a key is in the lock. Their folders sit on a shelf that protrudes from the pedestal, and bidders are welcome to examine it. Many of them will have copies already, sent to them for perusal before the actual sale. The folders contain the history of the slave, notes from trainers or former owners, and a copy of their contract.

The slaves are not bound, but are positioned on their knees with their hands behind their backs and their legs spread. Those who are not voice-trained are gagged. It is a mercy, really. The voice-trained may have to answer questions, and that is always so difficult under circumstances like these.

The bidding folders are actually in another room. There is no chance that any slave will even know how often he or she has been bid upon. Qualified buyers have until a certain time to write their high bid down, and they are permitted to return and bid again before the cut-off time. In our house, as in many older ones with an established clientele, we have a system of preferred buyers who are always given one opportunity to top the highest bid.

When a winning bid is determined, the new owner goes to their new slave, removes the tag, and may replace it with their own. But the one gesture that makes the sale complete is when they sign the three copies of the contract and take one.

The slave does not need to sign. They signed when they were free.

Chapter
Twenty-Three

The sale began at nine in the evening. There were twelve qualified buyers present, plus three preferred buyers who had placed advance bids and given instructions to bid up to a certain amount on their behalf. All of them had seen the two slaves before, so a lot of the pre-sale discussion was actually among themselves rather than with the slaves. Not that Sharon would have made interesting conversation. She was very securely gagged.

The buyers were a diverse group, quiet in their wealth, careful in speech, casual in dress. Grendel and Alexandra were dressed up, as good hosts should be, and mixed freely, introducing people and chatting amiably with old friends.

Mistress Madeleine arrived early in the day and Alexandra took her into her sunny office to chat for a while. When Madeleine was ready, Alex sent for Claudia, who arrived led by Chris. Chris was already in his suit for the night, dark and elegant, and next to him, Claudia could have been wearing a little black dress of the kind that women wore to fancy dress functions instead of the housekeeper's frock that it was. Her hair was up, and charmingly so, and her pleasure at seeing her mistress was so clear in her eyes that Alex had to smile. How could Madeleine have thought of sending the girl away?"

"I would like you to see something," Alex said, gesturing to Chris after Claudia had made her proper curtsy. Chris brought Brian in, and put him in a bent-over position, and handed Claudia a cane.

Madeleine stared in astonishment as Claudia gave Brian one hell of a formal caning, telling him to count and ask for the next, striking him in evenly spaced red lines, and holding the cane for him to kiss afterward. Chris sent Brian away with the cane, and followed him, leaving the three women in the room.

"That's just one thing we've done," Alexandra said, pleased with Claudia's performance. "I think you'll want some privacy to discuss things for a while. Please ring me if you need anything."

As soon as she left, Claudia ran to Madeleine and dropped to her knees. "Mistress!" she cried, bending her head. "I love you! Don't send me away, please!"

Madeleine lifted Claudia's chin and said softly, "Why, I wasn't planning to, little one. Alex told me all about how you've done. And I'm so proud. I want to hear all about it—when we get home. Right now, I want you to come upstairs to my room and show me what you can do."

Claudia's exuberance almost carried them both up the stairs. And when she appeared later, leashed at her mistress' side, her eyes glowing, Brian, Sharon, and Robert all envied her. Madeleine was every bit as beautiful as Claudia had claimed, and if Claudia was really as happy as she seemed, she had gotten what she dreamed of.

Sharon chewed on the mouthpiece on her gag, hating every passing minute. She hated the way people glanced at her folder and put it back down. She hated the way no one talked about anything in front of her, and the way people ignored her, and the way they paid attention to Robert. But she composed herself, thinking, soon. Soon.

"Bids will be collected in ten minutes, ladies and gentlemen!" Chris walked through the crowd, looking like a butler for once, instead of a working guy in a suit. A lot of people seemed to be friendly with him, and he smiled a lot. Robert's old mistress, for example, the woman Grendel called "Ali"—she seemed to think seeing the little bastard was a real treat. Sharon was the only one of the four not to feel any sympathy for the little man. She thought it was just fine that he would never get what he wanted. She straightened her back every time she saw him pass. Eat your heart out, Chris, she thought. I'm up where you wanna be. But he paid her no attention at all.

Robert had his mind full of old fears and new hopes and all the knowledge that had been shoved into him for the past six weeks. He answered questions in a daze, and even smiled at Mistress Allison when Chris brought her over to look at him. But he was elsewhere, waiting for it all to end. He envied

Brian, who was going to get another month of training before he had to do this. I'm not ready, he thought. I'm scared. What am I doing here? I can't do this! But he smiled and answered questions put to him anyway.

"Final bids have been accepted," Chris announced. "Thank you, ladies and gentlemen. High bids will be verified, and preferred buyers given their chance to bid now. Results will be announced in the main dining hall in twenty minutes."

Twenty minutes, an eternity.

Twenty minutes, gone in a flash.

Applause in the distance—no names, no clue what was happening. And then a low rumbling noise as people entered the hallway again, heading toward the front room, the ballroom, where the two slaves knelt waiting for hands and keys. Robert ached to stretch and felt hot and cold at the same time. Sharon felt like she could throw up.

Robert almost died when he saw the woman who was walking toward him, a pen in her hand. She was one of the women identified to him as a "friend of Madame's," a woman in an elite circle of mistresses who lived the life in a strict, almost Victorian milieu. She had another slave with her, a personal secretary, a woman in a high lace blouse, who followed her every step. And when the mistress signed the three copies of the contract, Robert felt tears forming in his eyes.

"How sweet," she said, lifting one finger to catch one as it spilled. "Emily, we seem to have purchased a romantic." Robert lightly kissed the tear away as his new mistress extended the finger to his mouth. Her hand dipped lower and closed the lock gently.

He closed his eyes in ecstasy.

"Well, here we are," said a gruff voice at Sharon's side. She turned slightly to look, even thought it was against the rules, and saw one of the men who had seen her earlier in the week. He was in his late fifties, she estimated, with longish brown hair speckled with white. he seemed to be in good shape, which was a relief. She tried to remember what he had been like. He had not used her sexually, but had read her file a lot. She remembered him sitting on a narrow chair, his briefcase in his lap, asking questions. She had him pegged as a voyeur.

Which wasn't so bad, really. Spending a lot of time jerking off wasn't a terrible vocation, but it might get dull after a while. More importantly, he was a widower, for many years, he had said. And he lived in Texas, but traveled back East a great deal.

"Let's make sure this is what I recall," he said carefully, pulling the contracts out of her folder. He scanned through one and nodded. "Yes, that's me. Someone get me a pen!" Chris handed him one and he signed all three contracts with a flourish. Sharon wished she could give him a great big smile, but she would wait patiently until he got around to taking the gag off. This wasn't going to be so bad! He was older, and a widower, so he was probably lonely. He lived in the South and traveled to the East, so he was probably very rich. And if he made few demands on her, so much the better. In time, she'd win his heart, and then who knows what could happen?

Then, suddenly, a hot-looking young woman appeared next to him. "Hi, daddy," she said, looking up at Sharon. "Is this the one?"

Sharon snorted out a sigh of relief. It was only his daughter!

"Yes, she sure is, honeybunch. You like her?"

The girl looked at Sharon critically. "I guess," she said finally. "I wish you'd let me pick them!"

"Next year," the old man said. Sharon felt bewildered. Her eyes shifted back and forth between the two people. "I had to buy this one because of the clauses in her contract, honey. Says here she wants a single fellow, and I guess that you getting married soon is gonna get in the way of your being single. But when you and Chet move into the big house, she'll be right there for you, honey. You just keep her for when I come visit, and that'll be just fine."

"Well," the girl said, her eyes narrowing, "I guess so. We can put her to work in the kitchen, I suppose, when you're not home. I wonder if we can train her to give a good pedicure. I could use home manicures and pedicures." Sharon felt those eyes boring into her. She panicked and started to snort air around the gag. Manicures? Daughter? Son-in-law-to-be? When you're home?!

"You can train her to do anything you want, sugar. All I need her for is a little warmth in the sack three or four times a year. Y'all can do whatever makes sense when I'm not there." Taking the contracts and his daughter, the man moved on, accepting the congratulations of his friends.

Sharon caught Chris looking at her out of the corner of his eye. She expected him to look triumphant. Instead, he looked sorry for her. She looked away, unable to bear it.

Chapter Twenty-Four

The house did very well on the two sales and on the money paid for Claudia's retraining. As expected, Sharon's stunning attractiveness had driven the bidding up a great deal. And Grendel couldn't help laughing over the situation she was sold into. It was petty and mean-spirited, he knew, but it felt good. He did not regret not fucking her.

In the nights after the sale, they finished up assorted old business and put the money away and took some time to figure out their fall schedule. Alex blocked out two weeks on her calendar for "Resort," and he knew better than to argue. Besides, the vacation would be needed. They expected at least two more applicants before then, and of course, there was Brian.

Brian was kneeling, his hands behind his back,

facing them as they worked on their schedule. They were doing patience and endurance training, dull but absolutely essential in a valuable slave. And he was showing his sustained excellence nicely, even under Chris's almost satanic supervision.

Part of being boss, Alex noted to Grendel with some amusement, is knowing how to motivate your people. You sure motivated the hell out of our butler. Grendel could only shrug. His long-awaited full reunion with his partner had taken place when the three slaves were taken away. He and Alex loved to come back after a separation like this. Still feeling pretty damn good about it, he wasn't about to argue anything. You know how to motivate the hell out of me, he admitted to her, and they laughed.

When it got late, Chris came looking for Brian and kicked him off to bed. Alexandra waited until Brian had left the room, and then said, "Why don't you take his place, Chris?"

It startled him, which was always good. But he recovered and went to kneel in the space vacated by the slave trainee, putting his hands behind his back. "Thank you, ma'am," he said softly.

"You're welcome. Chris, would you like to come with us to the resort?"

That too, caught him off guard. Better and better. He wasn't used to dealing with Alex on this level. His momentary confusion was reassuring to her—it meant that he was being handled well.

"If it would please you, ma'am. To help me make a more independent decision, would ma'am like to tell me why I would be there?"

"Because there, you can be our slave, and here you can't," she said, leaning forward. "I've discussed it with Grendel, and we'd like to reward you for your work on the four summer applicants." She looked at him seriously. "You can take your bonus as well, if you want it."

Chris took a deep breath. "Thank you, ma'am. I don't need a bonus." No surprise; he never took it. "But I accept your offer to accompany you to the resort as your slave, ma'am."

"Even knowing that the collar comes off when we leave and you get back to work?" Grendel asked.

"Even so," Chris nodded.

"Fine." Grendel shrugged. "Then we're settled. We'll go after the next two have completed training and Brian is sold. I'll bet you can't wait until the winter comes, eh Chris? In fact, I'm willing to bet you'd love nothing more than to start practicing tonight, and crawl all the way over to our bed and sleep at the foot of it."

"Gren," Alex said softly, "don't tease him any more." She got up and reached her hand out to her lover, who took it with a nod of acquiescence.

"We'll see you in the morning, Chris," he called over his shoulder. And the major-domo sighed, got up, turned the lights out, and went to lock the front door.

Have I told you that the mark of the best slaves is patience? Infinite patience.